PRAISE FOR A S

"Lee's lush romance is a delectable delight."

—*Booklist*

"Lee is a gifted writer, particularly when writing about the all-consuming power of desire."

—*Entertainment Weekly*

"Lee's latest is perfect for anyone who enjoyed Amy E. Reichert's *The Coincidence of Coconut Cake*. Readers will get lost in Aubrey's sugary creations while rooting for the characters to find their happily ever after."

—*Library Journal*

"Lee seamlessly spins a tale that offers her readers laugh-out-loud moments, with touching pages of raw honesty and heartfelt passion. A romance full of heart and second chances."

—*Kirkus*

"A perfect balance of impeccable wit, laugh-out-loud hilarity, and off-the-charts chemistry. *A Sweet Mess* is a sinfully decadent romantic comedy!"

—Helena Hunting, *New York Times* bestselling author

"A rich, vibrant romance that's a feast for all the senses!"

—Lauren Blakely, #1 *New York Times* bestselling author

"A wonderful twist on a classic romance . . . this is a fun summer read that is best enjoyed poolside or at the beach."

—Lit Up, Southern California News Group

OTHER TITLES BY JAYCI LEE

That Prince Is Mine

A Sweet Mess

A Sweet Mess
The Dating Dare
Booked on a Feeling

The Heirs of Hansol

The "I Do" Dilemma
The Not So Secret Crush
The Enemy Entanglement

Hana Trio

A Song of Secrets
One Night Only
Just a Few Fake Kisses

NINE TAILED

JAYCI LEE

Montlake

Text copyright © 2024 by Jayci Lee

Published by Montlake, Seattle

www.apub.com

Amazon, the Amazon logo, and Montlake are trademarks of Amazon.com, Inc., or its affiliates.

ISBN-13: 9781662523281 (hardcover)
ISBN-13: 9781662520747 (paperback)
ISBN-13: 9781662520754 (digital)

Cover design and illustration by Elizabeth Turner Stokes

Printed in the United States of America
First edition

To Matthew, my fellow fantasy fiend.
Thank you for being as excited for this story as I am
and holding me (literally) through the scariest parts of
writing it.

QUICK AND DIRTY GUIDE TO

PRONOUNCING ROMANIZED KOREAN

For the word nerds . . .

Pronouncing romanized Korean words is really hard, even for someone who is, like me, fluent in Korean. In *Nine Tailed*, I try my best to be consistent in romanizing Korean words, following the Revised Romanization of Korean system currently used in South Korea.

The consonants are pretty straightforward (until you get into the double *d*, *s*, *k*, etc., but let's not worry about that for now). How you sound out the consonants in your head will be close enough without tripping you up while you read. But there are a few tricky vowels that you might need some getting used to.

I think these are the most helpful ones to note:

a is pronounced "ah"

ae is pronounced "eh"

eo is pronounced "uh"

i is pronounced "ee"

o is pronounced "oh"

u is pronounced "oo"

The cool thing is that those vowels will always sound like that, no matter what consonants you combine them with. So the word for *nine-tailed fox spirit*, *gumiho*, is pronounced "goo-mee-ho"; the word for *the world of gods, Shingae,* is pronounced "sheen-geh"; the word for *the god of Mountains, Seonangshin,* is pronounced "suh-nah'ing-sheen"; and so on.

Now, if I haven't confused you more, go forth and read *Nine Tailed* with confidence. You got this! Welcome to the Shingae.

GUMIHO

All she wanted was to be human.

The beautiful maiden walked through the open-air market, with her cloak draped over her head and her eyes lowered demurely to the ground. She didn't have to look up to know that he was there. All it took was one glance at her for the handsome young scholar to be bewitched—to think himself ardently in love with her. She promised herself this would be the last time she used her magic.

They had to live as man and wife for one hundred days. She only had to hide that she was a gumiho, a nine-tailed fox spirit, for one hundred days . . . then she would become human. She would truly belong to this world she chose to call her home. They were married within a fortnight. As the days passed—warm and tranquil, like nothing she'd known before—she believed she could learn to love her human husband.

The closer it drew to the hundredth day, the more frantic she grew. *Just a few more days. Please.* All she wanted was to be human. Her wish became a fervent prayer in her heart. All she asked for was to live out the rest of her mortal life loving her quiet, studious husband—to belong to him . . . to belong to his world . . . to just belong.

Only on the ninety-ninth day did she learn of her folly. Her husband knew she was a gumiho. He had known all along. All he wanted was the Yeoiju. He asked, then pleaded, then threatened, to no avail. She couldn't give him what she didn't have. The Yeoiju was a myth . . . a legend. He didn't believe her.

If she had been a second too late, she would have perished on the spot. If she hadn't taken her fox form, the impact of his dark spell would have torn her into a thousand pieces. But her gumiho was strong . . . and fast. Even as blood poured from the deep gashes in her side, she ran faster than she ever had—a mere blur to the startled villagers' eyes— and disappeared into the deep, dark woods.

CHAPTER ONE

My T-shirt is sticking to my back from the heat off the sidewalk. Even at nighttime, summer in Las Vegas is brutal. Not that I'm complaining. I'll take the soggy shirt over roasting in the desert sun any day.

It's 10:00 p.m., and the night is just getting started for most folks. They're probably packing the main strip like sardines in a can. I take the side streets, where I can walk without constantly getting bumped and knocked around.

The too-old and too-new buildings stand next to each other companionably on the street, promising cheap eats and loose slots. People restlessly pace the sidewalks, holding wads of advertisements to push into the hands of unsuspecting tourists for all sorts and manners of entertainment. I look straight ahead and step with purpose to avoid unnecessary waste of paper. Besides, I do have a very important purpose. Dinner.

My stomach growls, urging me to pick up my pace, and I weave past the glowing neon signs and the shifting darkness with hurried steps. I'm two blocks from my destination when my scalp tightens with the sensation of being watched.

I swivel in a half arc and freeze when two malevolent yellow orbs pierce through a dark alleyway. Green fire ignites in my eyes, and my incisors elongate as magic flares in my veins. I slip into the alley before anyone sees me, preparing to throw down, when a black cat hisses and runs off into the night.

"For fuck's sake." I sigh and douse the fire with a deliberate blink.

I slow my hammering heart and bury my magic deep inside me. I'm jumpy tonight. It might be intuition. Or paranoia. I'm not sure which. But both have been instrumental in keeping me hidden—and alive—for over a century. Even so, I should have more sense than to reveal even a hint of my powers like that.

I walk out of the alleyway and continue down the street with my shoulders hunched. My eyes dart around, scanning every inch of my surroundings, from the tourists carrying fluorescent plastic cups filled with sorry excuses for margaritas to the impatient locals stomping past them, shaking their heads in disgust or sympathy. Seeing nothing out of the ordinary, I let my guard down a notch.

Then I stiffen right back up. I sense a female dokkaebi's life force— the dark, red, and stormy gi of Underworld—pulsating within a cluster of excited young women walking toward me. The life force of humans flows soft and steady like a shallow stream, but the gi of magical beings roils and churns, powerful as crashing waves. I have no trouble spotting the goblin as she hoots with laughter, the lightness at odds with her tumultuous gi. When she walks past me, oblivious to my identity, I almost sag with relief.

It doesn't matter if the dokkaebi was a friend or a foe. I don't want to be recognized for who I truly am. But I don't know why I'm fretting. I've stayed hidden this long. That's not about to change tonight. I take a *calm the fuck down* breath. With my magic under lockdown, my life force becomes a colorless trickle until even magical beings can't differentiate between me and the humans. No one will find me. I detach my shoulders from my ears and resume my trek to my destination, letting my mind wander.

Contrary to popular belief, goblins look no different from humans on the outside. It's the magic they carry inside, such as their affinity for gold and silver, that differentiates them. They like to make and spend wealth as though their lives depend on it. I've seen more dokkaebis and their Western counterparts in Las Vegas casinos than anywhere else in the country, with Wall Street being a close second.

Magical beings of the Shingae—the world of gods that I hail from—walk among the humans and lead ordinary lives on the surface. Humans vastly outnumber us, so it's not too difficult to melt into the chaos. But we always abide by the rules of the Shingae: Never expose the world of gods. Protect the magic. Keep the Amheuk, an ancient force of darkness, at bay.

The Amheuk once threatened to destroy the worlds as we know them and to plunge all that lived into the dark. It would've meant death for most beings, and those who didn't die would have become twisted, depraved abominations feeding off pain and misery. The Cheon'gwang—the true light—and all beings born of its light came together to defend the worlds from the Amheuk.

The Endless War ended five centuries ago, and the forces of darkness have been subdued, but we stay vigilant against the Amheuk. Too many have perished to protect what we have. So I adhere to the rules of the Shingae, even though I'm hiding from it.

To stay hidden from the world of gods, I can't allow the nine-tailed fox inside me to awaken. If I do, she will unleash my magic, and anyone from the Shingae will be able to track me down. Luckily, my careless lapse in control over the alley cat was too minor to leave more than a dusting behind.

Even the most talented of the Suhoshin, the powerful guardians of the Shingae, wouldn't be able to trace it back to me. Thank gods for that. They're supposed to be the *good guys*, but the elite, magical beings that make up the order just rub me the wrong way. They think they're better than the rest of us just because they're blessed by the gods with near immortality.

I scoff out loud, making a fellow pedestrian shoot me a frown. I frown right back and stomp past her. I'm hardly the weirdest person walking the streets of Las Vegas. Besides, it's not my fault the almighty guardians are irritating.

The Suhoshin's only saving grace, in my humble opinion, is that they don't discriminate based on your source of life. As long as your gi originates from the sources created by the Cheon'gwang—Mountains, Sky, Water, or Underworld—you can join the Suhoshin's ranks, *if* you're powerful and talented enough. And if you break the rules, the guardians will come after you no matter what you are—no preferential treatment. That makes me feel a smidgen better about the probability that I'm one of the Suhoshin's most wanted.

I arrive at my destination, with its garish sign proclaiming **Roxy's Diner**, **Roxy's Diner**, **Roxy's Diner**, the blinding flamingo and turquoise lights blinking in precise rhythm—two seconds on, one second off.

Any lingering thoughts of the Shingae fade into the background as I pull open the door and step inside. The interior reminds me of every other run-down diner in the movies, but there's no Hollywood magic in Roxy's Diner. It is authentically tacky and run down, which gives it a unique charm all its own.

"Home sweet home." I squeak across the red vinyl seat and sit with my elbows on the white table.

"Your usual, Sunny?" Rachel pours coffee into my mug. She's been working at Roxy's for thirty-some years but doesn't look a day over forty, despite her salt-and-pepper hair. She rules the dining hall with an iron fist and an unfaltering smile, wearing her pristine pink-and-white waitress uniform like a badge of honor.

"Yes, please." I beam at her. Dinner at Roxy's Diner is my favorite part of the day. What can I say? I appreciate the simple pleasures of life.

My first sip of the scalding coffee makes me feel half-human, so I take a second sip, wondering if it'll make me fully human. I laugh at myself. Even though she's hidden deep inside me, I can sense my gumiho's presence. I can always sense her. No amount of diner coffee will make me human. I ignore the churning mix of relief and despair in my stomach and take another sip of my nonmagical coffee. Yup, still not human.

"May I join you?" The low timbre of the vaguely familiar voice sends a shiver of awareness down my spine.

Taken aback by my body's reaction, I slowly turn my head to glance up at the owner of the voice. I'm stunned into silence for three pounding heartbeats. The man I find standing by my booth looks even better than he sounds. Even so, he shouldn't elicit this kind of visceral reaction from me. It must be the shock . . . because he shouldn't be standing there in the first place.

I shake my head to clear it. I haven't seen him in nearly a decade—he's a few inches taller and much broader in the chest and shoulders—but I'm sure it's him. I drag my eyes away from said chest and shoulders with some effort. It's definitely the shock.

"Ethan? I . . . what . . ." I'm the epitome of eloquence.

"Have you ordered?" He takes a seat across from me and waves over Rachel.

Rachel is super chill. Nothing ruffles her. Nothing except Ethan, apparently. She stares at him, then at me, then back at him. Blushing to the roots of her hair, she needlessly pats down her neat french twist and offers him a coquettish smile. I scowl.

"What can I get for you, hon?" she asks in a singsong voice.

"I'll have whatever she's having." He tips his chin toward me. "Including the coffee."

"You got it, sugar." Turning her back to him, Rachel mouths *oh my God* to me.

I put on a smile for her, which shuts off the moment she walks away. The impossible is happening. I'm untraceable—even by someone from the Shingae—unless . . . *no.* The hair on the back of my neck rises, but I push aside my wild suspicions. There must be a logical, *nonmagical* explanation for how Ethan Lee is sitting in front of me.

The way his dark-brown eyes dart around my face reminds me of a man gulping down water after wandering the desert for days. A thousand butterflies take flight in my stomach, and I resist the urge to press the back of my hand against my heated cheeks.

"How did you find me?" I ask in a cool, hard voice to hide the confusion roiling inside me.

He goes completely still for a second, his unreadable gaze snagging on mine. He recovers so quickly that I would've missed his reaction if I'd so much as blinked. And I nearly forget what I saw when a sheepish smile spreads across his face, his eyebrows cresting above the bridge of his nose. A soft breath whooshes past my lips.

I remember his nose being strikingly perfect, straight and aristo-cratic, on his shuttered teenage face. But he's broken it more than once since I last saw him. The slight bump suits him. It gives character to his too-perfect features—high cheekbones, wide lips, and dark eyebrows—and rescues him from being pretty. But it does nothing to change the fact that he's gorgeous.

I stop myself short. Oh, he is good. He wields his charm like a finely honed weapon. I take note of it, then double down on my scowl. "Well?"

"Believe it or not, I'm quite good at my job," he says, scratching the back of his head. With his *aww shucks* smile, he's fucking endearing.

Stomping down on my instinct to melt into a puddle, I say, "So you became a PI."

I feel a pinprick of disappointment, which is ridiculous. I haven't thought about Ethan since I left Los Angeles when he was still a teen-ager. Well, I stubbornly turned my thoughts *away* from him and his older brother whenever they popped into my head. Same thing.

"Ben and I told you—no, begged you—*not* to follow in his foot-steps." The words are out before I can stop them. "You're so smart. You could've been anything you wanted. A doctor, a rocket scientist—"

"You're right." His winning smile disappears, and a hard, unyielding glint enters his eyes. "I could've been anything I wanted, so I became the only thing I wanted to be."

My nostrils flare with a sharp inhale, but I clamp my mouth shut. I. Don't. Care. It's none of my business. Instead, I ask him again, "How did you find me?"

"Call it a hunch." He shrugs, but a muscle jumps in his jaw. My stomach dips. A hunch, like sixth sense or déjà vu, is a way humans try to explain the inexplicable—such as a brush with the Shingae. "Look, it's not important *how* I found you. We should talk about *why*."

"Fine. Tell me why you're here." I don't say "and leave," but the message is pretty clear. I just want him out of the quiet, dull life I've worked my tails off to cultivate. It doesn't matter how he found me—even though not knowing makes my shoulders bunch up with tension—as long as he leaves.

He drags a hand over his short black hair, fingers spread wide, as though he expected to find a full head of hair. So it's a recent haircut. I liked the long mop of curls he used to have, but I might like his hair better this way. The thick, silken strands would feel warm and smooth between my fingers . . . I jerk my thoughts back. Since when do I notice people's hair?

Since this man walked back into my life.

I swallow and shift in my seat. I don't understand my reaction to him. My body feels like . . . like a live wire. It's strange but not unpleasant. Having lived for over a century, I thought I'd forgotten how to feel surprised. But this is definitely new and surprising. I can't decide if I like it or not, but it definitely makes me feel off kilter.

"I need your help." His eyes bore into me with an intensity that holds me hostage, erasing every other thought from my head. I blink to break the connection.

Taking a deep breath, I focus on the task at hand. He didn't try to bullshit me or make small talk to soften me up. He'd always been straightforward to the point of being blunt. But I always respected him for that—for facing everything head on. I take another moment to consider his request.

"No." Just because I appreciate his directness doesn't mean I'll help him. I left Los Angeles eight years ago for a reason.

I had answered the wanted ad on a whim. I was tired of working at restaurants with aspiring actors and models. They wanted to shine, when all I wanted was to disappear. Ben was a young, up-and-coming PI, whose business was growing faster than he could handle. His ad said he needed an assistant to answer phone calls and file paperwork. It sounded like a nice, dead-end job. My favorite kind.

I never signed up to become his friend, but that's what happened. There were many late nights, so it made sense for us to have dinner together. And it made sense for Ben to discuss his cases with me from time to time and for me to nudge him in the right direction. My hunter's instinct was sharper than ever.

And it was hard to ignore his teenage brother, since he came to the office every day after school. So when I caught Ethan cleaning up his cuts and bruises one day, it made sense for me to drag the truth out of him—how he'd been bullied ever since they moved to LA after their parents died. An orphaned Korean kid with only an older brother to call family made an easy target. Since he refused to tell Ben, it also made sense for me to teach Ethan how to fight off the assholes at school.

By the time Ethan was sixteen, already over six feet tall, he easily fought off the bullies—four, five at once—until no one dared to pick on him again. He even occasionally bested me during sparring. I never took it easy on him, only held back my preternatural speed and strength. Based on skills and technique, the student had become better than the teacher.

It hit me one night that I had stayed too long. It was nothing really. Ben and I were stealing fries off each other's plates when it escalated into a food fight. Ethan laughed so hard that soda came out his nose. The quiet sixteen-year-old rarely laughed those days, so Ben was thrilled to get a peek at the younger brother he used to know. I took in the scene with a smile and realized I was . . . happy.

I was growing too attached to Ben and Ethan, and it terrified me. I swore to never care about anyone again—to never grieve a loss again. I had to cut ties before it was too late. I left before the sun rose the next morning. But . . . leaving them hurt. I don't want a repeat now. I can't let them back into my life.

"No? I haven't even told you anything," Ethan protests with a huff of incredulous laughter.

"You told me enough. Find someone else to help you." I look away, searching for Rachel. Where is my damn steak? I could use some distraction to choke down the question clawing at my throat. *Shit.* "Is Ben here too?"

Ethan lowers his eyes, his full, dark lashes casting shadows on his cheeks. When he meets my gaze again, my breath catches at the cold fury shimmering around him like a mirage.

"Ben's dead." His expression is as stark as his words. "He was murdered."

I can't inhale. *Breathe.* I have to breathe. "When was he . . . when did it happen?"

"Two weeks ago."

"Who?" I'm shaking now, and I bite down on my bottom lip until I taste blood.

"I don't know." He doesn't look away, even as his Adam's apple bobs in his throat and shame clouds his eyes.

"You. Don't. Know?" I welcome the surge of fury, because it overshadows the aching sadness spreading inside me. "You don't know who killed your own brother? Didn't you mention something about being a good PI?"

"I said I was good," he snarls through clenched teeth. *Good.* I'm glad he's angry too. Anger hurts less. "I didn't say I was you."

"I am not a PI." I don't want to remember the thrill of helping Ben with his cases—the surprise on his face every time I spotted something he'd missed, followed swiftly by a wide, proud smile. *Ben.* I smother the sob gathering in my throat. "I sell cigarettes at a shit casino."

"Sunny, your instincts are sharper than anyone I know. Ben saw that. He used to say the only reason people thought he was the best PI out there was because they hadn't met you." Ethan leans close, and his voice drops to a harsh rasp as he says, "Ben is *dead*. Help me find his murderer."

"Here you go." Rachel places my plate too close to the edge, her eyes glued on Ethan. I'm too shell shocked to be annoyed. "And here's yours, handsome."

"Thank you." He forces a smile. "It looks delicious."

Rachel refills our coffee. "Let me know if you need anything else."

"Shut up and eat," I tell Ethan as soon as she's gone. I inhale my rare steak and sunny-side up eggs even though my stomach screams against it. Hurling would be much more pleasant than discussing Ben's murder. I gag and cough. *Shit.* I chug my coffee to push it back down.

"Are you okay?" He hasn't touched his food. He stares at me with his dark eyes, concern clouding their depths. Ethan is worried about me, when he's the one who lost his older brother. He'd hero-worshipped Ben.

"I'm fine," I snap, clenching my hands under the table. I will not grieve Ben. I can't. I left before I could care too much about him or Ethan so I wouldn't have to hurt again. Had it already been too late?

"Please." His voice breaks on the word as he implores past his pride. "For Ben."

I look across the table at Ethan and see the helpless sorrow beneath his hard, arrogant veneer. He's lost. Ben was his only family. Now he is as alone as I am.

"I'm late for work." I slap down three crumpled twenties on the table and scramble to my feet. I need to move. Stillness invites emotion. Ethan slides out of the opposite bench and reaches for his back pocket. "Put your wallet away and walk with me."

CHAPTER TWO

My uniform is hideous. Simple as that. It's green, gold, and *so* sparkly. My neckline is a sneeze away from befitting a topless bar, and my skirt goes all of two inches below my ass. I force my long, thick hair into a tight bun to keep it from soaking up all the cigarette smoke, but it reveals the curve of my neck and leaves my shoulders bare. My uniform strips me of all modesty, so I shouldn't care about showing a bit more skin, but I have to push away a twinge of discomfort as I walk out to the casino.

Ethan ignored my request to wait for me at the bar until my break. Instead, he's leaning against a column across from the employee locker room, his shoulders loose and his thumbs tucked in his pockets. But his relaxed pose doesn't hide the coiled energy emanating from him. My pulse picks up as though I've sensed a predator.

When he sees me, he pushes off the column and stalks toward me, his eyes drawing a line of fire from the top of my head down to my toes. My body heats and tenses under his gaze. He stops less than a foot away from me. Neither of us speaks. Neither of us looks away. What the hell is happening?

"Nice outfit." He recovers from whatever passed between us quicker than I do. "Are you supposed to be a sexy leprechaun?"

"You think I'm sexy, eh?" I force myself to smirk even as my stomach flutters at his offhand compliment.

"Yes." His full lips quirk into a lopsided grin, and my heart turns over. "For a leprechaun."

"Well, leprechauns are mean sons of bitches," I say evenly, then show him my teeth in a vicious smile. "So I suggest you go get a drink at the bar before I bite you."

"If you're trying to convince me to leave"—his eyes drop to my lips, which part without my permission—"you're not doing a very good job."

I growl and take a step toward him. Ethan laughs and walks away with a wink. Not a creepy wink but the kind that makes you want to giggle like a debutante behind a lacy fan. I don't own a fan, and I don't do giggles. So I snarl at his back, ignoring the warmth pooling low in my stomach.

With an exasperated huff, I strap my tray of vile, cancer-causing goods around my neck like the peanuts guy at a ball game and contort my face into a cheek-paralyzing smile. I need to *draw customers, not chase them away*, to quote my greasy manager.

I sell the cigarettes and cigars on autopilot while my mind mimics a gravity-defying carnival ride. Ben is dead. My breath catches when I remember his mischievous smile as he swiped a fry off my plate. But I shove aside the grief threatening to engulf me.

Did he get too close on a case? He was an incredible PI. He wouldn't have been sloppy enough to get made. Then what? Something personal? I exhale through my teeth. This is pointless. I'm not keeping Ethan around for the fun of it. I need him to fill me in.

My shift drags like it's anchored in wet cement. When I finally make it to the crowded bar, my eyes zero in on Ethan as though he has a spotlight shining on him. Or does he exude an inner light? I snort despite my apprehension at being able to pick him out in one second flat.

He's staring down at the beer bottle gripped in his hand, his grief written in the lines of his hunched shoulders. Or is it a defensive posture? Is he being followed? I scan his vicinity, adrenaline flowing, and sense no immediate danger.

But there are about eleven women and three men of varying ages—and a platinum blonde seraph, glamoured to hide the white wings folded behind her back and to dampen her otherworldly beauty—all undressing him with their eyes. I'm relieved to find that I'm not the only one until an unfamiliar instinct kicks in.

He's mine.

What the fuck, Sunny? He is *not* yours. I'm fine. It's nothing. I just don't like having other people lusting after him, even if I'm doing the same thing. Is that what I'm doing? Is this electric, jittery heat inside me *lust*? I honestly wouldn't know. I've never felt anything like this before.

Well, it doesn't matter what I'm feeling, because I'm not going to act on it. But that doesn't mean I have to stop glaring at the assholes staring at him. I *really* don't like it . . . so I'm going to make them stop. The good thing about being a nomadic loner who gives zero fucks is that I can do whatever the hell I want, when I want. No excuses necessary.

Lust has nothing to do with it when I take off in a run toward Ethan. He spots me a second before I proceed to smack loud kisses on his face, his head trapped between my palms. I try not to notice the woodsy musk of his scent but find myself breathing him in instead. His arms wrap around me like bands of hot steel and tug me close. I squeak and plant my hands on his shoulders to steady myself. I'm immediately distracted by the feel of his muscles bunching and shifting under his shirt, and my kisses slow and linger against his jaw as I surreptitiously spread my fingers and dig them into his skin. There's hardly any give, like he's carved out of marble. A shiver runs through me.

I feel the tremor of his laughter but don't understand the reason behind it until too late. The last thing I see before he kisses me squarely on the mouth are the crinkled corners of his eyes. I know he's just playing along with my ruse, but my lips part against his on a sharp inhale. He stills for a split second, then deepens the kiss, swirling his tongue inside my mouth. I bite back a moan, arching into him. His hands flex against my back as he spreads his legs to pull me flush against him. He tastes bitter and hoppy, and I want to drink him in like he's my last bottle of IPA. I want the worlds around me to fade away, so I can lose myself in this kiss.

The thought stops me cold. I don't . . . I can't . . . I push against the hard wall of his chest, and he releases me, his hands skimming my waist and hips as they drop to his sides. His expression is guarded as he searches my face. I arch my eyebrow in a way I hope conveys sardonic amusement. I might've ruined the effect with my heaving bosom.

"They'd never buy your act without a proper kiss." His tone is dry and easy, but his eyes linger on my lips, which feel swollen. I fight the urge to brush my fingers across them.

"You're welcome," I say, plopping down on the stool beside him. The indignant huffs and stomping feet tell me the lovers' act worked. An act. That's all it was.

"Your usual." The bartender sets down two shots of tequila in front of me, giving Ethan a hostile look. The burly redhead is probably assessing whether he could take Ethan out if the need arose. I did him a small favor a couple of years ago, and now it seems he'll protect me with his life. Humans and their sentimentality.

"Thanks, Ford." I pound both shots and suck the tangy juice from one of the lime quarters. Ethan's taste still lingers in my mouth, even after the tequila and lime. "That's it for tonight, though."

The bartender cocks his head but clears the empty glasses without any question, throwing one last glance at my companion. Ford is built to bulldoze through a crowd, all barrel chest and tree-trunk arms. But Ethan is covered in lean, corded muscles that speak of speed, strength, and agility. It wouldn't be easy for either of them to get the better of the other. Good thing they won't need to go at it.

"How many shots do you usually have?" Ethan sips on his nearly untouched beer.

"Two at the beginning of my break and two before I get back on the floor. It takes the edge off so I don't knock anyone's teeth out."

"What are you doing here?" He sweeps his hand out to the busy casino.

"Can't you tell?" I say, bristling. "It's my calling."

He tousles his imaginary head of hair again. His frustration tic.

"Tell me everything you know," I say to preempt any unsolicited lecture. I'm one hundred thirty-two years old. He doesn't know that, but I don't need anyone giving me advice on how to live my life.

"It's been eight years." He ignores my demand, moving on to yet another subject I don't want to discuss. "You look exactly the same. How? It's like you're still twenty."

"The last time you saw me, I was twenty-one," I correct him, even though age is meaningless to me.

From Ethan's perspective, I'm in my late twenties, but no one would buy that. I can pass for midtwenties at most. For flexibility on how long I remain in one location, I revert back to being eighteen years old every time I move to a new city. How old is Vegas me again? Twenty-two, I think. In reality, I actually *look* eighteen because that's when I stopped aging—the same time I left Korea.

But no one needs to know about my eternal youth, especially since the why of it has me thoroughly stymied. My mother was a powerful gumiho, but I saw the fine lines around her eyes deepen and the streaks of gray in her hair multiply as the years passed. So why not me?

"Now stop stalling, and tell me what I need to know about Ben's . . . case." My voice cracks on the last word, and I scowl. "Or I might change my mind about helping you."

"Ben was looking for you before he died." Ethan stares at me as if expecting a reaction. I keep my shock to myself. "He got close, and I picked it up from there. I can't believe you were only a few hours away all this time."

I have a feeling Ben hit a dead end, but Ethan somehow figured out where I was. How? The not knowing is making me antsy, but I don't know the answers to a lot of questions. I'll just add this one to my list.

"Why would he want to find me after all this time?" I say, not quite successful in sounding dismissive, as warmth seeps into my chest.

He didn't forget me. He wanted to find me. I crush the ridiculous hope uncurling in my stomach. None of that matters. He is dead. And I can't shake the feeling that it is somehow my fault, but I ignore the thought for the sake of my sanity.

"He wanted to find you from the moment you disappeared." Ethan looks away. "He never stopped wanting to."

"That's beside the point." My voice isn't quite steady. The confirmation that someone gave a damn about me releases a flood of regret and gratitude, but I stamp down on the useless emotions. "He *didn't* look for me when I disappeared. He knew I didn't want to be found. So why would he start looking for me all these years later? What changed?"

"Who the hell knows?" Ethan takes a long sip of his beer, holding my gaze.

My eyes trace the line of his throat as he swallows, and my pulse picks up. These . . . things he does to my body are doubly confusing because of all the emotions I don't want to feel. I'm happy to see Ethan. I've . . . missed him. But I'm gutted over losing Ben. Maybe that's it. Maybe I'm just trying to distract myself from my grief.

Because . . . fuck. If I let myself, I'd grieve. My closest friend in over a hundred years died. He was *murdered*. No matter how much I want to deny it, I'd have to be dead myself to feel nothing.

"All I know is why I wanted to find you," Ethan says in a low voice, and my breath catches in my throat. Lust, longing, or whatever it is I'm feeling toward him is a messy distraction I don't need or understand. But finding Ben's murderer? And making that motherfucker pay? *That* I understand.

"How . . ." I snatch the sweating bottle of beer from him and gulp some down. I hand it back to him and blow out a long breath. "How did he die?"

"I found him at the agency, collapsed on the floor." Ethan shudders, and all color seeps out of his face. "I couldn't do anything. I just . . . watched him die in my arms."

I reach for his hand but stop. He's holding himself together through iron will. My sympathy will only undermine that. "Did he say anything before he . . . he died?"

"He was delirious, rambling about not being able to serve me anymore." Ethan scrubs a hand over his face. "Then he gripped my hand and looked me straight in the eyes. And I thought he was going to tell me who did this to him, but all he said was to break the stone and something about tears. Break the stone of tears, maybe? Those were his last words. Just gibberish."

"He was already too far gone when you found him." The image of the two brothers on the floor of the agency guts me like a knife. *Gods.* I shouldn't have left them. If I'd stayed to watch his back, maybe Ben would be alive. "Do you know the cause of death?"

"That's the thing." His eyebrows draw together. "Other than a small laceration on his earlobe as thin as a paper cut, he looked completely healthy and uninjured. I even had an autopsy done, and they found no sign of a heart attack or a stroke. No traces of poison or asphyxiation either. His body just shut down, like someone flipped a switch."

I keep seeing Ben, pale and limp, in Ethan's arms. I swallow the painful lump in my throat. "Do you have a copy of the autopsy report?"

There are poisons from the Shingae that can kill like that, but I'm not going to jump to conclusions. Ben was human. The repercussions for murdering a human are dire. No one from the world of gods would do it lightly. I shudder and block out the image of bodies strewn across a faraway mountain.

"Yes, it's on my laptop back at the hotel." He looks askance at me. "But like I said, they found nothing."

"I'd still like to see it." I tap my finger on my chin while I think. I go through a mental list of poisons that can switch a human off. Focusing on the facts is far more productive than succumbing to feelings. Mourning is not going to bring Ben back. Finding the killer won't bring him back, either, but Ethan needs closure. So do I. "What about the cops? Did they find anything?"

"The cops wouldn't touch it. There was no sign of forced entry or struggle. They ruled out murder even before I got the autopsy done." He scoffs, shaking his head. "They don't want to sink time into finding out what really happened. Besides, they'd only get in the way."

"What makes you so certain it was murder?" *I* know, because the whole thing stinks of the Shingae, but how does *he* know?

"I found this taped to the door outside the agency." Ethan reaches for his phone and pulls up an image. "Does this mean anything to you?"

It's a picture of a handwritten note, and my blood freezes drop by drop.

미화야, 잘 있느냐?

"You can read Korean, right?" He doesn't wait for my answer. He already knows.

It takes me a few tries to swallow, then I translate: "Mihwa, are you well?"

Ethan nods, and I remember Ben taught him to read and write Korean. "My question is who the hell is Mihwa, and what does he—"

"*She*, not *he*. Mihwa is a female name." The name sounds foreign on my tongue, even though it belonged to me for the first eighteen years of my life.

"Right. What does *she* have to do with Ben?" Ethan is focused on finding his brother's murderer, his grief under control. "Why did the killer leave this note?"

Because of me. A scream rings through my head. Ben's dead because of me.

YEOIJU

"Do you know what a Yeoiju is?" the mother asked.

"Yeo . . . i . . . ju?" the child repeated hesitantly, before giggling into her small hands. "Is it something yummy to eat?"

"No." The mother tickled the child, and peals of luminescent laughter filled the lonely mountain. "Try again. Remember your lessons."

Her nose scrunched up in concentration, then her eyes lit up. "It's the magic pearl!"

"The pearl of enlightenment," the mother corrected.

"Yes . . . and if a gumiho . . . *kisses* someone"—the child stuck her tongue out in disgust—"and gives them the pearl, that person will become . . . smart?"

"Not quite." The mother smoothed a strand of hair that had escaped the child's braid. "If that person looks into the heavens, they will learn the secrets of the Shingae. If they look toward the Earth, they will understand the ways of the humans."

"But Mother"—the child opened her mouth wide and pointed inside—"I don't have a Yeoiju in my mouth. Do you have one?"

"No." She shook her head slowly. "I don't."

"Then it's not true." The child pouted. "It's just a silly story."

"Don't underestimate the wisdom of our ancestors." The mother returned to gathering herbs from beneath a young cypress tree. "Sometimes stories are more than just stories."

"Oh. I remember now." The child bounced up and down. "Halmeoni once told me that the Yeoiju is the most powerful magical object in all the worlds."

"She is not your grandmother." The mother paled and held firmly onto the child's wrist. "You must address her as Samshin Halmeom. In fact, you shouldn't bother her at all."

"Yes, Mother." The child cast her eyes to the ground. But when she glanced back up, mischief danced within their depths. "But it seems like the Yeoiju is the most *boring* magical object in the worlds. Who wants to *know* about this, that, and everything? Besides, it's not even real."

The mother's vision blurred with hot tears, but the child did not see them. She was too busy chasing after a butterfly, her laughter trailing her like a golden ribbon.

CHAPTER THREE

Ethan wanted my word that I'd help him find his brother's killer. I told him I'd take a look at the autopsy report. Knowing it was the best offer he would get from me, he went back to his hotel after arranging a time and place for us to meet later. I couldn't tell Ethan I didn't want him around if Ben's death really has something to do with the Shingae.

Left alone with my thoughts, I zombie walk through the rest of my uncharacteristically busy shift. Apparently, the vacant, out-of-it look draws customers. My tray is almost empty when I turn in the night's earnings and remaining inventory.

"You had a good night." My coworker sounds much too surprised, her puffy lips forming an unconvincing O.

"Yes, I'm filled with an overwhelming sense of accomplishment," I gush with a saccharine smile.

"How . . . nice for you." Her eyebrows draw low in confusion. "Congratulations."

"Yeah, thanks."

I should be kind and let her know she doesn't have what it takes to become an actress, but I turn on my heel and head to the locker room. I'm in no mood for a smackdown with the Mean Girl.

I have four hours to wrap my head around what's going on, and maybe take a shower, before I meet Ethan. Or I might ditch him and disappear again—I only have a few years left here anyways—but I don't want to. Las Vegas feels more like home than any other place I've lived since Korea.

Besides, the investigation will go nowhere until I see the autopsy report. Visiting the crime scene will be no use. Any traces of magic would be long gone, since Ben was murdered two weeks ago. An image of him lying still and empty flits through my mind—his life cut short because of me. I reflexively turn my head to the side, scrunching my eyes shut, but there is no hiding from the guilt. Even so, I avert my gaze from the mirror on my locker door as I change into my street clothes.

I trudge out of the casino and into the bleary dawn. The few people out and about are dragging their feet, bodies heavy with exhaustion or satisfaction. I feel as though mine is being sucked into the center of the Earth—into the hot, suffocating oblivion.

Everyone who knew Mihwa died over a century ago. I killed . . . everyone, including Daeseong. A chill passes through me. The price of his death was too high, but what's done is done. Even if the dark mudang came back from the dead—which is impossible—he wouldn't have used poison to kill Ben. It was too quick. Too painless. I shake my head until I see doubles. It's. Not. Him.

But poison is a favorite weapon of the Jaenanpa—a faction of humans obsessed with the Shingae and its magic. They torture and kill magical beings to steal their powers, justifying the atrocities they commit by arguing it's unfair for the Shingae to monopolize magic— they're fighting for equality between the worlds. Too bad they're actually power-hungry psychopaths intent on world domination.

What did the Jaenanpa want from Ben? He had no magic for them to steal. Then again, he was never their target. He was killed to send me a message—used like the sticky note left on the door. My fists clench at my sides, and violence shudders through me. A feral growl gathers in my chest like an impending storm, but I subdue it with effort. Maybe they were afraid to come for me directly. They might have heard of what I've done—what I'm capable of. Or maybe they just couldn't find me. It doesn't matter. Ben's murderer will pay the price, even if it means I have to come out of hiding and reveal myself to the Shingae.

The world of gods lies like gossamer over the human world—a shimmer in the corner of their eyes. The humans' stories of gods and beasts weren't born of wild imagination but woven together from the sudden goose bumps on their arms and the cold shivers down their spines. Human minds can't grasp the truth, but they also can't completely ignore the allure of the supernatural—the magic.

My mother told me the Shingae isn't a physical place but a state of existence. It's about knowing who you are. When my gumiho and I existed in harmony, I felt my connection to the Shingae like the reassuring tug of a warm hand wrapped around my own. My mother said that was because of gi, the life force that runs through all beings born of the Cheon'gwang.

Even though she and I led solitary lives away from other magical beings, I never felt less a part of the world of gods, its magic my constant companion. Now I hide from both worlds and belong to neither. The pull of magic, laced with bone-deep loneliness, hums a siren's song in my blood. But the memory of how quickly that beauty shifted into a nightmare chills me to my bones.

I breathe in and out through my nose and shake out my arms. One thing at a time. I can't let my emotions fog my mind. I need to look at Ben's autopsy report to find out *what* killed him, then I can narrow down *who* killed him. Maybe the Shingae isn't involved at all. *Ha!*

I cut through a narrow alleyway and reach my apartment building in twelve minutes, saving five minutes to add to my tedious eternity. Or at least, what I assume is my version of eternity. It doesn't look like I'll die of old age, but I doubt I'm immortal. Only the gods are immortal, and I'm no goddess. Fox spirits were once revered as deities in Korea, but that's ancient history. Nowadays, most Koreans believe in the myth that gumihos are treacherous demons who turn into beautiful women to manipulate and control men to do their bidding.

I close my front door and lean back against it with a sigh. Home at last. It's small, dark, and sweltering. The AC shut off again, and my one-bedroom apartment is a thermos filled with yesterday's heat. I push off the door and strip out of my T-shirt and jeans, leaving them on the floor. I walk through the living room to the tiny galley kitchen, wearing only my black cotton bra and underwear. They're inexpensive and comfortable. What else matters?

I grab a glass from the sink and sniff it. Clean enough. I rinse it out and fill it with fresh water. After chugging it in one go, I extend my arm to refill it.

One of the windows shatters with enough force to tear down the blinds, saturating my place with muted light. I see a red figure standing in my living room at the same time I spot the daggers flying toward me. I leap onto the edge of the sink and hear the triple thud of knives slicing into the kitchen wall—to the hilt.

I jump off my perch and attack, aiming my kick at the assailant's throat. She catches my foot in one hand, absorbing the impact without so much as a stumble. She's strong . . . much stronger than I am. I spin out of her grasp before she can snap my ankle. I angle my torso and raise my arms in a loose fighting stance.

I'm pretty confident in my close-combat skills. My mother taught me well, and I never stopped training—anticipating an attack like this, hoping it would never come. But I'm not sure I can win this fight.

"Who are you?" I pant and circle my assailant. If anyone came after me from the Shingae, I thought it would be the Suhoshin, but my visitor is definitely not a guardian.

Her skintight unitard covers every part of her, including her eyes. She looks like a member of the Blue Man Group with their eyes closed, but in red. Maybe she's part of a new Vegas show. I hold back a cackle. *Shit.* The adrenaline rush of a fight never fails to get me high.

"Show your true form, beast." Her voice sounds like an echo inside an empty cave, devoid of life.

Beast. Her words are a punch in the gut. Fire seeps into my irises and spreads through my veins, signaling the beginning of my transformation. *No. This is* my *fight. I don't* need *you.* I clench my eyes tight and grit my teeth.

"No." I extinguish the flame, but the effort has me swaying on my feet. It's hard to suppress my magic in life-and-death situations. "She's unavailable at the moment, but *I'm* ready to rumble."

"Let's see what you say when I hold your life in my hands," she taunts in an eerie, melodic cadence.

She launches a volley of attacks on me, but I evade every kick and punch. Okay. So I'm faster than her. At least I have that going for me. She whips out another dagger from gods know where—her skintight unitard can't possibly have pockets—and tries to harvest my kidney with it, but I swirl out of her reach.

I'm huffing and puffing. She's not even . . . breathing. Distracted, I block a kick but don't move out of reach fast enough when she grabs for me. The moment her hand wraps around my throat, I sense what she is. She reeks of the Shingae but isn't one of us. She was human but not anymore. There's something important at the edge of my memory, but I can't quite grasp it. I'm not too hard on myself about it, though. It's not easy to think when my feet are dangling over the floor, with a scary-ass woman trying to choke me to death.

I grab her wrist with both hands and swing back for momentum, curling my legs into my chest, then plant both my feet into her solar plexus with a satisfying impact. I crumple to the floor in a sweaty, half-naked heap. The bad guy is curled into a fetal position across from me. She's strong, but she can be hurt.

"Heh." My sorry excuse of a laugh and the blood gurgling in my throat tell me the assassin fractured my larynx. I struggle to my feet to finish the ass kicking, but she breakdance leaps to standing and catches me on the jaw with a roundhouse kick, sending me back to the floor.

That's what I get for gloating. I swipe her legs out from under her, crawl like mad to the sofa, and pat around its underbelly. *Hello, lover.*

I unsheathe my short sword, its weight reassuring in my hands, just as the assassin slashes her blade down on me. I'm definitely not going to ask where she pulled that sword from. I raise my hwando over my head to block her strike and push off the ground. She has longer range, so I have to use my speed to my advantage. I close in and cut her across the chest and stomach, my thin, curved blade dancing through the air. She hisses and retreats several steps.

"Who sent you?" I wheeze through my burning throat.

"You know who my master is." Her cackle chills the air and raises goose bumps on my arms. "Didn't you get his message?"

"You killed Ben?" I say in a hoarse whisper, my fury so overwhelming that it ices over me.

"No, my brother had that privilege." She raises her sword. "But the Post-it note was my idea. On behalf of my master, of course. Precious, no?"

I roar with helpless fury and run toward her, swinging my hwando in a too-wide arc. I know I'm being reckless and stupid even before she buries her blade in my shoulder.

I stumble back from the impact, but the sword protruding from my shoulder blade stops me from slamming into the wall. My mouth opens in a silent scream as agony rips through me in a burst of ice and fire.

"Ready to show yourself, gumiho?" she goads, twisting the blade. "I want to tell my brothers I defeated you in a fair fight. I'll take one of your tails as my trophy."

My eyes roll back at the pain, but I fight to stay conscious.

"Stubborn, aren't you?" The red assassin gives the sword another wrench. "Suit yourself then."

I bite my lip, but a whimper escapes. I can't help it. It hurts. It hurts so much. But I hate being told what to do. It makes me monstrously stubborn. Even as my instincts scream for me to change—to survive—I refuse to give her what she wants. Instead, I beam a bright, bloody smile at her, even as the edges of my vision go dark.

I'm jerked alert by the sound of crashing, and I blearily register Ethan rushing toward me. In the momentary confusion, the assassin loosens her grip on the hilt. To his credit, he doesn't hesitate as he twists her hand off the sword and throws her to the ground in the same motion. It draws a howl of pain from me, but he had to seize the upper hand to neutralize the enemy.

"Sunny, are you okay?" Ethan takes his eyes off her for only a second, but that's all she needs.

No.

She twists out of his hold with a sickening crunch. Her arm dangles at the wrong angle, but she still moves faster than Ethan and lunges toward him with a dagger aimed at his heart. My sword is by my feet where I dropped it. It's too far away. She's going to kill him.

I grab the blade in my shoulder and pull it out with a guttural growl. I move faster than I've ever moved, but the point of the dagger is already against Ethan's chest. I hear a distant scream. It's coming from me. How am I screaming so loudly with my messed-up throat? The red assassin, however, doesn't make a sound when I bury her sword in her back, piercing through her heart. She twitches once, then stops moving. I collapse and watch her body disintegrate into a pile of red dust.

"Don't move." Ethan's eyes are wild, but he runs to the kitchen and whips a towel off the oven door. He folds it into a lopsided square and pushes it down on my shoulder. The pressure makes blood gush from the exit wound. "Shit, she sliced clean through you."

My shoulder hurts like hell, but the good news is my throat is healing. No, wait. *Ethan.* I rush to my knees and run my hands over his chest. He's hurt. The assassin stabbed him. How is he okay? I find a small slash in the center of his shirt. I tear his shirt open to check for the wound, but there is none. Not even a scratch.

"But I saw her stab you," I say weakly, his face swaying in and out of focus.

"You stopped her before she got me." He gently settles me back onto the floor.

"No, I wasn't fast enough." The room is spinning. I've lost a lot of blood.

Ethan rips off his torn T-shirt and uses it to stanch the blood from my back, pressing down on both sides of the wound.

"Fuuuck . . . ," I moan.

"Stay still." His face is taut and pale. I probably look like I stepped out of a horror film, with bruises around my throat and blood matted to my skin and hair. "I need to stop the bleeding."

"There's no time." I try to sit up, but he restrains me with a firm hand on my good shoulder. I swat at him weakly, and a smile twitches his lips.

"You can fight me after we get you patched up." He lifts a corner of the kitchen towel and winces.

"I'm serious, Ethan. We have to get out of here." I struggle to sit upright, and this time he helps me.

With an aggrieved sigh, he gives up trying to tie his shirt around my shoulder and compromises by draping the towel over it to cover both wounds. He lifts my good arm and places my hand over the towel. I obediently press my palm against the entrance wound, gritting my teeth.

He wraps a protective arm around me, and I allow it. The warmth of his body, holding me steady, soothes my shattered nerves. I hate to admit it, but it's been a while since I engaged in mortal combat, and I'm pretty shaken. I can't believe he jumped into the fight like that. Doesn't he know he's only human? He could've been killed. I should shove the idiot away, but I stay put and grudgingly admit I feel more respect than anger toward him.

"Do you know what the hell *that* was?" he asks, eyeing the red dust.

"Later." I have no idea how to explain any of this to him yet. But I sound weary enough that Ethan lets it go, probably too worried about my injury to push. I know it won't last, though, especially since I heal at inhuman speed.

I lean against him for another moment, then struggle to my feet, with Ethan doing the bulk of the work. He's shockingly strong, even for a big guy. A quick glance tells me I only come up to his collarbone. He must be at least six feet four.

It's only when I'm standing that I remember my state of undress. I shake off his arm and stumble back a step, heat rushing to my cheeks. Maybe I should've invested in nicer underwear. I peek at Ethan and realize he's shirtless. I guess the dress code for this event is seminude. I feel faint and nauseous, but that doesn't stop my eyes from roaming hungrily over his broad chest and cut abs.

My gaze snags on the quarter-size jade disk hanging from his neck. He never used to take that thing off. I guess he still doesn't. Ben told me once that it was a gift from his mother. I secretly envied Ethan for having something of his mom's to keep close to him. The thin, black leather cord, though, is new—and indecently sexy against his tanned skin. I press my hand against my cheek. How do I have enough blood to blush?

"I need to put some clothes on so we can leave." My eyes skitter across the living room. I need *him* to put some clothes on so I can stop ogling him. But something else niggles at me. I really don't want to do this. It's not that I'm not grateful, but it's just embarrassing. This is why I hate peopling. Blushing even harder, I mumble, "And thank you. For . . . you know."

"Yeah, I know." A quicksilver grin flashes across his face. "But you shouldn't be standing."

"Hey," I squeak when I'm lifted off my feet. The bare skin of my side presses against his naked chest, and I practically sizzle. "Put me down."

"Okay." Ethan carries me to the couch and gently sets me down on it. "I'll go find you some clothes."

Relieved to have a moment apart from the distractingly hot man, I take a deepish breath, careful not to jostle my shoulder wound. But it does nothing to calm my frantic pulse. How can I even feel like this right now? I mean, it fucking hurts everywhere.

I lift the corner of the kitchen towel. The bleeding has slowed to a sticky trickle. I sigh with relief. Then I notice for the first time that I cut my hand from pulling the assassin's blade from my shoulder, but it's a shallow gash and is closing up already.

Ethan comes back and hands me a loose black shirt and a pair of dark jeans. Smart choice. The blood won't show through as easily. But also, pretty much everything I own is black. He takes in my pale upturned face, and his lips press together until the edges turn white.

"Do you have anything to wrap your shoulder with?" he asks brusquely.

"I think I have some Band-Aids in the medicine cabinet." I feel a bit sheepish when Ethan frowns at my joke. He doesn't know how freakishly fast I heal. He's understandably not in the mood for my flippant humor. I still grumble, "What? It's funny."

I actually don't have any Band-Aids. My medicine cabinet is empty. I don't get sick. And any nicks and scratches heal before I can clean them. I've never tested my healing powers to this extent before, but so far so good. I don't know if I would've survived a fatal wound, though. If I bleed out before I can heal, then I'll most likely die. Like I said, I'm no immortal goddess.

But there is no figuring out the why or how of my healing powers since I cut ties with the Shingae. Much like the not-aging thing, I first noticed the power after I came to the United States. It's almost as though I'm a Blessed, but I don't recall being accepted into the ranks of the almighty Suhoshin. All I know is something happened to me when I blacked out the night Daeseong came for my mother and me.

Blood blossoms like flowers across her silky white fur. One, then another. Stunned silence smothers the shrill voice of the mob. Lifeless bodies cover the ground . . . I shrink back from the memory with a gasp. That night is the last thing I want to remember. Ever.

Ethan moves around my place like he owns it, utterly confident and not the least bit self-conscious about being shirtless. He comes back with some old T-shirts and a soaked hand towel. He sits down next to me, and I almost scoot away, suddenly shy. Fuck that. I force myself to stay exactly where I am.

"I have to get you to a hospital." He turns me toward him. "That's a nasty wound."

"This?" I quirk my eyebrow and take off the kitchen towel. I act nonchalant, but showing him my power makes me feel more exposed than being in my underwear. "It already stopped bleeding."

"What . . . how?" Ethan draws back like I sprouted an extra head. He dabs at my shoulder with the towel, wiping the blood off. He sucks in a sharp breath when he sees the neat three-inch gash, barely oozing blood. He carefully turns me to the side to check the exit wound on my back. His chest expands as he inhales through his nose. My guess is that one's nearly closed up too. He has to be freaked out, but he only says, "Well, it's still no paper cut."

He tears one of my old T-shirts into thin strips and binds my wound. I watch his face, trying to figure out what he's thinking. But the man has his poker face mastered. When he's done, I wiggle into my jeans on my own, but I need his help buttoning up my shirt. I ignore the flutter in my stomach as the backs of his fingers brush against my bare skin and linger a second longer than necessary. I'm imagining things. He can't possibly feel as worked up around me as I do around him. My assessment is confirmed when he buttons me up with aloof efficiency and gets to his feet as soon as he's finished.

I take slow, small sips of air and try to quiet my mind. But my mind refuses to cooperate as the assassin's words ring in my head. *My brother had that privilege.* The little calm I fought for is shattered. I want to find that brother of hers and slaughter him—make him pay for killing Ben. My fists clench. But it's not the red assassin or her brothers that matter. They're mere puppets. It's their master I want.

I *will* avenge Ben's death, but I need to focus on the now. I can't do shit if I'm dead. I'm a target—that much is certain—so I have to stay on the move. What about Ethan? His best chance for survival is to dive under the radar and stay the hell away from me.

"Will you go away if I ask you to?" I glance up at him, knowing my chances are slim. If he were the sort to run from the terrifying unknown, he wouldn't have jumped into the fray to save my ass from the creepy woman in red.

He arches a single brow, holding my gaze. "No."

"I didn't think so." *Arrogant bastard.*

I wince as I reach under the couch for my sword belt and strap it on, loving the feel of the aged leather hugging my waist. It's been years since I've worn it. I can't exactly walk the streets nowadays with a short sword strapped to me. I inch my butt off the sofa and straighten up. Nausea rises to my throat, but I don't pass out, and I walk over to pick up my hwando. Swinging it in a smooth half arc, I sheath the sword in a single motion. There's no need to clean it.

The red assassin didn't leave a single drop of blood.

CHAPTER FOUR

We're heading toward the highway in Ethan's Jeep, and the silence is stifling. I wonder what blows his mind more . . . The terrifying assassin who turned into red dust when I stabbed her through the heart? Or the fact that I'm sitting next to him scrolling through his laptop instead of bleeding out from my shoulder wound?

I sneak a peek at him. My gaze lingers on his arresting profile before I take in the rest of him. He grabbed a T-shirt from a duffel bag in his trunk, so he's no longer half-naked. I'm relieved. Of course I am.

I continue studying the fully clothed man next to me. Other than the slight tension in his shoulders and the hard set of his jaw, Ethan appears collected and cool. While I admire his stoicism—hysteria is the last thing I need—I can't shake off the pestering thought that a human shouldn't be able to calmly process this kind of exposure to the Shingae.

But what do I even know about him other than the fact that he is aggravatingly arrogant and stupidly brave? He must have developed nerves of steel over the last eight years. What hasn't changed is his kindness. I recall his gentle touch as he tended my injury and note his patience now, as he holds back the million questions he must have.

"Where to?" He breaks the silence, making me jump a little, but keeps his eyes on the road.

"Northern California," I say matter-of-factly, pretending to be engrossed in the autopsy report. I have a vague plan that I don't want to put into words yet.

He nods and adjusts our route toward the I-15, then resumes brooding. I have a feeling he's mentally compiling a list of questions to grill me with once he deems me well enough. He isn't too happy I'm not sleeping like he suggested when we first hit the road.

I'm too wired to sleep. I feel a restless energy crackling between us, waking up every nerve ending in my body. Maybe it's just me. But being in such close confines with him makes it difficult to concentrate, which is ridiculous since it's just Ethan. I know him. No, I *knew* him . . . This man isn't the sixteen-year-old I abandoned in the dead of night.

I try to take a deep breath, but it feels as though my lungs have been knotted in half. I'm much too attuned to his every movement . . . to the heat coming off his body. I keep finding myself listing toward him as though I'm yielding to a powerful magnetic pull.

Maybe my body is malfunctioning because I kept my distance from people—both emotionally and physically—for too long. Plus, the news of Ben's murder and the death match with the red assassin—the grief shot through with adrenaline—must be messing with my head. That has to be it. But what about my visceral reaction to Ethan when he first showed up at Roxy's? Before I knew about Ben's death? Before the rest of the shit happened?

I clear my throat and focus on the laptop perched on my knees. The autopsy report, like Ethan said, doesn't reveal much, but I'm more interested in the photos. I lean closer to the screen when I spot the faded purplish tints on Ben's fingers and toes, just above his cuticles. His lips have the same tint to them, even when the rest of his features are dull and gray. My heart thunders in my ears.

"Weird question." I lightly run my fingertips across the keyboard, not disturbing the keys. "What did Ben smell like when you found him?"

"Funny you should ask," Ethan says after a pregnant pause. He must've added another question to his list. "I figured I was losing my mind, but he smelled like . . . flowers."

"You weren't losing your mind," I say quietly, looking at him from beneath my lashes.

"Thanks." The corners of his full lips curl up for a second, and I feel the vise clamped around my chest relax a fraction. "Good to know."

I click through the autopsy photos again. The memory of my mother pointing out a dark-purple flower as we gathered herbs flashes through my mind. She called it *doksacho*. It looked lovely and smelled exquisite . . . a lot like jasmine but richer and sweeter. It seemed improbable for something so beautiful to grow deep in the mountains, where only needles of sunlight made it past the dense canopy of trees. My mother told me to never ever touch it, much less pick it, because it was one of the deadliest poisons in all the worlds. Doksacho also happens to be the Jaenanpa's poison of choice.

The puzzle pieces fell into place when the red assassin disintegrated into a pile of dust without leaving a drop of blood. Now I have to look at the whole picture, even if I might not like what I see. The red assassin was a corpse raised from the dead by dark magic. Only those in the upper echelons of the Jaenanpa are powerful enough to wield such magic.

The doksacho, the undead assassin . . . they both point squarely to the Jaenanpa. An alternative possibility nudges against my brain, but I block it out. He's dead. It can't be him. So it seems we're facing a horde of ruthless sociopaths lusting after magic. I close my eyes and dig the heels of my hands against them.

If the Jaenanpa are indeed responsible for Ben's death, then this case comes under the jurisdiction of the Suhoshin—which means the guardians are probably investigating the murder already. If I interfere with their investigation, they'll come after me too. Then they'll realize I'm guilty of far more than mere obstruction of justice. Panic jangles inside me, screaming at me to run. But I open my eyes and press my lips into a stubborn line. I will avenge Ben's death, no matter the consequence.

I close the laptop with a sigh. The Suhoshin are formidable—they capture and subdue criminals with brutal efficiency—but they aren't ruthless killers. Their sworn purpose is to keep order in the worlds and protect all law-abiding beings, including humans. I may not belong in the *law-abiding* class, but I'm still entitled to a fair trial. Those are better odds than the Jaenanpa will ever give me. I lean against the headrest, fighting back a wave of nausea. I'll deal with the Suhoshin when the time comes.

"Are you okay?" Ethan asks, his voice sharp with concern.

"Yeah, I'm fine." The skeptical glance he shoots my way tells me he's not buying it. I close my eyes, pretending to invite sleep.

I'm exhausted and weak, but I can't turn my mind off. I was attacked mere hours after Ethan walked back into my life. The Jaenanpa must've followed him to Vegas. My stomach sinks. That was their plan all along. They killed Ben, hoping his grieving brother would somehow lead them to me.

I still can't figure out how Ethan found me, but that's not important right now. What's important is that I'm the reason Ben is dead and I'm going to get Ethan killed too. But there might still be a way. Now that they've found me, they might not be interested in him anymore . . . as long as he doesn't get in their way.

"Ethan—" I turn toward him in my seat.

"No." His fists and jaw and everything else clench into an obstinate, angry knot.

"I haven't even told you anything," I protest.

"You told me enough," he says, echoing the conversation we had at Roxy's. It's funny how your life can be upended in a matter of hours. Well, it's not funny actually. Not funny at all.

I decide not to push him. What he doesn't know is that I can do obstinate and angry better than him. I've had over a century of practice. If I can't convince him to leave, then I'll leave.

"And don't even dream about ditching me," he warns, as though reading my mind. "I showed up at your place because I had a feeling you might disappear again. I won't stop searching for you, especially now. I can't let you die too. Let me keep you safe, Sunny."

My heart clenches painfully at his earnest words. He means it. He wants to keep me safe. How long has it been since someone cared about my safety? *Eight years.* He and Ben cared about me . . . and I cared about them. That's why I got spooked and ran. But Ethan *still* cares. Gods, I wish I didn't want him to.

I look out my window without answering. He can't keep me safe from the Shingae . . . but maybe *I* can keep him safe. No matter how badly I want to believe it, it's too late for him to escape the Jaenanpa's notice, even if he stays away from me. He's a loose end that they'll want to tie up. The laptop creaks plaintively, and I ease my grip on it before I crack it in half.

Calm steals over me, my decision made. I wasn't there to save Ben, but I *will* protect Ethan—or die trying. I owe it to Ben. That means we have to get to the hidden cypress tree in Monterey. I need to seek an audience with the Seonangshin. I wasn't ready to admit it before, but we're already headed that way.

In the days of old, people in Korea worshipped the Seonangshin, a deity they believed to be the patron god of villages. They would consecrate a tree by hanging strips of blue, red, yellow, white, and black fabric on its branches and building rock cairns around it. At these tree shrines, called *seonangdang*, the villagers would pray to the deity to ward off evil, bring them good luck, protect loved ones, and whatever else humans prayed for. It was another part of the Shingae comfortably diluted for human consumption.

But the Seonangshin is not a friendly neighborhood deity. *They*— for they are many but the same—are the god of Mountains, who have existed since the creation of the worlds. No one truly understands the Seonangshin or the extent of their powers. Those of the Shingae— especially beings of Mountains, like the gumiho—revere and fear the formidable, omniscient beings.

You only dare disturb the Seonangshin for matters of life and death—not to rub their trunks for good luck. If the humans knew that the deity could take their life away with a passing breeze, they wouldn't seek them out so readily. Not that it makes much difference. While the Seonangshin have a soft spot for humans and will at times heed their pleas, they only materialize for beings of the Shingae in secret, secluded locations through mature cypress trees.

I know of one such cypress tree, but I never thought I would visit it. When the ship that carried me away from Korea arrived in San Francisco, I was so weary and homesick from the endless trip that I reached out with my magic. It was a foolish thing for me to do, since I was running from the Shingae, but I was only eighteen and so alone. And a solitary cypress tree answered my call. Just knowing that the Seonangshin were here helped me survive those first difficult years in this vast country.

The Seonangshin might not welcome me now, since I left the Shingae and effectively turned my back on them. But I need answers, and they have them. Whether they'll give me those answers and whether I'll understand their cryptic guidance are bridges I'll cross when I get there.

"Ask me," I tell Ethan. When the laptop protests against my iron grip again, I toss the poor thing into the back seat, where it'll be safe from destruction. I blow out a breath and shift in my seat. I can't tell him everything, but I can explain some things. "Are you wondering what I am?"

"You're Sunny Cho." He finally looks at me, and his expression is fierce. "You're the prickliest *Sunny* I've ever met, but you're also the most generous person I know. You taught me how to protect myself, bought me beer without my brother knowing, and gave me the oddest but helpful pep talks. You're my friend. That's *who* you are."

A painful knot unravels in my chest. I hug my arms around my midriff, because the alternative would be to throw them around Ethan's neck. "Well, then you're even denser than you look."

He lets out a strangled laugh, and the tension in the air loosens its choke hold on us. "Let me ask you this. Who was that terrifying woman in red?"

"I have a hunch, but I'm hoping I'm way off." I squirm in my seat, searching for a more comfortable position. With the pain receding, I realize how sticky and gross I am. I sniff myself as inconspicuously as I can, hoping I don't smell as bad as I look. "I'd kill for a shower right now."

He arches an eyebrow with a wry twist of his lips. "Quit stalling."

I flip him off to stall a bit longer. I'm not sure how much to tell him. An explanation of the Shingae will seem too theoretical at this point. But that's not the only reason I decide to hold that tidbit back. Explaining the Shingae to Ethan will mean that I have to tell him I used to be a part of that world and that Ben died because of me. So it has less to do with the Shingae being "too theoretical" and more to do with me being chickenshit.

"How much do you know about Korean culture and customs?" I ask, drumming my fingers against my thighs.

I can't bring up the Jaenanpa. And that has nothing to do with me being a coward. There's no point in telling him that a faction of evil, homicidal villains might be after us when I'm not even 100 percent certain.

So what *can* I tell Ethan that won't lead to questions that I can't answer yet? He wants to know who the assassin was. Then I only need to tell him about dark magic in a broad, general sense. I roll my eyes at myself. Sure, dark magic is so simple and straightforward.

"I learned the little I know about Korean culture from hanging out in K-Town," he says with a shrug. "I doubt Korean pop culture will help me much here, though."

That's good. At least he doesn't have any warped, preconceived notions about the Shingae—like fox spirits being evil creatures who devour the livers of innocent virgin men. *Ick.* Folklore. Humans sometimes have the grossest imaginations.

"That's okay. I can give you a crash course on the house." I pause to parse out my thoughts. "In Korea, there are shamans known as mudangs, who believe that both natural and supernatural forces influence human life."

I leave out the part that the supernatural forces belong to the Shingae and that the mudangs are the select few humans who can glimpse past the veil that hides the world of gods from the rest. The Jaenanpa was formed by mudangs corrupt with power, who hungered for more than a glimpse of the Shingae.

"The mudangs practice divination and perform elaborate rituals to commune with ancestral spirits and deities on behalf of people who seek their help. You can say Korean shamanism is the oldest religion that originated in the country." I take a deep breath before telling him the hard-to-swallow part. "But there are some corrupt mudangs who can wield dark magic through forbidden spells."

Ethan nods for a long time, as though forcing his brain to accept what I said. He finally stops nodding and coughs into his fist. "My guess is we aren't talking about the kind of magic that involves pulling a bunny out of a top hat."

"Well, maybe if you ask really nicely." I don't mention that the most powerful dark mudangs of the Jaenanpa can also absorb magic into themselves by killing Shingae beings in horrifying ritualistic sacrifices. "But no. Dark magic rarely involves top hats."

He laughs under his breath, more dumbfounded than amused. I ignore how much I like the deep, rumbly sound. "So that woman was one of those mudang folks?"

"Not even close." I appreciate him trying to believe me when every ounce of his logic must be rebelling against the notion of magic. "She was merely a puppet. They didn't dress like that in the old days, but I guess even minion apparel has evolved."

"In the old days . . ." He stops himself before he asks what I meant by that. Neither of us is ready to get into that yet.

"But some things haven't changed," I say, hurrying past my slip of the tongue, "like what happened when she died."

"She dissolved into red dust," Ethan says dismally. No matter how unbelievable, he saw it with his own eyes.

"She was a corpse raised from the dead by her master, a dark mudang." I watch him closely for a potential head explosion, but he nods again. "When I destroyed her—with your help—she returned to her intended form. A handful of dust."

"Why was she after you?" he asks after a moment, his hands tightening around the steering wheel.

Having a near-death experience via weird-ass shit must make humans more open minded toward weird-ass shit. It still unnerves me how well Ethan is taking the magical elements of my explanation. But I also know he's making a huge effort for my sake. His concerned gaze keeps shifting from my injured shoulder to my face, which I'm guessing is still pale. I try not to succumb to any feelings of the warm and fuzzy sort.

"A powerful dark mudang out there wants something from me." Realization dawns on me as I answer. If the Jaenanpa wanted me dead, the assassin would have stabbed my heart, not my shoulder.

His eyes dart toward me. "What do they want from you?"

Could it be my magic? But why would they go through all this trouble to find me if all they want is my magic? There are other gumihos around. Besides, gumiho magic isn't all that coveted—being able to shift into a fox might've been useful for its speed, strength, and hunting skills way back when, but it's not much use in the modern world.

The true strength of the gumiho comes from their cunning and intelligence, but those things have nothing to do with magic. And no one knows about my newfound powers of eternal youth and fast healing. A chill runs down my spine. Many would gladly kill for those powers.

"I have no idea," I finally say.

"But you think they'll try again." He doesn't phrase it as a question. He probably figured it out during his brooding session. "That's why we're running."

"We're not running. It's a strategic retreat until we figure out exactly what we're up against." It'll be hard to keep Ethan alive and avenge Ben's death if I'm dead. That's the only reason we're *retreating*. "But yes. They'll send two more—Blue and Yellow."

"The zombies color coordinate their outfits?" He scoffs as though that's the most unbelievable part of the story I'm telling him.

"They're not zombies. They're more like"—I snap my fingers—"golems."

"Gollum? As in *my precious* . . ." His Gollum impersonation is passable.

"*Golems* as in the Jewish folklore." The *you idiot* is plain on my face. "They're supposed to be made of clay and controlled by their maker."

"Ahh." He grins, his eyes crinkling at the corners.

"Dingus." I can't help but smile back at him, grateful for the moment of levity. We needed it. "And to answer your question, the mudang's assassins are created in triplets. Red, blue, and yellow. It's the colors of the mudang insignia, which looks like three drops of red, blue, and yellow paint swirling together to make a circle. We've faced Red, the weakest of the three. Blue and Yellow will come for us next, and they'll be much harder to defeat."

"The weakest one almost killed us both." He clenches his jaw in obvious frustration. "How are we supposed to defeat the other two?"

"I'm trying to figure that out." I hold back my apology, because it won't do any good.

Ethan's expression turns grim again. He tracked me down so I can help him find Ben's killer, but now we're on the run from dark powers that he can't begin to fathom. As far as he's concerned, we might die without ever finding out who murdered his brother. *The Jaenanpa killed Ben because of me.* The words rise to the tip of my tongue, but I swallow them back down.

I don't have enough information yet. Either Blue or Yellow killed Ben, but they're nothing more than puppets dancing to someone else's tune. We need to find their master. Does the Jaenanpa as a faction want something from me? Or does someone in their ranks have a personal vendetta against me? I have no idea what we're up against. When I figure out who exactly is behind Ben's murder, I'll tell Ethan everything. Until then, keeping him alive is my priority. I can't risk him taking off in anger, too disgusted to stay with me.

"We'll find Ben's killer," I say instead. "Once we get out of this shitstorm—and I promise you we will—we'll find out who murdered your brother, and they'll pay for what they did."

"I want *justice* for Ben." He catches my eyes. Yes, he's every bit as kind as I remember him—noble, even. But I'm neither of those things. *I* want vengeance. I don't know what he sees in my expression, but he turns back to the road and says, "Let's focus on staying alive for the time being."

BUJEOK

The mother stood before the man, with the child hidden behind her back, shivering on the edge of the cliff. But the man didn't see a mother and a child. Neither did he see his wife and their daughter. All he saw was power and the obstacle stopping him from obtaining that power.

Blind hunger thrummed in his veins, consuming him. He had to possess it. There was no cost too great. He drew the bujeok from the depth of his sleeve, hands shaking from the enormity of what he was about to do. The rectangular strip of paper held forbidden incantations and symbols that were shunned even by the most ruthless magic thieves. No one in the worlds would forgive him for using the talisman. But none of that mattered, because he would become the most powerful being in all the realms.

The shaking in his hands ceased as the ghost of his humanity dissipated—burned to cinders by his insatiable need for power. And as his mouth formed the terrible words, the dark magic erased the last of the man he had once been.

The bujeok floated above his outstretched palm, the filmy paper suddenly as stiff as a sheet of metal. He heard the scuff of feet behind him as his disciples stumbled away from him. Their cowardice didn't surprise him. They were unworthy. Only *he* was worthy of this power.

The mother shifted form into a white nine-tailed fox as large as a mare—the transformation too fast to mark with the human concept of time. Her eyes flashed with green fire as she bared her teeth at him, fierce and unafraid. She was glorious. The man he had been would have felt a prickle of regret for having to kill her, but the dark mudang felt nothing.

Flames as dark as blood enveloped the bujeok. The bloody fire burned higher and higher on his palm until it entered him as swiftly as a serpent striking. It pierced him like white-hot daggers through his eyes, his nose, and his mouth. He wanted to scream, but the sound that escaped his throat was inhuman—agony given voice.

Then there was silence. A stillness he had never experienced before. The gumiho growled into the silence, and the mudang felt the sound ripple around him. He *tasted* her fear. His lips peeled back in a smile that shimmered with violence.

The mudang couldn't see that his teeth were red with blood—that his eyes had turned into pools of it. He wouldn't have cared. He felt nothing but sharp, thrilling exuberance as he uttered the word that would kill her.

"Sa."

CHAPTER FIVE

The direct route from Las Vegas to Monterey is only about eight hours, but we're taking the back roads as a precaution, so it'll be at least eleven. The Jaenanpa would expect us to go to Arizona or the Sierra Nevada, where groves of more powerful Seonangshin are rumored to reside. The cypress tree we're headed for stands alone by the sea and is less than three hundred years old, barely awakening to its omnipotence.

"We need to stop for gas," Ethan says, checking the rearview mirror before changing lanes.

"Sure. That's fine." Thank gods. I have to pee, and I'm starving. Ultrafast healing takes a lot out of me.

The blue-and-red gas station sign juts high into the sky, calling all tired travelers. Ethan pulls up to an open pump—pump four. I push aside my knee-jerk reaction to the number. Koreans don't like the number four because it's pronounced "sa"—the same pronunciation as the word for death. But I'm a being of the Shingae. I can differentiate between superstitious bullshit and the real stuff, and the whole unlucky-number-four business is just some silly superstition. So I say nothing as Ethan parks the car and kills the engine at pump four.

"I'm going to run inside to pay with cash." He pushes open the driver's side door and steps out in one graceful movement.

"Good idea." I scoot to the edge of my seat and use the narrow step below the door to get off.

I'm glad Ethan is savvy enough not to leave a paper trail. Well, the man *is* a PI. I should give him more credit. Anyway, our enemies are probably tech proficient enough to track us if we leave electronic traces—we turned off our phones and took out the batteries before we left Las Vegas. Surely, more than their outfits have evolved.

Once he walks inside to the cashier, I make a run for the restrooms adjacent to the main building. After I relieve myself, I head straight for the minimart and find Ethan in one of the aisles.

"I got plenty for both of us." His arms are filled with bottles of water, protein bars, and bags of trail mix. *Ugh.*

"Great. Let me grab a couple more things." I need animal protein. Full-fat milk, the last two hot dogs spinning in the machine, and a fistful of Slim Jims should do. *Shit.* I almost forgot the liquor. That would've been a disaster. When I unload my provisions next to his at the cashier stand, Ethan cringes for a millisecond. I know exactly what he's thinking. *Gross.* "I won't judge if you don't."

"Why would you judge me?" His eyebrows hike up in surprise.

"Protein bars and trail mix? You're so watching your figure." Even though I sink a lot of snark into my words, I can't stop my eyes from roaming over the biceps stretching out the sleeves of his T-shirt and the ridges and grooves of his muscular forearms. I catch myself and glance at him from underneath my lashes. He's looking at me with a knowing smirk. *Cocky bastard.* Irritation overshadows whatever I was feeling.

"I'll get this," I mumble, digging out some crumpled bills from my pocket.

"I need to see your driver's license," the cashier says, stifling a yawn.

"Are you kidding me?" While I remembered to grab some emergency cash on my way out, I left my wallet and driver's license in my apartment. Ethan shakes with silent laughter beside me. I dig an elbow into his side, hoping he feels some discomfort through his ridiculously hard obliques, and mutter, "*You* can pay."

Back outside, Ethan opens the passenger door for me, and I hesitate. "You must be exhausted. Should I drive the rest of the way?"

"You got stabbed in the shoulder," he says, his voice rough. "I think I can manage driving a bit further."

Not bothering with an answer, I climb into the passenger seat. He's right. My wound is closed, but my range of motion isn't fully restored. And the trip to the restroom and minimart drained me enough to make me dizzy. It might be safer for him to drive until I'm fully recovered. That reminds me. I'm famished. I need to get some protein in me if I want to heal properly. I rip open a Slim Jim and wolf it down.

I move on to my next one as Ethan pulls out of the gas station. When I'm on my fourth stick of dried meat, I notice the silence in the car and his sideways glances. "What?"

"Are you going to wash that down with some milk?" he asks with a grimace. "Or with a couple shots of Johnnie Walker?"

"The liquor isn't for me," I snap, pulling out one of my shriveled hot dogs. "It's for someone else."

"Where exactly are we going?" He stares at the hot dog with horrified fascination.

I roll my eyes as I rip off some of the dry meat and stale bread with my hands and teeth. Ethan holds back a shudder. He can judge all he wants. I can't be a woozy mess for what lies ahead.

"Just outside Monterey." We aren't headed for the famous Lone Cypress in Pebble Beach. The cypress I seek lives on a secluded cliffside on an outcropping a long way down from the road.

"And you know someone who can help us there?" With a sharp shake of his head, he tears his gaze away from my progress on the hot dog and focuses his attention on the road. "Someone who's fond of Johnnie Walker?"

"Yes." I don't elaborate. I'm too busy masticating rubbery meat.

The Johnnie Walker is an offering for the Seonangshin. I can't show up empty handed. It would be disrespectful. Why booze? Beats me. Sometimes tradition is just tradition. In Korea, humans offer food and liquor to their dead ancestors in an elaborate memorial ceremony called *jesa*. When they visit an ancestor's burial site, they bring a truncated version of jesa food and liquor, which is poured on the grassy mound of the grave. Maybe the Seonangshin developed a taste for the liquid fire soaked up by the earth. Whatever the case, one never visits the Seonangshin without an alcoholic offering.

"Will I get to meet your friend?" His head moves as though he's turning toward me again, but he jerks it back to keep looking straight. He can't face the horror of my gas station hot dog again.

"No, my . . . friend doesn't like meeting strangers." I can't risk bringing a human along. The Seonangshin might snuff his life out if he so much as blinks wrong. Besides, all he would see is a cypress tree. He won't be able to hear the Seonangshin or feel their presence. "Look, I know you have questions. I appreciate you not bombarding me with them right now. I promise I'll tell you more once I figure some things out."

His hands clench and unclench around the steering wheel, then he nods once. I release my breath. I bought myself some time, but not much. He needs an explanation. I can't blame him. He sure as hell deserves one.

I munch on my hot dog in silence. It's like gnawing on a leather belt, but I can't be picky, considering the amount of blood I lost. I open up the carton of milk to help wash it down. I feel some of my strength returning. Good. I'm going to need it for my audience with the Seonangshin.

Ethan's Jeep eats up the road, and I grow more anxious by the mile. I'm walking back into the world that I turned my back on over a hundred years ago—the world I've been hiding from all this time. Once I go back, there will be no hiding from my past. There will be no hiding from myself.

We make good time to Monterey as night descends around us. My stomach lurches with nerves. Or it could be the hot dogs. I wipe my damp palms on my jean-clad thighs and blow out a long breath. A part of me wants to bolt . . . but I know there's no running from the dark magic after us. At least, not for long. So back to the Shingae I go.

"Turn onto that dirt road," I say in a resigned voice. Ethan maneuvers the car into the shadows of the woods. "Okay. You can stop here."

"Where are we?" He peers out the windshield, but the headlights are swallowed up by the dense fog.

"Get out of the car," I tell him. He swivels his head around so fast I'm sure he gave himself whiplash. "I'm not ditching you. We're switching seats. I need to drive the rest of the way."

He nods and gets out of the driver's seat without any questions. Ethan is handling this strange day much better than I ever would have in his shoes. I feel unworthy of his patience and trust. Our eyes meet as we pass each other at the front of the car, but I look away first. Once I'm in the driver's seat, I move it closer to the steering wheel to compensate for my shorter legs. My barely five-feet-tall human body can be annoying as hell sometimes.

"Buckle in." I shift the gear into drive and close my eyes. "Here we go."

I need my spirit eyes to find the Seonangshin. My physical eyes will only get in the way, making me doubt and second-guess what my spirit senses. We're getting close. I can feel the Seonangshin's power pulsating around us, and the magic within me strains to answer. I grit my teeth and fight the primal call to transform into my spirit form—gumiho, the nine-tailed fox.

Ethan is tense and alert beside me, as though he can sense something too. Or he might be a tad bit concerned that I'm driving through a thick forest with my eyes closed. He doesn't know that I can perceive more topography with my spirit eyes than my physical eyes could ever see. When I maneuver the car toward the edge of the cliff, I feel his alarmed glance on me.

"Don't worry. I see it." I slow to a stop, shift into park, then turn off the engine. I brace myself before I open my eyes and face him.

"Your eyes are on fire," he breathes. I'm impressed by how he barely flinches.

"I know." My voice cracks, ruining my chill vibe.

I step out into the night, and Ethan comes to stand next to me. A knot loosens in my stomach at his quiet acceptance. To him, I'm Sunny Cho—his friend—even when my eyes are on fire.

Power is stirring within me, and I can't completely contain it. It's been over a century since I've actively used magic, and the small taste makes me hungry for more. But I don't give in to it.

"I have to go down the cliff," I say.

Ethan's eyebrows climb up to his forehead. He steps forward and peers down the cliff. "How far does it go?"

"Pretty far." I gulp.

He rakes his fingers through his hair. "And how do you plan on climbing down?"

"Very carefully." I'm not being flippant. I truly intend to go down very carefully.

He pivots and walks a few steps away before stomping back to me. "Can I go down instead?"

"Nope." I shake my head, as a squishy feeling fills my chest at his offer. Even if he was a being of the Shingae and could communicate with the Seonangshin, I would still go down myself. I couldn't stand by and watch him risk his life. It's easier to risk my own.

"Is it absolutely necessary for you to make the climb?" he says through clenched teeth.

"Yup." I nod.

"Fuck," he shouts, kicking the ground.

"I agree with that sentiment." I nod some more.

"Sunny, this isn't funny." His exasperated smile tells me he's resigned to my plan. He's stronger than I am.

"I know, but this is the only way I can get some answers." And I need answers to keep us alive.

"I won't be able to do a single thing to help you from up here." His voice is pained.

"Don't watch, and don't wait." I'm asking him to be completely helpless. It's a lot. "Go sit in the car, and get some rest. Whatever I find out down there, we'll have a long journey ahead of us."

"Sure. Some shut-eye sounds great." Sarcasm drips from his words.

I let it go. Like I said, it's a big ask. "I need to borrow your backpack."

"Be my guest." He crosses his arms over his chest and stands rooted to the spot as if to say, *I'm not lifting a finger to help you plunge to your death.*

I scoff before I trudge over to the car. I understand where he's coming from, but that doesn't make him any less immature. But I kind of like seeing this side of him. It makes him seem more human.

I dump out everything he has in his backpack and place the bottle of Johnnie Walker inside. I adjust the straps so the bag fits closely to my body. I tighten my sword belt and check my hwando. I would never lift a weapon against the Seonangshin, but the weight of my sword against my thigh calms me. With my preparations complete, I walk back to the cliff and begin my descent without glancing at Ethan. Because, come on. What the hell am I supposed to say? *I'll see you soon if I don't die?*

My physical eyes are useless in the dense, foggy night, so I close them again. My hands and feet find impossible holds as I climb down inch by painful inch. My foot slips, and I slide down the cliff, clawing at the rocky wall. I dig my hand into a thin crevice to stop my downward trajectory. My injured shoulder screams with pain as it bears the brunt of my body weight, and the closed wound rips open again. My other hand finds purchase on a minute protrusion, and I maneuver my feet onto whatever bumps and dips won't collapse beneath me.

I take a few seconds to catch my breath. The blood from my shoulder wound soaks through the front of my shirt, and my raw fingers make my grip tenuous. Still, I lower myself toward the outcropping below with the guidance of my spirit eyes, because the longer this descent takes, the less likely I am to make it down safely.

My shirt clings to my torso like a second skin from the blood and sweat, but I'm making progress. The hum of magic now brushes against my skin—the power almost palpable. I'm close. My sigh of relief turns into a scream when my foothold suddenly crumbles beneath me, and I'm free-falling. My eyes shoot open in panic, and I spin in the air to face downward. But I can't even see the ground rushing up to meet me with the thick fog cloaking the night.

I feel heat spreading in the center of my chest, as though an orb of fire is glowing inside me. It compels me to change my form—to allow the fire to consume me. *No.* I can't give in to it. If I do, everyone in the vicinity might die. Ethan might die. *No.* I won't allow it.

I stop falling a hand's width away from the ground, my scream hitching in my throat. What's happening? The puffs of my ragged breath create dust whorls on the rocky surface as I float, suspended in the air. I don't move a muscle. I don't make a sound.

"You would have died," the lone cypress says, "and you still didn't change. You would rather die than accept your destiny?"

The Seonangshin just confirmed that I *can* die. It's reassuring to finally know for sure. But yes, I was willing to die rather than take my gumiho form. Fuck destiny. Besides, what does my choice of going furry or not have to do with my destiny? Who says selling shit at a casino in a tiny, hideous dress isn't my destiny?

Of course I say none of this out loud. I don't dare speak before I pay proper respects to the young cypress. And she already knows my answer anyway. I inhale and exhale carefully through my nose. I'm a little emotional—I almost died, for fuck's sake—and I'm scared shitless to be in the presence of the Seonangshin.

While I calm myself down, she spins me in the air and places me feetfirst on solid ground. My knees buckle when she releases me from her hold, but I manage not to fall. Once I feel steady enough, I unhook the backpack from my arms with a wince and pull out the bottle of Johnnie Walker.

I avoided doing so until now, but I raise my eyes to face the lone cypress. Tall, sinewy, and jagged. Her harsh beauty takes my breath away, and the powerful pulse of her gi compels me to kneel. With my eyes downcast once more, I pour the entire bottle of whiskey on the edges of her roots and pay my respects, bowing with my forehead pressed to the ground.

"Rise, my child." The young cypress speaks through the wind and the waves.

I lift my head off the ground, but I stay kneeling and keep my gaze glued to the ground. I don't want to take any chances and offend the god of Mountains. With my voice wavering, I say in rusty Korean, "Sacred One, I seek your guidance."

"You have hidden from us, but we never lost sight of you," she intones.

My eyes shoot up to the lone cypress in alarm. "I never imagined I could hide from the Seonangshin."

"We witnessed the cruelty of your fate and your suffering, but turning your back on your destiny will bring you no peace."

"It is not peace I seek. I don't deserve it. You must know what I've done." My voice breaks as hot tears trail down my cheeks. I wipe a hand across my face and stare down at the moisture. The last time I wept, I was on a boat headed for America. "You showed me too much mercy in saving my life just now."

"There is much you do not know. But you will know in time," the Seonangshin says. "For now, know that your old enemy has risen."

"Ris . . . risen? Daeseong is dead. I extinguished his life force." I clench my fists on my lap and fight against the tidal wave of panic building inside me. "There can be no resurrection. That is the law of the Shingae."

"Do not presume to explain the law of the Shingae to me." Thunder booms in the dark sky, and I bow my head again. "Daeseong has returned. Even we could not interfere with his resurrection, because he has drawn from the powers of the Amheuk."

"The Amheuk?" I gasp, the hair on the back of my neck standing. The Amheuk—a force of true darkness—was defeated to *end* the Endless War and was banished to the edge of the worlds. How can this be possible? "But the price . . . so much blood has to be shed. How could he pay that from the beyond?"

"His followers," she answers.

None of this makes sense.

Daeseong was once a scholar driven by his quest for knowledge. When he discovered the existence of the Shingae, his quest was twisted by an insatiable hunger for magic, becoming something sinister and bloodthirsty. He became a powerful dark mudang and joined the Jaenanpa. He then led the faction in a rampage against the Shingae. But Daeseong's vision became too horrific even for the Jaenanpa. They cut him out of their ranks, and only the most loyal of his followers stayed with him.

"But how?" I whisper.

I killed the last of his followers when they came after my mother and me. But it had been too late. *I* had been too late. The memories of my past breach my defensive walls and flood my mind until I'm drowning.

No traces of the friendly, smiling villagers remained as they formed a violent, angry mob—their eyes slashes of hatred, their mouths black pits of rage. The stones they threw cut and bruised us.

It was when we were cornered against the sheer drop of a cliff that Daeseong stepped forward. He withdrew a strip of paper from his sleeves. It was a bujeok—a talisman. I couldn't make out what it said, but my mother stepped in front of me and transformed just as the paper combusted on Daeseong's palm, his lips moving silently.

"The women and children had remained behind." The Seonangshin's soft voice echoes in the night, startling me out of my waking nightmare into an even darker, bleaker present. "It took them over a century, but their faith was fanatical. They did nothing out of line. They lived, procreated, and recruited—nothing even the gods could interfere with.

"But once their numbers reached five thousand with the birth of a child, they acted without hesitation." The wind moaned around me. "We sensed the first dark ritual immediately, but it was too late because it was also the last. Daeseong's followers had synchronized the blood sacrifice down to the second and performed it at the exact same moment. Five thousand humans, including the newborn, took their final breath as one."

I can't tell if I'm crying or if it's the rain pouring down from the ripped sky. The Seonangshin lament as well. In the far recesses of my mind, I recall the news of a South Korean cult committing mass suicide. The blood sacrifice and the powers of the Amheuk resurrected Daeseong, and now he's after me. My head jerks up as terrifying understanding dawns on me.

"Sacred One, if Daeseong's life was drawn from the Amheuk, how can we destroy him?" I'd imagined my worst-case scenario to be finding out that I needed to take down the entire Jaenanpa faction. If that were the case, I might've been able to target the top tier of their ranks to stop whatever ploy they had against me. But if Daeseong was resurrected from the Amheuk . . . "Can we defeat him with the sacred ashes?"

"Not ones from my young limbs." The cypress sways and shakes her branches in the once-more-clear night. "You need the ashes from the roots of an ancient cypress tree."

An image of a grove of cypress flashes and settles in my mind. She has shown me the location of the ancient cypress grove. "Will their sacred ashes be enough?"

"Nothing might be enough to forestall the coming of the Amheuk." The wind howls, low and mournful.

I shake my head in confusion. *The coming of the Amheuk?* Does the Seonangshin mean Daeseong's resurrection? How do you forestall something that already happened? But what else could she mean?

The dark mudang's hunger for power has no end. He will wreak terror and destruction on the worlds. I know this to be true. But maybe this time I won't have to be the one to end him. There are plenty of heroes in the Shingae, and I'm not one of them. Isn't this the kind of shit the Suhoshin signed up for?

"Why . . . why does he seek me?" I need concrete answers, not riddles.

"For the same reason he sought you all those years ago," she says.

"I don't understand," I whisper. "He wanted to capture my mother to steal her powers—"

"He wanted *you*. Not your mother," the Seonangshin cuts me off, growing impatient. "He still seeks a power within you—a gift of the Cheon'gwang."

"The true light? The Cheon'gwang sacrificed itself half a millennium ago to vanquish the Amheuk. How can I bear its gift?" It can't be me. My mother was the most powerful gumiho of her time—a healer and a warrior. I'm not special. I'm not . . . good. "I don't understand."

"You will in time." The Seonangshin see all, but they do not impart their knowledge indiscriminately. "Be brave, my child."

With so many of my questions unanswered, the lone cypress transports me to the top of the cliff, my audience with her at an end.

CHAPTER SIX

"Sunny." Ethan's voice is hoarse with relief.

He pulls me back from the edge of the cliff and runs his hands over me, checking to make sure I'm still in one piece. His touch is urgent but so gentle that my heart twists a little. Darkness is threatening to overtake my mind, but all I want is to lean into his touch. A shiver runs through me, and his eyes shoot up to meet mine.

Whatever he sees in them changes the tenor of his touch as he resumes sliding his hands down my arms. His fingers linger at my elbows, his thumbs caressing the sensitive skin at the crooks of my arms. The slow circles make my skin catch fire, and heat gathers low in my stomach. I want to let it spread and undo me. Ethan takes a step toward me, narrowing the gap between us, and I release a ragged sigh. His hot gaze holds mine as he draws his hands back up my arms, and I sway toward him. But he suddenly stills and draws one hand away.

"Goddamn it, Sunny." He looks stricken. "You're bleeding."

"The shoulder wound tore open while I was climbing down. It already healed shut again," I explain woodenly. With his touch gone, nothing stands between my mind and the horrors of what I learned. "I'll be fine."

"Hey." He guides me closer to the car and peers into my face by the beam of the headlights. "Are you okay?"

"No," I force past my tear-clogged throat.

Nothing is okay. Daeseong came back from the dead—stronger and nearly invincible—through the blood of five thousand people. Even a newborn. And now . . . I know he orchestrated Ben's murder. The note—*Mihwa, are you well?*—is more than a taunt. It's a threat, telling me he can and will take the people I care about away from me unless I . . . what? Give him what he wants? But how can I if I have no idea what he wants from me?

And I have no more excuses left to keep the truth from Ethan—other than trying to keep him safe. But can I protect him from Daeseong? I don't even know if I can keep myself alive. This isn't my decision to make. I have to tell Ethan the truth so he can decide what he wants to do.

"Do you have a T-shirt I can borrow?" I ask, moving toward the trunk of the car where he keeps his duffel bag. "Let me clean myself up a bit, then we can be on our way."

"Sunny . . ." He stops me with a hand on my good arm and searches my face. I look away, pressing my lips together. I can't do this right now. With a sigh, he walks to the back of the car and opens the trunk. "On our way where?"

"Back to Las Vegas." I come stand next to him, grateful he let me change the subject.

"Won't the assassins come looking for us there?" He hands me a navy blue T-shirt and turns his back to me.

I unbutton my shirt and shrug out of it with a grimace. I use a dry patch of the cloth to wipe the blood off my skin the best I can. Some blood soaked into my bra, and I reach back for the clasp, but I hesitate. The heady buzz of desire still lingers in my veins, and the pebbled peaks of my breasts press against the confines of my bra. The thought of Ethan seeing how much he affects me makes me blush. And it's not only embarrassment that's making blood rush to my cheeks. A part of me *wants* him to see. I blush harder and decide to leave my bra on. I don't want to have my arms crossed over my chest for the entire drive back to Vegas.

"Hopefully, they won't expect us to go there, because it's so obvious," I say, thinking out loud. Focusing on strategy soothes my frayed nerves. I pull on the T-shirt. It falls halfway down my thighs, and the sleeves end just a couple of inches above my elbows. "Besides, if the assassins have any tracking skills, they'll find us no matter where we go, now that I've used my magic. I'll leave a trace for at least a few hours."

"So it's magic," he mutters almost to himself. He must've run through a hundred possibilities in his head. I could've been a mutant or an alien. But knowing that I can use magic probably raises even more questions for him. "I didn't hear you incant any spells. Did you perform a ritual when I wasn't looking?"

"My magic doesn't come from spells or rituals. It's a part of who I am." As the words leave my mouth, I know them to be true. I've been denying a part of myself—a part that defines me—for over a century. Without my magic, I am not whole. But do I want to be whole, knowing what I'm capable of?

"A part of who you are . . ." Instead of demanding to know what the hell that means, he asks a more productive question. "Your healing power—if that's magic—shouldn't that have alerted them back in your apartment? Do you think they followed us here?"

"I'm decent. You can turn around." When Ethan faces me again, I answer, "My passive powers aren't detectable. It's only when I actively use magic that it leaves a mark. But using my spirit eyes definitely counts as active magic."

"Then we better get out of here." He ushers me to the passenger seat with a hand on the small of my back and opens the door for me. "It sounds like we need a head start."

I nod and get into the car. I don't bother offering to drive. The second bucket of blood I lost has me feeling lightheaded and woozy. Even I know when to tap out. I reach into the paper bag from the gas station. When my hand wraps around the last two Slim Jims, I sigh with relief. It's not nearly enough to refuel me, but hopefully I'll stop seeing double. I scarf one down in record time and tear into the next one.

Ethan gives me a bemused look as he maneuvers the Jeep back onto the road. "Do you have a plan for when we get back to Vegas?"

I chew carefully before I swallow with a gulp. "That depends on what you decide to do."

"What *I* decide to do?" His eyebrows pull low over his eyes.

"Ethan, I need to tell you something." The words leave my mouth before I can stop them.

"Good, because I have questions." He huffs a relieved laugh. "So many questions."

He thinks I'm about to explain everything to him. He's right. I plan to . . . but there's something he needs to know first. My nails dig into my palms. Gods, am I doing this now? I guess I am. "Ben was killed because of me."

The car swerves with a screech of wheels as he whips his head around to stare at me. With a curse, he jerks his eyes back to the road and rights the car. It feels like an eternity before he speaks. "You don't know that."

"I do." I grip the half-eaten stick of dry meat as though it's a lifeline. "Someone from my past—someone from the Shingae—is after me."

"The Shingae?" His voice rings with frustration. "Where the hell is that?"

"It means the world of gods in Korean." When Ethan doesn't comment on my answer, I take that as my cue to continue. "There are many names for it across the worlds, but there is a world of magical beings unknown to humans.

"All the folklore, fairy tales, mythology . . . they're mostly *not* bullshit. The stories are bastardized and sensationalized, but they're based on the truth. It doesn't matter which culture the lore originates from—that's just semantics. The Shingae and the beings from there . . . like me . . . we're the source of those tales."

"Beings from the Shingae"—he wipes a hand down his face—"like you?"

"I'm a gumiho," I whisper, tears springing to the surface. "A nine-tailed fox spirit."

Beast. Monster. Spittle flies out of their snarling mouths as they pelt me with stones.

I push away the unwelcome memory and release a strangled breath. "I . . . I was born a gumiho, but I haven't taken my fox form in over a century."

"A . . . century?" Ethan repeats slowly.

"I left Korea and came to the US when I was eighteen. I've been roaming the country for over a century," I say. "I move from city to city every few years before anyone can suspect that I don't age."

He breathes in and out through his nose. "You're a hundred-something-year-old gumiho who doesn't age."

"One hundred thirty-two years *young*," I quip, then cringe. He doesn't laugh. Of course he doesn't laugh. I clear my throat. "Yes."

"Your spirit eyes, your ability to heal, your immortality are your powers—your magic—as a gumiho?" He sounds clinical . . . detached. Like a PI gathering evidence to get to the bottom of a case.

"The spirit eyes, yes. The rest . . . I don't know. And I'm not immortal." My hands are shaking, so I clench them in my lap. "I turned my back on the Shingae when I left Korea. There are a lot of things about my powers that I don't understand."

"And there are other beings from the Shingae . . . like you . . . living in the US?" He continues with his line of questions.

"Not too many and not exactly like me . . . but yes. Most magical beings prefer to remain in their originating countries, where their lore lives on strong. They're more powerful—in magic and in numbers—in their homeland.

"Plus, being an immigrant is just plain hard. It's just easier to stay in your comfort zone, you know?" I glance at Ethan with a strained smile, but he doesn't look at me. "But sometimes, we need . . . change. Humans come to the US to fulfill their American dream. We mostly come here to get lost in the masses. Either way, America is still a melting pot, even for magical beings."

The silence stretches on, and I fold first. "I know this is a lot—"

"It is," he cuts me off, his jaw clenched so tight I'm worried he'll crack a tooth. "Maybe more than I can ever wrap my head around. So let's focus on the important stuff for now. Tell me how any of this makes you responsible for Ben's death."

"Ben was poisoned. The thin cut on his earlobe, it was made by a dark mudang's poisoned dagger. The autopsy picked up nothing, because the poison is from the Shingae. Humans have no way of harvesting it or detecting it." I heave a shuddering breath. "And in my old life . . . I was known as Mihwa."

After a few seconds of stunned silence, Ethan makes a series of harrowing lane changes—I smell tire burn—to exit from the freeway.

"What are you doing?" I gasp.

He doesn't respond. Instead, he speeds down the dark, deserted road leading off the highway before screeching into the parking lot of a run-down diner. Other than a few semis, the lot is empty.

"There had to be a restaurant nearby," he says, killing the engine. "You're so pale, your lips look almost blue. You need a steak."

That is about the last thing I expect him to say, but my stomach growls loudly in agreement. "It's the blood loss. I need animal protein to recover."

"I figured as much from your gas station haul." The very evenness of his voice sends a spike of fear down my spine.

He gets out of the car, and I follow suit. Sure, there's a homicidal megalomaniac after us, but my instinct is screaming that Ethan is the person I don't want to cross right now. It makes no sense, but he is vibrating with a tightly controlled strength I don't want to see unleashed.

I look down at my legs to make sure the T-shirt is long enough to hide my hwando. Only the tip of the sheath peeks out. That's good enough. I can't risk being weaponless even for a short while.

I have to skip to keep up with Ethan's long strides. He notices with a frown and slows down, and we walk into the diner together. A tired-looking waitress meets my eyes and waves around a half-full pot of coffee. I assume she means we can choose any of the many empty booths to park our asses in.

Roxy's Diner is run down but brightly tacky. This diner is just run down and morose. A pang of homesickness hits me. I pick a booth near the back of the restaurant—it's close to a side exit in case we need to make a run for it—and I sit down facing the main entrance. Ethan slides in next to me. For a second, I feel trapped, but I realize it's a protective gesture. I can feel the heat emanating from his body, and I want to press myself against him. Seriously, what the fuck is wrong with me? I scoot a few inches away. He won't appreciate me rubbing up against him after everything I told him.

We order our food after a cursory glance at the sticky laminated menu. When the waitress brings us our coffee, I cradle my mug between my cold hands and stare down at it. The black coffee looks as dark as my soul. I hold back a nervous cackle. My stupid humor, I can handle. My newfound lasciviousness, not so much. I jump a little when Ethan finally speaks.

"You knew the note was for you, and you knew a poison from the Shingae killed Ben." He stares down at his coffee too. "Why didn't you tell me earlier?"

"I wasn't sure about anything. That note . . . it didn't make any sense. It could only have been someone from my old life, but that wasn't possible. Everyone I knew was . . . was dead," I stammer, blood rushing to my cheeks. I know I'm making excuses. "I needed to know what we were up against before I told you."

I leave out the part that I was afraid he'd hate me. And I didn't want him to—I *don't* want him to—hate me. As selfish as it sounds, I don't want him to leave. I can't do this alone. I don't want to *be* alone. But I can't tell him any of that. I don't even want to admit it to myself.

"We're up against a dark mudang," he says, working out the facts. "A mudang's assassin came after you, and a mudang's poisoned dagger killed Ben."

"Yes." I'm impressed he can think straight under the circumstances. I'm not sure I can. "But it's a little more complicated than that. There's a faction of dark mudangs called the Jaenanpa. Their primary purpose is to steal magic from beings of the Shingae by any means necessary, including torture and murder."

"So you needed to know whether we were up against a rogue dark mudang or an entire bloodthirsty faction." He sums up my thoughts neatly. "What did your alcohol-loving friend have to say about that?"

"I was seeking guidance from the Seonangshin, the god of Mountains."

"You went to have a drink with a *god*?" He gapes at me.

Is it wrong of me to feel a tiny bit satisfied that I finally made him lose his cool? Probably. But I like this Ethan so much more than the icy, distant version.

"The Johnnie Walker was an *offering* for them," I say primly. "The Seonangshin is more powerful than we can fathom, and I had to show them proper respect."

"So?" He arches a brow at me, lingering frustration sparking in his eyes. "Was it worth risking your life to go see this god?"

"I'm not sure if it was *worth it*, but I did get some answers. Unfortunately, what I now know makes facing the whole Jaenanpa sound appealing." I take a scalding sip of coffee, wishing I could've spared him from the helpless fear on top of that cliff. Hell, I wish I could spare him from this whole fucking nightmare, but he needs to know all the facts before he makes his decision. "But it's not the Jaenanpa at all. We have something much worse on our hands. Daeseong, the most powerful dark mudang who ever lived, came back from the dead."

"Came back from . . ." He cradles his forehead in his hand. "Should I even ask how that works?"

"To resurrect someone, a bloody ritual has to be performed to awaken the powers of the Amheuk, an ancient darkness." I don't soften the truth because, despite my worries, I know he can handle it. "Five thousand of Daeseong's followers committed mass suicide to bring him back from the dead. They . . . they even killed a newborn baby."

Ethan curses under his breath. "And why is this one mudang the worst thing that could happen to us?"

"Other than the fact that he's an unhinged megalomaniac?" A shiver of dread travels down my spine. "He was resurrected by the Amheuk, which means some of its powers passed on to him. Who knows how much. My guess is that he has grown immeasurably powerful and he's going to be nearly impossible to defeat."

"He *is* the worst," Ethan says dryly.

There's an edge of hysteria to my laughter. "But there might still be a way to stop him. The Seonangshin showed me a path . . ."

If we go our separate ways, it might be better if he doesn't know the details of my plan. Besides, I'm winging it as I go. I don't even know how to get from point A to point B, yet. Maybe going to Vegas is a bad idea, but I need a reminder that I still have a home to protect. That I still have things in my life worth fighting for—worth dying for. Like Roxy's Diner. I smirk down at my mug.

"Is Daeseong your old enemy?" Ethan asks, a muscle twitching in his jaw. I understand his unspoken question.

"Yes." My voice breaks on the single word. "And one of his undead assassins killed Ben."

He turns toward me with deliberate calm. "Was it the red assassin?"

"No, she said it was one of her brothers, which means it's either Blue or Yellow." I glance down at my hands and blabber more useless excuses. "I'm sorry I didn't . . . I should've . . . I didn't know how to tell you. And I wanted to find out who their master was—the real murderer—before saying anything."

"You're right. The assassins don't matter. Daeseong is the one I want." Ethan loosens his death grip on his mug and takes a sip of his black coffee. He grimaces as though he's not used to the bitter acidity. I wonder how he really takes his coffee. He used to have a sweet tooth. "Do you have any idea what he wants from you?"

"I don't know." I slide the sugar jar toward him, and he shoots me a surprised glance. A corner of his mouth quirks, and he dumps an alarming amount of sugar into his coffee. "The Seonangshin said something about a gift of the Cheon'gwang, the force of true light, but I have no idea what that means. I wish they didn't speak in riddles."

Ethan grunts his agreement. "That might be helpful."

"And . . ." I shift in my seat, making the vinyl bench squeak. No more secrets. No more hiding. "And he probably wants revenge."

"Revenge against you?" After everything I told him, he still looks bewildered. Like I'm not capable of doing anything that would inspire vengeance in someone. "For what?"

"For killing him over a century ago," I say, correcting his misguided faith in me.

He takes a moment to process that, pinching the bridge of his nose. "Is that . . . is that why he killed Ben? To get back at you?"

"I think that's part of it." I nod, my shoulders hunching forward. "I don't know how he found you guys, but I must've left some traces behind. I stayed too long. Daeseong somehow knew Ben mattered to me . . ."

"A part of it?" Ethan's eyes narrow as he puts together what I'm not telling him. "They killed Ben so I would lead them to you. They couldn't find you, and I led them straight to you like a fucking idiot."

"You're not doing this. You're not going to blame yourself for *any* of this," I say through gritted teeth, stupid tears filling my eyes. "You're supposed to hate me. Ben died because of *me*."

"That bastard killed Ben," he growls, then goes completely still—his face going blank with shock—as he figures something else out. "You thought I was going to leave you. That's what you meant when you said our next steps depend on what I decide to do."

"You have every right to walk away." My voice sounds hollow. "To keep yourself safe."

"You actually think I'll walk away knowing who killed Ben?" he asks in a near whisper. "Knowing that you might be next?"

"Ben would be alive if it wasn't for me." I draw back my shoulders and go for the kill. Why delay the inevitable? He's going to leave me eventually. "He was used as a calling card for me to see."

Ethan sucks in a quick breath and turns away from me. He sees now. He can't possibly want to stick with me. I ignore the ache in my heart and blink away the prickling behind my eyes. It's for the best. If I can't keep him by my side and protect him, the best thing I can do is draw Daeseong and his minions away from him. I need to get Ethan off the radar somehow. That way he might have some chance at survival, however slim.

Before the silence shrivels up my insides, the waitress shows up with our food and drops the plates in front of us. If I didn't know better, I would have thought she waited for a pause in our conversation to bring us the food. But I don't think this diner is about that kind of quality service. The food at least looks decent.

I pick up my utensils and cut into my steak. It's actually cooked perfectly rare. I was expecting an overcooked piece of well-done leather. I take a bite and chew. My eyes flutter shut. I break the yolk in my sunny-side up egg and dip a piece of steak in it before I pop it into my mouth.

I steal a glance at Ethan. He's digging into his western omelet with gusto. My steak gets stuck halfway down my throat. How is he so nonchalant about this? I pound my hand against my chest and gulp down some coffee. Maybe he's glad to get away from me—a monster from the Shingae.

I slice viciously into the steak and stuff a giant piece into my mouth. I chew as though I have a vendetta against the cow who sacrificed its life for the meal. Even as I fume in silence, I notice the new occupant who walks into the restaurant. He stands about six feet tall, but the breadth of his shoulders and his muscular build make him look bigger. But it's his face that makes my jaw go slack. Those pretty boy K-drama actors would pull brown paper bags over their heads in shame if they saw this guy.

"Fuck." Ethan jumps to his feet and drags me toward the side exit.

As I stumble after him, I glance over my shoulder and see the stranger's eyes light with silver fire. If I had time, I would smack my palm against my forehead. How did I not see it right away? But there's no time to call myself names. A suhoshin is after us.

TEARS OF BLOOD

The Queen of Mountains shed her tears in secret. Her people needed her to be strong. And it would be foolish to reveal her vulnerabilities to her husband. More than anything, she kept her pain and her tears to herself, because these were one part of her that were hers and hers alone. It was a miracle that she could still *feel*—that she could still hurt and cry.

But as she held her newborn son for the first time, she learned that love could not be hidden. All this time, she thought she was meant to give her life to protect the worlds . . . but she was wrong. She was meant to give her life to protect *him*.

"Your Highness." The lady-in-waiting fell to her knees, shock and distress plain on her face—for her queen was weeping.

Tears as red as blood fell in an unending stream down her cheeks. One by one, they dropped onto the white blanket that swaddled her newborn son.

"There must be another way," the lady-in-waiting said, her own eyes soaked with grief.

"There is no other way." The queen raised her face, her gaze clear and determined despite her heartbreak. She held out the sleeping prince to her lady-in-waiting—to her friend. "You will be his mother. He will know nothing. Not until it is time."

The queen's hands shook as she placed her son in her friend's out-stretched arms, knowing she would never hold him again . . . never see him again. She clawed at her throat as a sob tore from her. She was saying goodbye to her baby—her everything. She curled into herself as pain ripped through her.

With every ounce of her will—with every ounce of her love—she gathered herself and sat up tall. She didn't have to call for the tears that she needed. She didn't need a knife to draw her blood. Her fissured heart provided her with both. She cupped her hands and filled them with her tears of blood.

Her eyes churning with silver power, she blew into her hands until her tears caught fire, burning bright green. When the flames subsided, a disk of pure jade, a little bigger than her thumbnail, lay on her palm. Her breath coming in shallow pants, she threaded a yarn through the jade disk and placed it around her sleeping son's neck. Then she placed her lips on his downy head and closed her eyes.

"It is done." A fine sheen of sweat glistened on her forehead as she drew away from her baby. "Now you must go."

"Your Highness . . . he will kill you," the lady-in-waiting choked out.

"He wouldn't dare," the queen lied. "Go, before anyone finds out the baby was born. I can shield you until you are beyond the mountains."

"I cannot leave you."

"But you must, my dear friend," she said with a tremulous smile. "Who you hold in your arms is bigger than you or me."

The lady-in-waiting inhaled a shuddering breath, then steeled herself. "I will serve you both until my dying breath."

"Go."

CHAPTER SEVEN

We sprint across the empty highway into a field bristling with dry, overgrown weeds. There are no streetlamps, and the moon is hidden behind dense clouds. We run blindly in the dark as the light from the diner fades away behind us.

"Head toward the woods," I shout as I pick up pace.

Even in my human form, I retain some of my gumiho's speed. I grab hold of Ethan's hand to pull him along, but he keeps pace with me. I shoot him a surprised glance. He is freakishly fast for a human. But he won't be able to last long in a dead run.

My panic recedes into the background as I focus on finding a way for us to survive. No matter how fast we are, we won't be able to outrun a suhoshin. He is faster and more powerful than me in every sense of the word. I won't be able to defeat him in hand-to-hand combat . . . unless I unleash my fox spirit. As my gumiho, I'm bigger than a full-grown lion and can run fast enough to leave the woods in a blur behind me. But I won't need to run, because the suhoshin would find me a formidable opponent.

A savage smile slashes across my face as power thrums in my veins. I gasp and stumble. Ethan steadies me without slackening our pace, and I regain my balance in two jerky steps. I'm shaken. Not from the near face-plant but from the violence that thundered through me. *This* is why I must never awaken my fox spirit . . . my inner monster.

I hear the near-silent steps of our pursuer closing in on us. I scrounge in my brain for a way out, but I come up blank. The moon at last peeks out from behind the clouds, as though to show me that there is nowhere to run. We reach the edge of a sorry little pond at the same time as the guardian says from behind us, "Halt."

I squeeze Ethan's hand once in . . . reassurance? Apology? I don't know for sure. All I know is that my past has finally caught up with me. Time has come for me to pay the price for what I did. We turn around and face the suhoshin.

In the moonlight, he is even more arrestingly beautiful. He is a seonnam, an angelic being of Sky. Even if his ethereal good looks weren't a dead giveaway, the silver fire in his eyes would've confirmed which life force flowed through the seraph. The gi stemming from the four life sources each exude a different light—silver for Sky, green for Mountains, blue for Water, and red for Underworld.

Unlike the seraphim of the West, a seonnam's wings are invisible, made of air and wind. The subtle shifting of the suhoshin's black, shoulder-length hair is the only sign that his wings are flared wide behind him—ready for combat. I instinctively reach for my sword.

"There is no need for that," the suhoshin says, carelessly waving his hand.

My arms are pinned to my sides, and my legs are bound together. I belatedly remember what my mother taught me about the Suhoshin, the formidable guardians of the Shingae. They have the power to restrain their suspects with unbreakable binding. I snarl and writhe against the magic, but the invisible rope digs into my skin and doesn't give an inch.

"Why don't you settle down?" the suhoshin suggests.

"Why don't you go fuck yourself?" I say, mimicking his gratingly calm voice.

"What do you want from us?" Ethan steps in front of me, shielding me with his body.

I gasp, wondering how the hell he broke free from the binding. The suhoshin stumbles back half a step before he catches himself. Something like wonder and fear flits across his face. His stoic mask slides back into place as he says, "There is no time to talk. You must come with me."

Ethan reaches behind and presses his hand into my lower back, pushing me up against him. His protective gesture makes emotion clog my throat and shatters the helplessness holding me as immobile as the invisible binding. Ben died because of me. If I'm captured, I will never see the light of day again. I will never be able to avenge his death. I promised Ethan I'll find Ben's killer. I *will* find Daeseong. He'll pay for what he did.

I'm acting out of desperation, but I don't care. I wiggle my fingers and find that I can still move my hands. I grip either side of Ethan's shirt and drive all my weight into my upper back until we are falling . . . and falling. Time slows to an excruciating crawl as Ethan and I topple toward the pond.

Everything has to happen just right for this to work. I hope the suhoshin is a second too late reacting to our unexpected move. I hope the moon is reflected on the meager pond behind us. I hope whatever happened during my battle with Daeseong gave me the power to use high magic. I hope I don't get us killed.

Moon shifting is a form of high magic used to travel from one location to another by moving through the abyss. It's meant to happen in an instant, but I'm not too clear on the details since I've never tried it before. If I fail completely, Ethan and I will fall flat on our backs in the shallow pond behind us and into the waiting hands of the suhoshin. If I fail halfway, we will get stuck in the abyss, never coming out on the other side. I can't decide which failure would be worse, but hopefully, I won't have to pick.

Please, let this work.

At last, my back meets the water with a splash, and I feel Ethan's body on top of mine, but his weight doesn't push me down into the pond. Instead, warm, silken darkness surrounds us, and we float weightless in it. I can't believe it. It's working. I'm moon shifting us. I wrap my arms around Ethan's waist and hold on as though my life depends on it. The silence around us turns into the sharp howl of wind, and we're propelled through the abyss.

Air rushes out of my lungs as I'm plunged into the water, much too deep to be the pond in the wilds of Northern California. I thrash around for a second before I realize it really worked. I moon shifted us to Las Vegas.

I'm not quite sure *where* in Vegas, though. I just aimed for a body of water in Sin City with the moon reflected on it. I guess I'll see. I kick my legs toward the light above my head and break through the surface, gasping for air.

Well, I'll be damned. I brought us straight into the Fountains of Bellagio. The luxury hotel and casino's fountain show is one of the most spectacular sights in Las Vegas. More than a thousand water fountains line the 8.5-acre man-made lake, and the water shoots up as high as 460 feet in the air, dancing in time to music and light. There is no magic in the human world, but the Fountains of Bellagio have always seemed a little magical to me.

I might've accidentally orchestrated the coolest moon shift in the history of high magic. But it also means we don't have much time. Bellagio's highly trained security team will soon descend upon us for swimming where we shouldn't be.

"Come on, Ethan. We have to get out of here." But I don't see him anywhere. "Ethan?"

Oh, gods. Did I lose him in the abyss? I whip around in a circle in the water, scanning the lake.

"Ethan." His name rips out of me. "Ethan!"

Before the scream building inside me breaks free, he bursts out of the water a few yards from me. His head spins left and right until he spots me, and relief spreads across his face. I can't help it. I smile like a dork.

I tread water, still smiling, as he swims toward me. He grabs my face between his hands, and I stop breathing. Then I resume breathing . . . really loudly. I'm positively panting as anticipation courses through me. Ethan lowers his head, holding my gaze. I know what's about to happen, but I'm not even tempted to turn my head. My lips part of their own volition, and my eyes start to slide shut. But the shrill blow of a whistle jerks me out of my daze.

"Shit." I push him away before I can grab him to cross out the *almost* from that almost kiss. "We have to get out of here."

Not waiting for him to respond, I swim across the lake toward the side farthest from the Bellagio security guards running toward us. Ethan thankfully is right beside me. Glancing around, I adjust my course to head toward the roped fence surrounding a small portion of the lake.

My lungs burn in protest, but I don't slow down until I reach the edge of the water. I heave myself out on trembling arms and climb over the ropes with the grace of a panda bear, the innate elegance of my fox eluding me in my exhaustion.

As soon as our feet touch dry land, the fountains blast to life as though we timed it. I release a tiny huff of relief. The towering streams of water will hide us from the guards' view and give us enough time to get away. More importantly, the suhoshin won't be able to moon shift after us because the dancing water dispels even a hint of the moon's reflection. It's a short reprieve but a reprieve nonetheless.

Ethan's jaw drops. "Did we just take a dip in the Fountains of Bellagio?"

"Yup. Come on. We'll catch the show later." I grab his hand and race toward the crowd of tourists clogging the Strip. "We have to get somewhere safe."

By *safe*, I mean where there is a shit ton of humans around. Maybe—oh, I don't know—someplace like a casino? I wonder if Vegas has any of those. As I halt my loopy thoughts, I remember I didn't get to finish my steak. An adrenaline rush coupled with blood loss isn't a good combination for mental clarity.

I need to focus on getting us to safety. Nothing confounds magic more than the humans' disbelief of it. And there is no one as hard-headed and cynical as my favorite bartender, Ford. So it's decided. I'm going in to work. I might even put on my sexy leprechaun dress for old time's sake. *Yeah, hard pass.*

We fight our way through the Strip, weaving in and out of the throng. I worry Ethan and I'll get separated in our headlong rush. He must have the same concern, because he has an iron grip on my hand. I wince when a man passes by too close, jostling my still-tender shoulder. He shoots me a dirty look, like I'm the one who rammed into him. But he pales and raises his hands when Ethan cuts him a lethal glare.

"Let's go." I tug on his hand, and he follows reluctantly.

"Asshole," he mutters under his breath. "Are you okay?"

"I'm fine." My insides turn mushy at his concern, so I shoot him a moody scowl. "Tamp down on the testosterone, eh, big guy? The point is to *avoid* attention."

"Sure. No problem." His voice is as dry as the Mojave Desert. I flinch like an idiot when he reaches for my face. His hand pauses for the briefest second. Then he arches an eyebrow and picks up a strand of my dripping hair. He drops it almost right away, but not before his knuckles brush my cheek. "Because we're not noticeable at all."

"We aren't." Fighting back a blush, I try to free my hand from his grip, but Ethan holds on tight. *Fine. Whatever.* I press my lips together to stop them from curving into a smile. Why do I want to smile, anyway?

But I'm right. People don't give us more than a cursory glance as we move past them, sopping wet. They probably think we did something idiotic, like jump into a hotel pool with all our clothes on. Just for kicks, you know. In our case, we had good reason to jump into the Fountains of Bellagio fully dressed. But for everyone else, there's a reason why what happens in Vegas stays in Vegas.

"Where are we going?" Ethan asks after a few blocks.

"My work." I pretend to look at my nonexistent watch. "I think I still might make my shift. I wouldn't want to mess up my perfect attendance over a silly evil mudang."

Ethan gives me a bland look that makes me feel like an immature ass. I heave a sigh.

"Present company excluded, the vast majority of humans don't believe in magic." My side-eye makes it clear I think he's weird. "Magic and disbelief don't mix. When all these people stomp over my trail with their skepticism and mundane logic, they'll scatter the magic enough to make it hard to track."

As with everything else, he accepts my explanation as though it makes complete sense. Weirdo. But he asks, "But why your work?"

"Because we need a ride from the most skeptical human being in the worlds." I'm feeling generous, so I clarify. "Ford."

"The bartender?" Ethan's eyes widen.

"After all the things I've told you, you're surprised over *this*?" I gape at him.

He gives an impatient shake of his head. "Why him?"

"Other than the reason I just gave you?" I shrug. "He's trustworthy, and he owes me a favor."

"And he'll crawl over broken glass for you," he grumbles, dropping my hand. I squash my disappointment at the loss of connection. "That guy's got it bad for you."

I laugh in his face. "I helped him out with something a couple of years ago. He's grateful. That's all."

"Yeah, sure." Ethan stares straight ahead, clenching his teeth.

I study him for a few seconds, then shrug. The past twenty-some hours have been a mother of a shitstorm. He has a right to be cranky. Feeling surprisingly uncranky, I grab his hand—I don't want to risk losing him—and pick up my pace.

Even at night, the desert heat dries our clothes to a respectable sogginess as we near the end of our long trek down the Strip. I take us through a crowded casino to deposit us onto a side street. Keeping to the busiest sidewalks, we reach my place of employment. I pull Ethan toward the main entrance.

"Isn't there a side entrance for employees?" He tugs on his shirt, separating it from his muscled torso. That's a pity. "We aren't exactly presentable."

I wave a hand in the vicinity of my feet, then at the mass of people crowding the smoky casino.

"Ah, yes." His lips curve into a teasing smile. "You need them to stomp on your pixie dust."

I give him the finger without breaking my stride. He chuckles. My toes try to curl at the warm, rumbling sound but . . . hells no. Keeping my toes straight and uncurled, I make a beeline for the main bar. I release a breath of relief when I spot a mop of curly red hair behind the busy bar.

"Hey, there." I'm all smiles—happy to see a friendly face, happy to be alive.

"Sunny," Ford wheezes, nearly dropping the tumbler he's drying. He puts the glass down and stares at me with round eyes.

It takes me a good ten seconds to figure out what the hell has gotten into him. He's shocked to see me smiling. I admit I don't do it often, but this is getting ridiculous. With a roll of my eyes, I settle my face back into a grumpy scowl.

He finally blinks and clears his throat. "Your usual?"

"No, just a glass of milk for me." My limbs feel weak. I think longingly of the steak I left unfinished at the roadside diner. Alcohol definitely isn't a good idea in my state. "With a splash of Baileys."

Good ideas are overrated, especially with the clock ticking on my certain demise. My scowl turns even grumpier.

"And you?" Ford's nostrils flare as he glowers at a point just past my shoulder, plus a foot and change higher.

I didn't realize Ethan was standing so close to me. I fight the urge to turn around and check how close.

"Club soda with lime." Ethan's voice is an octave lower than usual—dark and territorial. I ignore the shiver that courses down my spine.

"With a splash of vodka." I climb onto a free barstool and turn to Ethan. "You're understandably cranky after everything that's happened. Sit and have a drink. You'll feel better."

"I think slowing down will make everything much, much worse." Ethan swipes his hand down his face, then takes a seat next to me. Once Ford is out of earshot, he continues, "Let's set one thing straight before I become overwhelmed with this new fucked-up reality. You and I? We're sticking together. Period. End of discussion. Are we clear?"

He wants to stick with me. A one-hundred-thirty-two-year-old fox spirit with emotional baggage the size of Death Valley—plus the added bonus of having the most powerful dark mudang of all time on my tails. Only an idiot would want to stick with me.

"If you stay with me, you'll die." Anyone who wants to hurt Ethan will have to do it over my dead body. Unfortunately for us both, they'll probably get the opportunity to do precisely that.

"I'll die even if I don't stay with you." He holds my gaze. "Tell me I'm wrong."

"But Ben—"

"Daeseong killed Ben." Ethan slashes a hand through the air, cutting off my words. "And he'll kill me, too, whether or not I'm with you." He levels a steely gaze on me. "Go ahead. Tell me I'm wrong."

"I . . ." I fucked up. He's already in too deep. We both know it. "You're not wrong."

"Like I said," Ethan says with a grim smile, "end of discussion."

"Fine." I close my eyes to hide my relief. I won't have to do this alone. "We stick together."

If that makes him an idiot, then that's his problem.

CHAPTER EIGHT

I catch a glimpse of myself in the locker mirror. My cheeks glow with a rosy flush, and my hair shines like black silk. Even after the sleepless night and loss of blood, I look better than I have in years. The brief spurt of magic I used has done wonders. I almost look like the eighteen-year-old girl I used to be. Almost. There is no hiding the scarred, weary soul looking out from behind my eyes.

Averting my gaze from the mirror, I unstrap my sword belt and strip off my soggy clothes. I gingerly rotate my shoulder and wince. The wound is an angry red scar. It won't heal fully until I eat a proper meal or two. My stomach growls in agreement.

After glancing around the empty locker room, I spread out my dirty clothes on the floor and sprinkle the salt I filched from the bar over them. Humans in Korea use salt to ward off bad fortune by pelting it at people who come home from a funeral. In reality, salt merely masks magic traces when you're in a pinch. Like deodorant for stinky magic.

I hide my hwando in my locker and bunch up my salted clothes. I bury the bundle at the bottom of the trash can and head for the showers. One perk about my shitty job is that the employee showers have amazing water pressure. As steaming-hot water rains down on my hair and aching body, I'm tempted to linger. A nice long shower sounds too good to pass up, but time isn't on my side. After a quick shampoo and wash down, I dry off and walk back to my locker.

I pull out my emergency backpack from the bottom of the locker and tug on a clean pair of jeans and a black T-shirt. I plunk down on the bench and put my wet sneakers back on. I didn't have the foresight to have extra shoes handy. Then again, the chances of me taking a plunge in the Fountains of Bellagio after *moon shifting* had been slim to none. How the hell did I conjure high magic? What does it all mean? I dig the heels of my hands against my eyelids and blow out a long breath. I'll worry about that later.

I rummage around my backpack. A passport, a dozen rolls of cash, a flashlight, some duct tape, and a few mini bottles of hard liquor. Not exactly Armageddon ready, but it'll have to do. I stuff my hwando and belt inside my backpack since I can't exactly wear a sword, even a short one, without Ethan's shirt to hide it.

Slinging the bag over my good shoulder, I walk out of the locker room. The loud jangling of slot machines and cigarette smoke greet me like an old friend. I take a deep breath and release a contented sigh. I hated the same racket and stench just the day before. I guess what they say about perspective is true.

I check the casino for danger as I make my way toward the bar. Unless tackiness could kill, I find no immediate threat. Ethan stands leaning against the bar, his hair damp and heavy from his shower. Either Ford wears his clothes really tight, or Ethan is bigger than I thought. He fills out his borrowed Henley and jeans respectably. The short-sleeved shirt flaps open at his neck, revealing a triangular patch of golden skin with the jade disk blinking against it. My mouth goes dry.

When he spots me, his lips quirk into a grin, and I bite my cheeks to stop my answering smile. Out of the corner of my eye, I see my slimy manager scowling at me from across the floor. I'm late for my shift and out of my uniform. He stomps toward me with a pinched look that says I'm in for a firm talking to. At a roulette table behind him, a blonde goblin cocks her head as recognition flares in her eyes. Having used magic recently, there's no hiding that I'm a being from the world of gods.

Shit. Hopefully, the goblin won't be around later to be questioned by the Suhoshin. She isn't Korean, but the Suhoshin are famous the worlds over. She'll cooperate with them, more likely than not. I grab Ethan's arm and lead us to the closest exit, shooting a glance at Ford. He nods and follows us after clapping one of the bartenders on her shoulder. She must be covering for him.

We slip outside, and Ford takes the lead. Ethan and I follow wordlessly, scanning the vicinity. Ford parked his car in an alleyway behind the casino. He unlocks it and gestures for us to get in.

"Are you fucking with me?" Ethan barks out an incredulous laugh. "A 1962 Oldsmobile Starfire?"

Ford's barrel chest puffs out with pride. I take a small step back in case buttons start popping off his shirt.

"God, she's beautiful." Ethan runs a reverent hand over the hood. Ford nods like a proud papa, then looks expectantly at me.

"Um . . . yeah. It's very . . . blue," I mumble and hop into the back seat of the convertible.

"You can sit up front," Ethan protests, even though he's much too tall to fit comfortably in the back.

"Just get in." I turn to Ford as he settles into the driver's seat. "Thank you for helping us."

"Are you kidding?" He rounds on me with something like hurt on his face. "After everything you've done for us?"

"It was nothing." I look away, scratching my neck.

"If saving my niece's life was nothing"—Ford scoffs—"then this is less than nothing."

Ethan looks over his shoulder with his eyebrows raised. I pointedly ignore him. Ford's niece was abducted a couple of years ago. I hunted down the bastard who took her and got her back before the police finished their coffee and donuts. It wasn't hard. But I wish I could erase those few hours for Lily. I didn't give the abductor time to hurt her, but she was afraid for her life the entire time. A fourteen-year-old girl shouldn't have to live with those nightmares.

"For what it's worth," I say to move past the unwanted gratitude, "I promise we're the good guys."

"Then tell me how to get you away from the bad guys," Ford says with a stubborn jut of his chin.

"Head for the I-15." I buckle in. "We need to get the hell away from this casino."

"Say no more." With a screech of tires, the Oldsmobile Starfire shoots out of the alley, and I lurch back in my seat.

Once we're on the highway, I relax enough to worry about the logistics. I tap Ethan on the shoulder. "You wouldn't happen to have your passport on you, would you?"

"Not on me," he says, swerving in his seat to face me. "It's in my hotel room. I brought it with me just in case you were overseas."

"Your hotel room?" I squeeze the back of my neck. "A golem might be waiting for us there."

Blue should be somewhere between Las Vegas and Monterey if he's a capable undead assassin. But Daeseong's been dead for over a hundred years; his magic might be so rusty that he made an incompetent golem who's decided to wait for Ethan to return to his hotel room, with me in tow.

"A golem?" Ford chuckled. "You gave your bad guys nicknames?"

"Sure." I keep my resting bitch face firmly in place. "You know me. I'm all about fun and games."

"Yeah, right." Ford laughs harder. "But you do have a morbid sense of humor, sunshine."

"Call me *sunshine* one more time, and see how morbid my sense of humor gets." I meet his eyes in the rearview mirror.

The man with the tree-trunk arms chokes on his laugh. "Sorry, Sunny."

"Whatever." I feel a smidgen bad for snapping at him when he's sticking his neck out for us. "Let's go a few more miles before we turn back."

"Making sure we have no tails?" Ford asks.

I want to snicker because I, in fact, have nine tails. But my amusement is frayed around the edges, so I get a grip. "Yeah. No need to make it easy for the bad guys to track us."

Ethan turns in his seat again. "Why do I need my passport?"

I flick a glance at the back of Ford's head and meet Ethan's eyes. "I'll tell you later."

Ford exits the freeway, takes a few surface streets, then gets back on in the opposite direction. "Where are you staying, Ethan?"

"The Venetian."

"The Venetian?" I snort at the mention of the fancy Venice-themed hotel and casino. Its ceilings are painted to look like the clear blue sky, with tufts of white cloud above a miniature Grand Canal *inside* the hotel. "Did you ride the gondola while you were there? Wait, wait. Did a gondolier in a tight white T-shirt and red neckerchief serenade you?"

Ethan doesn't bother turning around to flip me off. "I called in a favor. A friend of mine gets complimentary rooms. Something to do with his job."

"A *friend*," I say extra earnestly. "Gotcha."

The moment of normalcy passes too quickly, and I feel the weight of fear and grief settle down on me again. I haven't forgotten that the blue assassin might be waiting in Ethan's hotel room. That he might be the one who killed Ben. I blot out the memory of my friend's smiling face and infectious laugh and focus on the bloodlust roiling inside me. I feel reckless with fury, but it's better than drowning in sorrow.

Ford takes the initiative to use the most roundabout route to get to the Venetian and pulls into the parking structure. I crack my neck and reach for the sword in my backpack. I almost wish the golem will be there.

"You stay," I tell Ethan as soon as Ford shifts the car into park. "I'll go."

Ethan glares at me. "Like hell I'll stay."

"Be reasonable." I try to remain calm. I really do. "It'll be safer this way."

"Safer for *whom*?" He somehow enunciates through tightly clenched teeth. "What happened to sticking together?"

"Do we have to be literally *stuck* together? All the time? Maybe we should go potty together too." My calm shatters, and I snarl. "Give me a fucking break."

"What's your room number?" Ford asks so matter-of-factly that Ethan answers without pause. "And where is your passport?"

"In the safe," Ethan says with the beginnings of a frown.

Ford types something into his cell phone. "What's the combination?"

"What are you doing?" I finally ask.

"I know someone who works in hospitality." He shrugs. "She'll grab his passport and bring it down to us."

"Oh," Ethan and I say at the same time. The assassin has no reason to go after a random human and blow his cover.

"Yeah." Ford smirks. "The combination?"

Ethan rattles off a string of numbers. And less than fifteen minutes later, a statuesque blonde leans down to kiss Ford on the cheek as she pulls the passport from her purse and drops it in his lap.

"Thanks, Caroline," he says as he turns on the ignition. Caroline throws him a wink over her shoulder as she sashays away.

I'm impressed. "That is the coolest handoff I've seen in a while."

"I take it you've seen a lot of handoffs?" Ethan arches an eyebrow.

I ignore him. I've lived a long life. I'm not proud of all of it. "Do you know where we're going, Ford?"

"Harry Reid International Airport." He confidently maneuvers the Oldsmobile through traffic. "Unless you just risked facing a 'golem' for thrills."

"I liked it better when you kept to one-syllable words and grunts for communication," I mutter. "Departures. Terminal three."

Ford grunts but ruins the effect by winking at me through the rearview mirror. My chest constricts. I stare out at the Strip and the rest of Las Vegas as we make the fifteen-minute trek to the airport. I don't know if I'll ever come back. I might never see Ford again. He's a good man. A good . . . friend. Making friends is a bad idea. I end up hurting them . . . or they hurt me. But some people slip through my defenses somehow.

He pulls up to the curb in front of terminal three. I hop out of the car and grab the second bottle of stolen salt from my backpack. I open the cap and throw generous handfuls into the back seat and anywhere I've touched the car. I hope the Shingae will stay clear of Ford and his unshakable disbelief of magic.

"Whoa." Ford stretches out his hands. "Is that salt? On my leather seats?"

"Yup." The poor man. He looks like he might pass out. I throw a handful of salt at him for good measure. It was either that or hug him. A lump clogs my throat. I clear it sharply, losing patience with myself. "Do me a favor and use a vacuum to clean it up. Then you can rub it down with oil or whatever the hell you do to keep the damn thing so soft. But vacuum it first."

Technology, like skepticism, is the antithesis of magic. The vacuum will help disperse my magic better than a towel.

His mouth opens and closes several times before he gets his voice to work. "A vacuum? Of all things. Fine. I got you. Don't worry about it."

Why do I keep wanting to hug the big oaf? *Ugh.* To my great relief, Ethan walks up and gives Ford a bro hug. The two have really bonded over the Oldsmobile Starfire.

"Thanks for the ride," Ethan says, stepping back.

"No problem." Ford tilts his chin toward me. "Take care of that one for me."

Ethan nods solemnly. "I'll keep her out of trouble."

I look back and forth between the two assholes, talking about me like I'm not standing right there. Surprisingly, I'm not all that mad. In fact, I don't mind having two friends who care about what happens to me. *No.* I'm not mad. I'm fucking terrified.

I've spent over a century running away from my past and my identity, avoiding any real connections, but I seem to be rushing headlong back toward everything I left behind. Receiving unwanted visits from Daeseong and company, reentering the Shingae, and making friends by accident. But nothing has changed. I still have every reason to run away from it all.

"Come on, Ethan. Say bye-bye to your friend." I walk toward the entrance and wave without turning. "See you around, Ford."

"See you soon, Sunny," he calls out. "Your next round of tequila is on me."

"Damn it all to hell," I mutter as tears blur my vision. I pick up my pace and make a beeline for the Korean Air counter.

"Now are you going to tell me where we're going?" Ethan says close to my ear, catching up with me.

"Korea." I meet his eyes. "The Seonangshin showed me the way to an ancient cypress grove. We have to get there if we want any chance of ending the fucker who killed Ben."

CHAPTER NINE

I tuck my hair behind my ears and approach the Korean Air counter with a bright smile. "Hi, we'd like two tickets to Incheon International Airport, please."

The man behind the counter nods slowly, eyeing me and Ethan. "For what day were you looking to fly with us?"

"Your next flight, if possible," I say with a breathless giggle. "There's no time like the present."

"I'm afraid that flight is fully booked, unless . . ." He trails off as though he sees no point in continuing.

"Unless?" I widen my eyes and flutter my lashes a couple of times.

"We had a cancellation for two first-class seats." The man purses his lips like he tastes something sour. I look like a college-age kid at best, and Ethan doesn't look much older in his Henley and jeans. And neither of us looks like we have money. "First-class seats, especially those purchased at the last minute, are quite expensive."

"I've been saving up for eighteen years to visit Korea. And lo and behold, my schedule cleared up unexpectedly. It's now or never." I plunk a roll of hundreds on the counter, then another. The man's beady eyes reach their maximum roundness. "I have a huge family, and that adds up to a lot of birthday money."

"My girlfriend is a force of nature." Ethan picks up a lock of my hair and wraps it around his finger. My toes curl up like roly-polies at his hooded glance, even though he's just putting on a show for the airline man.

Well, my toes are being ridiculous. It's just Ethan. He used to get choked up every time that car commercial with the golden retriever came on. Never mind that I did too. I refuse to be dazzled by his sex appeal. I lean into his touch and nudge my cheek against his hand, playing along with the act.

"I . . . um . . ." Ethan's heated glance drops to my lips, then he shakes his head. "When she sets her sight on something, she won't stop until she gets it."

The man sniffs and clacks something into his computer. Then he flashes us a smirk that begs to be punched off his face. "So she'll pay twenty-two thousand dollars? In birthday money?"

"Yes, she will," I say and slam three more rolls of cash onto the counter. The airline man jumps a little. "Like I said, *so* much birthday money."

I take my time counting out the twenty-two thousand in hundreds as the dickhead watches with his mouth gaping. Once I'm done, I push the money across the counter to him. He takes it, with his Adam's apple bobbing. He moves around in a nervous rush, then produces two tickets and boarding passes for us.

"Thank you so much," he says with a sad excuse for a smile. "Have a safe flight."

Having gotten what I came for, I drop my smile and turn my back on him without replying. I'm proud of myself for not giving him the finger.

"Do you think he'll report us?" Ethan says once we reach the security check line.

"He doesn't have the balls." I pull off my damp sneakers as we inch toward the conveyor belt. "Besides, our flight already started boarding. Once it takes off, no one can get us, and we'll have thirteen hours of peace."

I unzip my backpack just enough to put my hand inside and grab the hilt of my sword. A spark of magic pulses out of my palm as I glamour my hwando. It's a necessary risk.

"Is that"—Ethan's eyes go wide—"a recorder?"

"I like to play for relaxation." I close my backpack as we near the front of the line.

"Did you use . . ." He makes a hapless gesture with his hand. His hesitation rubs me the wrong way, and I rise to my tippy-toes, grabbing onto his shoulder.

"Magic?" I breathe huskily into his ear. A muscle jumps in his jaw as I move away from him. I sigh. I shouldn't have taunted him. He has every reason to be hesitant. "Don't worry. Remember what I told you about magic and disbelief not mixing?"

Ethan nods curtly.

"Well, science and magic confuse the hell out of each other, and we're about to board an airplane. It takes a lot of science and technology to make two hundred tons of metal fly. What does all that mean?" I ask like I'm in an infomercial. "Airplanes eat magic traces for breakfast."

He doesn't laugh. We didn't have a chance to talk since we ran from that sad little diner. And I just reminded him that I still owe him a shitload of answers.

"Not even the Suhoshin will be able to track me while I'm flying in one," I babble on, because Ethan's stoic expression is making me nervous. "Maybe I should become a flight attendant in my next city."

His brows furrow above the bridge of his perfectly imperfect nose. "The Suhoshin?"

It's our turn to go through the security check. I put my backpack and my soggy shoes onto the conveyor belt and step through the metal detector. Ethan follows behind me with bare feet. My recorder passes the x-ray scan without issue. He grabs both our shoes and shoulders my backpack, despite my impatient scoff. We find a bench against the wall and sit down.

"The Suhoshin are the guardians of the Shingae. They are sworn to protect all beings and maintain order in the worlds," I say quietly. "That guy from the diner with his eyes on fire?"

"Silver fire," Ethan says darkly. "Never mind. Keep going."

"Well, he's a suhoshin." I shrug, pulling on a damp shoe.

"Why is a suhoshin after us?" He gives me the side-eye. "Did we break some law from the Shingae that I'm not aware of?"

"Ben's murder is under their jurisdiction. They might see our . . . activities as interference with their investigation." I hesitate for a moment, then bite the bullet. No more lies. I respect him too much to lie to him. And I . . . trust him. "Or they might be after *me*. When I killed Daeseong over a century ago, I hurt . . . others. That's why I fled to America. That's why I've been hiding from the Shingae."

It's incomplete and oversimplified, but it's the best I can do while sitting in a crowded airport. I haven't allowed myself to think about that night, much less talk about it with anyone. But when Ethan doesn't say anything, I feel icy shame slither down my spine.

"I didn't mean to," I choke out, my lips trembling. "I don't even know *how* I did it. I passed out—"

"Shh." Ethan wraps his arms around me, pressing my head against his shoulder. "Of course you didn't mean to. I know you. You don't need to explain."

More than anything, I want him to keep holding me—to tell me it wasn't my fault. I want to *believe* him. So I have no choice but to push him away. "Either way, I can't let the Suhoshin catch me until Daeseong pays for what he did to Ben."

Ethan searches my face for a long moment. "Then we better get on that plane."

"Yes." I stand, eager to move past my memories, then grimace at my sodden shoes. "But first, we need new shoes."

We walk into a duty-free shop and split up to find our shoes. We meet at the checkout line, each of us holding a pair of Converse. Mine are red high-tops, and his are a classic black.

"Great minds . . . ," he says with a grin.

I smile back at him. "Like Converse?"

We both jump when the cashier coughs. We sheepishly place our shoes on the counter. I pull some crumpled bills from my pocket—the change I got from the salty airline man—and pay for both of us.

"I'm out of cash. I'll pay you back," Ethan says, rubbing the back of his head. "After."

"Of course you will." I narrow my eyes at him to hide the ache burrowing into my chest. What I wouldn't give for there to be an *after*. "With interest."

Even though we run to our gate in our new shoes, we're the last to board. The flight attendant barely has time to give us our hot towels before the plane prepares for takeoff. I put the hot towel on my neck and squeeze the tight muscles. My eyes slide shut, and I moan. I open them to find Ethan staring at me, his lips parted.

He blushes. "Do . . . do you want my towel?"

"What? No." Why the hell am *I* blushing? "I'm fine."

"May I take your towels?" The flight attendant has impeccable timing. "I don't mean to rush you, but we're about to take off."

"Sure." Ethan quickly wipes his hands and places his towel on the tray she holds out.

I reach over and drop mine on it as well. "Thank you."

"We'll be serving supper as soon as the captain turns off the 'fasten seat belt' sign," she replies with a bright smile. "Please feel free to peruse the menu."

"Have you ever flown first class before?" Ethan asks once the flight attendant hurries off.

"No." I try not to gape at my surroundings. "You?"

"Uh, no. PIs don't make that kind of money." He chuckles. "Man, look at the size of these seats."

They are huge. My seat even has an ottoman at the front—which my feet barely reach. Each row has four seats in a 1-2-1 configuration. Ethan and I have the middle two seats, so we're next to each other, with a small partition down the middle. Our eyes meet across the cozy setup and hold. My heart rate picks up. I look away and grab the menu for something to do.

I don't know what to make of this connection I have with Ethan. It feels different from the friendship I used to share with him and Ben all those years ago. But maybe it's because I regret leaving them . . . because I've missed them. I don't want to admit it, but having friends and then losing them made the last eight years almost too lonely to bear. And now my guilt over Ben's death and the way I'm endangering Ethan laces every other feeling I have.

"Oh my gods." I force a laugh. "They have caviar service."

"Holy shit." Ethan opens up his menu. "They *do* have caviar service."

"I've never even had caviar." I can't stop laughing now that I've started. It's too much.

In the span of hours, I went from being attacked by an undead assassin to nearly plunging to my death over a cliff to moon shifting in terrified desperation. And now we've arrived at the *caviar service* portion of the programming.

I laugh harder, and Ethan joins me. We shush each other. I clap my hand over my mouth, and he presses his lips together. Our eyes meet, and we burst out laughing again. I turn my back to him to get myself under control. I wipe the tears off my face and take a deep breath.

"Okay." I don't look at him until I'm sure my laughing fit has passed. "A hard pass on the caviar service, but I'm eating everything on the menu, then sleeping until we land in Korea. I suggest you do the same. I don't know when we'll have another chance to eat or sleep once we get off this plane."

I shouldn't have worried he might make me laugh again. He doesn't have a trace of mirth on his face as he nods. "How do we get to the cypress grove from there?"

"I haven't thought that far ahead." I do some quick math in my head. "We'll land in Incheon around five a.m. It'll be too close to sunrise for me to moon shift us."

"Moon . . . shift," he says, rubbing his forehead. He looks as exhausted as I feel. "Is that what you did? To take us from Northern California to Las Vegas in . . . in an instant?"

I nod, holding back a guilty cringe. Ethan knows nothing about the Shingae and its magic, even though he's been neck deep in it since he walked into Roxy's Diner. I can hardly believe it's only been a little over twenty-four hours. His head must be spinning.

"Beings of the Shingae could travel from one reflection of the moon to another," I explain.

I don't mention that you need high magic to moon shift, because I still have no idea how *I* did it. My mother said only the Suhoshin can conjure high magic. Besides, the *how* doesn't matter at this point. I'll take all the advantages I can get. Doubting my powers will only weaken me.

"In Korea, the humans sometimes fill a bowl with water to pray to the moon," I say to stop the silence from stretching on. "They might not understand everything, but they sense that there's magic in the moon and its reflection."

Ethan is quiet for a while, then asks, "If you can't moon shift, then how will we get there? Is it very far from Incheon?"

"Only about a hundred miles." I worry my bottom lip, wondering how much to tell him.

"Well, that's not too far." He shrugs. "We can take a taxi."

"To a certain point. The thing is . . ." Oh, fuck it. "The grove is in North Korea."

"North . . ." He clears his throat and asks in a hoarse whisper, "North Korea? How?"

"The Seonangshin have been around for much longer than the thirty-eighth parallel," I say dryly. "There's only one Korea to them."

My old village also lies in North Korea, although there was no North and South back then either. I take a shuddering breath. Reentering the Shingae wasn't easy for me, but going back to my birth country is something else entirely. My life force is irrevocably tied to Korea—to its soil and its mountains. It will call to my magic, and I don't know what will awaken inside of me. I shiver and wrap my arms around my torso.

"Hey, you okay?" Ethan grabs a blanket from a storage compartment and drapes it over my shoulders. "They should be serving food soon."

"Thanks," I say instead of answering his question. I'm not about to tell him that I'm far from okay.

To distract myself, I focus on figuring out how to get to the cypress grove. Landing at 5:00 a.m. blows. We can't wait around for fifteen hours until nightfall. Our frolic through the Las Vegas Strip and the plane ride bought us some time, but it isn't enough to keep the blue assassin and the Suhoshin off my scent for long. We have to keep moving.

After the meal service, Ethan and I head to the lavatories with our airline-provided toiletries and pajamas while our flight attendant prepares the turndown service. When we return, our seats are transformed into fully reclined beds with fluffy pillows and cozy comforters. I lie down and raise the outer partition, and Ethan does the same on his side. I don't close the center partition, and neither does he.

Once we're cocooned in our self-contained pod, I whisper to him, "I need to figure out a way to get us into North Korea."

"How?" he whispers back.

"I should be able to find us a way in using my spirit eyes." I give a decisive nod. "I'll try it now."

"Are you sure?" His voice deepens with worry. "You're still a little pale."

"It won't take long." I tamp down on the fluttering in my chest. Having someone give a damn makes me feel cherished. It would be dangerous to get used to such feelings. "The plane is probably the safest place for me to use magic without getting us caught. It'll be foolish not to take advantage of it while I can."

"I'll keep watch, but promise me you'll stop if it gets too much." Ethan sits up and shifts toward me, his gaze fiercely protective. My insides melt against my will.

I give him a thumbs-up to avoid making a promise I can't keep. And before I do something stupid like blush, I shut my eyes and take a deep breath. My spirit eyes burst open with zero finesse—wide and edgy. I see the heartbeat of every passenger. I smell agitation, excitement, anger . . . The gi of the people around me thrums in my ears and in my veins.

My breath whooshes out of me. *Ethan.* His life force is . . . There's another layer of gi pulsating beneath the quiet tendrils of his life force. I don't understand. Human gi doesn't have any discernible color—their gi is as faint as a soft breeze—but I can sense . . . *something*. A color. Or . . . colors? I can't make it out. It's obscured. What *is* that?

I hunch in on myself like I'm recoiling from a too-bright light. Ethan grabs the partition between us and leans over me, his pulse kicking up in alarm. I feel his eyes skip over my body as his hands hover in the air, not knowing what to do. I force myself to relax and rein in my sight. I'm so out of practice I'm tying myself into a knot over nothing. I don't know how I managed back in Monterey. Maybe the proximity of the Seonangshin centered me.

I shut out everything else and focus on crossing into North Korea without getting caught. One image after another flashes past my vision—knowledge imprinting itself on my mind. A desolate beach. An abandoned mine scarring the side of the mountain. Endless tunnels deep in the earth. With a gasp, I open my eyes, but my vision is blurred and swimming. I see too much—images layered over each other, obscuring the physical world—and I can't make out anything.

"Shit," Ethan hisses and claps his hand over my eyes.

Shit is right. With my spirit eyes open, the green fire still burns brightly in my physical eyes. I exhale a long breath and close my spirit eyes. I wait until my magic settles beneath my skin again.

I open my eyes again, but everything is dark. I tug on Ethan's wrist. "You can take your hand off now."

He complies—slowly—staring at my face. He huffs a sigh of relief to find the green fire banked. "How does that work anyway? Are you looking into the future or something?"

"Pffft." I laugh. "Looking into the future? Don't be absurd. No one can see the future. How can anyone see something that hasn't been written yet?"

"*I'm* being absurd?" He glares at me, mouth gaping. "After the day I've had, I wouldn't be surprised if unicorns are real." I hold up my index finger to confirm the existence of the magical creatures, but he grabs my hand and pushes it down. "Besides, looking into the future isn't that far fetched. There are such things as fate and destiny. When something is meant to be, it might as well be written in stone."

You would rather die than accept your destiny? The Seonangshin's words ring in my ears.

"Bull. Shit." I snatch my hand out of his grasp. "There is no such thing as destiny."

"Suit yourself." He shrugs, and my upper lip curls in irritation. "If not the future, what exactly did your spirit eyes show you?"

My mind flashes back to the moment I saw two layers of gi flowing through Ethan. But that's not possible. I shake my head to clear it. "I guided my spirit eyes to the border between the two Koreas to search for a way into the North that wouldn't get us shot."

"And did you find us a way in?" He leans toward me, his face alight with fascination.

I sit up in a sudden panic, and he shifts back before our foreheads crash. "Are you claustrophobic?"

"No." He cocks his head to the side.

"Okay, good. Then yes." I yawn and lie back down. My eyelids feel like they're weighed down by iron ingots. "I found us a way in."

"That won't get us shot?" he asks wryly. "Sunny?"

Yes, but I'm too far gone to respond.

LITTLE PRINCE

"My little prince." The lady-in-waiting knelt down to wrap her arms around the boy, her eyes sliding closed at the feel of his warm, small body. "Did you have a good day at school?"

"Mom, why do you always call me that?" The boy crinkled his nose, pulling out of her embrace much too quickly. "School was fine."

"Always with the *fine*." She ruffled his hair. "What does it even mean? This *fine*."

"*Fine* means *fine*." He dropped his backpack on the floor and trailed after her to the kitchen. "*Fine* also means that I can't wait to grow up and be done with this school business."

The lady-in-waiting poured the boy a glass of milk when he climbed onto the stool at the kitchen island. She pushed a plate of warm chocolate chip cookies toward him. He promptly stuffed a whole cookie into his mouth. She smiled, her eyes misting. Sometimes she couldn't believe he existed—this miracle—grumbling about school and eating cookies like any other boy. She couldn't believe that *she* got to be his mother.

She spun away from him and turned on the faucet when her tears threatened to fall, overcome by the memory of another mother's tears. She washed the lone coffee mug in the sink and turned back to the boy, her emotions under control once more. He didn't need to know any of that yet. The heartbreaking sacrifices already made for him and . . . those yet to be made. No one person should bear the weight of that responsibility alone, but it was his to carry one day.

She looked at the boy's narrow shoulders and gangly arms. It was much too heavy, and she feared he would falter beneath it. But that was just the mother in her. He would rise triumphant over all, as foretold. Still, she wanted him to be free for as long as possible. For as long as she could protect him.

She smiled at him—she couldn't look at him and not smile—and said, "Don't be in such a hurry to grow up. Stay my little prince for a while longer."

"Mom." He rolled his eyes but couldn't hide the grin that curved his lips. "Okay, fine."

The lady-in-waiting soaked up the boy's sweet smile like it was sunlight. "Fine."

CHAPTER TEN

"I can't take you any farther," the taxi driver says in Korean.

"This is fine." My Korean is slowly coming back to me. "You can drop us off here."

The fishing town he drops us off at is just waking up to the day, delivery trucks and motorcycles weaving through the small streets as merchants open up metal shutters with practiced ease. Street vendors set up their wares on the sidewalk, and the smell of rich bone soup boiled overnight fills the air.

An old lady with her white hair bound into a neat, low bun carries a basket overflowing with gimbap on top of her head. When she reaches an empty spot by a lamppost, she shifts the basket, preparing to put her load down. Ethan reaches her side in a blink.

"Here," he says in English. "Let me help you."

"Eh?" She squints up at him.

"We'll help you, halmeoni," I repeat in Korean.

"Ah, thank you." The grandmother smiles, watching Ethan place the basket on the ground with a hand pressed against her lower back.

"You're here again?" A gentleman from the produce store behind us rushes out with a small plastic stool. "Your fancy businessman son sends you plenty of money from Seoul. I don't see why you insist on keeping this up."

"This is what I've done all my life. What else am I going to do? Lie around at home and wait to die?" The old lady sits on the stool behind her basket of gimbap—rolls of rice and seaweed filled with marinated meat and seasoned veggies.

"You're as stubborn as they come," the store owner grumbles with affectionate exasperation. "Come sit in the store for a bit if it gets too hot out here."

She scoffs and waves her neighbor away, then smiles at us. "What a beautiful couple you make—and kind too. You'll have beautiful children."

"No, no. We're not . . ." I wave my hands frantically, my cheeks burning. "We're just friends."

The halmeoni chuckles, obviously not believing a word.

"What did she say?" Ethan says close to my ear, making my blush deepen.

"Nothing." I stare at my shoes.

"Here, take some gimbap for the road. I made them this morning." She loads a Styrofoam plate with beautiful disks of sliced gimbap and wraps it up in a black plastic bag.

She pushes it into my hands and clicks her tongue when I try to pay. Not wanting to disrespect her, I put away the money and accept the gimbap with two hands. Even after a hundred years, I still remember my manners.

"Thank you, halmeoni," I say and bow from the waist.

Ethan bows as well and repeats in hesitant Korean, "Thank you."

I ask her for directions to the small mountain we have to cross to get to the beach on the other side. The mountain with the burial mounds at the top. The halmeoni is surprised I know about the burial site but gives me clear and concise directions.

"Make sure you pay your respects at the seonangdang at the base of the mountain," she warns. "There are some old spirits up there you don't want to offend."

I thank her again but don't pay much heed to her warning. The seonangdang is probably just an old tree the townspeople used to pray to back in the day, forgotten by the younger generation. As for old spirits, they're harmless . . . for the most part.

I put away the gimbap in my backpack and walk into the produce store. After buying some bottled water from the gruff store owner, we head for the mountain.

"Man, my Korean is so awful." Ethan grimaces, scratching the back of his neck.

"You were born in America." I shrug. "Don't beat yourself up about it."

"I was actually born in Korea," he says. "Ben told me I was like a day old when we flew to the US."

"A day? I'm sure he was exaggerating." I roll my eyes. "You were *at least* a month old. In Korean culture, new moms aren't allowed to leave their beds for a month, other than to use the bathroom."

"What?" His face goes slack with shock.

"And they even get their meals—seaweed soup and rice—served to them in bed. Three times a day. Every day."

"Miyeok guk for a month?" He sounds horrified. "I mean, I love seaweed soup. But I can't imagine eating it for every meal for a month."

"Right? Anyway, like I said, you had to have been at least a month old." I nudge him with my elbow. "Which is still not long enough for you to have picked up Korean."

"I guess not." Ethan huffs a small laugh. "It's strange, though. I've never been back in Korea, but it all somehow feels . . . familiar."

"Yeah, I know what you mean." It feels *too* familiar.

I lower my gaze and suppress the memories clamoring to rise to the surface. I feel my mother's presence here, but I don't let myself acknowledge it. Not yet. I can't avenge Ben if I fall apart. I can't keep Ethan safe. *I'm sorry, Mother.*

We reach the base of the mountain. As I suspected, the seonang-dang is just an old tree decorated with strips of blue, red, yellow, white, and black fabric. But I inhale a sharp breath as something brushes against my life force. There's no such thing as *just* an old tree. Its gi rushes forth, imbued with wisdom and strength. I should know better. Nature is powerful in its own right and should never be taken lightly.

"Does this mountain somehow lead into North Korea?" Ethan asks as we hike up the narrow path through the woods. "You fell asleep on the plane before I could ask you anything."

"No, there's a secluded beach over this—"

The hair on the back of my neck rises. I suck in a sharp breath, glancing swiftly left and right. After a moment, I exhale and unclench my fists. I sense no immediate danger. Other than the trees and the wildlife, it's only us on the mountain.

"Sunny." Ethan grips my hand, his gaze sweeping the woods. "What's wrong?"

"Nothing." I felt something, but . . . it must be my paranoia flaring up. "We should be able to find a cave at the beach that's connected to an abandoned mine. One of the tunnels inside leads all the way into North Korea."

"That's why you wanted to know whether I was claustrophobic."

I nod, still on edge. Maybe I'm more spooked by the gimbap halmeoni's warning about old spirits than I want to admit.

For there to be life, there must be death. This balance is immutable—a fundamental truth. Underworld is as much a part of the source of life as Mountains, Sky, and Water. But its gi stems from the loss and sorrow of death . . . from the grief of those who lost their loved ones. That pain is born of love, so the resulting gi is *good*—as much as the gi flowing from the other sources of life.

But sometimes grief becomes corrupted into something darker. It becomes han—grief perverted by resentment and vengeance into something that haunts the soul. The gi wrought from han is twisted and foul, and it feeds the stranded souls that humans call *ghosts*. The stranded don't do much other than scare the shit out of people, but they are . . . not my favorite. Their gi feels off—cold and slithering—and they creep me out.

I shake off a shiver and walk on, with Ethan close by my side. His presence soothes my jagged nerves, and I feel more myself as we continue our climb up the small mountain. I pick up my pace. He keeps up easily.

I steal a glance at him. "Are you a runner?"

"Why?" He snorts, catching my drift. "Because I can keep up with you? You think you're that fast, huh?"

"I *am* a fox spirit." I shrug smugly. I have . . . issues with being a gumiho, but I don't mind it so much when I'm using it to egg him on.

"A fox spirit with short legs." Despite his teasing, his gaze travels up and down my body with blatant appreciation. We both know my legs are long and lithe for my height. A blush rises to my cheeks. "You barely come up to my chest. You have to take two steps to match one of my steps."

I break into a dead run. It takes him a second to catch up, but he keeps pace with me. I'm impressed and push him a little harder. I smirk when his breathing becomes labored. Taking pity, I finally slow down.

"Don't feel bad." I pat him on his shoulder. *Pat, pat, pat.* "You tried."

"Pick on someone your own size." He holds out a hand and lowers it, *and* lowers it, until it's at his knee height.

"Asshole," I mutter, the corners of my lips twitching. I can't deny the man has a great sense of humor. Considering the circumstances, I'm shocked at how much I've been smiling thanks to him.

I'd forgotten about it, but I had a crush on a village boy when I was ten or eleven. Other than being mortifying—I was a stuttering mess when he was near—the crush was harmless and short lived. My thing for Ethan is starting to look a lot like that crush. A slightly more grown-up version, but a crush nonetheless. I'm sure it'll be equally harmless and short lived.

Our breakfast on the plane feels like ages ago, and my stomach gives a warning growl. I unhook one strap from my shoulder and hug my backpack to my front. "Do you want some gimbap?"

"Yes, I need some sustenance after that workout," he says with a grin.

I pull out the gimbap and shoulder my backpack again. The mouth-watering scent of toasted sesame oil assails my nostrils. Nothing smells better in all the worlds. I hold out the plate to Ethan, and he takes a piece of the sliced gimbap. I pop one in my mouth and moan. The sticky rice, marinated beef, and crunchy veggies meld harmoniously into a perfect bite.

"This is so good." I stuff another gimbap into my mouth. "That halmeoni should get a Michelin star."

"My mom made the best gimbap." Ethan grabs another piece. "But this is a close second."

He rarely mentions his mom. I resume chewing and swallow. "Do you miss her?"

"Every day." He takes a swig of water. "I was eight when she died, and there's a lot I don't remember. But when I close my eyes, I can still see her smile. It was open and serene like the blue sky and green pastures. She smiled all the time and never lost her temper with us."

"I'm glad you have that memory of her," I say quietly. I wish I could remember my mother's smile when I think of her. Instead, all I see is her white coat soaked with blood—the dark stain spreading wider and wider no matter how hard I pressed down on her wounds. I swallow my rising nausea. "Your mom sounds like she was a lovely woman."

"She was." Ethan smiles, and my heart stutters.

"I think you have her smile," I whisper, staring at the soft curve of his lips. I force myself to meet his eyes. This is a passing crush, probably born of loneliness.

"Thanks." He holds my gaze until my breathing grows shallow, and I wonder if he feels it, too—this maddening pull of attraction. He looks away and snatches a gimbap off the plate. *I guess not.* "This is definitely the best gimbap I've had in years."

We walk in companionable silence, enjoying our delicious meal. We are as relaxed as two people can be while running for their lives. Not comfortable enough to settle down for a picnic in the mountains but at ease enough to appreciate good food. Or maybe near-death experiences heighten your senses and make everything taste better.

Ethan offers me the last gimbap, and I get a little choked up. Nothing says *I care* better than giving up the last serving of food. *I would've fought him for it.* I try to savor the last piece, chewing slowly.

With the food gone, I become more aware of my surroundings. The morning sun dappling through the lush green leaves, the crisp mountain air, the birds making a ruckus with their song. Goose bumps prickle across my skin. I feel at once alert and calm. The gi of the small mountain calls to mine—our life force, ancient and new, is one and the same—and my magic thunders in my veins, wanting to be unleashed.

"Ethan!" I barely have time to push him behind a tree as I spin away from the deadly blade.

The blue assassin is here. If my magic wasn't so close to the surface, the dagger would've buried itself in my shoulder before I even realized it was coming for me. Ethan would've been next, but the dagger wouldn't be in his shoulder. They don't need him alive. The blood drains from my face, fear making my knees weak.

Ethan somehow pins me against the trunk, reversing our positions, and covers me with his body until his height and breadth cocoon me like armor. I hear the thunk of two more daggers piercing the side of the tree, much too close to us—to him. I'm suddenly furious, and I welcome the flare of violence that erupts inside me.

"Listen, you idiot. I'm stronger and faster than you. I heal quickly. You? You. Will. Die. Do you understand?" For a split second, I'm tempted to knock Ethan out and keep him away from danger, but I respect him too much for that. So instead I snarl at him, "Stay behind this tree. Save yourself for Daeseong. This isn't your fight."

I don't have time to wonder if he'll listen to me. I step out into the clearing as the assassin streaks toward me in a blue blur. These fucking golems and their unitards. But unlike the red assassin, he's not wearing a full face mask. The dark slash of his mouth is curved in an off-kilter smile, and the hollow depths of his eye sockets burn with malice. I can't stop the dread slithering down my spine. Oh, what I would give for a blue beanie to pull over that hideous face.

"Slow down, Speedy." I unsheathe my recorder. *Shit.* I shake off the glamour and raise my sword in front of me. "I wouldn't want you to trip and get a boo-boo."

I'm lying, of course. I would like nothing better than for him to trip—preferably on top of my hwando—and die. But Blue doesn't seem to be in the mood to be obliging. He doesn't even bother engaging in some witty repartee.

Without slowing down, he throws three more daggers at me. I punt two away with my sword and twist away from the third, but it grazes the side of my neck. Damn, he's fast.

"Hey, that could've killed me," I say with mock outrage and swing my blade down on his head. He effortlessly blocks my hwando with his long sword. "You got a little sloppy there. I thought Daeseong wanted me alive."

The blue assassin finally responds in shrill outrage. "How dare you speak my master's name? I will rip your tongue out for that, you filthy beast."

His sword slices and cuts through the air with harrowing speed. I barely evade his blade, grunting from the strain, and can't get in a single strike. *Fuck.* I put space between us with two backward flips. I struggle to even out my breathing as I circle Blue. He leisurely swings his sword in front of him, drawing an infinity symbol in the air. The asshole is taunting me.

"You've already forfeited your tongue, but I might let you keep your eyes"—his black tongue slithers out to lick his lips, and his breath quickens into eager pants—"if you come with me willingly."

"Gross." I gag. "You're not only lying but you actually want to *eat* my eyeballs. Don't you? Ugh. I can't even."

Blue releases a piercing screech, and pain claws at my chest as though a thousand glass shards are tearing into me. I double over, blood spewing from my lips. It hurts so much that I want to weep and beg.

On second thought, I would rather have him kiss my dead ass. I struggle into a fighting stance, even as warm blood trickles from my eyes, nose, and mouth. The assassin shuts off his unholy shriek, and the pain mercifully stops. But I don't think it's mercy he has in mind.

"It'll be so easy to kill you. I wouldn't even have to raise my sword." A chilling smile stretches his black mouth far too wide for his face. "But where's the fun in that?"

The assassin launches himself at me, sword flashing. I block and parry, but he pushes on relentlessly. I stumble back, step by step, until I back into a tree.

Don't be a stubborn fool. I hear a familiar voice in my head. *What use are you dead? You want to avenge Ben's death? You want to keep Ethan safe? Then transform.* I know that voice. It's Mihwa, the girl I used to be. The girl who loved the gumiho inside her. *We are strong. We are glorious. Don't be afraid.*

But I am. I'm so afraid.

I grip my hwando with both hands and meet the assassin's sword. I swing in a downward arc to push his blade toward the ground. A strategy forms in my head. It's risky, but I have to take the chance. I just need to be faster than him and attack before he responds. *Simple.* I take the weight of my hwando off his sword and step close, thrusting my blade into his stomach.

But the golem has no sense of self-preservation. It might have something to do with the fact that he's already dead. Rather than blocking my attack, he merely grunts as my sword pierces his gut, and he proceeds to slash my thigh, clean to my femur. I scream as agony reverberates through me, and I drop to my knees, withdrawing my sword from the assassin to break my fall.

My vision goes hazy, and bile rises to my throat. I bear my weight on my good leg and the hwando digging into the ground, but my butchered thigh screams with pain, and I sway. Beyond the shock of pain, I realize I'm kneeling at the assassin's feet like I'm awaiting my execution. That won't do. No fucking way. With a roar of fury, I lift my sword with shaking arms.

"This is *too* easy." Blue cackles like a hyena and knocks away my hwando with a careless swing of his sword. "I'm almost embarrassed for you. I don't know why my master wants you alive. A feeble, pathetic, *foul* thing like you."

He reaches down and squeezes my cheeks between his fingers, forcing my lips apart. I jerk my face away, but he holds tight. I don't stop struggling even though I can barely stay conscious. I see a flash of silver and gold behind the assassin. I must be hallucinating.

"A beast like you wouldn't understand honor, but I am a man of my word." He digs his cold, dead fingers into my mouth, and I gag, tilting my head away. "I will take your tongue, as I promised."

"And I will take your hand for touching her," Ethan says in a steely voice I hardly recognize.

The undead assassin's mouth gapes wide in a soundless scream as a golden axe slices through his shoulder in one powerful strike. The golem's arm falls to the ground like a branch snapped away from a tree. But the arm still attached to Blue's body is holding a sword, and he spins around to block the silver axe coming for his neck.

My vision clears enough to see Ethan standing in front of the assassin, wielding an axe in each hand. The muscles in his neck are bulging, as though he's straining to hold the axes aloft. He raises the golden axe with effort, like he's fighting against an invisible rope pinning his arm to his side.

"Did you kill my brother?" Ethan roars as he swings his axe toward Blue's head.

The golem's injuries have slowed him down—black wisps of smoke escape from his armless shoulder and the wound in his stomach—but he's still faster than any human. With a gleeful cackle, he draws back his sword and drives it toward Ethan.

In the end, it is as easy as exhaling a long-held breath. There is no need to think or *do*. I simply *am*.

My lips pull back as I snarl at the assassin, power and violence pulsing through me. My nine tails move in unison and sweep the sick bastard aside like he's nothing more than a gnat. He slams against a tree with enough force to make the trunk splinter, before falling face-first into the earth. He lies limply like a blue rag doll, but he won't stay down for long. I have to finish this.

I reach his side before the golem can get to his feet but not before he opens his mouth. A screech as dark as death fills the air. My injured hind leg nearly gives out. I heal faster in my spirit form, and the femoral artery has already mended itself, but blood still flows steadily from the gash. It's not my leg that worries me, though.

My eyes, nose, and mouth bleed until my white fur is soaked red. I take another step toward the assassin before I stumble and crash to the ground, blood gurling in my throat. His head swivels to an unnatural angle to face me, and his mouth opens past unhinged jaws—hideous and gaping—and his scream climbs to a fevered pitch.

I fight against the dark magic tearing up my insides and swipe my claws at the golem's head. The side of his face is slashed open like a half-peeled orange, but he doesn't stop his assault. The shriek intensifies until the agony is unbearable.

Ethan. He's fallen to his knees. He can't take much more of this. I have to kill the assassin. I try to push myself up, but my legs won't carry my weight. *Ethan.* I want to take my human form so I can hold him in my arms, but I don't have enough strength left in me to wield my magic. This can't be the end. A keening noise rips out of me as darkness edges in on my vision.

Please help. Save him. Please.

The trees tremble around us, branches swaying and leaves shivering. I feel the gi of nature pulsate beneath the ground. The entire mountain comes alive with it. No, it's not *just* a mountain.

A root bursts through the ground and pierces the assassin's throat. The shrieking stops abruptly as he struggles against the root skewering his neck. I rise shakily to my feet and stand over the golem's writhing body. Helpless fury still courses through my veins. This *thing* nearly killed Ethan. I pause for a heartbeat—not because I'm hesitant but because I want the golem to understand that I'm about to end him.

"M . . . my master will . . . find you." His voice hisses and rattles, soaked in hate and fear. "He will l . . . leech every drop of your power—power a beast like you c . . . can't begin to understand—until you wish you w . . . were—"

I rip his heart out with my teeth and spit it on the ground, grimacing from the taste of death and rot. It's done. But I don't feel satisfaction . . . just a heavy weariness. Chest heaving with labored breathing, I watch the terror on the assassin's face fade as he disintegrates into a pile of blue dust.

CHAPTER ELEVEN

Ethan groans as he rises to his feet, and I almost sag with relief. He looks unharmed. I don't even see dried blood on his face from the assassin's heart-shredding screams. I squint to see straight as my head spins from the blood loss. Did he wipe it all away? But I don't see any blood on his hands or shirt. I sway on my feet as the adrenaline seeps out of me.

"Sunny?" He steps toward me.

I startle and turn away from him, tucking my tails close to my body. I don't want him to see me like this. I shrink in on myself.

Monster! Even the girl who'd been my friend since we could barely walk had thrown stones at me. *Beast!* Her round, smiling face had been contorted into an angry mask. I had implored her with my hands outstretched. *Please, I'm your friend.* But all she had seen was an abomination, something she feared and hated.

"Sunny," Ethan repeats, coming to stand in front of me.

I force myself to hold my head up high and face him, flaring my nine tails wide. *I am not a monster.* Even so, when he reaches out a tentative hand, I have a hard time not flinching. I hold my breath and wait. He lowers his hand on the back of my neck and smooths it down to my shoulder blades. I can't hide my shiver, my fur fluttering as though rustled by an invisible wind.

He catches my eyes, and I want to close them—to hide. But I stand still and hold his gaze. Little by little, I feel myself thawing, as though shedding an armor of frozen fear. I see no judgment in his eyes—no disgust, no fear. He runs his fingers through my fur, his face full of wonder. His parted lips curve into a smile when my tails swish of their own accord.

"You're so beautiful." Ethan drops to one knee and presses his forehead against mine. "And God, I don't think I've felt anything as soft as your fur."

I am not a monster. This time I almost believe it. I feel naked standing before him as a gumiho but not ashamed. The violence that churned through me disappeared with the blue assassin. The only person I hurt was the bad guy, who was already technically dead. *I am not a monster.* I might not wear this form with ease, but I'm still me. I feel a raw, gaping hole inside me begin to mend. When tears fill my eyes, I know it's time to end this touching moment.

"You can stop rubbing up against me," I say telepathically. "I'm not a therapy dog."

Ethan startles and falls on his ass. I snort. It's never *not* funny to see someone falling on their ass. I list sideways before I right myself. I lost a lot of blood and feel as weak as a newborn fawn. If I'm not careful, I might fall on my ass too.

"How did you do that?" He picks himself off the ground and crouches down in front of me.

"Do what?" I cock my head. When he arches an eyebrow, I huff out a resigned breath. "I can speak telepathically in this form."

After two beats of silence, he says, "I have to admit that's kind of awesome."

"Does that mean you think *I'm* kind of awesome?" If I wasn't in my gumiho form, I might have dissolved into a fit of giggles. *Gods help me.* I need to find food. Fast.

Ethan smirks but quickly sobers. "Your thigh. The wound is closing up, but it's still bleeding."

"Don't worry about it. I heal even faster as a gumiho," I rush to say before he can rip apart his only shirt to wrap up my leg. I can't afford the distraction of a bare-chested Ethan. "What about you? Are you okay?"

His eyes don't leave the gash on my hind leg—he's clearly still worried about it. I lower myself to the ground, tucking my leg close to my body even though it hurts like hell to do so. He finally looks at my face and says, "I have a pounding headache, but I'm otherwise fine. That screech . . . It felt like my head was about to explode."

"Along with the rest of your internal organs. We wouldn't have lasted much longer without the mountain's help." I lay my head down on the ground and feel a soothing pulse beneath me. "Can you pour a couple of mini liquor bottles on the roots of this tree? I want to thank them."

"Was it the Seonangshin?" Ethan walks over to pick up my backpack several yards away.

"No, it was this mountain." I breathe in the scent of earth, my eyes sliding closed. "Gumihos are beings of Mountains. We share the same life force, this mountain and I. Much of nature isn't sentient, but I must've somehow awakened their primal need to protect one of their own."

"Lucky us." He pours the liquor on the ground and puts his hand on the tree trunk. "Thank you."

I almost doze off but jerk awake with a snort. "The axes. Where did they come from?"

"I found them," Ethan says, looking down at his hands. "You were fighting the golem, and I needed to help you, but I had . . . nothing. No powers. No weapons. I was about to rush out with rocks in my hands, when I saw something glinting in the forest.

"It felt like I walked for miles following the light, but I couldn't have. I could still see you behind me. I finally found a golden axe and a silver axe nestled in some moss under a tree. I would've come for you then but I . . . couldn't lift them.

"They were impossibly heavy, and I was about to give up. Then I saw you fall to your knees and . . . I don't know what happened. I just . . . picked up the axes and went after the bastard." He drags an unsteady hand through his hair. "I'm sorry I wasn't there sooner. I should've stopped him before he slashed your leg—"

"Stop, Ethan." I go to him and nudge my nose against his hand. He cradles my head against his side, burying his fingers in my fur. I press closer to him, and we stand like that for a long moment. I sigh and break the silence. "I would've been pissed if you came running brandishing little rocks."

He chuckles a bit wearily. "I guess the axes came in handy."

Axes. *A golden axe and a silver axe.* A memory rises to the surface—an old, weathered face whispering strange and wonderful tales to a little girl.

"There's a Korean folktale about a humble woodsman." My thoughts drift far away, even though I'm still standing beside Ethan. "The woodsman loses his axe in the mountains, but the Spirit of Mountains, Sanshillyeong, comes to his aid.

"First, he shows the woodsman a silver axe, but the woodsman tells him that it's not his axe. Then, the spirit shows him a golden axe, but the woodsman still tells him that it's not his axe. Only when the Sanshillyeong returns with his old metal axe does the woodsman claim it as his own.

"The tale goes that the Spirit of Mountains gave the woodsman both the golden axe and the silver axe to reward him for his honesty."

That isn't the real ending to the story. At least, not the way my halmeoni told it. What was it? I chase the faint memory, but it floats away—again and again—just out of reach. It doesn't matter. It's just an old story.

Ethan has gone still next to me. "Are you telling me that the Spirit of Mountains left me those axes?"

I realize that's exactly what I'm telling him. *Then what does that make Ethan?* Nothing. It doesn't make him anything. Ethan is just . . . Ethan. I shake out my fur and say with forced nonchalance, "All I'm saying is that someone out there is looking out for us."

"We could use some of that." Ethan straightens up, then frowns. "Where *are* the axes?"

"What?" I glance around.

"I dropped them on the ground right over here." He circles the area where he'd fallen to his knees.

It's the right spot. I see a puddle of blood across from it, where the assassin sliced through my thigh. What I don't see are the axes.

"The Spirit of Mountains or not . . . it's not nice to give someone a gift, then . . . take it back," I complain in my head, groggy from exhaustion.

The ground rumbles beneath us, and I immediately duck my head. I am definitely not thinking straight. Sanshillyeong is one of the manifestations of the Seonangshin. If the Spirit of Mountains had indeed given Ethan the axes, then I need to keep my mouth shut—even if they took the axes back. The ground could've swallowed me whole for disrespecting the Seonangshin.

"Whoa," Ethan says. "I didn't know Korea had earthquakes."

"Only when I mouth off." I shake my head. "Well, it sounds to me like the damn things are too heavy to carry around anyway. Who knows? Maybe the axes will appear again when you need them."

Ethan pinches the bridge of his nose. "At some point, this shit is going to get too weird for me to handle."

"I'm surprised you're handling any of it at all," I admit.

"Surviving something and handling it are not the same thing," he says quietly. I can't see his face because he's sheathing my hwando and putting it away in my backpack. "Anyway, are you okay to move on?"

"I'm not going to get far if I don't eat something." I sniff the air. There's a hare nearby. "Keep going down this trail. It'll take you to the beach. I'll meet you there."

I take off into the woods before he can respond. Even in my weakened state, it's thrilling to run through the mountain, my feet kicking up dirt and the trees blurring past me. I slow down to a trot when my prey is close. Then I slink around the line of trees, silent and unseen. I haven't hunted in over a century. As hungry as I am, I feel queasy at the thought of killing and eating a mountain rabbit. But there's no time for squeamishness.

I let myself recede into the background, and instinct takes over.

◆ ◆ ◆

I splash into the cold ocean. I don't like swimming in my fox form, but I need to wash off the blood. I dunk my head underwater and emerge a second later, sputtering. I repeat the head dunk several times until the stiff dried blood washes off my face. How did Ethan not get any blood on his face? Maybe he wiped it off with his hands. Did I get a good look at his palms? I was barely conscious from the blood loss. I could've missed it.

I'm not sure I believe myself. But what's the alternative?

My head is throbbing, and the saltwater burns against my wound. I turn around and swim back ashore. After shaking the water out of my fur, I climb onto a sun-kissed boulder. I return to my human form, even though it's easier to walk on my injured leg when I'm down on all fours. The beach is secluded, but I can't risk being seen by humans. A snow-white nine-tailed fox the size of a lion cannot pass for an average fox. A freak-out would ensue. I don't need to give the Suhoshin any more reason to come after me.

I lie down on the warm surface, spreading my wet hair behind my head. The sky looks impossibly blue, with perfect cotton candy clouds scattered across it. I should stay alert—taking my gumiho form was like sending up a flare to the Shingae—but my eyes flutter shut. The hare went a long way to replenish my strength, but I'm far from 100 percent. The last few days have been rough on my body.

I don't know if I fell asleep, but I hear a shuffling noise beside the boulder. I shoot up to my feet and reach for my hwando before I remember I left it with Ethan. Luckily, he's the one who made the noise as he climbed onto the rock beside me.

He scans me slowly from head to toe, then says, "Huh."

"What?" I touch my wet hair but catch the self-conscious gesture and drop my hand.

"You still have your clothes." His brows draw into a frown.

"And?" I know what he's getting at, but I'm not going to make it easy for him. It's a matter of principle.

"I mean"—Ethan blushes—"didn't they get ripped apart when you changed forms?"

"Were you hoping to find me sprawled out on the beach . . . naked?" I can't deny I'm having fun.

"Not hoping . . ." He cringes, turning even redder. "I was planning for contingencies. I figured I could give you my shirt until we find you some clothes. You're so short it would come down past your thighs—"

"It's magic," I say, cutting him off. I'm not totally merciless.

"What?" He blinks. "Being short?"

"When I transform, whatever I'm wearing changes with me," I grit out through my teeth. *Bastard.* This is what I get for taking pity on him. I should've let him squirm some more. I narrow my eyes. "So when I change back, I return to being exactly as I was."

A slow smile spreads across his face. Damn it. I walked right into that one. When he opens his mouth, I slash my hand across the air. "If you say 'To being short?' I swear I'll bring down a world of hurt on you."

Ethan wisely keeps his mouth shut, but I want to kiss that cocky smirk off his face. No, not kiss. I meant punch. Like really, really hard. With my fist. *Fuck.*

Anyway, by *exactly as I was*, I meant *back to wearing jeans torn at my thigh and stained with blood.* My little dip in the ocean was hardly enough to get a blood stain out of a pair of jeans. You need club soda for that, right? Thinking of laundry hacks clears my mind of unwanted impulses.

"Can you help me rip this off?" I ask, pointing at the torn leg of my jeans. "I can't walk around in bloody jeans."

"Sure." Dropping my backpack on the rock, Ethan sinks to his knees at my feet. "How are you feeling?"

I stare down at his dark bent head, and my stomach swoops with . . . lust. My cheeks—as well as some other parts—grow uncomfortably warm. This is definitely lust. And I'm all out of laundry hacks to combat it. Thoroughly flustered, I answer without thinking. "Strange."

He glances up at me, with his head cocked to the side. When he sees my expression, understanding dawns on his face, and his eyes darken. Holding my gaze, he runs his hands down the backs of my legs, starting from the fold below my ass down to my calves. I shudder, and his grip tightens around my legs.

Oh, gods. I panic and take a step back, almost stumbling off the boulder.

"Whoa." He tugs me back and holds me steady by my hips. Then he closes his eyes and blows out an unsteady breath. When he speaks, his voice is carefully neutral. "So you want me to rip this off here?"

"Yup." I nod too many times . . . still panicked, still turned on.

With the help of my hwando and some brute force, we repurpose my jeans into really short shorts. Like *behold, my butt cheeks* short. Ethan gets to his feet, but his gaze is glued to my legs.

"Hey," I snap before I'm tempted to like it. "Eyes up here."

"Sorry." His pupils are blown wide. I feel a mixture of nerves and triumph that he isn't immune to the attraction flaring between us. But nerves win out.

"We need to hurry." I stuff the remnants of my jeans into the backpack. My magic traces are everywhere, but I don't need to leave an arrow pointing to the cave. "We still have a lot of ground to cover, and the Suhoshin will find us sooner rather than later after our scuffle with Blue."

"And the yellow assassin?" Ethan jumps off the rock and offers me a hand.

I roll my eyes and leap down. I immediately regret not accepting his help when pain radiates from my thigh to my teeth. I cough to cover up my whimper. "I'm going to avoid thinking about him for as long as I can."

"A wise plan." He sounds so droll I can't help but grin at him.

"Come on." I jerk my head toward the cave and lead the way.

The cave entrance is strewn with rocks and tree branches. When we pull them aside, inky darkness greets us. The cave doesn't look very big as we walk in. Ethan has to slouch not to hit his head on the ceiling. But as we make our way down the dark path with my puny flashlight guiding our way, I realize looks can be deceptive.

CHAPTER TWELVE

If avoidance were an Olympic event, I'd be a record-breaking gold medalist. I've had over a century of practice, after all. The tunnels are dark and dank, and we walk single file through the narrow path—me up front and Ethan behind me. It's not conducive to conversation, especially since we've been trudging on for hours.

In the tomb-like silence, I have plenty of time for self-reflection, but I turn my thoughts to food instead. I could really go for a juicy, sloppy cheeseburger right now. Or my personal favorite, rare steak with two sunny-side up eggs.

When I first came to the States, I didn't . . . talk. I didn't want to hear my voice. I didn't want to see my reflection in the mirror. I didn't want to be reminded that I was me. Besides, no one understood Korean, and I didn't know how to speak English. But I listened. And soon the words started making sense to me.

The missionary couple who took me in thought I *couldn't* speak. Then one day, I pointed at the fried egg on my plate and said, "Sun." The bright-orange yolk of the eggs I'd gathered from the henhouse looked like the sun. It made me happy that I could still have a thought so pure and innocent, because maybe it meant a part of me remained good.

The couple took to calling me Sunny after that, and I guess the name stuck. It wasn't until years later that diners began serving "sunny-side up" eggs. Since I came first, the eggs were technically named after me.

Before my mind takes a proper stroll down memory lane, I glance over my shoulder and break the silence. "You doing okay?"

Ethan grimaces, hunched over at the waist to avoid hitting his head. "It's torture on my back, but I'll live."

As though the earth heard the plea in his voice, the tunnel opens into a cavern . . . with two passages. I curse under my breath.

"Oh, thank God." He straightens up with a groan, pounding his fist on his lower back. "I seriously considered crawling after you on all fours if it didn't let up."

"Here." I hand him a bottle of water before I drink from my own. Then I sit against a wall and glare at the fork in the path.

"Any idea which way to go?" He settles down beside me and takes a long gulp of water.

"Give me five minutes," I say and close my eyes.

"Are you stalling?" The teasing lilt in his voice hatches butterflies in my stomach.

"Yes?" I didn't mean to say that like a question. And I definitely wasn't going for a husky whisper. I open my eyes and turn toward him. We're sitting closer than I'd realized, our faces mere inches apart. He stares at me for a long moment, his throat working.

Just when I think he's going to speak, he jumps to his feet and walks to one tunnel opening, then the other. "I feel a breeze coming from this one."

"You're right," I say, coming to stand beside him. "We have to be close to North Korea by now. Hopefully, this tunnel leads us out into the open."

But when we walk down the path, it deposits us into another cavern that looks suspiciously like the one we've left behind—with another set of tunnels to choose from.

"Is there folklore about Daedalus building a second labyrinth in Korea?" He peers into one of the tunnels. "More importantly, are we going to run into the Minotaur down here?"

"Why, chickenshit?" I smirk. "Are you scared?"

"Why should I be scared?" He doesn't miss a beat. "Your gumiho can take the Minotaur."

I roll my eyes. I don't bother explaining that minotaurs are perfectly nice guys. Besides, I wouldn't mess with the Greeks. Their mythology is part of the US public school curriculum. When it comes down to it, they are harder to kill than a mythical creature only people in Korea know about.

"Do you have a coin?" he says, running a hand through his hair. "Maybe we should flip for it."

"Shh." I press myself against the wall, tugging Ethan beside me. "I hear something."

The sounds of footfall and a murmur of voices are our only warnings before two men step into the cavern. The twin looks of shock on their faces instantly morph into hard, ruthless masks. These guys aren't amateurs. Not bothering to ask us who we are or what we're doing down here, they draw their guns.

Ethan and I jump headlong into the tunnel next to us. Gunshots ring out in rapid succession. Debris of dirt and rock showers down on our heads as the bullets lodge themselves into a wall, too close for comfort. I scramble to my feet and break into a dead run, with Ethan at my heels.

The gunshots continue to echo in the tunnel, ricocheting off the walls. It's impossible to discern how close the men are—they might still be right behind us. I pick up speed. We didn't come this far to let some random dudes shoot us. That would be beyond anticlimactic.

When the tunnel forks left and right, I let gut instinct choose the path and push on. Even when I don't hear them chasing us anymore, I keep running, with Ethan close behind me. I realize this isn't about losing the bad guys anymore. I wait and wait for him to fall behind, but he doesn't.

Thoroughly winded, I stop with one hand against the wall and the other on my side. Ethan doubles over with his hands on his thighs, wheezing like he can't get enough air into his lungs. But he's right there beside me. I didn't hold back, even when my injured thigh burned like hell. I hear the rush of blood pounding in my ears. The nagging suspicions I've had since his appearance at Roxy's . . . could they be true? It makes zero sense, but that doesn't mean I'm wrong. Then what *does* it mean?

"I thought . . . this was the way into the North . . . *without* getting us shot," he pants.

"Do you see any bullet holes in either one of us? No? I didn't think so." I push away from the wall and shuffle down the tunnel. We have to get to the cypress grove. Everything else can wait. "We *didn't* get shot. We just got shot *at*."

Ethan shakes his head at me, not wasting precious oxygen on a response. But he knows I'm right.

"Come on, slowpoke," I say over my shoulder.

"*Slowpoke?*" He takes two long strides to catch up with me. "You need to work on your terms of endearment."

"Yeah?" I smirk. "How does *dumbass* work for you?"

"I prefer *dingus*. It makes me feel all warm and fuzzy when you call me that." He grins happily at me, even though he still sounds breathless. "Who do you think those men were? They didn't seem particularly magical."

"They're most likely smugglers, hawking South Korean goods to the North."

Ethan nods and falls quiet. It's heartbreaking to see a country torn in half, especially when one side flourishes while the other side struggles to feed its people. Korea had its share of problems before the divide, but at least it was the problems of one nation, one people.

The tunnel at this end is wide enough for us to walk side by side, but it's far from roomy. Our arms keep brushing against each other's, and I feel every touch like an electric zap. I held on to my flashlight through the one-sided shoot-out, and I can see Ethan in the dim glow. The man is unfairly hot—pretty much up there with the seraphim, minus the wings. Except you can only ogle perfection for so long before you get bored. With Ethan, his not-quite-straight nose and rugged edges make him infinitely more ogle worthy than a beautiful angel.

My breathing grows shallow, even though we're not running. These flashes of awareness are inconvenient, not to mention frustrating. I said I wouldn't act on this attraction—and I won't. But it's growing harder and harder to ignore. He catches me staring. I shoot my gaze up to the ceiling, but not before I glimpse a corner of his mouth curving up.

"See anything interesting?" he drawls.

Cocky bastard. "Just making sure the ceiling's not about to collapse and bury us alive down here."

"Thank you for that," he grumbles. "That's just the mental image I needed."

"I'm sorry." Not sorry. "I thought you weren't claustrophobic?"

He scoffs in disbelief. "Not wanting to be buried alive doesn't make me claustrophobic."

I have to admit, being buried alive is not my idea of a good time either. Maybe sinking morale wasn't the best way to deflect embarrassment. But as we trudge on, the air inside the tunnel changes—lightens. I can smell the mountains nearby. Relief rushes through me. We lucked out and chose the right path.

"Cheer up, Grumpy." I smile. "We'll be out in the open soon."

"Really?" His eyebrows hike up. "Thank God."

We march on with renewed energy until we spy the moonlit night at the end of the tunnel. I'm tempted to run outside to breathe in the fresh air, but I slow down and press myself up against the wall. Ethan flattens himself on the opposite wall, and we take silent, measured steps to the opening. When he holds up a fist, I freeze and listen for noise outside. I nod, and he peers out, scanning left and right.

"It's clear," he says.

Even so, he tucks me close behind him as we step outside. Warmth unfurls in my stomach, and I press my cheek against his back. I'm more than capable of taking care of myself. But would it be so terrible to let someone else do it for me once in a while? *Oh, hells no.* I swat his arm away and stomp to his side. I haven't had anyone protect me for over a century—minus the three years with the Lee brothers—and I don't need anyone now.

The tunnel deposits us into a field of wildflowers turned golden from the summer heat. A gentle breeze coaxes the flowers to sway, and shimmering waves dance across the field. The song of crickets and the smell of rich soil surround me in a warm embrace. I feel not so much a sense of homecoming—I've lived in the United States for too long for Korea to feel like home—but a sweet nostalgia for my childhood. For a moment, I'm hopeful . . . hopeful that I can hold on to the good stuff and let go of the rest at last.

"I'm guessing we're headed that way?" Ethan asks just in time to dispel my fanciful train of thoughts.

I follow his gaze across the field. A solitary mountain juts toward the sky, and I recognize it as the one the lone cypress showed me. *Oh, gods.* We're going to make it.

"If I were an old cypress tree, I'd want to live there." I grin as I hurry forward. "Come on. It shouldn't take us more than an hour to reach the base of the mountain."

After what feels like a good hour, I look over my shoulder at the long stretch of flowers behind us. My lungs and thighs burn like I've been climbing uphill—not strolling across a flat field. The tunnel entrance has long since disappeared from view. We should be at least halfway to the mountain, but we aren't getting any closer.

"Is it me? Or is the mountain getting farther away?" Ethan wipes his forearm across his brow.

I frown, focusing my senses on our surroundings. I don't hear the crickets singing anymore. I don't hear a single sound other than the rasp of our labored breathing . . . like we're sealed in a vacuum.

"This isn't an ordinary flower field." My voice echoes in the silence but is muted like we're underwater. "It's enchanted."

The backs of my hands sting. When I glance down, I see a dozen scratches on them. My legs haven't fared much better. The pretty wildflowers have given me hundreds of shallow cuts. Without my healing powers, I'd have thousands. I scan Ethan's hands, but he doesn't have a single scratch on them. Maybe he's so tall that the flowers don't reach them.

"What do we do?" Ethan scans the seemingly endless field.

"I don't know." I shake away my disquiet and force myself to think. "The Seonangshin don't want to make it easy for people to reach the cypress grove. But I can't use my spirit eyes to find the right path . . ."

The salt from my dip in the ocean would've slowed down the Suhoshin, but they must be hot on our trail by now. We need to get to the ancient cypress grove before we're captured. If we get the sacred ashes, the Suhoshin might give us some time . . . or even help us find Daeseong. But if I use my magic now, they'll moon shift to a nearby body of water—the mountain must have plenty—and capture us, leaving us with nothing to barter.

"You could transform," Ethan says casually, like it's the obvious answer. "That way even if you use your spirit eyes, you'll be fast enough to get there before the Suhoshin track you down."

"You're pretty fast, but you'll never be able to keep up with my gumiho." Just the thought of transforming knots my stomach with shame and anxiety—the instinctive fear of my fox spirit rearing its head again. To hide my agitation, I quip, "And there's no way in hell I'm letting you ride me."

No. I did *not* just say that. But my flaming-hot face tells me otherwise. I stare at my toes, hoping he lets it pass. When I see Ethan's shoes stop just a couple of inches away from mine, I have no choice but to look up at him.

"I wasn't asking for a ride," he says in a low voice, his gaze dropping to my lips, then lower. "Besides, that's not the kind of ride I'm interested in."

My blood pounds in my ears in time with my heartbeat. Is he *flirting* with me? And he picked *now* to do it? I can't deal. But I'm tempted to ask him to explain in detail what kind of ride he *is* interested in. Now really isn't the time, though.

"Then what are you planning to do?" I ask instead.

He takes his time raising his eyes to meet mine, then says with a shrug, "I'll catch up with you."

"You'll *catch up* with me?" I gape at him. His dismissive little shrug annoys me to no end. "I just told you this field is enchanted. Once I'm gone, you'll never be able to find your way out of here on your own."

"I'll find a way." Ethan nearly shrugs again but catches himself.

I finally see through his nonchalant act. The idiot is asking me to leave him. To fucking *abandon* him in an enchanted field full of sharp, bloodthirsty flowers. If we weren't in a time crunch, I would throttle him.

I settle for narrowing my eyes and snapping, "What happened to sticking together?"

"We don't have to be literally stuck together," he says, throwing my words back at me.

Considering the circumstances—where he's being an unreasonable, noble asshole—maybe I can make time to throttle him. My hands rise of their own accord, with my fingers curled into claws. Before I can find satisfaction, something flits past us, and a faint cackling rings in the distance.

"Did you see that?" I whip around in a half circle.

"See what?" His brows draw together.

"Halmeoni," I breathe.

In the distance, she stands with her hands clasped behind her back, wearing a light-brown hanbok made of coarse cotton, with her white hair bound in a low bun. Her smile is both wise and full of mischief. Samshin Halmeom. She looks exactly as I remember her.

"Halmeoni," I call out and run toward her.

She flashes in and out of view as I chase her, a blur of white and brown. When I lose sight of her, I follow the sound of her husky cackle and find her again. But no matter how fast I run, she's just out of reach.

"Halmeoni," I shout. "Wait."

Other than my mother, Samshin Halmeom was the closest thing to family I'd known. She would come to me whenever I was playing alone in the woods near our little house in the mountain. She always asked me to help her find a particular flower, a rare herb, or a one-of-a-kind stone. As we searched for one elusive treasure or another, she would tell me the most wondrous stories. My mother said they were just fanciful tales. But sometimes . . . they felt more real to me than our quiet life in the woods.

"Samshin Halmeom!"

I chase after her until she's . . . gone. Why would she run from me? Does she resent me for leaving the Shingae? Is she horrified by what I've done? I shake my head. It would be weird if she *wanted* to see me—not the other way around—especially considering who she is. Even so, I can't stop the hurt sob that slips past my lips.

I'm so bereft it takes me a moment to realize I'm standing at the base of the mountain. Alone. Where's Ethan? I spin left and right. My chest seizes, and all the air is squeezed out of my lungs. After all that, *I* left him. Now he's lost, and I don't know how to find him. Just as I'm about to scream and kick something, he sprints out of the field and lurches to a stop next to me. Shock paralyzes me for a heartbeat before relief rushes through me, making me choke on stupid tears. My feet carry me toward him without my consent, and I have a sinking feeling that I'm about to throw myself into his arms.

"Who was that?" Ethan pants, holding a hand to his side.

His question startles me enough to chase away my sentimentality. "You *saw* her?"

"Yeah." He squints at me, his chest still heaving. "The grandmother in a traditional dress. A hanbok, right?"

I nod slowly. "Right."

When I grew too old to play in the woods, deciding only little kids did that, Samshin Halmeom stopped coming to me. It wasn't until years later, when I'd almost forgotten about her, that my mother told me my favorite storyteller was a manifestation of the Seonangshin.

I still can't reconcile my halmeoni with the fearsome god of Mountains. And I don't understand why Samshin Halmeom had appeared to a precocious little gumiho in the first place. Maybe she'd really needed that flower or herb or stone. And maybe she showed herself to us tonight—and led us to the cypress grove—because *someone* has to stop Daeseong.

But before I go back to the *why me?* of it all, I have to accept one thing first. Even though I had my suspicions, especially after our run through the tunnels, I didn't really believe it. But there is no other explanation for it. Only beings of the Shingae can see the gods and . . .

Ethan saw Samshin Halmeom.

CHAPTER THIRTEEN

"That was Samshin Halmeom," I say in a small voice, my gaze unfocused. "She's one of the manifestations of the Seonangshin."

"She led us out of the enchanted field." Ethan straightens and looks around us, his breath evening out. "That means the Seonangshin wants us at the cypress grove. That's good news, right?"

"Maybe." *Ethan is a being of the Shingae.* The realization rattles deafeningly through my head. But I force myself to continue. "Or whatever shit that's about to hit the fan is so horrible that the Seonangshin will help *anyone* to stop Daeseong."

Why can't I sense his gi? Did he hide his life force so deep inside himself that his magic isn't detectable? It's possible to hide your magic. *I* did it for over a century. But that would mean Ethan knows about his powers. It means he can control his magic. And he's been doing it since he was a teenager when I was with him. That's not too far fetched. I was only eighteen when I had to hide my magic for the first time. I steal a glance at Ethan.

"Well, fuck," he says, then runs a hand down his face.

I don't want to believe it. What reason could he have to lie to me? *So many,* whispers a cynical voice inside me. But that's not true. People only lie to you when they want something from you—or to keep something from you. I have nothing he wants. He has nothing I want.

I double down on the idea. I was perfectly content working at a crappy casino—eating my rare steak, drinking my tequila. I wanted and needed nothing. I was a solitary island. Why would anyone lie to me? *They wouldn't.* Ergo, Ethan did not lie to me.

The only person who has any reason to lie to me is Daeseong, because he wants something from me. *But what if Ethan is working for Daeseong?* What? No. That psychopath killed his brother. *What if Ethan is somehow involved in Ben's murder?* No way. No. Fucking. Way. My paranoia is having a field day. Maybe my blood sugar dropped or something.

I can't act rashly. I have to think this through with a clear head. I can't let on that I know his secret. For now, I'm going to operate under the assumption that he's my friend. And friends don't accuse friends of killing their own brothers.

"Let's get on with it," I mutter and stomp into the woods.

He matches my stride. "Is there anything I should know before we face the Seonangshin?"

"Just follow my lead," I say.

The one upside to Ethan being from the Shingae is that he won't drop like a fly by merely being in the presence of the Seonangshin. But if he turns out to be an evil bastard, then maybe it'll be better if the god strikes him down. My hands curl into fists, even as my elongated claws dig into my palms. In my mind, flames engulf the cypress grove, and the Seonangshin burn. I realize with a chill that I would destroy anyone who tries to hurt Ethan. Even the gods.

I take a deep breath, and my claws become fingernails again, allowing the little bloody crescents on my palms to mend. I glance at Ethan. He's so beautiful that my heart skips a beat. And he's a good man . . . no, male. I *know* this in the marrow of my bones. Then why would he hide his identity from me? Nothing makes sense.

"Is everything all right?" I feel his eyes on me, so I continue looking straight ahead. "You seem . . . quiet."

"When have I ever been chatty?" I shrug, super chill.

"Are you nervous about going to the cypress grove?" he asks gently.

"Ha!" I pause because I actually *am* nervous about going before the ancient cypress grove, like any sane being of the Shingae. Besides, he just gave me the perfect excuse for my weird mood. "Well, yes. I *am* nervous. Very."

He reaches for my hand and links his fingers through mine. Emotions of the squishy variety invade my heart, and I don't protest. I accept the quiet comfort he offers, because it loosens the vise tightening around my chest.

"Everything will be okay." He gives my hand a reassuring squeeze. "The Seonangshin in Monterey was helpful, right?"

"Yes, but you can't predict the temperament of the Seonangshin." I manage a small smile. "Each manifestation is unique, and not all of them are kind."

"But aren't gods supposed to be . . . *good?*"

"Aww, you're sweet." I pat his cheek.

So quick that I can't pull away, he presses his hand over mine and turns his head to plant an open-mouthed kiss on my palm. I feel the barest flick of his tongue and gasp despite myself. He doesn't stop me when I snatch my hand away, but his half-hooded glance makes me exhale a shaky breath.

"It's not as black and white as that. Gods let horrors occur for the *greater good*—whatever the fuck that means," I say once I can speak in a normal voice. "Sure, their end goal might be good, but they don't always get there by doing good things. That might make them practical but not exactly *good.*"

He nods as he absently swipes his thumb over the back of my hand. I hope he can't see my blush in the dark. Besides, the hike up the mountain is a workout. Anyone would be flushed from the exertion.

The air suddenly changes, and the moonlight turns liquid, drenching the woods around us in a silvery glow. Our hands tighten around each other's. The Seonangshin's power is palpable—it vibrates in my bones—and I don't need my spirit eyes to know which way to go.

Ethan walks quietly at my side. He must feel the tidal wave of gi too. *Who are you? What are you hiding? Were you and Ben hiding the truth from me all those years ago? Or were you keeping it from your brother as well?* I turn my wayward thoughts to the present. I can't be distracted in the presence of the Seonangshin. Such disrespect will not go unpunished.

The deeper we hike into the woods, the denser the trees grow. They block out the light of the moon and turn our path pitch black. Ethan closes the distance between us until our shoulders brush with every step. We weave in and out of the trees with halting gaits, like we're finding our way through a maze blindfolded. But the hum of magic inside me reaches a fevered pitch. We're close.

All of a sudden, we're standing in an open field, the trees forming an enormous circle around us. And at the opposite end, a grove of twelve sprawling cypress trees stands apart from the rest. I fall to my knees and lay my forehead on the ground. I feel Ethan kneel beside me and can only hope that he's paying obeisance to the Seonangshin as I am.

Keeping my head bowed, I open my backpack and grab all the remaining mini bottles. One by one, I pour the liquor onto the ground with two hands. Once the last bottle is emptied, I feel a bony hand grip my elbow. I gasp but don't jerk my arm away. At the prompting of the hand, I rise to my feet before I lift my gaze from the ground.

"Halmeoni," I choke out as tears fall down my cheek. She's here. She wasn't avoiding me after all.

Samshin Halmeom pulls me into her arms and smooths her hand down my hair. "Hello, little fox."

I wail and spill a hundred years' worth of tears. She holds me through it all. Samshin Halmeom is the Seonangshin. I should be terrified of her, but all I feel is joy and relief at seeing her after all this time. It's almost like seeing my mother again.

"Halmeoni—" I straighten when she drops her arms after one last pat on my back. "I mean, Samshin Halmeom. My mother . . . she's . . . gone."

"Yes, I know," she says, her hands held behind her stooped back.

"And I . . . I . . ." I swallow back a sob. *I took so many lives.*

"I know it all, child." Her expression is unreadable, but she sounds weary. Then her gaze shifts, and she barks out a dry, cackling laugh. "Tell that boy to stand up."

Ethan is looking up at us with wide eyes, but he's still on his knees. Although she spoke in Korean, he gets the gist and stands up. He bows from the waist and says, "Samshin Halmeom."

She peers at him for a long while with a tinge of sadness in her mischievous smile. Then she turns to me and says, "You got yourself a looker."

"I didn't . . . He's not my . . ." I glance down and press my lips together. There's no use lying to the Seonangshin. I don't think he's my anything. I'm not even sure if I want him to be. But regardless of what I want, I might be falling for him without having any idea who he really is or what he's playing at . . . My head jerks up. Samshin Halmeom has to know. "Do you—"

She cuts me off with a stern gaze. "Why don't you focus on why you came here, little fox?"

"We're here to ask for your help," I say, chastised. She's not a carnival fortune teller. "We need the sacred ashes."

"Do you?" She clucks her tongue. "Is it worth the price you have to pay?"

"The . . . the price?" Apprehension prickles down my spine. My mother never taught me about any price that had to be paid to obtain the sacred ashes.

"Severing a part of our roots means severing a part of our gi," Samshin Halmeom says. "Do you think we will hand you a portion of our life force without a price?"

Severing a part of their gi? I shake my head slowly. I had no idea I was asking the Seonangshin to sacrifice so much.

"You must relive the worst moment of your life." Her voice echoes with the rustling of restless leaves and the baying of wind caught in a hollow trunk. "It will be more than remembering. You will feel every emotion, every pain, like it was happening to you again."

I suck in a sharp breath. "But why?"

Samshin Halmeom's eyes burn in every shade of green, beautiful, terrifying, and eternal. "You dare question my decision?"

"N . . . no." My teeth chatter with fear. I know with devastating certainty what the worst moment of my life was. Reliving it will wreck me. "No, Samshin Halmeom. I . . . I will pay the price."

Ben didn't deserve to die. Neither did my mother. My hands fist at my sides. I killed Daeseong once. I will kill him again. I will pay *any* price to avenge their senseless deaths and protect Ethan from him.

"Sunny." Ethan grips my shoulders and turns me to face him. "What's going on?"

"The sacred ashes . . ." My voice breaks. "I have to pay a price."

"What price?" He shoots an enraged glare at Samshin Halmeom and roars, "What are you going to do to her?"

"Ethan! No!" I step in front of him, but it's too late.

Samshin Halmeom's nostrils flare, and Ethan slams into a tree at the farthest edge of the field. Branches snake around him, binding him to the trunk. Despite his furious struggles, he is cocooned in a wooden prison within seconds.

"Sunny, don't do—" Leaves plaster themselves across his mouth, silencing him.

"Please don't hurt him," I beg, more afraid than I've ever been in my life. "He doesn't know the ways of the Shingae. He meant you no disrespect."

"Oh, the boy meant me disrespect." The deity snorts. "Don't fret, child. His destiny has yet to play out. I will not interfere."

Before I can ask her what she means, the field and the cypress grove dissolve around me, melting away into my nightmare.

THE GIRL WHO RAN

The girl was full of joy and light. The mountain rabbit and its puffy white tail. The ribbon of leaves dancing in the wind. The song of birds and the flight of butterflies. They all made her laugh and laugh. With her world filled with such beauty, there was no room for fear or sorrow.

"Why must we train endlessly?" The girl panted even as she swung her sword over her head to take her fighting stance. "There's never anyone here but us."

"Would you rather gather more herbs?" the mother asked. "Winter's approaching. The villagers will need more cough tonic."

"When an adversary attacks from behind, what is the best defensive strike?" the girl asked, changing the subject with cheeky mischief. Without waiting for her mother to answer, she spun with fluid grace, proving she already knew the proper technique.

The daughter's silken hair was braided down her back like a proper maiden's, but she wore the hanbok of a man, with loose pants and a top that fell below her waist. Even the coarse brown cotton of a commoner did nothing to diminish the girl's exquisite beauty. In the moonlight, her dark laughing eyes twinkled with vivacity while she wielded her hwando with the deadly precision of a seasoned warrior.

There stands hope born of despair, the mother thought with wonder. Then she shook her head and hid the smile tugging on her lips. She loved her daughter more than life itself. She prayed she would always shine—bright and beautiful. She hoped her daughter would never forget that she was *good*.

But that didn't mean she should take her training lightly.

The mother opened her mouth to scold her, when the roar of an angry mob echoed in the distance. The blood drained from her face. *Oh, gods*. It couldn't be. *Please no*. The girl was only eighteen. *It's too soon*. She closed her eyes against a wave of dizziness. He had come for her.

She should have taught her more. *No*. She should have told her the truth. In her soul of souls, hadn't she known this day was inevitable? But she hadn't wanted to believe it. She had thought only of protecting her beloved daughter. Now it was too late. How was the girl to face what lay ahead?

"Forgive me." She pressed a shaking hand to her mouth.

"Mother?"

The mother gripped the girl's hand and ran . . . even though there was no running from this. The light from the torches and the ugly shouts of hatred drew closer and closer.

"You must run, Daughter." They skidded to a stop, steps away from the plunging cliff. "You must never stop running."

The mother knew her daughter couldn't run from her destiny forever. She only hoped that the girl would find happiness along the way to sustain her through the devastation that would follow.

CHAPTER FOURTEEN

I know who the man is. I raise my arms to shield my face as the villagers pelt me and my mother with stones. He is Daeseong, the dark mudang whose hunger for magic led to the murder of countless beings of the Shingae. The mudang who drove so many of us into hiding. I thought he was a make-believe villain in a dark fairy tale that my mother told me to keep me in line. But he is very real and here for us.

My mother hides me behind her back, and I let her, even as shame crawls over me. I should be strong and brave, but I'm scared. I've never been more scared in my life. I still have my hwando, but it hangs limply by my side.

"Give her to me," he snarls.

"She does not have it," my mother says, her voice breaking. "You can walk away, Daeseong. It's not too late."

Something like regret softens his face, but a demented scowl overshadows the fleeting glimpse of humanity. "It *is* too late."

"Monster!" someone shrieks.

A stone hits my mother's forehead, and blood slides down her temple. I drop my sword and step in front of her with my arms spread wide. I peer into the crowd, my eyes frantically scanning the sea of angry faces.

When I see my friend in the crowd, I sag with relief. It's going to be all right. She will explain to everyone that my mother and I are good people. We always bring the poor meat after a hunt, taking the bare minimum for ourselves. My mother helps the sick with tonics and acupuncture, and I provide whatever care I can. But I feel my blood chill as I recognize the hateful glares of the very people we helped.

"Beast!" My friend screams and launches a stone at me. "This scholar told us *everything*. You and your mother are abominations. You will destroy our village."

"No, that's a lie. You know that's not true." I hold out a shaking hand. "Please, I'm your friend."

The mob roars with fury and closes in on us. We retreat, one halting step at a time, until the lip of the cliff snatches at our heels.

"Be brave, Mihwa." My mother wraps me in a tight embrace. "I love you."

"Mother . . ." I shake my head. It sounds too much like goodbye. "No . . ."

Daeseong withdraws a rectangular piece of paper from his sleeve, dismissive of the villagers raging around him. My mother gasps and pushes me behind her again. Before I can protest, she takes her gumiho form. Screams erupt, and the mob breaks apart, as some villagers run back into the woods while others scramble to gather more stones.

The paper catches fire, and black flames engulf the mudang. The men flanking him scamper back with horror on their faces. The fire is extinguished in a heartbeat. Blood drips from Daeseong's mouth, dribbling down his chin, and his eyes are filled with it, violence screaming within them.

My mother growls, low and fierce, but I can feel her body trembling against mine. Whatever dark magic this is, she might not be able to withstand it. I have to do something. With jerky, broken movements, I pick up my hwando and take my fighting stance. But the smile on Daeseong's face brings up bile to my mouth.

"Sa," he hisses.

My mother rears up and wraps her body around mine. My breath comes in rough pants against the soft coat of her stomach. And slowly—oh so slowly—she slides off me. I stare down at her body. The wounds look like crimson poppies blossoming over her white fur, until the blood runs together and there is no white left on her.

"Mother?" I fall to my knees. "M-mother?"

"Now come with me, little one," Daeseong says, his bloody smile stretched across his pale face.

My growl bristles down my spine, and I stand over my mother's body, my gumiho unleashed. My consciousness curls up into a little ball in my head—the gut-wrenching grief unraveling the stitches of my sanity—and mindless fury explodes inside me. Searing heat spreads in my chest. All I feel is hate. Because love hurts too much. All I want is destruction. Because I can't bring my mother back. Love is sorrow. Sorrow is rage. I close my eyes, and everything goes white.

When I come to . . . I am me again. A hint of fuchsia outlines the distant mountaintops, sunrise nudging against the inky darkness. And a sea of death lies before me. My breath leaves me in a shaky moan. I stumble to my knees as I lurch toward the bodies and crawl on all fours, even though I'm back in my human body.

Daeseong lies prone on the ground with his bloody eyes still open. I reach out with a trembling hand and feel for his life force. Gone. He is dead. All the men he brought with him—his followers—are also dead. Dead. Dead. I snatch my hand back and clutch it against my chest. The villagers . . . all of them . . . lie deathly still. But I don't reach out for their gi, afraid of the silence I'll meet.

Did I . . . did I kill them? All of them? I don't remember what happened. Or how it happened. I wrap my arms around my stomach and rock back and forth on my knees. What frightens me the most is that my first thought isn't of guilt—or remorse for the horror I've committed. *No.* My first thought is that I should've killed them sooner. Before they killed my mother. If I had such power, I should've used it when it mattered. I don't . . . I don't know who I am. I don't know who this . . . this killer is.

I rise to my feet and turn haltingly toward the cliff. I clap a hand over my mouth and whimper against it. My mother lies crumpled on the ground, her blood dried in dark-brown clumps. I don't need to reach for her gi. I already know she's gone. I don't feel her anymore. The line that was once tethered from my heart to hers now hangs limply from me, with nothing to anchor the other end.

I pull her head onto my lap and wail, "Mother."

You must run, Daughter. You must never stop running.

I don't know what my mother meant, but I intend to do as she said. I bury my mother by our little house. Then I run.

CHAPTER FIFTEEN

I return to the ancient cypress grove, raw with pain and horror. Time had dulled the sharp edges of my grief, but now I feel the pain as though my mother just died in my arms. In a way, she did. Do I have to live another hundred years for it to hurt less? I stand swaying on my feet, with unseeing eyes.

"The price has been paid," Samshin Halmeom intones.

I instinctively take a step back when she suddenly grunts in pain. She holds out a trembling arm as her fingers stitch together, melding into one. The half-moon-shaped sleeve of her hanbok rips to shreds as her arm twists and thickens into the root of a tree, with deep grooves scored along its dark length. I scream when green fire engulfs the root from its tip to where her elbow had been.

Samshin Halmeom's eyes flicker back and forth under her eyelids, and sweat beads on her forehead. Her thin lips move in an ancient tongue that I don't understand, but she speaks with rising urgency as the flames grow.

The smoke stings my eyes, and the smell of burning flesh and wood coats my nostrils and throat. Nausea lurches me forward, and I vomit on the ground. I didn't realize this was what I'd asked of her. I want to tell her to stop, but the pain of the price I paid—and why I paid that price—stays my tongue. All this because of Daeseong. What evil does he intend to unleash in the worlds that the Seonangshin would make such a sacrifice?

I hear muffled shouting behind me. *Ethan.* He twists against the branches roped around him. He's afraid for me. I shake my head, silently telling him to wait. Samshin Halmeom isn't going to hurt me. But he struggles harder, and something inconceivable happens. The branches splinter and split, and Ethan tears through them. The leaves fall from his mouth as he shouts my name and runs to my side.

"Are you hurt?" He grasps my shoulders as his eyes dart over my face, then my body. "Are you okay?"

"I'm . . ." I can't make myself say I'm okay. "I'm not hurt."

He pulls me into a rough embrace, and I bury my face in his chest, taking the solace he offers. My mother bled to death in my arms, and my halmeoni is being burned alive in front of me. I can't bear this on my own. I can't even try.

Then it all stops. The fire, the smoke, the smell. It's all gone. The sleeve of Samshin Halmeom's hanbok is whole again, but the place where her forearm had been lies flat. She holds out the palm of her one remaining hand, cradling a silk bokjumeoni. It's a round rainbow-striped pouch tied off at the top—the kind children carry on New Year's Day to stash the money their elders gave them.

If I wasn't an empty husk of a person at the moment, I would've laughed at the irony of it all. Something begotten by so much suffering stuffed inside a colorful lucky pouch. I step away from Ethan and accept the bokjumeoni with both my hands.

"How do I . . ." My throat feels raw. "How do I use the sacred ashes?"

Samshin Halmeom told me stories of brave heroes defeating evil villains with the sacred ashes, but she never told me the logistics of how they did it.

"I am weary." The one-armed deity sighs. "Stop Daeseong. Fulfill your destiny."

"What—"

Without another word, Samshin Halmeom waves her hand, and the world spirals out from under us.

"No, no, no," I yell when my feet land on solid ground. I spin in a wild arc. Samshin Halmeom and the cypress trees are gone. More accurately, she made *us* gone. I bury my face in my hands. We got the sacred ashes. But what do I do with them? Eat them? Throw them in Daeseong's face? "Oh, gods."

"Hey." Ethan wraps me in his arms, and I let him. Again. "It's going to be okay. We'll figure this out."

He's right. The toughest part is over. We can figure out the rest. And now that we have the sacred ashes, we might even be able to enlist the help of the Suhoshin. I peel my hands away from my face and rest them against his hard chest. Without thinking, I spread my fingers wide, reveling in his strength. He shivers and pulls me tighter against him, trapping my hands between our bodies.

We can't stay like this forever. I have to make a decision. I could either brush my cheek against the solid wall of his chest and soak up his warmth. Or I could push him away and quit being a baby.

"Are you . . ." I step away from him, averting my gaze. I'm no baby, but I'm not going to tempt myself by looking at him just yet. I scrape the tip of my sneaker on the ground until I scrounge up the guts to look him in the face. "Are *you* okay? Those branches were squeezing the hell out of you."

"I'll live." He shrugs, his face hardening with the memory of his helpless fury. "Do you know where we are?"

"Looks like another mountain . . ." I'm too tired to care, which isn't smart, considering we have some very scary people after us. I glance around with half-hearted interest until goose bumps spread across my arms.

"How . . ." I sprint through a copse of trees and skid to a stop. "It can't be."

But it's true. The thatched-roof hanok, a traditional Korean house, that my mother and I used to live in stands in the small clearing, no worse for wear after over a century. There's even smoke coming out of the chimney.

"Mother?" I scramble to the kitchen, knowing she won't be there . . . hoping she will be there. "Mother?"

But she isn't there. Of course she isn't. She died. She's dead.

Ethan picks me up from the dirt floor of the kitchen. I don't know how I ended up there. He carries me into the only room in the house and sits on the floor with his back against the wall. I somehow end up settled on his lap, my head against his shoulder, with my face tucked into his neck.

I realize I'm crying when he brushes a rough thumb across my cheek. I try to take a deep breath but only manage a shuddering hiccup. I should be embarrassed to be seen like this, but the only thing I feel is . . . safe. I squeeze my eyes shut and wrap my arms around his waist. He rests a warm hand on my back and smooths my hair with the other. His breath ruffles the top of my head.

"What happened, Sunny?" His quiet question places no pressure on me to answer. It's as though he's wondering out loud to himself. "What did they do to you?"

"I had to relive my worst memory," I whisper. "I had to relive the day my mother died."

"That fucking—"

I sit up and press my fingertips against his lips. "Do *not* disrespect the Seonangshin. It was a high price to pay, but their sacrifice was greater."

I drop my hand when the fury dims in his eyes. But his mouth is pressed into a mutinous line. "If you say so."

"I do say so." I sigh and let myself take in the room that I shared with my mother.

"This place . . ." He studies my face for a long moment, his eyes gentle with understanding. "Is this where you and your mother used to live?"

"How . . . how did you know?"

"You looked like you saw a ghost when we came up on this house." He reaches out and brushes the hair out of my eyes. "Then you ran into the kitchen calling for your mother."

I shake my head. "I don't know why Samshin Halmeom sent us here. It seems needlessly cruel . . ."

"Or kind," he interrupts. "Maybe she thought being in your old house will console you."

"Oh, now you're taking her side?" I smirk, but my smile fades away as I realize why she chose this house. "You're right. She was being kind."

"Yeah?" He seems surprised by my quick acquiescence.

"This house is enchanted." I notice for the first time that there's a candle lit on the low dresser and the floor is warm from the woodfire burning in the kitchen. Even in the summer, the mountain grows chilly in the evenings.

"Enchanted?" He cringes. "Like the field?"

"No, not like that." I put my hand against the wall behind Ethan's shoulder and speak to the house. "You took good care of yourself all these years. Were you waiting for me to come home?"

The candle flickers and makes happy shadows jump across the room.

"This house is *alive*?" Ethan pushes away from the wall, jostling me on his lap.

"Not how you think." I climb down from his thighs, mortified at how comfortable I'd made myself there. "It doesn't have a life force of its own. My mother . . ." I clear my throat. "My mother imbued some of her magic into the house."

"Okay. It's not alive, but it's *sentient*." He gazes warily around the room, like the walls might close in on us at any moment.

"Yes, but it exists only to serve me and my mother. Well, just me now, I guess." When Ethan's eyebrows shoot up to his forehead, I add, "And my guests."

"It . . ." His brows furrow. "It understands English?"

"Understands English?" *Of all things.* "It doesn't need to because it understands our needs."

As though reminded of its manners, the house rattles the round brass handle on the door leading to the kitchen. It takes me all of one step to reach the hanji-papered door—the room is no more than three hundred square feet—and open it.

A short-legged wooden table laden with piping-hot food sits on the small landing. I reach down and bring it inside the room.

"See, it even made us food." I sit by the table and wave Ethan over. "Come on. Let's eat."

He sits facing me and glances down at the simple but plentiful meal. "Is this chicken soup?"

"What gave it away?" I tear off a drumstick and dip it in a side of salt and pepper. "The whole chicken in the bowl?"

"Smart-ass." He dips his spoon into the soup, then snaps his fingers. "Samgaetang. It's chicken soup with ginseng."

"Mm-hmm." I don't even look up from my chicken. My injured thigh still throbs stubbornly, and I'm ready to heal. But I look up when Ethan places a drumstick in my soup bowl.

"You need it more than I do," he says.

I swallow a mouthful of chicken with a gulp. A warm cup of barley tea appears on the table when I pound on my chest. I clear my throat and drink some tea. Mostly, I'm trying to blink away the tears welling in my eyes. My mother always gave me one of her drumsticks when we ate samgaetang. Chicken leg is a love language all its own.

"Thanks," I mumble. I'm being ridiculous. It's just some chicken. He knows I need the protein to heal.

We finish our meal in silence and push the empty bowls away from us. We didn't leave even a drop of soup. I lean back on my hands and consider lying down all the way. I haven't been truly full in days, and I welcome the food coma like a long-lost friend.

Ethan puts the table away in the kitchen and comes to sit beside me. "Why don't you go to sleep? I'll keep first watch."

The sleeping mat folded up in the corner unrolls itself onto the floor. Two pillows and a light blanket flutter down on top of it. I'm suddenly wide awake and very aware of the man . . . no, male . . . sitting by my side.

"You don't need to keep watch," I squeak. "The house is warded. I mean, it can't keep us hidden forever, but we should be safe spending a few days here."

I feel his eyes on my face. I stare at a corner of the ceiling. The air becomes saturated with a current of awareness, and I'm afraid he can hear my heart thumping in the small room. My eyes are crossing from the effort to keep myself from meeting his gaze. I can't look at him. If I do—I sit on my hands to keep from fanning my face with them—I might do something rash.

He grabs a pillow from the bedding and tosses it toward the opposite wall. "Then we better get some sleep."

I hear the death sizzle of my libido—Ethan's words a bucket of cold water over the flames of my horniness. My cheeks burning with mortification, I crawl over to the bedding and lift the blanket to slide under it, and I realize that my clothes are still crusty from the dip in the sea. *I* am crusty from the dip in the sea.

Thank the fucking gods.

"I'm taking a bath." I jump to my feet and run into the kitchen. "Good night."

CHAPTER SIXTEEN

I sigh as I slide into the deep wooden tub filled with steaming-hot water, my sore muscles loosening in the warmth.

When I escaped into the kitchen earlier, the bath was already waiting for me, complete with a towel and a change of clothing laid out on the landing. With no one to teach it the wonders of modern toiletries, the house prepared milky rice water to wash my face with and fragrant orchid oil for my hair.

I warily eye the neat pile of clothes, because I'm almost certain it's a hanbok. I hide my grimace so as not to hurt the house's feelings, but the voluminous skirt that ties over the chest and the cropped jeogori shirt have never been my favorite—they're cumbersome and uncomfortable. But I'll worry about that later.

Using a muslin cloth, I scrub one arm, then the next. It feels so good to get the grime off my body. As I run the cloth down my neck, my thoughts drift lazily to Ethan. About how good it felt to be in his arms—sitting on his firm thighs, with his chest under my hands. I gasp when the muslin cloth brushes the sensitive tips of my breasts, and desire throbs between my legs. I clench my thighs together and squirm on my ass, my hand sliding down my stomach toward my . . .

What the *hell* am I doing? It's not that I'm shy about pleasuring myself. It's the only kind of release I know. But . . . it's the fact that a real live person inspired this ache inside me. I never wanted anyone like this before. Not even close.

And the only thing separating the kitchen from the aforementioned real live person is a wood-slatted door covered with opaque paper. *Maybe he's asleep.* Nope. Nuh-uh. I scour my legs with more force than necessary. I refuse to get off thinking about Ethan with him sitting behind a thick piece of hanji no more than ten steps from me.

I dip my head underwater to soak my hair, loosening the gritty bits of the sea. I sit up and dribble some orchid oil into my palm. But when I raise my arms to work it into my hair, my injured shoulder screams. Only a thin raised scar remains of my wound, but I'm still sore as hell. I'm sure climbing down cliffs and sword fighting undead assassins haven't helped the healing process. I massage the heel of my hand against the shoulder, trying to ease the ache, and grunt in pain.

The kitchen door flings wide open, banging loudly against the wall. Ethan sits directly across from the door, leaning against the opposite wall. And I'm lying in the tub, facing him. His eyes widen when they meet mine and travel down to my . . . I squeak and hug my arms around my breasts. He starts and claps a hand over his eyes.

"I'm sorry," he cries. "I didn't see anything."

"Yes, you did," I say, outraged.

"I did. Yes." His hand still firmly covers his eyes. "But I didn't *mean* to see."

I snort. I can't help it. He looks so freaking adorable. I sink deeper into the tub until the water reaches my chin. "You can uncover your eyes."

He splits his fingers apart and peeks through them. His lips quirk into a grin as he finally drops his hand. "Why did that door fling open? Was it the wind?"

"No." I glance around the kitchen with narrowed eyes. "It was the house."

"The house? Why?"

"I . . ." This is a bad idea, but my hair is a tangled mess. "I need to wash my hair, but my shoulder is still a bit sore. I think the house wanted me to ask for your help."

He swallows. "Do *you* want my help?"

"Yeah, sure." I scoot around in the tub and hug my legs to my chest, offering him my back. "You have to use that orchid oil. The house doesn't know about shampoos because it's been alone for more than a century."

I hear him push off the floor and walk into the kitchen. The back of my neck tingles when he comes to stand behind me. I see him pick up the oil from the corner of my eyes. As the heady scent of orchids fills the kitchen, his fingers dig deeply into my hair and massage my scalp in slow, sinuous circles.

I moan and lean into his touch. I hear his breath catch, but he doesn't stop his gentle ministrations. He pours a few more drops of oil into his hands and works his fingers through my hair, untangling the knots. I sigh, slowly melting into the tub.

"Lean back," he says in a husky rasp. "I need to rinse the oil off."

"But I . . ."

"Look up at me." He smooths his hands down my shoulders. "My eyes won't leave your face."

I stretch out my legs, grabbing the lip of the tub with both my hands, and tilt my head back until my hair is submerged in the water. I meet his gaze, and my heart lurches. The black of his pupils nearly obscures his dark-brown irises as he stares down at me with pure, unadulterated lust. I'm a feast spread out before him when he hasn't eaten in days. Still, his eyes never stray from mine as his hands massage and comb my hair.

"Sit up." He suddenly steps back from the tub and hisses out a breath. I obey unthinkingly, hugging my knees to my chest. "I'll dry your hair, then help you get out."

I blink rapidly and shake my head. "I'm perfectly capable of—"

"I want to take care of you, Sunny." The heat of his words brushes against my ear, and my toes curl under the water. "Let me."

I don't protest when he wraps the towel around my hair and wrings out the moisture. Then stepping to the side, he holds the towel open wide and turns his head away. "Stand up."

His eyes fly to mine when I stand and hug the towel against my chest. The intensity of his gaze is hotter than the water as he wraps the towel around me and bodily scoops me out of the tub.

"Put me down," I croak. "I'm getting you wet."

"I don't care," he growls.

He carries me all the way into the room before he sets me down. Then he places the hanbok on the floor and leaves, closing the door behind him. I scoff in disbelief. That's it? He turns me on until I have steam billowing from my ears, then he *leaves*? I drop the towel and open my mouth to call him back inside.

What am I thinking? We have a madman after us. Samshin Halmeom's departing words echo in my head. *Stop Daeseong. Fulfill your destiny.* I have shit to figure out. And what about Ethan? He's a being of the Shingae, and he's keeping it from me. I'm going to blithely disregard all that for a moment of carnal bliss? I clench my thighs together, considering the question. *Oh, for gods' sake.* I snatch the hanbok skirt off the floor. The answer is *no*. I'm not disregarding a single damned thing.

I wrap the floor-length skirt around my body and tighten the stays over my breasts. I pick up the cropped jeogori and stare at the baggy sleeves, straight at the top of the arms and rounded at the bottom. After a pause, I toss it to the corner of the room. The night is too warm for layers of cumbersome clothing. Besides, I'm basically covered from armpits to toes. Only my shoulders are bare.

"Ethan, come inside," I call out. "I'm decent."

When the door flings open, he blinks at me from the other side of the threshold, his hand suspended halfway to the door.

"Will you stop doing that?" I snap at the house. The house shifts with a low, whining sound. I sigh. "We'll manage from now. Thank you."

Ethan steps inside but forgets to close the door, gaping at me. I look down at myself. My small breasts look like luminous, forbidden fruit, not quite spilling over the top of my skirt. I'd inadvertently done a better job of showcasing my breasts than a V-neck shirt and a push-up bra.

"House," I say in a resigned voice, and it closes the door behind Ethan.

I swing my damp hair over one shoulder, and that seems to break my boobs' hypnotic hold over Ethan. He meets my gaze evenly, with only a slight flush to his cheeks. His control is admirable but also slightly annoying. Pursing my lips, I settle down on the floor. When I motion for him to sit beside me, he cocks his head to the side but complies with a shrug, sitting close enough for our shoulders to touch.

This is ridiculous. He's my friend. This heightened awareness between us is fleeting. I have to focus on the important stuff. Such as . . . Who the fuck is he? And there's no need to drive myself crazy trying to figure out why he's keeping his identity a secret from me. We can talk, like normal people.

"What are you hiding from me?" I ask him point blank. Maybe normal people ease in to this stuff, but I'm not normal people.

His brows pull down low over his eyes. "What am I *hiding* from you?"

"Yes, that's what I asked." I keep my voice nice and level.

"Why would I hide anything from you?" he says with a bewildered shake of his head.

"You tell me." My eyes narrow. Is he stalling to come up with a convincing lie?

"Where is this even coming from?" He stares at me as though I might've hit my head on the bathtub.

"Will you stop asking me questions and answer *my* question?" I throw my hands up, losing my patience. "Just tell me the truth."

He grabs his head with his hands. "The truth about what?"

"I swear I will strangle you if you ask me one more question," I say in a vicious whisper. "I know you're a being of the Shingae. Why have you been hiding it from me?"

Ethan freezes for a heartbeat, then bursts out laughing. "You have the oddest sense of humor, Sunny."

I scan his face for signs of guilt, unease, or calculation—the signs of someone who is lying—but all I see are the traces of his laugh and a hint of worry in his eyes. Does he really not know who he is?

"I'm not joking, Ethan." I enunciate carefully, not knowing what to think anymore.

He jumps to his feet, shaking his head. He spins left and right, pacing the small space of the room. I stand up and take a gentle hold of his hands. He turns his head away, his Adam's apple working. *Oh, gods.* If he didn't know, then I did a really shitty job of breaking the news to him.

"You didn't know?" I cup his cheek and turn him to face me. "You had no idea?"

"About *what*?" His voice breaks. "I don't . . . understand."

"Maybe I don't either." The hurt and confusion on his face make my throat tighten with the threat of tears. I'm not sure how to explain, so I start at the beginning. "I've had my suspicions since you showed up in Vegas. I don't know how, but you must have tracked my magic. I mean, how else would you know I'd be at Roxy's Diner, of all places?"

"I pored over Ben's notes, but I kept hitting dead ends. I . . . I went to Las Vegas on a . . . a wild hunch." He pulls away to pace again with short, tense steps. "I couldn't sleep that night, so I went out for a walk—to clear my head—but my steps led me straight to you. It was as though I could *feel* you were there."

"Didn't you think that was weird?" I keep my voice level, even though he just confirmed that he traced my small burst of magic to find me. Something no one should be able to do. I tuck away that mystery to solve another time.

"I don't know." He stops at a wall and leans his head back against it. "I think I convinced myself that a good private investigator has to rely on his gut sometimes."

"And the red assassin stabbed you," I continue, moving on to the next piece of the puzzle. I hold up my hand when he opens his mouth to argue. "I *know* what I saw. She stabbed you, but her blade didn't pierce you. Even when the blue assassin screeched that soul-shriveling scream, you didn't bleed. And the wildflowers on the enchanted field didn't cut you even though they slashed through me."

"Red didn't get me. You don't remember clearly, because you were hurt." Ethan pushes off the wall, warming up to the idea. "Her dagger only grazed my shirt. And . . . and maybe Blue's scream affects beings of the Shingae more strongly than humans. That's why you bled, but I didn't. It makes sense, doesn't it? That's got to be it."

"What about the flowers?" I ask softly. He's making the same excuses I had been making, but I can't hide from the truth anymore. And neither can he.

"I was wearing these jeans, and . . . and the flowers weren't tall enough to reach my hands." He comes to stand in front of me, wearing a taut smile. "See? You're way off the mark, Sunny."

Nothing I know about the Shingae can explain his seeming invincibility, but I know magic when I see it. And I don't remind him about the mythical golden and silver axes—something I didn't even believe were real until I saw them in his hands—appearing before him when he desperately needed them. Besides, I can't explain their sudden appearance either . . .

A memory claps through my head like thunder, and I remember how the lore of the woodsman ends. *Ethan can wield the axes.* My mind scrambles with the knowledge, its significance taking root. *Oh, gods.* I can't begin to fathom what that means—what it means for *him.* I clear my throat and meet his gaze.

"I'm sorry, Ethan." I can't tell him about the axes. Not right now. This must already be too much for him. It's more than *I* can handle. Time to flex my avoidance muscles. "I can't explain everything, but I'm afraid I got it on the nose."

"No, you're wrong," he rasps, his smile dissolving. "I don't know what makes you think I'm a being of the Shingae, but I'm *human.*"

"Only beings of the Shingae can see Samshin Halmeom. And you saw her," I whisper, but Ethan winces like I'm screaming in his ear.

Everything else could be explained away, but this is the incontrovertible truth. This is what finally convinced me that Ethan is a being of the Shingae. "Humans can't hear the Seonangshin. But you heard her speak."

Ethan backs away from me, shaking his head. My heart breaks for him. I know what it's like to want to hide from yourself. My brows pull into a frown as a thought occurs to me. But if he doesn't know who he really is, how is he hiding his true life force?

"I can't sense your magic. Your gi is somehow hidden," I murmur, thinking out loud. I link my fingers tightly together. "Or *bound*."

Why would anyone bind his magic? Who even has the power to do that? But I see Ethan standing a few steps away from me, looking pale and haggard, and I pack up the questions for another time. Everything else can wait. I need to be here for him.

"I thought you were hiding your magic the way I had been," I confess. "I thought that meant you knew you had powers. Even back when we were together in LA . . . But you really didn't know, did you?"

"Do I look like a man who knows the first thing about magic?" His laughter holds no humor. "You seriously think I have *powers*? What powers? I was about to rush the blue assassin with rocks in my hands, for fuck's sake. No, it can't be true. It *can't*."

"Everything will be okay." I take a tentative step toward him. "We can figure this out together."

His eyes jump wildly around the room before he drops his head into his hands, his shoulders hunching forward. "God, Sunny. How can that be? I . . . What *am* I?"

"You're Ethan Lee." I pull his hands away from his face and force him to meet my gaze. "You're smart and funny, but stubborn as hell. You're *infuriating*, but loyal, brave, and kind to the core. Ethan, you're my friend. That's *who* you are."

He's so still I can't even feel him breathing. I just hope my words mean as much to him as his words meant to me. I hope he feels seen the way I felt seen. I want to take away his hurt. I want him to know that he will always be Ethan to me.

"Ethan." Holding his face between my hands, I press my forehead against his. "Say something."

When he reaches out and pulls me toward him, I go to him without hesitation. With tenderness that wrenches my heart, he runs the pad of his thumb across my cheek, then traces the outline of my lips.

"Sunny," he says in a broken rasp. "I need to kiss you."

"Then do it." I entwine my trembling arms around his neck. Then, not wanting to sound too bossy for once, I add, "Please."

I thought his kiss would be soft and gentle, like the first rays of sunshine brushing awake the worlds. But I'm wrong. His lips are hot and hungry against mine, and every nerve ending in my body lights up. When I gasp at the sharp flash of pleasure, he plunges his tongue into my mouth, possessive and greedy. I whimper and push onto my toes.

I didn't realize kissing could feel like this. My first few decades in the United States were about survival, much of it spent disguised as a boy. When the human world slowly changed and being a young, single woman wasn't a danger in and of itself, I began to breathe a little easier, live a little more. So there have been stolen kisses, some drunken groping. But nothing has ever felt like this kiss.

Ethan's hand slips free from my hair and smooths down my side to the dip of my waist, to the flare of my hips. His touch is greedy, curious, and reverent all at once, and I can only think, *More*. When his hand slides back up and cups my breast, I lean into his touch and grind my hips against him, led by pure instinct.

His low growl reverberates through me, and moisture gathers between my legs. He dips his head and kisses the swell of my breasts spilling over the top of my skirt. I dig my fingers into his hair and hold him against me. His tongue slips under the fabric and brushes the hard tip of my breast and I moan, throwing back my head.

When he crushes his mouth against mine, I know whatever control he has left hangs by a precarious thread. With a trembling hand, he reaches for the tie at my chest holding my skirt up. I freeze, my heart stuttering. *If you do this, imagine how much more it'll hurt to lose him.* Losing him will already hurt more than I'm ready to admit.

Sex is an indulgence I never allowed myself. I never let anyone get close enough—I never trusted anyone enough—to experience this kind of intimacy. And there has never been anyone I wanted to share myself with. Until Ethan.

But is this passion even real? Maybe we're just desperate to escape from the horrors of reality. And being on the run wreaked havoc on our equilibrium and probably amped up our libido. Adrenaline makes you horny, right? We both want a distraction . . . a release. That's all this is. Even if any of these feelings are real—and they aren't—they can't possibly last. Whatever this is, it's fleeting. It has to be.

I trap his hand against my chest, and he stills immediately, dropping his other hand to his side. His eyes are wild, but he'll never push me to do anything I'm not ready for. I trust him. And I *desperately* crave this closeness with him. That's why I can't have this—I can't have *him*.

"Ethan," I whisper.

"God, I'm sorry." He presses his forehead against mine, fighting for his breath and his control. When I let go of his hand, he grasps my bare shoulders, his thumbs moving in slow circles. "Are you okay?"

"I'm fine. I just . . ." I stumble over my words. "I'm not . . ."

"You've been through a lot today," he says, pressing my head against his chest. I feel the reassuring thud of his heart against my cheek. "Hell, I've been through a lot. I shouldn't have let things go so far when you're vulnerable."

"Hey, don't act like I had no part in this." I lean back and glare up at him. I might headbutt him if he says this was a mistake. I might've put a stop to things, but I didn't regret a single moment of it. "And don't you dare apologize. I wanted you to kiss me."

He smiles shyly and tucks a lock of hair behind my ear. "I hope I haven't done anything to stop you from wanting me to kiss you again."

"You haven't," I mumble. He must've felt me catch fire in his arms. If anything, I wanted him to kiss me more. I step away from him and wave a hand toward his pillow. "And don't be ridiculous. There's plenty of room for both of us on the sleeping mat."

He glances at the bedding the house has so kindly set out for us and huffs an embarrassed laugh. "I guess I can manage to keep my hands off you for one night."

After a mumbled good night, I scamper under the blanket and turn my back toward him so he won't see my stupid blush. I squeeze my eyes shut, and Ethan steps quietly out of the room. I hear the soft splash of water outside as he washes up.

I'm still wide awake when he returns to the room and slips under the blanket beside me. I pretend to be asleep, forcing my breathing to slow and even out, but I can feel the heat of his body next to mine.

"Good night, Sunny," he whispers and drops a featherlight kiss on my temple.

It's all I can do not to shiver at the fleeting touch. How can I ever fall asleep with Ethan next to me . . .

CHAPTER SEVENTEEN

When I blink open my eyes, the soft morning sun is filtering through the latticed doors of the hanok. I lazily rub my cheek against the warm, smooth skin beneath me and smile at the comforting feel of a strong arm tightening around my back. I burrow deeper into the embrace, breathing in the woodsy musk of his scent.

I go completely still the same moment I come fully awake. Sometime in the night, my skirt had ridden up to my thighs, and I had tucked one leg snugly between Ethan's. At least he still has his pants on, but I can't say the same about his shirt. He must've chucked his bedraggled T-shirt before he climbed beneath the blankets last night. I can't blame him. In fact, I want to applaud him for a decision well made as I lay draped over his naked chest, a hand spread possessively over a perfect pec.

I want to do all kinds of things. I want to run my hands down his torso to feel the ridges of his ridiculous abs and then lower to his . . . My eyes flicker down of their own volition, and I suck in a sharp breath. His hard length is straining against the confines of his pants. Gods, I want to slide my leg over his waist and grind my core against him until the ache coiling in my sex eases.

I do none of those things because my sanity is intact. With a wistful sigh, I sit up and slap him on the chest with a resounding thwack. "Wake up, lazy ass. We've got work to do."

"What kind of work?" Without opening his eyes, he shoots out his hand and pulls me back down against him.

"I forget," I say weakly as he nuzzles my neck. I tilt my head to give him better access. "But I think it has something to do with not dying. Oh, yes. I remember now. We need to figure out how to use the sacred ashes. Samshin Halmeom didn't make that part clear."

Ethan sighs against my neck and stops the delicious thing he is doing. I tell myself it's for the best, but I kind of want to pout and sulk. He flops back on his pillow and throws an arm over his eyes. "I guess that means the last few days weren't a bad dream."

"What kind of sick mind would dream up something like that?" I scramble to my feet and straighten my skirt, patting it down and shaking it out much longer than necessary.

He sits up on the sleeping mat, one arm resting on his drawn-up knee, and watches me with hooded eyes. "But that means I did taste your sweet lips last night."

"Oh, man." I smack my tongue against the roof of my mouth. "My mouth feels gnarly. I should go brush my teeth. I don't think salt is going to be enough to get rid of my hideous morning breath, but the house probably doesn't have any toothpaste."

I run outside like a coward even as Ethan's low laughter licks at my skin. Wait, what if I really have morning breath? Cupping my hand over my mouth, I huff and sniff. It's respectable, but I might as well brush my teeth since I said I would. The house provides me with a small bowl of coarse salt, a washbasin, and a pitcher of water. Tucking my skirt between my legs, I crouch on the ground and dutifully dip my finger in the salt. I rub it over my teeth and tongue, grimacing as my mouth goes numb. I pour some water into the basin and rinse out my mouth, then scrub my face clean.

I plop down on the raised platform in the courtyard. Now what? *Oh, for fuck's sake.* I can't hide from him forever. We actually have work to do. Really important work. We have to find out how to use the sacred ashes to defeat Daeseong. We can't live on the run forever, and we sure as hell can't let the dark mudang get away with Ben's murder. But where can we learn more about the sacred ashes?

The *Book of Answers*. Of course. I scramble to my feet. How could I have forgotten?

I run to the house and jerk open the door, just as Ethan pulls a pair of hanbok pants over his bare ass. When he spins around in surprise, I don't have to manufacture the scowl on my face. It happened too fast. I didn't get a proper look.

"Sorry about flashing you," he says, misinterpreting my expression. He hurriedly pulls on the matching shirt, covering his glorious torso. I frown harder. "I asked the house for some clean clothes, and it gave me this hanbok."

I mutter something incomprehensible as I stomp past him and go to the low dresser at the back of the room. I yank on its small door, and the house creaks in protest, affronted by my rough handling of its furniture.

"Sorry." I gently open the door the rest of the way and sigh in relief. The handsewn booklet is still there. "Thank you for keeping it safe."

Mollified, the house scoots a low table toward me, and I place the book on it. Its cover is made of only slightly thicker paper than the pages within, looking as innocuous as ever in faded brown. Without my having to ask, a tray with a block of ink and a brush appears next to the book.

"What is that?" Ethan sits down next to me.

I turn to him and open my mouth to answer, but his eyes drift down to my shoulders, then my breasts. I'm still not wearing a jeogori. Blushing bright pink, I scramble for my cropped top and push my arms through. I botch the single-looped bow in the front, but at least I'm all covered up.

I reclaim my seat in front of the table and answer him as though I'd been fully dressed all along. "It's the *Book of Answers*."

He opens the cover and frowns as he flips the pages. "It's blank."

"That's because we haven't asked it any questions yet." Excitement bubbles up at sharing the book with Ethan. He hasn't seen much good in magic, and we both could use some good in our lives right now. "What do you want to ask?"

As a child, I never sought any life-altering answers from the book. I asked things like *Why do I have to study?* It answered, *So you can eloquently ask ridiculous questions like this.* Or *What do you do when you're not answering our questions?* It said, *I wait with bated breath for your next scintillating question. Except I'm a book, so I don't breathe. Nor wait.* What can I say? The book had an attitude problem. Hopefully, the years have mellowed it out.

"I could ask anything?" A corner of his mouth quirks up in a lopsided smile filled with wonder.

"I think so." I hope I'm right, because I really could use some answers. But before I delve into the mysterious powers of the sacred ashes, I want Ethan to have his fun. "Come on. Try."

"Wait, can I write in English?" He picks up the brush and frowns down at it.

"I have no idea." I take the brush from him and wet it with a bit of black ink. "Here, I'll write it for you."

"Thank God. I can read Korean by sounding it out, but that is the extent of my foreign-language skills." He chuckles sheepishly. "Okay. Ask it how old I am."

"Oh, wow. That is deep," I deadpan.

"Just ask, smart-ass." He bumps shoulders with me. "I want to establish a baseline."

"Now you just sound like a nerd." I duck my chin to hide my smile and write his question—in English, because I'm curious now.

How old is Ethan?

The answer appears on the page just below my question. It's in Korean, but the book obviously understands English. *Cool.*

"It says twenty-four. Is that right?" I think it is, but I want to make sure.

"Yeah, I just turned twenty-four." Ethan and I grin at each other, giddy like children. He shifts closer and leans toward the book. I try not to breathe in his scent. I fail. "Ask it . . ."

But the book isn't done.

The second evolution of the dragon.

The letters look uneven, like it's written in a shaky hand. My brows draw low over my narrowed eyes. The book always has meticulous penmanship.

The peak of power. Unleash—

The last letter slashes across the page, like someone physically wrestled the brush out of the book's metaphorical hand.

"What the hell? What is it talking about?" I flip through the book and check it cover to cover. By the time I turn back to the first page, the question and answers are already erased, like they've never been there. Anything written on its pages disappears as the ink dries, leaving the book a blank slate for the next question. "It must be rusty because it hasn't been used in over a century. Let me ask it something else."

I write, *What's my favorite color?* The book doesn't hesitate. *Is it still pink? Never mind. Of course it is. PINK.* The lettering is crisp and clear. I slap my hand over the words.

"What? What did you ask?" Ethan tries to peel my hand away.

"None of your business." I duck low and cover the page with my upper body. "But it's working."

We tussle awhile longer, but Ethan grows silent and stills beside me. "Ask it who I am."

"Ethan . . ." I shoot him a worried glance.

"It's okay," he says grimly. "I'd rather know."

"Just take its answer with a grain of salt." Nerves churn my stomach. But what can possibly go wrong? All beings of the Shingae are born of the Cheon'gwang, the true light, and belong to one of four life sources—Mountains, Sky, Water, or Underworld. So no answer can be *bad* unless the book decides to provide an existential soliloquy. "The book does better with precise, unambiguous questions. Your question bears some philosophical weight. There could be many answers."

"I understand." He nods. "You don't have to worry."

I chew my bottom lip as I write out the question, *Who is Ethan Lee?*

As we watch, black ink splatters onto the page like fat drops of rain. I glance at the ceiling, expecting to see a black cloud hanging ominously above us, but there's nothing there. But the ink keeps falling until the entire page is drenched in black. I desperately flip through the book. Every page is drenched.

I feel it now. A magic outside the book is silencing it. And that magic is flowing from . . . the house? I cover the book with my hands spread wide, like I can protect it from the raining ink.

"No, no, no."

Ethan's eyes widen at the alarm in my voice. "What's happening, Sunny?"

"Don't do this. Not now. I still need answers. How do you use the sacred ashes? How do I stop Daeseong? Tell. Me." I shake the *Book of Answers*. It can't break now. I scream at the house, "What are you doing to it?"

"Me?" Ethan draws back as though I slapped him. "I'm not . . . I'm not doing anything."

"No, not you. The house." I look around the room with frantic eyes. "I think it's doing this."

"The house?" He looks bewildered and . . . disappointed. I realize the book never answered his question. "Why?"

"I have no idea." I slump, planting my hands on the floor.

The magic choking the book finally dissipates, and the house goes still like it went into hiding.

"I'm sorry," Ethan murmurs. "I know you wanted answers about the sacred ashes."

"It's not your fault." I draw myself up and squeeze his hand. "I'm sure the ink will dry off by tomorrow."

"Yes, let's try again tomorrow morning." He flips his hand and laces his fingers through mine. "Well, what should we do until then?"

Just like that, the air between us hums with charged awareness, and my entire body tingles like a humongous nerve ending. I jump to my feet before I do something I'll regret.

"Um . . . laundry? Yeah, we need to do laundry." Laundry helped dampen my horniness before. It can do it again. "We can't keep wearing hanbok."

Of course, the house would've been happy to do our laundry, especially after the weird stunt it pulled. I'm not even sure if it was the house that ruined the *Book of Answers*. It certainly felt as though the magic was coming from it, but my mother's gi wouldn't allow it to do anything that would cause me harm. Unless it was trying to protect me by drowning the book in ink. I huff a frustrated sigh. It makes no sense. At any rate, I'm peeved enough not to want its help. And I need a distraction from my infatuation with Ethan.

"Sure." He draws out the word. "Why not? Let's do some laundry."

He helps hand-wash both of our clothes even though he must know I'm making up excuses to keep my distance from him. But the mindless, mundane work actually feels pretty nice after the week we've been having.

I look around my old house, with the humble courtyard and the woods surrounding it. I feel a pang of longing for simpler times, when I only had to worry about harvesting herbs and practicing sword fighting . . . when I had someone who loved me unconditionally. I know she's gone, but being here makes me feel closer to my mother. It's both painful and healing.

I reach out with my senses and check the wards on the house, careful not to let my gi leak outside the boundaries of my mother's magic. The wards hold strong. Staying put in one place when you're on the run is never a good idea, but resting for a few days might not be a *bad* idea.

Ethan wrings the water from our clothes, and my eyes catch on the muscles of his forearms. *Gulp*. Then again, this might be the worst idea ever. Giving into this attraction will complicate an already impossibly complicated situation. The distraction might actually put our lives in danger. Well, in even *more* danger.

With renewed determination to keep my hands to myself, I help hang the laundry on a line outside the kitchen. Once we're finished, I glance nervously around the courtyard. What can we do now?

The house comes to the rescue. There's a table laden with food waiting for us on the raised platform. And there's ssam. Ssam is an art form of food wrapped in red lettuce and perilla leaves, topped with ssamjang, a sauce made with soybean paste and gochujang. The widely accepted goal of ssam is to build the perfect bite, which I suppose holds some truth. But we all know the *ultimate* goal is to wrap as much food as you can in the leaves and stuff it into your face all at once. It's glorious and fucking satisfying. Plus, it's impossible to have sexy vibes with your mouth so full that you look like a greedy little chipmunk.

"I guess we earned ourselves a break." I laugh with relief. "Let's go eat."

I sit cross-legged at one end of the table and wait for Ethan to settle down across from me. Saliva pooling in my mouth, I lay a piece of red lettuce and perilla leaf on my palm and top it with a spoonful of steaming white rice, a generous chunk of spicy pork bulgogi, and a dollop of ssamjang. I wrap the whole thing into a pouch of deliciousness and stuff it into my mouth, wiggling it side to side to make it all fit inside.

My moan is muffled by the food. It's insanely good. There's no giant bite more perfect than a well-made ssam. Ethan chuckles across from me, shaking his head, but he soon follows my example and adds his own muffled moan to the quiet of the late morning.

I give him a smug grin, dipping a green chili into the ssamjang. I bite off half of the crunchy pepper, and my smile slowly dims . . . then dies. Torturous heat spreads across the inside of my cheeks, over my tongue and in my esophagus. Even my lips burn.

"Is this cheongyang gochu?" I yell at the house. "Are you trying to kill me?"

The house creaks in alarm and hurriedly produces a cold pitcher of makgeolli, a milky fermented rice wine. I pour some into a ceramic bowl and gulp it down in one shot. Then I pour some more and hold the cold drink in my mouth, hoping to douse the fire.

"What's cheongyang gochu?" Ethan asks, wide eyed.

I swallow the makgeolli and answer in a husky rasp. "It's like the Korean version of serrano chili. It's tasty in small doses but not if you eat half of it at once."

He bites his cheek to hold back his smile. It's a smart move on his part, because I'm irritated enough to force the other half of the chili down his throat if he dares laugh at me. He avoids an untimely demise by cheongyang gochu and focuses on wrapping a ssam.

"Here, eat." He holds it out to me. "It'll help with the heat."

I lean forward and open my mouth. His eyes twinkle with suppressed laughter as he stuffs the ssam into my mouth. But I forget to be grumpy because I'm enthralled by the symphony of happy-making flavors and textures. Ethan is a ssam *genius*.

"Is that makgeolli?" He points at the pitcher. I can only nod with my mouth so full. "Can I have some?"

I pass him the pitcher, and he reaches across the table to refill my empty bowl—Korean drinking etiquette number one—before he pours some for himself. He raises his makgeolli in the air, and I clink mine against it.

Feeling magnanimous, I toast, "To the house."

"To the house." Ethan drinks deeply from his bowl.

Susceptible to flattery, the house happily keeps the pitcher of makgeolli topped off, no matter how many bowls we pour. Full and toasty drunk, we lie down on the platform after the house clears away the table. The tree branches arching over us are filled with enough leaves to shade us from the heat but sparse enough for us to see glimpses of the blue sky beyond it. My limbs grow heavy, and my eyes slide closed.

"Ethan?" I whisper, half hoping he's asleep.

"Mmm-hmm." The warm, intimate sound rumbles in his chest, inviting me to talk to him. To tell him anything.

"I'm sorry I dragged you into all this." It's easier to apologize—to make myself vulnerable—with my eyes closed, cocooned in the soft darkness of my own making.

"I don't think you did," he says after a long pause. "If I'm really a being of the Shingae, then maybe I was meant to be a part of this all along. Besides, you didn't drag me into anything. I chose to be with you."

"Do you wish you chose differently?" My voice is as small as a child's, and I hold my breath as I wait for his answer.

"I'll always choose to be with you, Sunny." He reaches across the small gap between us and links his pinky with mine. Like a promise. "There is no other choice for me."

I take a shuddering breath as hot tears rush to my eyes. It shouldn't make me happy—but fuck it all—it makes me so terrifyingly happy that I can't find the saltiness to call him an idiot.

CHAPTER EIGHTEEN

The *Book of Answers* doesn't clear up the next day. So we decide to wait and try again after another day. And another day. And another day after that. We play house like this for several days—eating in the courtyard, talking for hours, falling asleep beneath the blue sky.

In the space between sleep and wakefulness, I tell Ethan things I've never told anyone. And he listens as though he wants to soak up every word that comes out of my mouth. He tells me things too—about the years after I left him and Ben. About the years before I met them.

"How did your parents die?" I ask, staring up at the wispy clouds.

"Car accident," he says simply. "It happened when I was eight. I was at school, and the principal called me into her office. I thought I was in trouble for drawing a caricature of my homeroom teacher. But Ben was there . . ."

I reach for his hand. He laces our fingers together.

"He said it happened quickly and they didn't suffer. And they were together, so they didn't feel lonely." Ethan clears his throat. "Ben dropped out of college to take care of me, and we moved to LA. I don't remember why we moved, but I'm glad we did, because you came into our lives a handful of years later."

"I was happy with you guys, you know." I turn my head away. "That's why I left. I . . . I got scared."

"I want to make you happy again." He cups my cheek and turns me to face him, shifting to his side. "And I won't let you run away this time. I'm going to *keep* you happy."

I crush my lips against his so suddenly that he gasps with surprise. I had to shut him up. He can't say things like that. It makes me feel things I can't acknowledge. It makes me long for things I don't deserve. But I also kiss him because I want to . . . I want *him*. That, I can acknowledge. The quiet of the last few days has taught me that I care about him. That he's my friend. But I also desire him with every cell in my body. I want to touch him and be touched by him. I hunger for him. I burn for him.

And I'm beginning to understand that being his friend and lusting after him don't have to be mutually exclusive. I'm inexperienced, but I don't have to experience things firsthand to *know* things. It's hard not to learn all kinds of stuff when you've lived as long as I have. So I know friends with benefits is a thing. It's actually a very practical, mature thing.

I've been lonely, even though I never admitted it to myself. Being with Ethan has eased that loneliness. I'm also horny as hell. It might have something to do with the fact that I'm a one-hundred-thirty-two-year-old virgin. That was a choice I made. *This* is also a choice I'm making. I want to have sex. With Ethan. He might as well ease my horniness too.

Ethan is so still, I'm not sure if he's breathing. Slowly, so slowly, he raises his hand to cup the back of my head with a featherlight touch. He brushes his lips back and forth against mine as though he's memorizing the feel of them . . . memorizing every last detail of this moment. I whimper and lean closer, but he draws back, breaking the kiss.

"Shhh." He presses a kiss on one closed eye, then the other while his thumb traces the outline of my bottom lip. "Be patient for me."

Exhaling a shaky breath, I force myself still. I can be patient. When his lips at last find mine again, my patience is put to the test. He kisses each corner, murmuring how sweet I taste, and moisture gathers between my legs, slick and hot. He eases my lips apart and sucks my lower lip into his mouth. He groans and burrows his fingers deeper into my hair.

Even if my heart is beating too fast and tears prickle my eyes, it doesn't mean that this is anything more than satisfying a physical need. Attraction is fleeting—that's another thing I know. We need to keep this casual so no one gets their heart broken. I turn my head away, but Ethan trails kisses down my neck, undeterred. I bare more of my neck to him.

"This doesn't have to change anything," I pant, and he freezes, his lips pressed against my skin.

He leans back to look at me, his eyes shuttered and unreadable. "Explain."

"Things are . . . not normal right now, and we don't know if this"—I manage to wave my hand in the narrow gap between our bodies—"is real or whatever. I don't want you to think I expect anything from you. We can . . . move on with our lives when things become normal again."

He goes taut against me. And he feels distant even though he's close enough for the heat of his body to seep into mine. "I see."

He *sees*? What the hell does that mean? And why am I disappointed? Did I expect him to balk and argue? To insist that this is more than scratching an itch? It doesn't matter. I needed him to know where I stand. Now he knows. But I'm afraid he's going to pull away. Afraid he'll stop.

"Ethan?" I brush my nose along his. "I just want you to make this ache inside me go away. Please?"

I think I see devastation in his eyes before he crushes his lips against mine, all searing heat and desperation. There are no more tender whispers or soft lingering kisses. He's done with his slow exploration. This is what I wanted, right? I don't want to be cherished. I want to be ravished.

I arch my body against his and, gods . . . he's already as hard as steel. His tongue delves into my mouth with decadent, sinuous strokes. I moan, and he captures the sound with another devouring kiss. He runs an unsteady hand down the dip of my waist and cups my ass, hauling me closer. I grind my hips against him, and he growls deep in his chest.

Ethan holds on to his control by a fragile thread. I can feel it in the faint tremors running through his body and the sweat beading on his forehead. I writhe against his body, desperate for release. It feels raw and erotic to skirt the edges of our control again and again, waiting for it to crumble and send us tumbling.

He sucks my tongue into his mouth, and I scrape my nails down his back, hard enough to draw blood from anyone else. He hisses, his hips jerking against mine. I take advantage of his momentary distraction and push him onto his back, straddling him. I ruthlessly deepen the kiss and rock against him.

With a helpless groan, he pulls me against his chest as he surges up, his control shattering at last. I smile in triumph, but he kisses it right off me. His tongue tangles with mine, and our teeth clash as our kiss turns frantic. I wrap my legs around his waist and cling to his shoulders. Fisting his hand in my hair, he tilts my head to the side and licks and suckles his way down my neck. When his lips meet fabric at my shoulder, he grunts with disapproval and rips my shirt off with a sharp tug.

Wrapping an arm around me, he lowers me down until my back presses into the platform and I lie beneath him. He rakes his eyes over my naked breasts with such hunger that I don't even feel embarrassed about baring myself to him. He runs his hands down from my shoulders to my breasts and palms them greedily. And I moan my approval when he squeezes them none too gently. He drags his hands down farther and stops at the top of my shorts.

"I need to see you." He's breathless and wild eyed, but he waits for my answer.

"Yes." I lift my hips off the platform.

He fumbles over the button of my jean shorts and tugs them down with rough, jerky movements. He's kneeling at my feet, his chest rising and falling with rough pants. "Beautiful. So fucking beautiful."

He pulls his shirt over his head and nearly falls between my legs, pushing my thighs apart. He glances up at me. "Yes?"

When I falter, he smooths slow, gentle circles on my inner thighs with the pads of his thumbs. Then he drops kisses where his thumbs had been. An ache spreads in my core, and I squirm beneath his hands. He looks up at me again—patient, worshipful.

"Yes." I shiver, half with nerves, half with need. I don't know what it'll be like, but I know I *need* it.

"Good girl," he drawls with a wolfish grin, then dips his head.

"Oh." I gasp when he sweeps his tongue in a long, leisurely line across my swollen clit. "Oh."

He continues to lick, suck, and gently bite me as I become a creature of mindless pleasure. I make incoherent, unrecognizable sounds and grip his hair in my greedy fists. My hips jerk up, and he pushes them back down.

"Ethan." It's a question and a plea.

"Let go, Sunny." His breath is hot against my core, and the cool swipe of his tongue that follows is a delicious shock. "Come for me, sweetheart."

I shatter.

Waves after waves of my orgasm shudder through me, and he eases me down with the gentle pressure of his palm, moving in slow circles over me. I lie utterly spent as Ethan slides his body over mine, until he's looking down at me with heart-wrenching tenderness.

"Are you okay?" He smooths my hair away from my face, bearing his weight on one forearm.

"Mmm." I thought I was spent, but my body lights up again at the feel of his thick length pressing against my thigh.

He leans down and kisses me softly on the mouth. I scoff at the audacity and stick my tongue down his throat. He growls and kisses me back with appropriate hunger, my taste still lingering in his mouth. With impatient hands, I tear at his jeans until he sits back to shove them off, along with his boxer briefs. He throws them to the side, and I drink in the perfection of his naked body.

I can look at him forever, but I also can't complain when he lowers his body over mine and resumes kissing me with a touch of wildness—coarse and clumsy in his need. I reach down and eagerly wrap my hand around his erection. I gasp. How can something so hard be so soft? I run my hand over his cock again and again. I can't get over the incongruity of his hard thick length and his silky skin.

Lost to the wonder of my exploration, I'm startled by the almost painful sound of his groan as he lurches helplessly into my hand. On pure instinct, I tighten my grip around him, and he shudders.

"Sunny, can I . . ." He grinds his hips. "I need . . ."

"Yes." I'm not sure what he's asking, but I want to give him whatever he needs. When he pumps into my fist, I finally understand.

I move my hand along his cock in rhythm with his thrusts. His lips peel away from his teeth, and his eyes clench shut as the muscles in his neck tighten and cord. He moves faster and faster, sweat dripping down his chest. Curious and greedy, I run my free hand down his chest and push myself up to sink my teeth into his quivering shoulder.

"Fuck," he rasps.

I want to taste more of him, so I drag my tongue from the base of his throat to the top of his neck. "Mmm, salty."

"God, Sunny." He swivels his hips and groans deep in his chest. "You're going to be the death of me."

"There's no need to be so dramatic," I whisper, my lips brushing against his ear. A shudder runs through him, and I smile with wicked triumph. "All you need to do is fall apart for me. Completely and utterly. Then . . . I'll let you live."

He comes . . . undone. He jerks wildly into my hand, and my hips undulate with him, my thighs slick with my arousal. He leans his weight onto one forearm and reaches his hand between our bodies. His thumb unerringly finds my throbbing clit and rubs me in deep, sure circles.

"Gods . . . Ethan," I whimper.

"I got you." His voice is a gravelly rasp. "I need you to come for me again. I need—"

We shout together as our bodies arch and warmth spills across my stomach. Our climax rocks through us until I go limp beneath his trembling body, my head lolling to the side. Ethan shifts off me and uses his T-shirt to wipe my stomach clean. Then he nearly collapses onto his back. We lie side by side, fighting to catch our breath.

"Wait," I say once I can form words. Confusion tugs my brows into a frown. "I thought there's more . . ."

He emits a sound halfway between tortured and amused. "We can't. I don't have a condom."

"But—"

He abruptly pushes himself onto his elbow and catches my chin between his fingers. "There is nothing I want more than to bury myself inside you and fuck you until you come around my cock. But I can't risk . . . If you become pregnant . . ."

"You're right," I breathe, shocked that for a split second I wanted to take that risk. "Of course we can't."

"Later." He sighs and presses his forehead against mine. "I promise."

I want to cradle his promise in my heart. To hold it and keep it safe. But I swallow the emotion tightening my throat. I don't want to think about later. I'm supposed to be over this *infatuation* later.

"Let's not worry about later." It was just sex. Not even full-on sex since I'm technically still a virgin. See? Nothing changed. "This was pretty fun."

"Pretty fun?" Ethan looks down at me with a mock frown, even as something like hurt shadows his eyes. "I've got to do better than that."

"What?" I widen my eyes with innocence. *Now* is enough. "I thought it was *nice.*"

"That's it." His smile is pure wickedness, and relief runs through me. No one will get their heart broken. "I'm going to make you come so hard, you won't be able to see straight."

"Oh, yeah?" I squeak, pressing my thighs together.

His laughter tickles my skin as he dips his head to my breast. When he licks my nipple and sucks it into his mouth, I have no sass to give.

When my eyes flicker open, I'm groggy as I'm dragged out of a dreamless slumber. It's still dark as a crypt outside. I don't know what woke me, but Ethan has his big body curled against my back with his arm flung over my stomach, a possessive hand on my breast. I wiggle my ass closer to him and sigh, linking my fingers through his. The quiet stillness of the night ensconces us, and my eyes flutter shut, only to snap open a second later.

Mihwa-ya.

My mother is dead, but I would know her voice anywhere. I don't want to wake up Ethan. I'm most likely hallucinating anyway—which is disturbing, but I'll worry about that later. Holding my breath, I lift his arm off me and slip out of the blanket tangled around us.

Mihwa-ya.

I'm just hallucinating . . . Oh, fuck it. I run the rest of the way out of the room and into the small courtyard of our house.

"Mother?" I spin left and right. "Mother?"

I stare out into the dark forest, tears streaming down my face. She's not here. Of course she's not. Why do I keep doing this to myself? Because the house holds a hint of her life force and it makes me feel closer to her. But enough is enough. I dry my wet cheeks with impatient swipes of my hand. She's gone.

With a deafening crack, a rush of heat pushes me from behind, making me stumble and fall onto my hands and knees. Shaking my head to clear it, I get to my feet and turn around. Flames, hot and towering, are consuming my childhood home . . . with Ethan inside.

A shrill scream rises to my throat. "No."

Run, Daughter. I hear my mother's voice again. *You must run.*

This isn't an ordinary fire. I sense a tendril of her gi in the fiery heat. The magic from the last of her life force is burning the house down. Within seconds, a wooden pillar crumbles to cinders and collapses the roof over the kitchen. *Ethan.*

"Are you doing this? Why, Mother?" I shout into the night. "Stop. Please stop. Ethan's inside."

Run, Daughter, the voice repeats. I want to clap my hands over my ears.

"No. You're dead." I clench my fists. "He's all I have."

You must run.

She can't complain that I'm not listening to her, because I do as I'm told.

I run.

I run straight into the blazing house.

GOLDEN AXE, SILVER AXE

One fair morning on a cloudless summer day, the steady thud of an axe rang out in the deep emerald mountain. A woodsman was chopping down a sturdy tree, not too old and not too young. His body was strong, and his swing steadfast.

His arms burned, and his back ached, but he did not complain, for he took quiet pride in working hard. Sweat dripped from his forehead, and his palms grew slippery, but he did not stop chopping.

Just ten more strikes, he promised himself, *then I'll take a break*.

But on the ninth strike, he lost his grip on the axe, and it flew out of his hands. As he watched in dismay, it sank into a nearby spring—a deep and fathomless one—with a gentle plop. The woodsman dropped to his knees, burying his face in his hands. Losing his axe meant losing his livelihood. He wasn't rich, but he made an honest living for himself.

Sanshillyeong, the Spirit of Mountains, emerged from the water in a flowing white robe. His long white hair and long white beard billowed in the breeze. He didn't have a drop of water on him as he floated above the spring, holding aloft a silver axe.

"Is this silver axe your silver axe?" His question echoed in the silent woods.

"No, that is not my axe," the woodsman answered in a clear, ringing voice. He was afraid to be in Sanshillyeong's presence—for he was no fool—but he would not be cowed.

The spirit disappeared underwater and rose again a moment later. "Is this golden axe your golden axe?"

"No, that is not my axe," the woodsman said once more.

When Sanshillyeong returned with his old metal axe, the woodsman sighed with relief and bowed his head to the ground in gratitude. "That is my axe. Thank you for finding it."

"You have proven your honor," the Spirit of Mountains said with a benevolent smile. "The golden axe and the silver axe are yours to keep."

"But they are not mine." The woodsman shook his head. "I did not earn them."

"You have proven your integrity." Sanshillyeong nodded, his smile growing. "Take the golden axe and the silver axe. I have been burdened with them long enough."

"Burdened? Are they too heavy for you?" The woodsman rushed to take the axes from the spirit's hands—to take the burden off him.

"You have proven your compassion." The Spirit of Mountains laid a hand on the woodsman's shoulder. "Now you shall rule the Kingdom of Mountains."

The woodsman's humble hanbok transformed into a royal gown, resplendent in emerald silk. The golden axe and the silver axe merged in his hands and became a crown of gold twines and jade leaves. He fell to his knees before Sanshillyeong, accepting his destiny with the courage of a true king.

"Rule with honor, integrity, and compassion." The spirit took the crown from the woodsman's calloused hands and placed it on his head. "Be worthy of the crown."

CHAPTER NINETEEN

The fire burns my fur and singes my skin as I burst through the doors, my nine tails fanning away the smoke. Ethan is crouched low on the floor, covering his nose and mouth with his shirt. He sees me and knows what to do without my asking. When he wraps his arms around my neck, I leap through the flames, out into the courtyard.

Even before I land, I hear the house crashing down behind me, the wooden beams snapping and cracking. I face the ruins of my childhood home, and an icy shudder runs through me. Ethan was in there only seconds ago. I crumple to the ground.

"Sunny." His frantic face—unmarked by the fire—swims in front of me. *Good.* He's not hurt. "Tell me how to help."

The pain is too unbearable for me to answer right away. But soon I'm able to catch my breath as my skin begins to mend. I raise my head and search the woods with bleary eyes. I sigh with relief when I find it.

"That tree with the oblong yellow leaves . . ." I tell him telepathically. "The sap will . . . help with the burns."

I swear the golden axe materializes in Ethan's hand before I finish speaking. I hear the thud of an axe against the tree. The rhythmic sound calms me, but I hurt too much to fall asleep. Soon I feel the cool press of tree bark against my skin, one by one, as the searing pain seeps out of my burns. I whimper with relief.

I drift in and out as I lie in the courtyard. I feel a warm, calloused palm smoothing down the fur between my ears. I want to lean into the touch, but I'm too weak to move my head . . . I startle awake. Green and silver flames burst from the ruins of the house. The house is on fire again, but I can't keep my eyes open. Why is the fire green and silver? Where's Ethan? I try to stand but can only manage a long, plaintive whimper. I feel the hand on my head again. I fall asleep.

When I come to, my body is warm from the midday sun, but my face feels cool. I glance up to find a sunshade made of four branches and a man's shirt over my head. The bare-chested owner of the shirt sits by my side, with his arms resting on his raised knees.

"I see you've been having fun with your new axe," I speak into his mind.

"Sunny." He runs his hand over my muzzle, his touch so gentle that it brings tears to my eyes. "How are you feeling?"

"Fine . . . I think." I push off the ground and stand, toppling the sunshade in the process. "Oops, sorry."

"Don't worry about it." He picks his shirt up from the ground and shakes off the dirt. "It's not exactly a masterpiece."

"How long have I been out?" I study the shift and ripple of his muscles as he pulls his shirt on. There's something . . . different about him, but I can't put my finger on it.

"An eternity." He runs a hand down his face, then offers me a rueful smile. "A few hours, I think. My best guess is that it's just past noon."

"You should've woken me." I look up at the sky as unease shoots through me. "The fire destroyed the wards along with the house."

"The rest did you good," he says with a pointed glance at my body.

I can't argue with that. My burns have healed, and even my coat is as good as new, white and gleaming. I shift back into my human form. I click my tongue in frustration when I realize I'm wearing my hanbok skirt. With no top. Ethan ripped my T-shirt, and I was too shy to sleep with my boobs hanging out.

"Even so, we need to leave," I say, surprised someone hasn't found us already. But the edges of my vision go dark, and I sway on my feet as realization slams into me. *Gods, no.* "The sacred ashes. They were in my backpack."

Ethan lifts my backpack into the air. I snatch it from his hand and dig through it. I release a ragged breath when my hand wraps around the lucky pouch.

"How?" Tears of relief sting my eyes. I don't have to relive that night again. Samshin Halmeom doesn't need to lose another arm.

"I managed to grab it before we leapt out of the house." He shrugs as though it's no big deal.

The lone cypress's cryptic warning rings in my head. *Nothing might be enough to forestall the coming of the Amheuk.* But with the sacred ashes, we still have a chance of taking down Daeseong.

"Ethan, you might have saved the worlds," I say in a husky voice.

"I guess I overshot a bit." His lips curve into a wry smirk. "I was just trying to save our asses from a megalomaniac."

I smile back, and my eyes drop to his mouth. My grin fades as I remember the feel of his hands on my body and the hungry crush of his lips against mine. The more pleasure we shared, the more ravenous we became. We couldn't keep our hands off each other as day turned to night. Only exhaustion finally lulled us to sleep.

His throat works to swallow, and I know he's remembering too. My tongue flicks out as I take in the lush curve of his lips, and he takes a step toward me. *The wards.* We can't do this now. I force my gaze lower and focus on the triangle of his chest where his shirt flaps open. Ethan stills. I blink. Then I blink again.

"Your jade disk," I gasp. "Where is it?"

"It must've fallen off in the fire." His eyes flit away to the remnants of my old home. I spin toward the house, ready to launch into the hot embers, but he grips my arm.

"Let go, Ethan." I swat at his hand. "We have to find it. It was your mom's."

"My mother's," he murmurs, not loosening his hold on my arm. "It's no use. I looked for hours while you were out. I couldn't find it."

"I could take my fox form. My senses are heightened as my gumiho—"

"Leave it, Sunny." The sharp edge in his voice makes me pause. He sighs. "There's no time. Like you said, we need to leave. It's . . . it's just a necklace."

"But . . ." My heart cracks a little. He's never taken it off before. He must feel incomplete without it—his last connection to his mom.

He wraps his arm around my waist and pulls me close to his side. I lean into him without thinking, and my body hums happily. I'm distracted enough to let him lead me away from the ruined house.

"Where to now?" He runs his hand up and down my bare arm. I can't decide whether it's soothing or arousing.

"Hmm?" I say as his question sinks in. "We need to . . ."

Shit. Where to, indeed? We have the sacred ashes, but I still have no idea how to use them. Even if I did, I don't know where to find Daeseong. Where are the damned Suhoshin when I need them? They must have intel on the dark mudang's whereabouts. But we can't risk waiting around for them because the third assassin might show up first. I could use a break from being stabbed, slashed, and burned—although the bad guys had nothing to do with the fire.

Run, Daughter. You must run.

Why did the last of my mother's life force tell me to run? Why did she try to *kill* Ethan?

Frustrated and desperate, I ask, "Did you by any chance grab the *Book of Answers* too?"

"Sorry, no." He kisses the top of my head. "And I'm so sorry about your house."

"Me too." I sigh. "Let's get out of here."

"Lead the way." He drops his arm from my shoulder, then grabs hold of my hand.

I pick a direction and walk, lifting my floor-length skirt off the ground with my free hand. I'm still missing a jeogori, but I feel far less self-conscious about my luscious cleavage. Oh, what a difference a day of naked shenanigans makes.

As I trudge on like a topless Joseon maiden, Ethan walks silently at my side. I glance at his profile and down at his hands. "Hey, where did your golden axe go?"

He shrugs, keeping his gaze forward.

"I guess it comes and goes as it pleases," I murmur when he doesn't elaborate. "Let's go this way. There's a spring nearby."

As we walk on, his expression grows distant and hard. *He* feels distant and hard. My teeth dig into my bottom lip. I tsk and shake my head. He's upset about losing his necklace. How could he not be? The only reason I'm semi-okay with my childhood home burning down is because I have Olympic-level avoidance skills.

I want to hug him tight until he thaws, but something holds me back. The rigid set of his shoulders and the inflexible lines of his face tell me he might not welcome my comfort. Something inside me withers a little. Does he . . . regret what happened yesterday? My stomach drops at the thought, and my heart drums with fear. No, this won't do. I clench my jaw and pick up my pace.

I don't care what he thinks, because I don't intend to repeat the . . . the mistake. I tug my hand out of his grip, but he doesn't seem to notice. I bite the inside of my cheek to keep my lips from wobbling. We're in this together for now, but once it's over—and we manage to live through it—I'm going back to my life *alone*, and he'll go on with his.

But the life he left behind won't be the one he'll return to. That life doesn't exist anymore. He's a being of the Shingae with untapped powers I can't even begin to fathom. Nothing can wound him. Even the Blessed get hurt—they just heal fast like me. And he can wield the legendary axes.

I know Ethan is *more*, but I can't make sense of it. The Kingdom of Mountains from the old story doesn't exist. There is no *King* of Mountains. There is no crown. But until a few days ago, I thought the golden axe and the silver axe weren't real.

Although my mother kept me secluded from the rest of the Shingae, she taught me everything I know about the world of gods—from history and politics to medicine and martial arts. But what if Samshin Halmeom had been teaching me too? What if the tales she told me were based on the truth? I shiver. Some of her stories were dark and bloody. I would have nightmares for a week after hearing one. That didn't stop me from asking for more, though.

I can't help glancing at Ethan again, my heart twisting. I don't know if it's for myself or for him. *Who are you?* I press my lips tight. He's Ethan Lee. My friend. That's all that matters. And I'm going to do everything in my power to make sure he survives this shitshow so he can have a life to live—whatever life awaits him. *Without me.*

"Hey." The back of his hand brushes mine. "Where have you gone?"

"Just . . . strategizing," I murmur, drawing myself out of my thoughts.

Ethan nods. "Now that we have the sacred ashes, don't you think it's time we bring the fight to Daeseong?"

"That'll be suicide until we figure out *how* to use the ashes," I say, arching my brow. What's gotten into him? "Besides, I have no idea how to find him."

"Maybe we let him find us." A muscle tics in his jaw. "Once we dispose of his final assassin, he'll have no choice but to come after us himself. And when he does, we'll make him pay for killing Ben . . . for hurting you."

I feel it again. He's . . . different. The Ethan that walked into Roxy's was kind, even in his grief. He wanted justice for Ben, not necessarily vengeance. It's true that things have changed since we learned the truth about Daeseong's resurrection. He isn't someone we can just turn over to the local law enforcement. No, the dark mudang has to be stopped at all costs. But this Ethan is vengeful, angry . . . sorrowful. He's like a stranger.

"Hey." I put a hand on his arm, and he stops walking. "Daeseong will pay for what he did to Ben, but there might be more at work here than we know. I need you to be patient for just a bit longer."

"Patient?" His soft scoff is as bitter as crushed aspirin. "I think I've been patient for far too long."

"I . . ." My words catch in my throat. "I'm sorry. This is . . . this is all my fault. I'm so sorry."

"None of this is your fault." He spins me to face him, his fingers digging into my bare shoulders. Then he sighs, bowing his head. His grip loosens, and his thumbs brush across my skin. When he raises his eyes to meet mine, they are full of remorse. "I'm being an asshole."

"Yes. Yes, you are," I say without rancor. I glance around the woods because I can't seem to look at him. "I bet you didn't sleep since the fire. You must be exhausted. Once we get to the spring, we can rest and regroup."

We climb the mountain in silence, each of us lost in thought. Neither my mother's teachings nor Samshin Halmeom's stories explain how to use the sacred ashes. Maybe I could draw a circle on the ground with them and entrap Daeseong inside, paralyzing his powers. Or I could coat my hwando with the ashes and drive it into his heart. Or I could dip bulbs of garlic in them and wear them around my neck, splashing around holy water. *Gods.*

"Halt," a uniformed man yells from the woods. "Hands in the air."

"They're spies," another shouts, panic in his voice. "Just shoot the bastards."

"No—"

Logic stands no chance of prevailing against panic. The first man's orders are resoundingly ignored, and shots ring out. A bullet ricochets off a tree just above my head. I can't believe I let them sneak up on us.

"Ethan." I reach for his hand. "We have to run."

Chilling power, roiling with violence, emanates from Ethan as he stretches out his free hand in front of him. I don't know what he's about to do, but I can't wait to find out. I grab his arm and bodily drag him behind a tree.

"Don't hurt them." As I say the words, I realize that he *can* hurt them. His power rolls off him and reverberates through me like the pounding of a war drum. "They're human. Feel their gi. They're just some North Korean soldiers who think they're doing their job."

"They tried to kill you," he snarls. *His eyes.* They're swirling with silver-and-green fire. "I won't lose you too."

Before I can wonder about his eyes—I've never seen anything like them—a half dozen shots ring out behind us. They're closing in on us. A low growl starts in his chest. *Shit.*

"Please, Ethan," I plead.

He allows me to tug him away. We dart between the trees, but a bullet skims my shoulder. My heart plummets when Ethan spins his torso and raises his hand, bellowing with rage. But the soldiers don't crumple to their feet. They keep running toward us, firing their guns.

Ethan wraps his arm around my shoulders and says against my ear, "Run."

We take off through the woods. The trees thin out, and I cringe, anticipating more bullets to find their mark. But . . . nothing. I risk glancing behind me and see the bullets bouncing off the air behind us. A shield. Ethan raised some kind of shield around us.

There's no time for questions, so I keep running. The soldiers and their guns can't keep up with our preternatural speed. We escape them before long and stop to catch our breaths.

"Your shoulder." Ethan wraps his hands around my arms and turns me to face him.

"It's just a scratch," I mutter, stepping out of his hold. "It scabbed over already."

He stares at the curve of my shoulder where the bullet grazed me, running his thumb underneath the scab to wipe off the blood. He grits his teeth so hard, it's a wonder he doesn't crack a molar. I can still sense his rage, but beneath it is a trill of fear and worry . . . for me. I can tell by how close he stands to me, shielding me with his body as he scans the woods. But even that doesn't thaw the ice hardening around my heart.

I get my bearings and lead us to the spring. It's inside a yawning cave, shallow but tall. The afternoon sun filters in from the gaping mouth, providing enough light for us to make our way to the spring. It's not an ideal hideout, but the cave will shield us from view long enough to ready ourselves against unwanted visitors.

But right now, I don't give a fuck about the bad guys. All I care about is the male standing next to me. He *lied* to me. He knows how to use his powers—that shield he erected to stop the bullets proves it. That means he knows what his powers are. He knows *who* he is. Gods, he must've known all along. Betrayal, dark and bitter, taints my fragile trust in him. In us.

I turn to face him and ask the question I promised myself I wouldn't. "Who *are* you?"

CHAPTER TWENTY

"Sunny." Ethan reaches out for me, devastation in his eyes, and suddenly . . . I don't want him to answer. I don't want to know who he is. "I—"

Before I can tell him to shut up—tell him I take back my question—he snaps his mouth shut and turns into that hard, tortured stranger again. I follow his line of sight and take an instinctive step back. Apparently, a shallow cave offers no protection from the guardians of the Shingae if they feel like ambushing you. The suhoshin from the diner arrived at the mouth of the cave unseen and unheard.

"Shit." I drag out the word, putting a wealth of frustration into it. It's true I was distracted because . . . Ethan. But this is the second time in less than half an hour that I let an enemy sneak up on us.

The suhoshin glances at me with the barest arch of his perfect eyebrow. My memories of him from our brief encounter—where we were actively running away from him—didn't do him justice. He is stupendously gorgeous in a fitted white T-shirt and jeans. Nothing as pedestrian as *pretty* but a masterpiece of masculine beauty with high, sweeping cheekbones, a straight, aristocratic nose, and long, wide eyes framed by lush, black lashes.

"What do you want?" I sound like a petulant child, but he has no right to be that good looking.

I have enough of my faculties to notice that the silken curtain of his black hair lies unmoving against his shoulders. He doesn't have his wings out. I also note that he hasn't bound us. Maybe this is a friendly visit. Or at least the kind where I don't get thrown into a windowless cell for all eternity.

But he turns his insolent gaze away from me without answering and studies Ethan for a moment. Then he draws his head back, his eyes flashing with . . . recognition? With relief? Drawing a sharp breath, he stands straighter, which is quite a feat.

"At last." The suhoshin steps one leg forward and moves to . . . crouch? My mouth goes slack. What's he doing? Are his shoelaces untied? "My pr—"

"What is your name?" Ethan asks tersely, halting the suhoshin midmotion.

The suhoshin straightens once more, his gaze flitting toward me for the briefest second before returning to Ethan. "I am Song Jihun, son of Taehun, from the Kingdo—"

"You're a suhoshin?" Ethan cuts him off. My eyes jump back and forth between them.

Frankly, I'm surprised the suhoshin is allowing Ethan to talk to him like this. This authoritative side to Ethan is admittedly hot, but the guardian is bound to snap any minute. The Suhoshin are an arrogant lot. I inch closer to Ethan. I don't know what I'll do if this Jihun guy decides to immobilize me, but I'll think of something. The handsome bastard is not getting Ethan.

Wait. I'm angry . . . no . . . *furious* with Ethan. Why do I want to help him? Because, damn it all to fucking hell, he's still my friend.

"Yes, I am a captain in the Order of the Suhoshin." He cocks his head to the side with the faintest frown. "Your hi—"

"Don't." Ethan holds up a hand and glances at me with pleading in his eyes. Pleading for what? I tilt my head to hold his gaze, but he turns away from me. His voice is firm when he says, "Not yet, Captain. I need to—"

"Look what we have here." The cold, slithering voice echoes in the cave.

"Give me a fucking break," I grit out. The yellow assassin is somewhere above us, but I can't see him. "You all have to stop sneaking up on me."

"I'm actually a little hurt that no one invited me to this playdate," he simpers. Now he's somewhere low to the ground.

"Oh, wow. A rotting corpse with a sense of humor." I draw my sword and casually sling my backpack over a shoulder with my free hand. I can't let on that I have the sacred ashes in there. "How refreshing."

Ethan steps close to me and whispers, "Protect the ashes."

The suhoshin runs straight for us at breakneck speed. I raise my hwando to block his attack, but he leaps into the air a few feet from us, swinging his long sword in elegant, lethal strikes. The yellow assassin flickers into view and thuds to the ground on all fours, his unitard sliced open at his chest and thigh.

Ethan pushes me behind him and stretches his arms wide. The golden axe and the silver axe appear in each of his fists. I stumble back a step. He can summon the axes at will? Why am I even surp—

Before I can finish the thought, he lunges for the assassin.

The golem shifts like a shadow—a bright, school bus–yellow shadow—flickering in and out of view as he evades Ethan's axes and Jihun's sword. Ethan has a shitload of explaining to do, but we have to survive this first. I switch my sword hand to slip on both straps of the backpack and tighten it against my body.

I can't let the boys have all the fun, so I sprint toward the wall of the cave, kick off into the air, and bring my hwando down on the swirling mist of yellow, which I assume is the assassin. Ethan and Jihun stay their weapons just in time not to slice me up. I strike home with my blow and follow through with a roundhouse kick as I land. The assassin shrieks in pain and stumbles back to earth in his corporeal form, gripping his shoulder.

"Where is your master?" I point my sword at Yellow as Ethan and the suhoshin flank me.

His black lips stretch all the way to the edges of his jaw in an abomination of a smile. "I don't think I want to play anymore."

The assassin bursts open like a balloon filled beyond its capacity, his body shattering into fine powder that envelops the cave in a noxious yellow fog. The plants shrivel and fall to the ground like flakes of black snow. And the trees outside decompose from the tips of their branches down to their roots. I stare in horror, reminded of Samshin Halmeom's arm burning to ashes. He can't do this. He's killing this mountain. He's killing . . . us.

A racking cough tears through my body, blood spewing from my mouth. My legs give out, and I fall to my knees. Ethan kneels beside me and pulls me toward him, his arm wrapped around my shoulders. Jihun plants his long sword on the ground and sways on his feet.

"Captain, bind the assassin," Ethan snaps. "Now!"

The suhoshin draws himself up, even as blood drips down his chin, and holds his palm out. The fog of poison converges toward the center of the cave, growing denser and thicker until a blob of yellow—like the sinuous wax in a lava lamp—flows and shifts in the air. Jihun's hand is gripped into a shaky fist, and he grits his teeth to hold on.

Ethan walks toward the yellow blob with long, determined steps.

"No." My voice is a ragged whisper, my throat raw from the poison. "Don't . . ."

He raises the axes—he doesn't seem to feel their weight—and brings them down on either side of the shifting mass, stopping just shy of burying the blades in it. In a cold, imperious voice, Ethan commands, "Show yourself."

The undead assassin materializes in his corporeal form, holding himself stiffly away from the axes on either side of his neck. His sneer is strained as he says, "The gumiho I know. And anyone can see the angel boy is a self-righteous suhoshin. But who are you, I wonder?"

"So poison is your little power." Ethan presses the blades of his axes against the golem's neck. "Did you enjoy killing my brother?"

Oh, gods. It makes perfect, sickening sense. I draw in breath after breath of clean air. The yellow assassin killed Ben with his poison. Rage burns through the fog in my head. I drag the back of my hand across my mouth, wiping off the blood. I'm going to end the fucker as soon as I can stand.

"Ah, you're our messenger boy." Yellow preens. "We were hoping you'd run to the beast. But however did you find her? Have you secretly been in touch with her? Behind your brother's back." He shrieks with unhinged laughter. "Two brothers with a hard-on for an *animal*. It would be sweet if it wasn't so revolting."

"Of course you enjoyed killing him," Ethan continues, as though the assassin hasn't spoken. "But not as much as I'll enjoy watching you die. First thing first, where is your master?"

"Oh, don't worry your pretty little head over it." The undead's eerie smile spreads. "He'll come soon enough for the beast."

I don't even feel his dig as my magic struggles to clear the poison from my systems. It's slow going and painful, but I can't complain. I would've been dead in mere seconds if Ethan and Jihun hadn't stopped Yellow. I clench and unclench my hand around the hilt of my hwando, testing my grip.

"Where is the dark mudang?" Ethan asks, his expression chillingly calm.

The yellow assassin cackles with delight, the sound as charming as a bed of wiggling maggots. I gag and throw up a mouthful of blood and bile. That's one way to expel more of the poison. I do feel much better. I put my legs under me, but they can't quite bear my weight yet.

Yellow points one hand at me, the tips of his fingers elongating into long, sharp needles, and digs the other clawed hand into his own chest. Everything happens too fast for my poison-addled brain to follow.

I think the needles are meant for me . . . but is the golem trying to kill himself as well? Jihun shifts forward, raising his sword. Ethan grips the undead assassin's wrist before he can bury his claws in himself. Then without taking his eyes off Yellow, he shouts, "Protect her."

Before I draw my next breath, the suhoshin throws himself in front of me, swinging his sword in lightning-fast arcs. I struggle clumsily to my feet. What do I do? Who do I help? During my split second of panicked indecision, Ethan and the yellow assassin disappear into thin air. And Jihun falls to one knee with a pained grunt. It's all over, and I don't even understand what happened.

"Ethan." I stumble toward the mouth of the cave. "Ethan!"

He . . . he left me. This new Ethan—the one who is lying to me—didn't get the memo that we promised to stick together. But he sure knew how to summon and wield those axes. He fought like a seasoned warrior whose weapons were an extension of his body. When Blue attacked us in the woods less than a week ago, he acted like he could barely lift those axes. It had to have been an act, right? Because no one can master their magic in a few short days. Maybe teleportation is one of his many hidden powers.

Unbidden, the story of the humble woodsman becoming the rightful King of Mountains flashes through my mind, but I shy away from it without knowing why. Instead, I allow my humiliation and anger at myself to scorch my insides black. Ethan lied to me, then left me. How could I have been so stupid? *This* is why I choose to be alone.

It takes me a moment to hear the wet cough. I spin around just in time to see the suhoshin spew blood from his mouth and crumple to the ground.

"For fuck's sake," I hiss.

With one last desperate glance around the woods, I run back to Jihun and tip him over onto his back. One long, yellow needle protrudes from his side. Covering my hand with the fabric of my skirt, I pull out the poison needle and throw it onto the ground, noticing that there are more needles scattered around us. If the suhoshin hadn't deflected them, those needles would be embedded in my body. I wouldn't have had the speed to evade them in my human form. Everything happened so fucking fast. I still should've transformed and defended us, but becoming a gumiho still doesn't feel . . . right. I don't trust my gumiho, her power . . . her rage.

Jihun's eyelids flutter closed, and his body goes limp and heavy. *Shit, shit, shit.* My hesitation to shift might've cost this male his life. *No.* I'm not going to let that happen.

"Hey." I slap his cheek. The bases of his fingernails are starting to turn purple. "Don't go to sleep. *Open. Your. Eyes.*"

To my relief, his eyes snap open. But then he plants one hand on the ground and struggles to push himself up. He collapses onto his chest with a pained groan but tries again.

"Hey, stop that." I roll him onto his back again and press his shoulders into the ground. The more he moves, the quicker the poison will spread. "I need you to stay still."

I scramble to the spring and bring back water cupped in my palms. I dribble it into his mouth. "You have to drink this. This is a medicinal spring. The water has healing properties that will slow the progression of the poison. Drink."

Jihun swallows and coughs, then drinks some more as I run back and forth from the spring. His eyes are bleary, but at least they're open. That's good.

"I have to . . . ," he rasps, his lips turning a deep purple. It's like someone pumped doksacho into his veins. That's not good.

"Don't talk. Stay very, very still." I look out at the setting sun. The yellow assassin's poison has the same effects as doksacho, the poison that killed Ben, but is much more potent. Daeseong somehow reanimated Yellow's corpse to hold the essence of the poisonous flower. What a sick bastard. "I have to find the antidote."

His eyes roll back in his head, but he lowers them again and focuses on me through sheer willpower. He's one tough son of a bitch. "Too . . . dangerous . . ."

"Oh, shut up." I know the mountain like the back of my hand. Or at least I did over a hundred years ago. But it seems untouched by civilization, the vegetation growing as it had all those years ago. "If you even think about moving, I'll kick your ass. I'll be right back."

"No . . ." He reaches for my hand, cringing in pain.

I evade his hand easily and sprint into the woods as a gumiho. Every time I transform, I rest a little easier in my skin. My gumiho is strong. I can protect the people I care about. Maybe the dangerous power that lies deep inside me will stay dormant if I transform only to help others. I have no idea if that's the way it works. That uncertainty scares the shit out of me. What if I'm wrong? What if I still hurt people despite my good intentions? But I'm not going to let fear stop me from helping someone, especially when that someone risked his life to save mine.

The higher temperature of my fox form burns away the remaining toxin in my body. I run fast enough to blur my surroundings. But my heart feels hollowed out, and I can't stop thinking about Ethan. I saw him moments ago. I'm still furious with him. But I miss him. I miss him so much, even as betrayal, doubt, and fear churn into a mess inside me.

Did he *choose* to leave me? Did he do it to protect me? Or was he blinded by his thirst for vengeance? That doesn't sound like the Ethan I know, but the enraged, sorrowful male I saw earlier in the woods might have chosen revenge over our . . . friendship. I remember the icy rage in his voice. *Where is the dark mudang?*

Still, all I can think is I don't know where he's gone. Is he hurt? What if he's . . . No, he has to be alive. I just need to know he's safe. I can deal with everything else, but I *need* him to be safe. I should leave the suhoshin and go find Ethan.

But I don't stop searching for the bright-green leaves of the seungmacho. For whatever reason, Jihun fought against the yellow assassin alongside us. Then he jumped in front of the poison needles intended for me. Now, he might die because of me. I don't understand, and I hate the thought of owing someone my life, but I dash higher up the mountain. The herb thrives in high elevation.

My body goes limp with relief when I find the familiar green leaves. I dig up a thick clump of the herb and streak down the mountain, my paws barely touching the ground. There is almost no light left in the day, but I use my spirit eyes to find the cave. There's no reason to hold back my magic at this point. I shift back into my human form and walk inside to find the suhoshin lying eerily still where I left him. I run to his side, throwing an orb of light into the air.

"Jihun." I shake his shoulders. His eyes flutter open, and I exhale long and loud. "Gods, I thought you were dead."

The suhoshin manages to arch a haughty eyebrow and says, "You told me to be still."

His voice is softer than a whisper, but he nails the arrogance. I smirk at him. "What a good boy you are."

I glance around the cave, looking for something to pound the herb with. Jihun coughs, choking on blood. *Shit.* There's no time to be timid. I wash the seungmacho in the spring and stuff a handful in my mouth. I chew it into a pulp, grimacing at the swampy bitterness, then hold it against his lips.

"Eat," I say gruffly. "There's no time for me to look for a mortar and pestle. I know it's gross, but it's better than dying."

With another arch of his brow, Jihun leans forward and eats the herb off my hand. My face heats when his lips brush my palm, but I hold my hand still until he takes every bit of the seungmacho. Once he lies back down, I wash the rest of the herb and masticate it. I lift his shirt and spread the pulp on his punctured side so the antidote penetrates through the open wound. I finish quickly and pull his shirt down past his sculpted abs. *Sculpted?* How can I notice his six-pack at a time like this?

When I look up at his face, I find him staring at me. I hope my blush isn't noticeable in the glow of our makeshift light. I scowl for good measure and mutter, "What?"

"Thank you," he says.

"You took a bullet for me—so to speak." I shrug, embarrassed. I'm still no good at peopling. I don't know if I'll ever be. "I wasn't going to let you just . . . die."

"Huh." He tilts his head to get a better look at me. I wish he'd close his eyes again. "Gumihos aren't exactly known for their loyalty."

"What the hell is that supposed to mean?" I snap. Maybe I should've let the arrogant bastard die.

"That's not what I . . . I didn't . . . I meant no offense." His words trip over each other. He's blushing. *Shit.* If I can see him blushing, that means he saw me turn into a beet a minute ago. "You're just not what I expected."

My sanity returns to me in a rush. This male is a suhoshin. There's a reason I was running from his kind. It's my turn to arch an eyebrow, but I can't match his mastery. Neither can I keep the slight tremor out of my voice. "You don't think the other mass murderers would've fed you disgusting chewed-up leaves?"

His stoic expression doesn't change, but his voice gentles when he says, "You aren't a mass murderer."

I don't know what he means. Does he not know about what I did? I stay silent, afraid of giving something away.

"Yes, you killed Daeseong and his followers *in self-defense.*" The intensity of his gaze holds me captive, as though willing me to believe what he's saying. "But you didn't kill any of the villagers."

I squeeze my eyes shut. My lungs are broken. I can't breathe. What is he saying? My blood pounds too loudly in my ears. I don't know what he's *saying.*

"Mihwa?"

"Don't call me that," I whisper. "My name is Sunny. I haven't been Mihwa in over a century."

"Why can't you be both?" he says softly, as though he understands my turmoil. But he knows nothing about me.

"Because I . . . can't." I keep my eyes closed. I concentrate on not hyperventilating.

"Sunny." He reaches out and covers my hand with his. "The villagers lived. Daeseong and his followers died because their humanity was too far gone. The rest of the people woke up in the morning with no memory of the night before and went back to living their lives. You didn't hurt them."

A sob escapes me. I clamp a hand over my mouth, but I can't stop sobbing. I can't stop the hot tears from spilling down my face. I didn't . . . The hope that blossoms is terrifying. I didn't kill those people?

I stop fighting. I let go. I cry and wail as though I will never stop.

CHAPTER
TWENTY-ONE

I'm on the ground, curled up in a fetal position. The night has deepened, but the moon drenches the cave in its silvery light. I'm hollowed out. I open my swollen eyes, blinking as though waking up from a dream. I take a shuddering breath, my chest heaving from the storm of tears.

Ethan. I scramble upright. He's gone. Devastation slams into me before I remember his lies . . . his betrayal. I dig the heels of my hands against my eyelids, then take a deep breath. He's going to explain. Once I find him, he'll explain *everything*. And I *will* find him. That's all I can focus on right now.

Jihun can help me find Ethan. The Suhoshin are the best trackers in all the worlds. *Jihun.* I spin to my side to find him lying next to me, quiet and still. I can barely see his shadowy outline in the moonlight. My light orb must've gone out when I . . . fell apart. I throw another one into the air to get a better look at him.

A relieved sigh whooshes out of me when I see his chest rising and falling. He didn't die. He's just sleeping. I need him alive to help me find Ethan. I lean in close to study his face. It's hard to make out his complexion in the silvery light, but the purple tint under his eyes and on his lips seems to have faded. Thank gods.

"Ahh!" I scuttle back when his eyes open.

The corners of his mouth twitch in a hint of a smile that disappears almost immediately. "Are you okay?"

"I'm fine," I mutter sullenly. I don't know if I'm more mortified that he saw me crying like a baby or heard me screaming like a little girl. Maybe I'll get lucky, and he'll still die. I sigh. There's no time for wishful thinking. "It looks like you're going to live."

"Thanks to you." He struggles to sit up and winces, pressing his hand against his side.

"Hey." I rush over and help him, gripping his biceps with both hands. "Take it easy."

He glances at the sky outside. "We need to leave."

"You're not well enough," I protest, even though I'm anxious to find Ethan.

"I'm not that easy to kill," he says. I drop his arm as soon as I'm relatively certain he won't topple over.

"Well, aren't you lucky?" I croon, remembering why I don't like the Suhoshin. They are a bunch of arrogant, privileged bastards who have been made nearly immortal by the gods—the fucking Blessed. Unfortunately, this one saved my life, and I need his help. With an annoyed grunt, I walk over to the spring and bring back water cupped in my hands. "Drink."

Jihun wraps his big palm under my hands and drinks the water, his stubble tickling my fingers. I withdraw my hands the minute he leans back. I return to the spring to put some space between us and drink until my stomach feels sloshy. That should kill the asshole butterflies in there.

I don't know what the hell is wrong with me. Is the frightened eighteen-year-old inside me in awe of his strength? Maybe it's my current butt-scared self who admires his stoic fearlessness. Who the hell knows? But I can't deny there is something solid and steadfast about the suhoshin that makes me want to lean on him.

Loneliness stabs at me with a suddenness that makes me gasp. *Where are you, Ethan?* Damn it, I'm missing the lying bastard again. I want him to be safe—because I'm a decent person—but I'd be a total loser to miss someone who deceived me.

I glance back to find Jihun watching me. He has some color in his face and seems to be improving exponentially. Good. Now he can answer some of my questions. I'm not stalling to let him rest longer.

"If I didn't kill all those people"—I hug my arms around my stomach—"then am I *not* wanted by the Suhoshin?"

"No." He shakes his head. "You are not a fugitive of the order."

But even if the villagers lived, I killed Daeseong and his followers. What kind of power lies in me that I can wreak such destruction? How do I know it's not evil? How do I know *I'm* not evil? All these years, I haven't been running from the Shingae. I've been running from that question. And I still don't have an answer. Alas, the soul-searching has to wait.

"Then why have you been following us?" I ask.

"I'm not at liberty to share that information," he says with stiff formality, and the back of my skull tingles with a hunch.

"Were you following me?" I narrow my eyes. "Or were you following Ethan?"

The suhoshin holds my gaze with no intention of responding. His expression says he can do this all day, but he already gave everything away with his silence.

"What do you know about Ethan?" I don't expect him to answer, but I still want to throttle him when he presses his lips together. "Who *is* he?"

"I need to take you to the realm." He pushes to a stand with barely a cringe.

"The realm?" My brows furrow in confusion. Did he just change the subject on me? It worked, though. "What realm?"

"I can't guard him while I'm protecting you." He walks to the middle of the cave and stoops down to pick up his long sword. He flicks his wrist, and it disappears.

It reminds me of how the axes appeared in Ethan's hands—how sure footed he'd been in the face of the yellow assassin's horrifying magic. I press my hands against the sick lurch in my stomach. Later. I'll figure all that out later.

Jihun continues, "I need to take you someplace safe."

"I need your protection like I need to be audited by the IRS." In a single motion, I push off the ground and get in his face. "And I sure as hell am not going *someplace safe* with you."

"Audited by the IRS?" He cocks his head to the side, his brows furrowing.

"You don't know . . ." Of course he doesn't know. He's a suhoshin. He has bigger villains to contend with than the IRS. Wait. How does he even speak English so well? I click my tongue. "Never mind. You're taking me to Ethan. *Now.*"

"Enough." The suhoshin waves a graceful hand through the air. I already know before I try to move. He's bound my arms and legs. "We are leaving."

"Cock*sucker.*" I strain against the invisible bonds but only manage to knock myself off balance. Jihun catches me before I crash to the ground, his big hands nearly spanning my entire waist as he holds me steady.

"My apologies . . . but time is of the essence." He sounds sincere, but I don't care.

"Unbind me, you self-righteous prick," I snarl, thrashing against the binds.

With his jaw set, he lifts me off the ground as though I weigh nothing, his arms like iron bands across my upper back and beneath my thighs. When I buck against him, he tightens his grip on my body and holds me close to the wall of his chest.

"Stop struggling." His tone is terse, as though he's fast losing his patience. "I don't want to hurt you."

I go limp in his arms as fury overtakes logic and all my hesitation dissipates. I *will* find Ethan. I close my eyes. *I am gumiho.* Blessed or not, I can take the suhoshin in my spirit form if I move faster than he can bind me. I'll knock him around a bit, then tie *him* up—how would he like *that*?—until he's willing to take me to Ethan. But nothing happens. Panic flashes through me. *I. Am. Gumiho.* I glance down at my scrawny five-feet-tall human body. What the fuck? Why can't I transform?

"What did you do to me?" I turn wide, frightened eyes on the suhoshin.

He gazes straight ahead as he marches us out of the cave. "I've restrained your magic as well as your body."

"I will *kill* you." I have hidden my magic for over a century, but it has always been my choice. To have my magic suppressed against my will is a . . . violation. "You have no right. I am *not* a fugitive."

"No, you're not. But you are under my protection." He finally glances down at me. "And I will not let anyone—including you—interfere with carrying out my duty."

"I don't know what the fuck you're talking a—" My words die on a sharp intake of breath as Jihun's wings flare and we take off into the sky.

I fight against the instinct to squeeze my eyes shut as the ground grows farther and farther away. My arms remain tied to my sides, so I can't even cling to the suhoshin's neck. With no magic to help break the fall, I'm dead if he drops me. I'm at his mercy, and I hate it. I hate *him.*

If only looks could kill. I glare at him until my eyeballs hurt, but he won't even meet my eyes. *Coward.* Why is he doing this? Why is he suddenly obsessed with protecting me? Something flickers at the edges of my mind.

Ethan's words ring in my head—solemn and commanding. *Protect her.*

Is that why Jihun risked his life to save me? Is that why he's kidnapping me? Or, as he liked to call it, "taking me somewhere safe." But why would he obey Ethan as though it were his . . . duty? It can't be . . . *Shut up, shut up, shut up.* I don't want to know. I just have to figure out a way to get away from the suhoshin and find Ethan on my own.

I take a fortifying breath and glance around me. We are very, very far off the ground. And Jihun seems to be headed toward the highest peak of a distant mountain. There's something odd about the clouds surrounding the mountain. They shimmer and shift as though they're glamoured to hide something. But no one is powerful enough to glamour an entire mountain. Not unless you're a god.

But the air thrums with power as though the life force of thousands—no, tens of thousands—of beings of the Shingae are gathered in one place. Fear spreads like frost from the back of my skull to the base of my spine. Something isn't right. There is something unnatural about this power.

"Are you taking me to the Suhoshin headquarters or something?" I quip to hide the nerves shuddering through me. "Do you guys all live together in one house, fighting over who gets to use the bathroom first? Oh, do you use your super-guardian skills to track down the roommate who ate your last strawberry yogurt?"

A huff of surprised laughter escapes his lips before he schools his features into cool indifference. "Breathe. Holding your breath makes it much worse."

"Makes what wor—"

The suhoshin tips his body and plunges toward the mountain. My lips part on a silent scream as he descends fast enough to make my ears pop. My body reacts without my consent, and I end up with my face buried against his neck. And as far as I can tell, we're still careening to our deaths.

My stomach shoves itself into my throat, and I hold my body tense, waiting for the impact. I only realize I'm holding my breath when my lungs start to burn. I force myself to breathe—with sharp little gulps at first, then I deepen my breathing with effort. But the asshole lied. It doesn't make anything better.

I lift my head a bare inch but wish I hadn't. Jihun is about to get us bashed against the cliff face. At the last possible second—my dangling feet skimming the mountainside and sending pebbles raining—he straightens in the air and shoots toward the sky like a rocket blasting off into space.

The creepy clouds loom over us, and we head straight into them. At the speed we're flying, I expect us to pop out into the open sky within seconds, but the clouds just close in on us, growing colder and denser.

"Jihun?"

My voice is swallowed up by the dense gray clouds. No, they're more like gray water? Whatever it is, it's cold, so cold, and it's above us and under us—it surrounds us. There is no way out. The suhoshin still holds me close to his chest, but I know I'm drowning. My head spins in dizzying circles, and my eyes roll back.

"Breathe." I feel Jihun's warm breath against my ear. How is that possible? We're underwater. "Breathe, damn it."

I have to hold my breath. I'll die if I breathe. My chest lurches, and my shoulders draw back as my body convulses—like invisible defibrillators are pumping electric currents through my body. But I'm not dead. My eyes fly open against the cold burn of the gray water. I listen for my heartbeat.

"Breathe, Sunny." I feel strong arms tighten around me.

Then I hear it. *Thu-thump*. My heartbeat. *Thu-thump*. My blood pulses in my ears. I'm alive. But not for long. Not if I don't breathe. I'm terrified to open my mouth. I don't want to let the water rush into my body. *Fuck it.* I suck in a full breath . . . and sweet, sweet air fills my lungs. I take great, heaving breaths.

"There you go." I hear the relief in Jihun's words. "Just keep breathing."

The chilling lap of water recedes from my skin, and a warm breeze brushes against me. I sigh as the aching cold seeps out of my bones. I can finally breathe without effort, and my body feels like mine again. As my head clears, I realize we're out of the clouds.

Jihun still holds me tightly against him. I would never admit it, but his strength and warmth are reassuring after the ordeal with the gray water. Or was it the clouds that threatened to drown me? I'm not eager to find out.

I gaze around me. There is a clarity to everything I see, like someone outlined the world with a black Sharpie. The very air around us hums with gi—like a gong was struck in the distance and the air is shimmering with the reverberation. Brilliant stars as sharp as diamonds spill from the inky sky. And the crescent moon illuminates the night, leaving no room for darkness. And the clouds at our feet stretch on and on . . .

The clouds . . . at our . . . feet. I look down. Jihun is floating so close to the clouds that his feet seem planted on top of them. But I don't hear the rustle of his wings over his shoulders. No, he's not floating—he's *standing* on the clouds.

My eyes dart to his face, and he meets my gaze with steady calm. Without breaking eye contact, he gently sets me down *on the clouds* and takes a few steps back, like he's trying to give me space.

"Welcome to the Kingdom of Sky." Jihun bows his head with solemn formality.

Dread shivers down my spine, jolting through my shoulders and arms. *Wait.* I can move them. The binds. They're gone.

"It is one of four kingdoms in this realm," he explains.

What is he? A fucking tour guide? I don't care where I am or what he has to say. I just know he has taken me far away from Ethan . . . somewhere I know I can't reach him.

"It's where—"

My fist connects with his jaw, and he widens his stance to keep his balance. But he's ready for my jab to his kidney, and his hand wraps around my wrist. My other fist flies at his face again but meets only air. Then his hand closes around my fist and forces my arm down. I jerk my arms, trying to free myself, and draw my leg back to knee him. He twists me in his grip and yanks me until my back presses flush against his front.

"This has been diverting, but we don't have time for—" He grunts and stumbles back two steps, unable to hold on to me any longer . . . the other me.

I spin to face him and growl low in my chest, my hackles rising like daggers ready to fly. I shift low onto my haunches, preparing to launch myself at him. I force myself to face my rage—to feel the pulse of violence in my veins. I will fight for the people I care about. And I will fight for myself. My nine tails swish back and forth in anticipation. I intend to lay him out on his back, with my claws at his throat, before he so much as raises his hand to bind me again. I charge toward him in a blur and leap into the air.

I crash to the ground hard enough to make my head ring. Who knew clouds were as hard as cement? I shift to stand, but something forces me back down. Twelve seonnam soldiers surround me in a circle, tightening a silvery net over me. The soldiers are outfitted in traditional Korean armor but in a dark-blue material with pinpricks of light shimmering across it—it looks eerily like they are wearing the midnight sky.

Confused—no, terrified—I snarl, baring my sharp teeth at the seraphim soldiers, my eyes burning green. Their wings of wind rustle as they shift nervously on their feet, but they don't loosen their grips on the net.

"Captain," a deep, booming voice calls out in Korean. While the male only appears to be in his early thirties, the commanding tone alone marks him as someone powerful. But his towering stature and the way he wears his midnight armor like a second skin make him undeniably formidable. Only a fool would want him as a foe. "What is the meaning of this? Why did you bring this creature of Mountains into the Kingdom of Sky? Trespassing in the realm is punishable by death."

Creature? The slur raises shame and rage inside me, and I very much want to be the fool that calls this male my foe. I shift into my human form, and the soldiers startle enough to slacken the net. I sit up with my legs crossed in front of me, my hands lying loose and open on my knees. I cock my head to the side and stare at the powerful male until he meets my eyes. I hope the smile I offer him truly creeps him out.

"General, she seeks amnesty pursuant to the Code of the Realm." Jihun steps in before I can open my big mouth. It's the first time I hear him speak Korean. He sounds even more stern and formal. I'm annoyed that it works for him. But what the hell is he talking about? *I'm* seeking *what?*

"Amnesty?" The general's eyebrows rise. "Is that why she was trying to rip your throat out? To seek *amnesty?*"

"That was a matter of private dispute." Jihun coughs into his fist, hiding a ghost of a smile. My eyes narrow on him. Did he find our *private dispute* amusing? "Pursuant to the code, any and all beings of the Shingae may petition to join the Order of the Suhoshin."

"And they may seek amnesty in any kingdom of the realm for the duration of their training and participation in the trial," the other male finishes. "You do not need to instruct me on the code, Captain."

"Of course not, General. My apologies." Jihun stands with his hands clasped behind his back in due deference, but there is steel in his voice. "May I present to you the Suhoshin's newest recruit, Cho Mihwa."

THE SEONNYEO AND
THE PRINCE

Long ago in the days of old, a lovely seonnyeo—an angel of the heavens—and a handsome prince lived in the Realm of Four Kingdoms.

The seonnyeo was full of laughter and spirit, sometimes too much for her poor widowed father to bear. She loved her home with the sun and the moon, the clouds and the stars, all within hands' reach. But the beauty of the Kingdom of Sky was fleeting—slipping through her fingers every time she reached for it. She couldn't help but long for the majestic nature of the Kingdom of Mountains. She wanted to feel the green, vibrant life of the mirrored lakes and soaring mountains against her skin, visceral and real.

The Prince of Mountains didn't appreciate the lakes and the mountains of his home. He took the bounty of the Kingdom of Mountains and the privileges of his birth for granted. No, he did not cherish all that he had, only lamented what he lacked. Nothing was ever enough. He wished for greater wealth. He wished for untold power. He wished for a beautiful wife who could give him both. But no maiden in the Kingdom of Mountains could live up to his ideals. And with the feud between the four kingdoms, the prince could not find a wife in any other kingdom.

One day, an enchanted deer running for its life asked the prince for refuge, promising to grant him one wish in exchange. Eager with greed, the prince hid the deer from the hunter, saving its life and sealing the bargain. He then told the grateful deer that he wished to wed the daughter of the most powerful seonnam in the Kingdom of Sky.

Too late, the deer saw the endless hunger in the prince's heart, but there was no undoing the bargain. It told the prince that on the night of the fullest moon, a seonnyeo would visit the Kingdom of Mountains. She would bathe in the lake at the peak of the highest mountain. And if the prince did exactly as the deer instructed, he could claim his heart's desire.

So on the night of the fullest moon, the prince hid among the woods at the highest mountain and waited impatiently for his unwilling bride. As he grew weary of the passing hours, he vowed to hunt down the deer if its promise proved false. But deep in the night, an ethereal seonnyeo descended from the Kingdom of Sky, her wings of wind caressing the surface of the mirrored lake.

After a furtive glance around the lake, the seonnyeo quickly disrobed and entered the lake, until only her milky shoulders remained above the water. With her back to the woods, she washed herself, humming a haunting song echoed by the wind and the leaves.

Beguiled by the seonnyeo and her song, the prince watched and listened with tears raining down his cheeks. Maybe winning the seonnyeo's heart would be . . . enough. But his gnawing hunger for more shattered his fragile dream of happiness. He would never be content with her love alone. The prince wanted her family's wealth and power to bolster his own. With an angry swipe of his arm, he dried his tears and remembered what had to be done.

When the seonnyeo finished her bath and turned to come ashore, the prince stood at the edge of the water with her clothes gripped in his hands. With a horrified gasp, the seonnyeo sank deeper into the water, shielding her body with her hands and arms.

She wept and pleaded with the prince to return her clothes, but he refused again and again. The seonnyeo nearly lost all hope as she crouched, cold and shivering, in the lake, but at long last, the prince revealed his true intent.

"I will return your clothes and turn my back to allow you to dress. Your honor will remain unsullied . . . if you agree to marry me," he said.

"But are you not a being of Mountains?" She shook her head in confusion. How could he wed a being of Sky?

"I am the Prince of Mountains," he replied, a cold smile curling his lips.

In that moment, the seonnyeo understood the prince's dark nature—saw his cruel, brittle heart. But he held the honor of her family in his greedy hands, because of her foolish choices. Her beloved father would bend his knee to the prince to protect his only daughter.

"I will marry you," the seonnyeo said in an unwavering voice. She might have dishonored herself, but she would not be quelled by the prince.

She wanted to cry. She wanted to laugh. Her impulsive sojourn to the Kingdom of Mountains—her small act of rebellion, her little adventure—bound her to a bleak future she'd never dreamt possible.

CHAPTER TWENTY-TWO

I walk on my own two feet, my hands free at my sides. After Jihun's invisible binds and the soldiers' silvery net, it's a luxury I don't take for granted. I glance at Jihun for the tenth time, but he stares straight ahead as he walks beside me, his expression stoic. I want to shake him until his eyeballs rattle, but the general rides only a few yards ahead of us, looking back every few minutes. I don't want to risk being pinned down by the silvery net again.

Where am I? And when did I apply to become a suhoshin? Because I would remember if I made such a dumbass move. But I bite my tongue because Jihun's lie got me out of the net. He obviously did it to get me amnesty, but I have a feeling I won't like whatever it is I'm going to have to do. And there's no way in hell I'm joining the Order of the Suhoshin, so he better have a plan B.

Anxiety claws at my chest. Ethan is out there somewhere with a deadly assassin. I don't have time for this bullshit. I shoot another angry glare at Jihun, but chilling realization halts my thoughts. I hear Ethan's voice, hard with determination. *Where is the dark mudang?* I was too busy feeling betrayed and hurt to grasp his intent. He wanted the assassin to take him to Daeseong.

Whoever he is—whatever his powers may be—Ethan can't fight the dark mudang on his own. The sacred ashes are our only chance at stopping Daeseong. My hands tighten around the straps of my back-pack. I'm still pissed at him, but I want him safe above all else. But he'll get himself killed if I don't find him in time. I *have* to figure out how to use the sacred ashes and save Ethan.

I throw Jihun a panicked glance, and he raises an eyebrow. He can help me figure out how to use the sacred ashes against the dark mudang. We have to go back. We have to save Ethan. But I can't say any of that in front of all these strangers. I give him a curt shake of my head. *Not now.*

Later—when I get the suhoshin alone—he'll tell me everything I need to know. I'll beat the answers out of him if I have to. Or maybe even if I don't *have* to. I blow out a long, frustrated breath. What if Yellow already took Ethan to Daeseong? No, I don't believe that. The yellow assassin is a nasty piece of work. He won't take Ethan to his master so easily. There's still time.

I try to distract myself by taking in my surroundings. The clouds beneath my feet shift and swirl but are somehow solid as I walk on them. I hope I don't fall through and go splat on the mountaintop—*if* we're still above the mountain we flew over. I can't be sure. I can't be sure about a damned thing.

As we march on, surrounded by the general's soldiers, a gleaming city of pearlescent buildings with gold-tiled roofs rises in the horizon along with the sun. The soldiers' armors shift with the sky, becoming clear blue with tufts of white cloud. No matter how beautiful the sight, I want to pretend I'm dreaming and that all of this will be gone when I wake up. It's all so overwhelming—the fear of the unknown warring with the hunger to know *more.*

Is this how the humans feel when confronted with glimpses of the Shingae? Is this how Ethan felt? Or did he already know everything? Anger and concern war inside me. I miss him. I want to kick his ass. If I let myself dwell on it, my insides will burn into cinders. I clench my hands into fists at my sides. I have to focus on the now.

Drums beat in the distance, deliberate and precise. *Da-dum . . . boom. Da-dum . . . boom.* My walk of shame—whether I'm shackled or not, this definitely feels like one—takes longer than I expect, the city farther away than it first appeared. As we approach its fortified walls, the towering golden gates open without delay. The drums must've been announcing our arrival.

I recognize the architectural style of the city. It's filled with the kind of hanok buildings I saw growing up in Korea but on a much grander scale. I imagine the wealthy and the powerful lived this way even in the late 1800s, except for the part where the walls glow like moonlight and the roofs shine golden as the sun.

Seonnams and seonnyeos, male and female seraphim, walk the streets in silk hanbok in every shade of the sky, dazzling in their unearthly beauty. No, it's not just that they're beautiful. These angelic beings are literally *shining*—luminous as the moon. I sigh, too exhausted to be stunned. Whatever this place is, I wish I had my shades.

"Is everyone here seraphim?" I whisper out of the corner of my mouth. Jihun, a seonnam himself, graces me with a barely perceptible nod. I grit my teeth. "Then why aren't you lit up like them?"

His expression turns even more shuttered than usual. "I've been away for too long."

I don't know if he's talking to himself or answering my question. "What does being away have to do with anything?"

Jihun proceeds to ignore me again. I'm so annoyed I want to knock his teeth out, but I take comfort in the familiar emotion. I used to daydream regularly about punching the casino patrons in the face. I never thought I would miss my job as the tobacco wench.

The general dismounts at the gates of a grand estate and hands over the reins to one of his soldiers. As I stare wide eyed at the sprawling hanok, he says, "Captain, you cannot present her to the council in this state."

I glance down at my topless hanbok. He makes a fair point. I'm not presentable to anyone, much less the . . . *Wait.*

"What council?" I blurt out in English, then cringe and switch to Korean. "Why do I have to be presented to anyone?"

"She will have a chance to wash away her journey before I request an audience with the council." Jihun addresses the general, ignoring me yet again. I surreptitiously dig my elbow into his side, but he doesn't so much as wince.

"I presume you will petition to be her sponsor." The older male purses his lips. "Do you need a reminder as to what that entails?"

"No, General." Jihun lifts his chin. "I am fully aware of my responsibilities."

"Responsibilities to whom, I wonder?" the general muses. "I hope you do not forget where your true loyalties lie."

"Never." Jihun stands impossibly straight. "It is my true loyalties that prompt me to protect her."

"Are you two done talking about me?" I snap. "Because I'm standing right here."

"I know we have much to discuss, Lady Mihwa," Jihun interjects smoothly. "Once you have rested, I will present you to the Council of the Suhoshin. Until then . . ."

Keep your mouth shut and play along. I hear the rest of his sentence as clearly as if he'd spoken it out loud.

"Of course, *Captain* Song," I concede, coming to a decision.

A gumiho's greatest strength is her cunning. Giving in to my emotions will only cloud my judgment. I'll comply for now while I devise a plan to find the answers I need and save Ethan from his stupid self. Does he really think he can take Daeseong by himself? I swallow my worry and impatience.

Jihun nods, even as his eyes narrow in suspicion. But what is he going to do? Tell me not to agree with him?

"I trust your judgment, Captain, but tread lightly with the council on this one." The general claps him on the shoulder. "It's good to have you home, son."

"Yes, General." The captain's expression softens. "Good to be back, sir."

My brows furrow when the general remounts his horse and trots down the street with his soldiers in tow. "Where is he going? Isn't this his house?"

Jihun arches an eyebrow at me. "This is my home."

"Yours?" I blink in surprise. Do all the Suhoshin live this large? Or did Jihun inherit his wealth through a noble birth?

"Yes." Of course he doesn't elaborate.

I clench my teeth at his taciturn response and follow him into the estate. Then it's all I can do to keep my mouth from falling open. The outdoor courtyard is massive, surrounded on all sides by hanok structures with slanted gold-tiled roofs and their sweeping eaves. At least a dozen latticed hanji doors and windows face the courtyard, with a semi-open sitting room in the middle of the central building.

Four indigo floor cushions made of shimmering silk—fabric that commoners like me never even dream of *wearing*—surround a low table in the sitting room. It's the perfect spot to have tea and admire the stunning trees with gold branches and jade leaves that stand in clusters around the yard. Two archways to my left and right show that this is just one wing of the estate.

Jihun has a muted conversation with a young male, who is wearing a long white robe and a gat, a wide-brimmed hat made of black mesh. He's not dressed like a commoner, but he holds himself slightly stooped in deference to the captain.

When our eyes meet briefly, Jihun offers me a curt nod and heads toward the archway on the right without another word. I scoff in outrage and take a step to follow him, but a soft cough halts me in my tracks.

"My lady, allow me to escort you to the guest quarters," the male in white says, focusing his gaze somewhere toward my left ear.

"But . . ." I sigh. Maybe it'll be best to have this conversation with Jihun when I'm fully clothed. Ethan will be okay for a little while longer. I believe in the nasty golem's spite. I take a calming breath and force a polite smile. "Please lead the way."

Beyond the left arch, there is an open grassy yard with a walkway that leads to a detached hanok a quarter mile away. My breath hitches at the picturesque sight. The building, which I assume houses the guest quarters, is backed by a stand of bejeweled trees, while the front looks onto a rectangular lily pond surrounded by a bramble of flowers in every shade of pink.

The male stops just short of the three-tiered stone steps that lead up to the sitting area. I notice that the silk cushions here are in a shade of burnt orange. A pretty young female in a white jeogori and a light-blue skirt stands at the top of the steps, with her hands loosely clasped at her front. When her eyes alight on me, I expect to see judgment on her face for my altogether inappropriate attire, but only a soft smile curves her lips.

"Welcome to the Sunset Pavilion," she says, bowing at her waist.

When I start to bow back to her, the female startles and waves her hands in front of her. "Please, my lady. I am only a handmaiden."

When I halt midbow and straighten, she offers me a warm smile tinged with relief. Even so, I insist, "I'm not a lady."

"But you are a guest of the captain, my lady," she corrects me in a tone that brooks no argument. The female has backbone.

She glances past my shoulders and nods at the male in white. When he bows and takes his leave, she waits patiently for me to take my shoes off and join her in the sitting area. But my Converse remind me of Ethan, and I freeze on the stone steps, filled with that mix of helpless anger and worry. A soft cough snaps me out of my torment, and I finally walk up the steps.

The female leads me through sliding doors to reach the interior of the Sunset Pavilion. After a short walk down a hallway, she draws open another set of doors, leading me deeper into the building. Two younger females in matching white-and-gray hanboks stand on either side of a high wooden tub filled with steaming water.

"These two will assist you with your bath. If you need anything, please don't hesitate to call for me. My name is Miok."

After Miok closes the door behind her, one of the females—the one with a round face—gestures for me to step into the tub while they both avert their eyes. I'm grateful to them for allowing me my modesty despite the fact that I came to them topless. I unknot the tie at my chest and drop my hanbok skirt to the ground. I can't hold back a moan as I submerge my sore body into the fragrant bath.

The taller of the two females giggles softly. "There's nothing like a hot bath after a long journey."

"Tea and sweet treats make it even better," the round-faced female says with a smile as she lays a wooden plank across the tub and presents me with a veritable feast.

A soothing, sweet scent rises from the teacup. One of the attendants waves a hand over the cup, and a yellow chrysanthemum blossoms at the top. My eyes widen at the casual display of magic, then slide shut as I swallow the warm tea past my parched throat. I can get used to this kind of magic.

Once I quench my thirst, I realize I'm famished and immediately feel ashamed. Ethan is out there facing gods know what, and I want to stuff my face with food? But I need my strength if I'm going to save him. Starving myself isn't going to help anyone. Despite the logic in my thoughts, my blood pounds in my ears.

Every time I think of Ethan, I become a panicked mess, which is a problem since everything seems to remind me of him. I have to get a fucking grip. I'm no use to him without a clear head and a strong body. *I will save him. There's still time.* I breathe in and out through my nose until a steely calm settles over me.

The attendants let me eat as I soak in the tub. I savor the round pillows of white, green, and pink rice cakes filled with honey and sesame seeds, the crisp mounds of fried cookies dusted with citron rinds, and a flower-shaped dessert that's a cross between a donut and sticky toffee pudding—dense, chewy, and oozing with syrup.

Once I finish, the kind attendants get to work on scrubbing a layer of skin off me, leaving my modesty in the dust. Feeling fresh, pink, and generally floppy, I step out of the tub and let myself be wrapped in a warm towel. They quickly dress me in a simple white hanbok that feels as soft as petals against my skin.

"I don't even know your names." I glance askance at the females.

They titter and blush as though they don't get their names asked often. The taller one says, "My name is Seonah, my lady. And that's Yoonah, my younger sister."

"Nice to meet you." I smile, even though the introduction feels a bit odd coming after stripping naked in front of them. "Thank you for the bath and snacks."

"It was our pleasure." Yoonah beams at me.

"I hope you had a relaxing bath, my lady." Miok enters the bathing chamber as though she's been waiting outside the door. The sisters step back and bow to her. "Allow me to escort you to your chambers to prepare you for your audience with the council."

Shit. I'd forgotten about that part. My loose muscles tense up again, but I force a smile and say, "Of course. Lead the way."

We walk down to the opposite end of the hallway, and my hand-maiden—I can't fucking believe I have a handmaiden—slides open the double doors. When she bows and stretches her arm toward the open doorway, I take it as my cue and step into the chambers. I draw in a sharp breath, my hand fluttering to my chest as though to grab a fistful of pearls. I drop the offending hand with a grimace, even as my wide eyes continue taking in the room.

The sight of the serene pond greets me through the open windows facing the front of the pavilion. The room is elegantly furnished with a low wooden desk, a silk embroidered room divider—which I instantly *covet*—behind the desk, and an exquisite wooden dresser and armoire with brass appliqués standing against one wall. I see the room as my eighteen-year-old self would have. It's the most beautiful room I've ever seen, luxurious in its simplicity. I would take this room over a presidential suite on the Vegas Strip any day.

"Is the room to your liking?" Miok's soft voice brings me back to the present.

"I love it," I say, feeling guilty again for enjoying the comforts of this place when I don't even know if Ethan is dead or alive. *Alive.* He's alive. *I will save him. There's still time.* I hang on to that mantra like a lifeline.

"My lady?" Concern lines her forehead.

"I'm sorry." I shake my head and ask, "Am I going to see the council now?"

Miok smiles. "Not until you're ready."

"What more do I need?" I'm freshly washed and dressed in this lovely silk hanbok.

"Well, I would need to do your makeup, style your hair, and help you into your dress."

Makeup and hair—I guess I get that—but the dress? "What's wrong with this hanbok?"

"You want to meet the council in your sleepwear?" Her eyes go round.

"This is sleepwear?" My jaw drops.

A huff of laughter escapes Miok's lips before she claps her hands over her mouth. Smoothing her face into a deferential mask, she removes her hands from her mouth and says, "Forgive me, my lady."

"Don't worry about it." I give her a wry smile that she returns with a warm one of her own.

"Now"—her expression turns all-business—"let's get you prepared for an audience with the council."

She has me sit on one of those pretty floor cushions and brushes my hair with a double-sided, fine-tooth comb until it gleams. Then she braids my hair at one temple, then the other and weaves it into a three-strand braid from the base of my head all the way down my back.

Miok turns me to face a rectangular mirror she propped open on the desk and studies my face with pursed lips. "You already have such lovely skin. There isn't much we need to do in terms of makeup . . ."

She reaches for a tray lined with white rose petals and waves her hand over it in a graceful loop. The rose petals turn into a palette of various shades of pink. She picks one petal up and holds it against my cheek, then another in a different shade. Nodding in apparent satisfaction, she brushes the second petal against my skin, and my cheeks take on a rosy complexion. Then she takes the petal in the deepest pink and brushes it against my lips, turning them into the same color.

I have no words. I've never seen magic like this—for simple, practical uses. "Does . . . does everyone know how to do that?"

"Do what, my lady?" My handmaiden blinks.

"Use magic like that," I croak.

"Everyone learns minor magic suited to their station and duties," she says lightly, tidying up the tray and mirror.

I nod, letting that soak in. What kind of magic would I have learned if I grew up in this place? What really is this place? Why did my mother never mention it? She must not have known about it.

"Now for your dress." Miok can barely suppress her excitement as she pulls a hanbok from the armoire.

The jeogori is in a lovely shade of pink, similar to the petal that she applied to my cheeks. But the skirt . . . It glows and swirls with all the colors of a sunset, like they took a square of the sky at dusk and made it into a skirt. I touch the fabric, and the silk slides across my fingers like water.

Once she finishes dressing me in the breathtaking hanbok, Miok turns me to the tall floor mirror. I don't recognize the female staring back at me, soft and lovely. I don't glow like the seraphim in this realm, but I'm nevertheless beautiful.

"Now, my lady"—my handmaiden smiles broadly—"you are ready to meet the council."

CHAPTER TWENTY-THREE

I step into the sitting area of the Sunset Pavilion, smiling at something Miok said. But I falter when I find Jihun outside with his gaze on the pond. He's dressed in a navy silk robe with a gat tied neatly under his chin. He looks like a handsome nobleman from a Korean fairy tale, and my breath catches in my throat.

"My lord." Miok bows at my side.

Jihun turns toward us with his usual stoic expression, then freezes in place, his eyes going round. I would think he'd turned into a statue if it wasn't for his gaze dipping slowly down my body, then back up to my face. I want to scowl or do *something* to hide the blush rising to my cheeks, but it's hard not to be flattered by the unmistakable appreciation in his eyes.

I'm not sure if I'm relieved or disappointed when he abruptly descends the stone stairs and steps into his elegant black boots. "Come with me."

Miok hurriedly places a robe, the same color as my skirt, over my shoulders and helps me into a pair of embroidered silk slippers. I murmur a quick thanks and hasten after the long-legged male, who is already halfway to the main courtyard. I'm tempted to kick off the delicate slippers to catch up with him, but he slows down and turns to face me.

"Would you mind walking to the Celestial Palace?" he asks in English once we're alone. His eyes roam over me once more before he snaps them back to my face. "It's a few miles from here. It should give us time to speak."

"If we don't walk, then how would we get there?" I'm relieved to speak to him in English. The old-fashioned Korean and the honorifics were tripping me up. Besides, it would feel weird to use honorifics with Jihun like he's my elder or superior. But we're not close enough to speak familiarly. Yes, English is much simpler.

"We could take those." He waves at two exquisite wooden palanquins sitting near the main gates.

"Let's walk." I crinkle my nose. "I don't want to make someone carry me for miles."

"They wouldn't carry you physically." Jihun's lips twitch, as though he's tempted to smile. "They use minor magic to maneuver the palanquin."

"Fancy." Sarcasm drips from my word. "We should still walk and talk."

The male in white opens the gates for us and whispers something to Jihun. The captain's eyes narrow, and a muscle jumps in his clenched jaw. But he nods curtly at the male, then extends his arm toward the gate, with his solemn gaze on me. "After you."

I roll my eyes at Jihun but remember to thank the male in white before I step out to the street. "Who is he?"

"He's my man of business. He takes care of all my affairs." He waves an elegant hand toward his estate.

"What's his name?" I ask.

"His family name is Gim." Jihun casts a curious glance at me.

"I was getting tired of thinking of him as 'the male in white.'" I worry my bottom lip. Now that I have Jihun alone, something's holding me back from asking him about the sacred ashes. How do I know I can trust him? "Okay. Why don't we get down to business? You and the general spoke of a realm and four kingdoms, and we're in the Kingdom of Sky. Are we no longer in the same realm as Earth?"

"No. We're in the Realm of Four Kingdoms, a realm that exists across the abyss." He pauses, but I nod for him to continue. I'd figured as much and just wanted confirmation, so I don't need time to process. "Besides the Kingdom of Sky, there are the Kingdom of Mountains, Kingdom of Water, and Kingdom of Underworld."

"There's a kingdom for each source of life . . ." I think out loud, nodding slowly. The beings in this realm belong to an actual kingdom rather than just a life source. "Even the Underworld has a kingdom in this realm?"

"It *is* one of the life sources born of the Cheon'gwang, is it not?" We walk down what appears to be the busy main road. "So yes, the Kingdom of Underworld is part of the Realm of Four Kingdoms."

My mother always told me that the Shingae isn't a physical place—that it is a state of being—but here . . . it is very much an actual place. I'm *standing* in the Kingdom of Sky. Did my mother, a five-hundred-year-old gumiho, really not know about the existence of the Realm of Four Kingdoms? I give my head a sharp shake, trying to dislodge the thought. Of course she didn't know. She would never lie to me.

"This fortified city"—I sweep my hand out—"is this the entirety of the Kingdom of Sky?"

"No, we're in the capital. There are many cities and villages outside of these walls."

"Are the citizens of this kingdom free to enter any of the other kingdoms?" I study Jihun from under my lashes. The information could come in handy someday. I might need to escape to another kingdom if things go south with Jihun. "And vice versa?"

"It's like traveling between different nations in the Mortal Realm," he says with a one-shoulder shrug. "The ease of access is determined by the relationship between the kingdoms."

"If . . ." I'm distracted by a palanquin without bearers, floating past us in the streets. "If the realm we were in is the Mortal Realm, then are you saying that this is the *immortal* realm?"

"The humans and beings of the Shingae on Earth are mortal. Hence the name Mortal Realm," he explains with unexpected patience. I see no signs of him getting tired of my quick-fire questions. "But we don't refer to the Realm of Four Kingdoms as the 'immortal realm' since the Shinbiin aren't necessarily immortal."

"Shinbiin?" I try to keep track of everything he's saying, while juggling my options on how to find the answers I need to save Ethan.

"The beings of the Shingae in the Realm of Four Kingdoms are known as the Shinbiin."

"Am . . . am I a shinbiin?" I blurt out the question before I can stop myself.

"No." Jihun averts his gaze. "There are no animal spirits in this realm. That's why the general was so shocked I brought you here."

He didn't have to say it. Me and my kind aren't welcome here. A greasy feeling of shame spreads through me, but I grit my teeth against it. I'm not the one who should feel ashamed.

"And the *Shinbiin*"—I sink a world of disdain into the word—"are potentially immortal?"

"When the Shinbiin reach the age of twenty-four, the second evolution of our zodiac animal, we come into the peak of our powers." The wry arch of his eyebrow tells me that he didn't miss my disgust with his people . . . and that he doesn't blame me. "After the change, we do not know sickness and heal quickly. We also do not age, not at the mortal rate, at least. Many of us live for a thousand years."

"Like the Blessed," I breathe. *Kind of like me.* Except I stopped aging when I was eighteen, and I have no idea what my life span is. What if *I* can live a thousand years?

"Yes, the Blessed." He raises his hand, as though to rake his hand through his hair, but stops, remembering his hair is bound into a tight bun at the top of his head and covered by his gat. "That *myth* was perpetuated in the Mortal Realm to conceal the existence of the Realm of Four Kingdoms while the Suhoshin traveled between the two realms. The Blessed don't exist. Only the Shinbiin."

A . . . myth? I mouth the words, but no sound comes out.

I had it all wrong. My mother had it all wrong. But that seems to be the theme of my little field trip to this realm, doesn't it? If everything Jihun said is true, there is no such thing as the Blessed, and I'm not a shinbiin. Then what the hell do my powers make me?

"Who are you trying to hide the Realm of Four Kingdoms from? Humans or the beings of the Shingae in the Mortal Realm?" I spit out, suddenly disgusted. Jihun has the grace to look ashamed. "You don't need to answer that. It's obvious the Shinbiin want to keep the *unde-sirables* of the Shingae out of this realm. Let's move on for now. What is the council?"

"The Council of the Suhoshin is an oversight group that has to approve all major decisions relating to the order." He sounds relieved to have gotten past the whole *the Blessed is a myth* reveal. But my gut tells me that isn't even the real bombshell, and I have no idea when the real one will drop. "It's made up of five high-ranking officials from the queen's court, including General Bak."

"The general from the welcoming party?" I scoff.

"Yes." One corner of his mouth twitches, which I now recognize as his version of a smile. "General Bak and the others have to officially accept you as a suhoshin cadet before you begin your training."

"Are they going to give us trouble with that?" I ask, but Jihun doesn't answer right away. He's been honest and straightforward with me, even when he knew I wouldn't like his answers. This one must be a real stinker for him to hesitate. "Well, are they?"

"Generally, the audience is more of a formality," he says in a care-fully neutral tone. *Wait for it.* "They rarely reject any candidates, since the trial itself kills three-quarters of the cadets anyway."

"What? I thought the point of training and participating in the trial was to receive amnesty." I stop in the middle of the road and ignore the beautiful, shining faces glancing our way. "They'd only be sparing my life so I could die a wee bit later?"

"The trial only happens once a year on New Year's Day." He places a hand on my lower back, urging me to keep walking. I grudgingly comply, my head still spinning from all the information. "That's months away, so we don't need to worry about that yet."

"Sure." Or not at all, since I'll be long gone by then. "Whatever."

"If you're that excited to become a suhoshin, then I can petition to have you participate in the trial sooner."

"No, thanks." I snort. "I'd rather live."

"Suit yourself." His tone makes me think he's teasing me, and I don't stop the grin that spreads across my face.

My instinct tells me he's trustworthy. He already saved my life twice. Maybe he'll do it for a third time by giving me a fighting chance against Daeseong. He's the best option I have to save Ethan. The other options involve me dying a senseless death.

"I haven't forgiven you for kidnapping me." I side-eye him, coming to a decision. I'm going to trust him. "I'm just giving you *amnesty* from the ass kicking of your lifetime because you saved my life."

"Twice." He looks quite smug for such a stoic male. I'm beginning to think he might actually have a sense of humor.

"I don't think this second time counts, since I'm going to die in a few months anyway."

"I'm not going to let that happen," he says solemnly.

My stomach swoops to my toes, then back up, leaving my insides sloshy. The thing is . . . I believe him. I believe he'll die protecting me . . . and Ethan. So it's up to me to keep all of us alive.

"I'm going back to the Mortal Realm," I tell him. "I'm going to find Ethan. With or without your help."

"He can take care of himself," Jihun says quietly.

My breath catches in my throat. So my hunch was right. "You know who he is."

He nods once to confirm, even though it wasn't a question. "It is not my story to share."

"I didn't ask you to." Instead, I ask another question, already knowing the answer. "Does *he* know who he is?"

"Yes." Jihun's voice is calm and level, but my head rings from the single word. A part of me had still hoped . . .

It doesn't matter what I'd hoped. Ethan knows, and he kept it from me. Fresh hurt and betrayal spear through me. I bite down on my bottom lip hard enough to draw blood to hold the tears at bay. A few days spent running for our lives—and a day of naked shenanigans—don't make us mean something to each other. He doesn't owe me anything.

Even so, he stood by me like a stubborn ass when the odds were stacked up against us. I should get a chance to return the favor. But . . . something curls up inside me. His lies hurt me, but why he lied hurts more. Ethan doesn't trust me. And—if what Jihun says is true—he doesn't need me either.

But there is cold comfort in that thought. It means he'll be okay until I find him. Because I *will* find him. I don't give a flying fuck whether he *needs* me. We promised to stick together, and I intend to hold up my end of the bargain, no matter what.

"You're going back for him," I say with certainty. Jihun is somehow bound to protect Ethan. "And you're taking me with you."

"I can't help him if I have to protect you," he says grimly. "Staying here is the best way for you to help us both."

"You don't understand." I grab a fistful of his sleeve to stop him. "Ethan is going after a powerful dark mudang. We don't have much time."

"I realize that." He turns to face me. "That's why I need to go find him as soon as you're safe here."

"Do you even know who Daeseong is?" I shout, throwing up my hands.

"He is a dark mudang resurrected by the Amheuk. The one who had Benjamin Lee killed." Grief flashes past his face so quickly I almost miss it.

"Then . . ." I swallow my own grief, wondering what his meant. Did he know Ben? "Then you know that even an almighty suhoshin can't defeat him."

"I'll die trying," he vows.

"I know, and you *will* die. You'll both die if you don't help me." I pull out the colorful bokjumeoni from my sleeve and hold it up to him. "*I* can give us a fighting chance. Do you know what this is? It's the sacred ashes of an ancient cypress tree. The life force of the Seonangshin."

"You . . ." He stumbles back a half step, then reaches out a tentative hand. "How did you get that?"

"It doesn't matter." I stuff the bokjumeoni back into my sleeve. I'm not ready to let anyone touch it. And I sure as hell am not ready to talk about what I had to do—what Samshin Halmeom had to do—to get the sacred ashes. "All you have to know is that I'm the only one who has a chance of defeating Daeseong."

"Not if you don't know how to use it," he counters.

"How did you know . . ." It doesn't matter how he knows. He's right. And I *hate* that he's right, but I can't indulge in pride. The whole point of this conversation was to ask for his help. "All right then. Who can we beg, bribe, or threaten to tell us how to use the sacred ashes?"

"We're on our way to meet her now." Jihun sighs. He might as well serenade me. It's the sound of resignation. I'm going back to the Mortal Realm with him. "And if we ask nicely, she'll tell us what she knows. No drastic measures necessary."

"But where's the fun in that?" I widen my eyes innocently. He looks at me with a slight groove between his eyebrows, like he can't tell whether I'm kidding.

"Wait a minute." I grab hold of his sleeve again. "I thought we have an audience with the council."

"The council has postponed the audience," Jihun clips out, obviously displeased.

"Why?" I'm more confused than worried.

"Because they enjoy parading their power." Anger sharpens his features. "As long as they stall the audience, they can legitimately withhold granting you amnesty."

"Well, that's not very nice." I purse my lips. "Does that mean I have to watch my back? Are they going to try to off me?"

"To off you?" He looks so befuddled that I want to laugh.

"You know." I drag a finger across my neck, clicking my tongue at the end. "Kill me."

"You're not as funny as you think." Jihun presses his lips into a stern line.

"We both know I'm hella funny." I'm giddy that I'm finally making progress. We're about to get some answers. *Hold on, Ethan. I'm coming.*

"The council won't do anything rash," Jihun continues, without acknowledging my excellent sense of humor. "General Bak is my great-uncle. *Offing you* would mean declaring war against my family."

"I see the resemblance." I nod slowly. "The crotchety gene must run strong in your family."

"The postponement is just an inconvenience," Jihun says, sounding decidedly crotchety. "But until you are officially accepted as a cadet, you cannot leave the Kingdom of Sky."

"What?" I blurt, my bubble of happiness bursting. "For how long?"

"It wouldn't make sense to delay the audience for longer than a few days." His distaste for the council's games is palpable. "If they hold off much longer, their power display would become redundant."

"Sure," I drawl, my voice as dry as a well-done steak. "It's okay for them to be dicks, but they wouldn't want to be *redundant*."

The corners of his mouth quiver. "We'll just have to make good use of our time until then."

HIS ROYAL GUARD

I sense the danger even before I feel the breeze from the open door. My brother is coming later in the evening, but this isn't him. Thank gods it isn't him. He has less than two weeks until his coming of age—the time I've been desperately waiting for . . . the time he'll become powerful enough to fulfill his destiny.

It would be easy to dodge the dagger. Even outside the Realm of Four Kingdoms, I remain a shinbiin with strength and speed unknown to humankind. But that is exactly why I do not move away from my desk. The undead isn't here for me or my brother.

He approaches me as though I'm human, not bothering to stay silent or hidden. My magic fights to flare, but I bury it deep inside me. The assassin doesn't know who I am. He doesn't know who I serve. And it has to remain that way.

I continue flipping through my folder, then stack it neatly on top of my other files rather than locking it away in my drawer. He will find her. She will help him. My friend . . . my love . . . the beautiful, broken female, who is good and kind to her core.

My heart clenches in my chest. I do not fear death. I would lay down my life for my brother a thousand times if I could. I only mourn the fact that I will not be able to witness his ascent. But enough selfish indulgence. My duty is not to bask in his triumph but to protect him until he comes into his power. Only two weeks left . . . This final act is the best way I can serve him.

"Do not do this," my bonded brother speaks in my mind, his words a desperate plea. "Find another way."

"There is no other way," I tell him. "I can die with my eyes closed, knowing you will be there for him."

"NO."

The dagger flies through the air and nicks my ear. It feels as light as wind brushing past my head, but I know it's enough to kill me. Not as quickly as I have to pretend for the ruse to work, but quickly enough. I stagger to my feet and stumble to the front of my desk. I let my limbs go limp, crumple to the floor, and slow my breathing.

Evil chimes through the assassin's soft chuckle. "Come out and play, little fox."

With a chill, I realize my mistake. Fixated on keeping my brother hidden, I didn't consider why the undead came here. There wasn't enough time to think about anything else but protecting him. Now he is going to lead the assassin straight to her.

I know the moment I'm alone. I force open my eyes and try to push myself off the floor, but I'm too weak. The poison is working faster than I'd anticipated. Everything will be all right. They will take care of each other. My brother would've been pushed into the Shingae in two weeks' time no matter what. This way, he won't be alone when it happens. And she won't have to be alone anymore either.

"You are now his royal guard," I speak through the bond. "Protect him."

My bonded brother is quiet on the other end. I feel a flash of panic, but his solemn vow fills my mind. "With my life."

I float in and out of consciousness. I'm jerked awake when someone pulls me into their arms. My brother. I want to say, *Don't be sad, Little Brother.* But I don't have the strength. I only have enough strength left to tell him . . . tell him what? It's crucial . . .

"Forgive me, Your Highness. I can no longer serve you." I focus my gaze on his beloved face one last time before darkness edges in. "Break . . . the stone. You must break the stone . . . of tears."

It's time to join my mother and father. I protected him with my life as they protected him with theirs. We have served him well. That is all that matters.

CHAPTER
TWENTY-FOUR

Jihun leads the way to a bustling outdoor restaurant with a large raised platform underneath a sloping thatched roof. A crowd of people sit cross-legged on the platform, eating bowls of hearty soup with rice, stooped over low tables.

"You expect to find someone who knows about the sacred ashes at a jumak?" I gape at him.

"What's wrong with a jumak? They serve the best gukbap here." When my eyes narrow, he relents and says, "And the person I want you to meet usually has lunch here."

We circle the platform until Jihun approaches a seonnyeo drinking soup straight from a heavy earthen bowl.

"I knew I would find you here," Jihun says amiably. He must know her well.

The female seraph thumps the bowl down onto the table and loudly scrapes up the few remaining grains of rice with her metal spoon. She doesn't look up to acknowledge us, but Jihun sits down across from her and motions for me to take a seat. Then he waves down the owner as she bustles by with a stack of empty soup bowls.

"Jumo, we'll have two gukbap," he says.

"Right away, my lord." She bows and rushes off.

"What do you know about the sacred ashes, Minju?" he asks without delay.

The seonnyeo pushes her empty bowl away and finally meets Jihun's eyes. "They're extremely rare, to the point of being mythical."

He lowers his voice. "What if I told you someone obtained the sacred ashes?"

"And lives to tell the story?" Her big owlish eyes glitter with sudden focus. "I would say that's fascinating."

The seonnyeo is wearing a fine silk hanbok, but her skirt is hopelessly rumpled, and splotches of black ink stain the sleeves of her jeogori. And strands of hair have come loose from her untidy braid and hang down by her face. But even her disheveled appearance can't dampen her exquisite beauty.

I lean toward Jihun and whisper, "*This* is the person we're looking for?"

"What better person to ask than the Kingdom of Sky's foremost scholar of arcane magic and a historian of the Order of the Suhoshin?" Jihun arches an amused brow at my surprise. "Minju, this is Sunny. She has some questions for you."

A half hour conversation proves that Minju is whip smart and passionate about her work, beneath her sloppy appearance and distracted air. Unfortunately, she has more questions than answers for me at the moment.

"I'm sorry I can't be more help," she says with genuine regret. "But I promise to devote all my waking hours to finding you answers."

"Thank you, Minju." I offer her a wavering smile. Another dead end. I don't know what else to do. I fight against the hopelessness that threatens to drown me.

"I appreciate your help." Jihun nods at the historian. "Please update us as soon as you find anything."

Minju sits up straight with a gasp. "What if . . ."

"What if what?" I grip the edge of the table.

"What if we look into other ways to defend against the Amheuk?" she whispers.

"There are other ways?" A small part of me thinks, *I got the sacred ashes for nothing?* But really, I'll take anything I can get at this point.

"There's the Yeoiju . . ." The historian bites her lip.

"The Yeoiju isn't real . . ." A nervous laugh bubbles up my throat until I see that she's serious. "Are you saying the pearl of enlightenment really exists?"

"What did you call it?" Minju's gaze sharpens on me. "Who told you the Yeoiju is the pearl of enlightenment?"

"My mother . . ." I shake my head. "Why does it matter?"

"Not many people know about that facet of the Yeoiju." She taps her fingers on the table as though she's keeping time with a song in her mind. "The Yeoiju is many things, but at its core, it's the last of the Cheon'gwang—the true light."

"Why take the long way around when we already possess the sacred ashes?" Jihun interrupts, with a frown between his brows. "Even if the Yeoiju could be used to defeat Daeseong, no one knows where it—"

"*Who* it is," the historian corrects.

"The Yeoiju is a person?" I breathe.

"Not exactly, but . . ." She stares at me until I squirm.

"But coming back to the point, we don't have the Yeoiju. We have the sacred ashes." Jihun crosses his arms. "We need to focus on what we have to stop the dark mudang."

"Hmm." The historian drops some coins onto the table and rises to her feet, her mind already elsewhere. With a preoccupied wave, she hurries away, muttering under her breath.

I watch her disappear into the crowd, and I slump with disappointment.

"She'll find something soon." Jihun gives my arm a squeeze before quickly withdrawing his hand. "We still have time. He is stronger than you think."

I'm too disheartened to snap at him that I can't know what to think because I don't know who Ethan is. I just nod listlessly and take a bite of rice soaked in rich broth. "At least the gukbap's good."

"I'm glad you approve." Wry remark delivered, he gives his full attention to his gukbap and wolfs it down like he hasn't eaten in days.

Maybe he *hasn't* eaten in days, since he was busy tracking me and Ethan. And he nearly died less than a day ago saving my life. I watch him from beneath my lashes. The damned male even inhales his food with elegance. I should cut the guy some slack, but I don't know how to tell him that I don't want to kick his ass anymore. So with my nose to the bowl, I shovel rice and soup into my mouth instead.

I hear a faint cough beside me, but my eyelids are too heavy to lift. At Jihun's insistence, I came to my room to rest. I fell into a restless sleep after hours of tossing and turning, only to encounter endless nightmares. A hand gently shakes my shoulder.

"Ethan!" I sit up on my sleeping mat with a startled gasp. "What is it? What's happening?"

"Nothing, my lady." Miok wrings her hands. "I'm sorry I woke you, but you slept through the afternoon, and I wanted to make sure you had dinner before you retired for the night."

I press my hand against my forehead and breathe to calm my pounding heart. "You don't need to apologize, Miok. Thank you for taking care of me."

"Of course, my lady." Smiling shyly, she pours a cup of warm tea and sets it on a round wooden platter by my side. "I'll have the sisters bring in your dinner in a moment."

I obediently take the tea from the platter and sip on it. When Seonah and Yoonah bring in a table laden with food, I eat without protest. I cried myself to sleep after I came back to the Sunset Pavilion. It's like my body wanted to expel all the tears I'd kept pent up inside for the last hundred-some years. But I'm done with crying. I need to stay strong and alert. So I'll eat, sleep, and exist until I can return to the Mortal Realm and save Ethan from Daeseong.

After they clear away the table, I open my window and stare out into the courtyard. It's dark out, but the moon and the stars shine brightly enough for me to admire the lovely pond. Lost in my thoughts, I don't see Jihun until he stands directly in my line of vision and waves a hand at me. I stop myself from waving back like an idiot. He's not waving hello. He's beckoning me to him.

I walk out to the courtyard to meet him, smoothing out the skirt of my sunset hanbok. I fell asleep in it, but even wrinkled, it's still the most beautiful thing I've ever worn. Jihun watches my progress with a hooded gaze, and I stop a few steps away from him.

"What?" I sound a tad rude, but he doesn't blink an eye.

"I didn't want to anger you by not inviting you to our team meeting," he says mildly.

I scoff. "I'm not easy to anger."

He looks at me with astonishment and I give him the bird. With one of his almost smiles, he cocks his head toward the archway. "Come."

I follow him to the other side of the estate, which is just as beautiful as the guest quarters but with less pink all around. He leads me inside what looks like a study and . . . there are modern office chairs lining the long conference table in the middle of the room. I round on him with wide eyes. He just shrugs his broad shoulders.

"I spend a great deal of time in the Mortal Realm," he says, taking a seat at the table. "I've grown accustomed to some of their ways."

"Don't tell me you have a bed in your room." I love my traditional room in the Sunset Pavilion, but I miss sleeping in a bed.

"Interesting." He tilts his head to the side. "Is there any particular reason you're curious about my bed?"

My eyes narrow into murderous slits. "I preferred it when you barely spoke a word to me."

"Seriously?" A tall, willowy female with luscious waves falling to her waist steps out from behind a bookshelf. She might as well have walked off the pages of a fashion magazine. Wearing a dove gray off-the-shoulder top and designer jeans that look spray-painted on her, she's the most stunning female I've ever seen. "He pulled that dark brooding act on you?"

"An act?" Jihun sputters.

"Hey, where d'you get those jeans?" Of all the things I could've asked, that's what pops out of my mouth.

"Gods, I don't remember." She blows a raspberry with her Cupid's bow lips. "At some mall in the Mortal Realm? They were on sale. You like 'em?"

"Yeah, I do." I clear my throat and belatedly register that the female is speaking English. "I . . . um, was mostly surprised to see mortal clothes in this realm. I'm not used to dressing like . . . this."

"Well, I think you look lovely." She winks at me. "Like a proper assi."

"A noble maiden?" I snort. "Hardly."

"But I can hook you up with some mortal clothes," the female says. "They're pretty simple for our seamstresses to make. They just aren't very popular here."

Jihun sighs from his seat, rubbing his forehead. "First Lieutenant Gim, meet Lady Cho."

"So formal." She crinkles her nose, then sticks out her hand. "Call me Hailey."

"Sunny," I say, shaking her hand. My grin falters, and goose bumps spread across my arms as her chilling gi brushes against me—gi born of grief. She's a being of Underworld. "You . . . you're a jeoseungsaja?"

"A.k.a. Grim Reaper, Death, or as people often call me, 'Oh, no. Please not you.' But yeah, I have the power to escort the dead to the Kingdom of Underworld."

Despite the turbulent nature of her life force, I like this female. "That's so badass."

"I like her," she says to Jihun, echoing my thoughts.

"If you two are finished, I thought we might talk about some pressing matters." He levels a stern gaze on us.

"Like how one uses the sacred ashes to take down a demented mudang resurrected by the Amheuk?" Hailey quips, not fazed in the least.

I reach into the sleeve of my hanbok and touch the bokjumeoni to make sure it's still there. "So you're up to speed on that shitshow?"

"Oh, yeah. We're the shitshow specialists," she says, sitting down across from Jihun. I take a seat next to him. "Minju is obsessively going through every scroll she could find on the sacred ashes as we speak."

"How is she doing?" Jihun asks, concern lining his face.

"She's so hyperfocused on the research that she won't even talk." Hailey sighs. Minju must have a tendency to fall down the rabbit hole, worrying her teammates. "I'll check back on her when we're done here to make sure she eats something. There's not much I can do about her not sleeping, though."

"Thank you for looking in on her." Jihun steeples his fingers. "How long do you think she'll need?"

"Who knows?" Hailey spreads her hands. "Let's just say that there are *a lot* of scrolls piled around her."

"We should take bets. I put my money on two weeks." A sharp-faced male in black leather pants and a white collared shirt, unbuttoned nearly halfway down his chest, swaggers into the study. I shiver as his shadowy gi brushes past me. He's a dokkaebi, another being of Underworld.

"Report, Second Lieutenant Cha," Jihun commands.

The second lieutenant sends Hailey a wary glance. "Has he been like this the whole time?"

"I'm afraid so," she says, cringing. "Sunny, this is Jaeseok."

"Well, hello there," the goblin drawls, taking me in with a hooded glance. *Holy shit.* He oozes enough sex appeal to make me want to fan my face. Maybe I've finally hit my sexual peak at age one hundred thirty-two.

I clear my throat. "Hi."

Jihun tsks impatiently. "Any luck tracking down Daeseong's location?"

"None whatsoever." Jaeseok pouts as he drapes himself into a chair next to Hailey. "I haven't even been able to flush out the creep in the yellow unitard."

I dart a glance at Jihun. "But Ethan . . ."

"Focus on the assassin." He keeps his gaze trained on Jaeseok. "He's our best bet for now."

I understand his strategy. If they find the yellow assassin, they'll find Ethan. Unless Ethan already killed Yellow and is facing off with Daeseong alone . . . *Stop it, Sunny.* These guys are the Suhoshin. They'll find Ethan before the dingus gets himself killed.

"Aye-aye, Captain," Jaeseok says with a jaunty salute. Then he turns to me with a lazy smile that raises the temperature in the room. "So tell me, Sunny. Where have you been hiding all my life?"

I fight to hold back a giggle. I would've had to kill everyone in the room if that giggle escaped. Instead, I arch an eyebrow and look down my nose at the sexy dokkaebi. "Far, far away, where your cheesy pickup lines would never reach me."

"Ouch." Jaeseok grabs his chest like he's been wounded, but he's grinning from ear to ear. He turns to Hailey and says, "I like her."

"I know," she squeals. "She'll fit right in."

I fidget in my seat, not knowing what to do with their ready acceptance of me.

"Captain." Minju bursts into the study, out of breath.

Jaeseok shoots to his feet and gapes at the historian, his smooth confidence nowhere in sight. "Min . . . Minju. Hey . . . hi."

Minju passes him with a mumbled hello and comes to stand in front of Jihun. "Captain, I need access to the imperial library. I've exhausted our resources at the headquarters' library."

"Have you found a lead?" He rises to his feet.

"I can't say yet." Her eyes flit to mine, then away. "I think I might have found one, but I need to confirm something first."

"Right now?" Jihun glances warily out at the night sky. "The palace will be locking down soon."

"*Now*," Minju says. "It's important."

"I agree." My pulse picks up. "If she's close to something, she should keep searching."

Every day the answer eludes us is another day spent away from the Mortal Realm. Away from Ethan. I don't even remember why I was angry with him. It all seems like a misunderstanding a long conversation could solve. I just want to be with him. *We're coming. Please stay safe until then.*

Jihun frowns but summons a brush and black ink with a flick of his fingers. The historian hovers next to him, peering over his shoulders.

"Come on, Minju." Hailey tugs her down into an empty seat beside her. She takes a small bundle from her bag and unwraps a handkerchief, revealing pieces of sweet rice cakes. She picks one up and holds it in front of the other female's mouth. "Eat."

The historian's eyes don't stray from the letter granting her access to the imperial library, but she obediently opens her mouth and eats the rice cake. When she's done, she opens her mouth again, and Hailey pops in another one. Jaeseok watches the oddly sweet scene with intense concentration, his lips softly parted.

When Jihun finishes the letter and stamps his insignia on it, Minju jumps to her feet and grabs the paper out of his hand. She takes a step toward the door but turns back abruptly.

"Hailey, those rice cakes are really good," she mumbles, a blush spreading across the bridge of her nose. "You should get some for Sunny."

Before any of us can say anything, the historian rushes out the door and into the night. Hailey and Jaeseok—and even Jihun—share wide-eyed glances, then they all turn to stare at me.

"I guess Minju likes her, too," Hailey says with something like wonder.

"*I* like rice cakes," Jaeseok mutters. *"Hey, you should get some rice cakes for Jaeseok too. He's such a cool guy."*

"Here." Jihun grabs the last of the rice cakes and tosses it to the other male. "Here's your rice cake."

Jaeseok ducks his head to catch it in his mouth and chews sullenly. "Thanks."

Hailey and Jihun burst out laughing, and I can't help joining in. Life is a dumpster fire, but these guys are . . . all right.

CHAPTER
TWENTY-FIVE

"We could've gone back to the Mortal Realm days ago if it weren't for those dickheads," I seethe.

I should be relieved the council finally scheduled an audience for us, but I can't get past my frustration that they kept me from Ethan for this long. What if he's hurt? Or worse? I inhale through my nose until my chest expands. *Come on, Yellow. Be the spiteful asshole you're meant to be.* I exhale slowly through my mouth. *I will find him. There's still time.*

"That's not necessarily true, although I tend to agree with your assessment of the council—my great-uncle excepted. Minju needed time to research the sacred ashes," Jihun says, annoying me with his logic. "Speaking of which, Hailey said she might have found something at the imperial library. We'll talk to them after the audience."

Busy muttering under my breath, I don't notice Jihun stop and walk right past him. He shoots out a hand to grab my arm and tugs me back to his side.

"We're here," he says.

Here is apparently the Celestial Palace. I was so worried about Ethan that I didn't even notice we'd arrived. The palace's enormous gates are flanked by two soldiers with long, menacing spears. When we step toward them, they extend their spears to form a giant *X* across the gates. Jihun withdraws an emblem of glowing white stone from his sleeve and holds it up to the guards. They click their heels and pull back their spears, then the gates open for us.

If Jihun's opulent estate is Disneyland, then the palace is Disney World. My eyes bug out as he takes assured steps onto the palace grounds. It's basically a walled city reminiscent of the Vatican, with miles and miles of land filled with stunning hanok structures of all shapes and sizes and scenic greenery.

All this—the Realm of Four Kingdoms, the Kingdom of Sky, the Celestial Palace, the Council of the Suhoshin, the *Shinbiin*—all of it is intimidating. *I* am intimidated. I don't like how little prepared I am for any of it. Like there's a gaping hole in my education. In my mother's teachings.

"Is there anything I should know before we go in?" I ask when we stop in front of a stand-alone hanok with sentries by the stairs.

"Just follow my lead, and let me do the talking." He holds my gaze, obviously trying to impart the importance of my cooperation.

"Consider it done." I smirk with forced confidence. I might be intimidated, but that doesn't mean I'm going to let anyone see it.

Despite the hanji windows lining the walls, the meeting hall is dark and somber. Maybe it's because of the air of the five men sitting at the long table facing us. General Bak and a male to his left look to be the oldest—around thirtysomething in human years. The rest appear to be in their late twenties, a few years older than Jihun. But the expressions on their faces make them all look like grumpy old men.

When Jihun bows from the waist, I *follow his lead* and bow as well. I straighten to find five sets of curmudgeonly eyes on me. I lower my eyes to my hands clasped in front of me, resisting the urge to glare right back at them.

"My lords, have any of you ever seen a gumiho before? She certainly is as enticing as they are rumored to be," one of the younger males says, an avaricious lilt in his voice. My head snaps up as a cold shudder slithers down my back. Jihun stiffens next to me.

"Yes, Lord Gweon," the male to the general's left answers in a booming, self-important voice. "It's been over five hundred years, but I have seen her kind before. As you say, they are alluring."

Five hundred years? I haven't fully processed that the Shinbiin are immortal for all points and purposes. I'd believed that the gods blessed the Suhoshin with near immortality because they risked their lives upholding justice in the worlds. But these males? What did they do to deserve immortality? What did any of the Shinbiin do to deserve it?

"There are reasons why *creatures* like her are not allowed into the Realm of Four Kingdoms." One of the males sneers, not bothering to hide his disgust. "She might be using her vile magic on us now."

I bite my cheeks to keep my fury in check. Jihun stretches his finger to brush the back of my hand.

"Lord Choe," General Bak interjects with a disapproving frown. "I believe only Lord Nam and I are old enough to remember the true reasons."

"May I propose we save this fascinating conversation for another time and proceed with the audience?" A pretty-faced male waves a graceful hand and nods at Jihun. "Captain Song, please introduce the applicant to the council."

"Thank you, Lord Yoon." Jihun straightens to his full height, linking his hands behind his back. "This is Cho Mihwa. She seeks permission to participate in next year's trial. She is a gumiho of extraordinary strength and powers. I believe she will be an asset to the Order of the Suhoshin."

I sneak a sideways glance at him. *Extraordinary strength and powers?*

"This is unheard of," Lord Choe says with an ugly snarl.

"It *is* rather unusual." Lord Gweon turns his creepy gaze on me again.

"The rarity of the situation does not make it unlawful. The Code of the Realm is clear on the subject," General Bak says. "*Any and all* beings of the Shingae may apply to join the Order of the Suhoshin. We have no lawful basis to deny the application."

Lord Nam shoots the general a disgruntled frown. "But how do we know she is trustworthy?"

"I petition to be her sponsor, my lords." Jihun doesn't seem the least bit cowed by the blustering officials in the room. "Now the question becomes whether the council trusts *me*."

"You risk a great deal." Lord Yoon cocks his head to the side like a curious bird.

"Maybe the young captain finds the risk worth his while." A lewd smile crosses Lord Gweon's face.

"No one here would dare question Captain Song's loyalty," General Bak says with steely authority. "If he trusts this female enough to sponsor her, we have no reason to keep her from participating in the next trial."

Lord Choe grumbles under his breath while Lord Gweon shrugs, neither of them raising an objection. The older male, Lord Nam, harrumphs and crosses his arms like a petulant child but says nothing.

"Well, this is going to be interesting," Lord Yoon murmurs as he gets to his feet. "If we are all in agreement to grant Captain Song's petition for sponsorship and Cho Mihwa's application to participate in the trial, I think I will take my leave."

"Both requests are hereby granted," General Bak declares. "You are dismissed, Captain."

"Thank you, my lords." Jihun bows, so I mimic him once more and follow him out the door.

We walk down the path that leads back to the gates. As awe inspiring as it is, I don't want to spend a single unnecessary second on the palace grounds. Something about the place feels sinister.

"Lord Choe is an idiot. Lord Gweon is creepy as hell. I would *not* want to run into him in a dark alley. Lord Nam vacillates between bragging and worrying but mostly only cares about his reputation." I tick them off my fingers one by one when the meeting hall is far enough behind us. "And Lord Yoon will go whichever way that benefits him. I don't trust him one bit. Our only clear ally is General Bak."

"You deduced all that from one meeting?" Jihun tilts his head and gives me an appraising look. "Impressive."

I clamp down on the urge to be flattered by his compliment. "What are you risking by sponsoring me?"

"Not much, I hope." His expression gives nothing away.

"Ugh," I groan in frustration. "Enough with these cryptic non-answers. What does sponsoring me entail?"

"I have in essence pledged myself to be your proxy for any infractions you might commit," he says, like he does this every day. "If you break a law of this kingdom, I will pay the price."

I spin on him, coming to a halt. "You what?"

"I don't see an issue." He presses a warm hand against my lower back, and I begrudgingly start moving down the path again. His hand lingers on my back for a few more steps. "You're not planning on breaking any laws, are you?"

"I don't know, *Captain*." I'm being a snotty brat, but I'm not sure how I feel about him sponsoring me. I already owe him so much. "Are there any laws *begging* to be broken?"

"Only a few." His lips twitch for a second.

I give him a shit-eating grin. "I'll be sure to get to them when I find some free time."

◆ ◆ ◆

Hailey is already in Jihun's study when we arrive. "How did the audience go?"

"They're a bunch of pompous assholes." I wiggle into my usual seat, then smooth out the beautiful hanbok skirt, the color of the sky moments before sunset. I can't believe I had to dress up for that circus show.

"It went well then?" she quips.

"*Well* isn't the word I'd use, but we got what we needed." Jihun drags a hand down his face. "What has Minju uncovered?"

"So we all know that the legendary Gwangdo, the only known weapon against the Amheuk, is very much lost," she begins.

"But?" He arches an eyebrow.

"*But* Minju found some obscure references about a way to forge another sword of light with the sacred ashes . . ." Hailey sighs. "And dragon scales."

"Is that supposed to be a joke?" I don't know whether to laugh or cry. Dragons are fantasy bullshit made up by humans.

"Might as well be." She shakes her head. "Yongwang, the Dragon King, has been asleep for more than a century."

"Yongwang, the god of Water, is a dragon?" My voice rises with every word.

"You know *yong* means *dragon* in Korean, right?" Hailey gives me a wary glance.

"Yes, but I thought it was just a badass name." I don't care how clueless I sound. "I didn't know it was an actual *description* of the god."

"But there are lesser dragons in the Mortal Realm," Jihun says, as though I'm not losing my shit over the whole dragon thing. "The dragon spirits."

"The dragon spirits?" I clap a hand over my mouth.

I have to stop freaking out. It shouldn't come as a complete shock that there are dragon spirits when I'm a fox spirit. There are bear spirits and tiger spirits, too, so why not dragon spirits? *Because dragons aren't fucking real.* I blow out a long breath. I didn't even know about the existence of the Realm of Four Kingdoms. There's a good chance I know nothing.

"*Theoretically*, there are." Hailey crosses her arms, worrying her bottom lip. "But we don't know the location of a single one."

"We *didn't* know." Jaeseok saunters into the study with a wink at me. I grin at him before I can stop myself.

An impatient grunt emanates from Jihun's direction. "What do you mean we *didn't* know?"

"It means I've located a dragon spirit. No, let me rephrase that." Jaeseok twirls his fingers like he's reeling his words back. "My super secret informant reported that *she* located a dragon spirit."

"Where?" Jihun snaps, barely hanging on to his patience.

"Where else?" Jaeseok smirks. "Heaven Lake."

"In Mount Baekdu?" Hailey's eyes grow impossibly wide, then a gleeful smile spreads across her face. "That's sick."

"You mean there really is a monster in the Cheonji?" I sputter. Like the Loch Ness Monster in Scotland, there is lore in Asia—human lore—that speaks of a monster in the depths of Heaven Lake.

"I don't think the dragon spirit will take kindly to being called a monster." Jaeseok pauses to grin with relish. "But yes. The Cheonji Monster is *real*."

"Ooooh." Hailey claps in delight. As shocked as I am, I have to agree with her sentiment. It's pretty fucking cool.

"We can't be sure until we confirm it for ourselves." Jihun taps his fingers on the table, predictably unimpressed by the wonders of the worlds. "We'll send a reconnaissance crew—"

"I'll be your reconnaissance crew." I push back from the table. I'm one step closer to saving Ethan from certain death. "If the dragon spirit is there, we can't waste time waiting for your crew to come back and report on their findings. We need to get those scales and forge a sword of light right away."

"A crew by definition has more than one person." Hailey glances at Jihun. "I'll go with her."

"I guess I'll have to come along too." Jaeseok peers at his nails. "My informant won't speak to anyone but me."

Jihun's sigh is heavy enough to sink the floor. "It looks like we're all going."

I stare at the three suhoshins with bewildered eyes. "Why are you guys helping me?"

"I think it's been established that we all like you, Sunny," Hailey says, and damn it, I feel warm and fuzzy all over. "Besides, it's our sworn duty to protect the realms. That includes bringing down Daeseong."

"Among other duties," Jaeseok murmurs.

Jihun cuts him a warning glance. "We'll meet back here in thirty minutes."

"No, we leave now." My tone brooks no argument.

"Are you sure you want to return to the Mortal Realm dressed like that?" Jihun argues with a swooping wave of his hand, encompassing my fancy hanbok.

I look down at myself and curse. I can't even run dressed in a hanbok, much less throw down with a dragon spirit.

"Come on, Sunny." Hailey cocks her head toward the doors. "Let's get you some sensible clothes."

"Thank gods." I follow with hurried steps to keep up with the taller female.

"Thirty minutes," Jihun calls after us.

"What does he think we're going to do? Paint our nails?" I roll my eyes. "Is he always this insufferable?"

"Pretty much," Hailey quips, but she quickly sobers. "And he's worried."

"About what?"

"Daeseong's resurrection is a headache we didn't anticipate. It's thrown a wrench into some long-awaited plans." Hailey gives me a sheepish glance. "Sorry I can't be more specific."

"Right. It's not your story to tell," I say sullenly. She doesn't understand the level of devastation the dark mudang will rain down on the worlds. Their secret plans will become moot if we can't stop Daeseong. But none of this is her fault. "Anyway, how do you guys speak English so well?"

"The suhoshins assigned to the Mortal Realm speak at least four languages. We never know where our cases will take us." She smirks. "I, for example, speak Korean, English, Mandarin, and Spanish."

"Impressive." I hike up my skirt so I don't trip over it. "Are most suhoshins based in the Kingdom of Sky?"

"The order is headquartered here, but there are bases in all four kingdoms and smaller outposts spread throughout the Mortal Realm."

"Why aren't you stationed in Underworld?" I glance sideways at her.

"I didn't have a choice," she says without rancor. "The idea is to assign everyone from Sky, Water, Mountains, and Underworld evenly throughout the kingdoms to build camaraderie among all of us. They want to drive home the fact that we no longer belong to a single kingdom but to the order."

"What if you're not a shinbiin?" I ask before I can stop myself.

"None of us are Shinbiin anymore." Hailey stops and turns to me, quiet understanding in her gaze. "We are the Suhoshin."

I belatedly notice that we've walked back to the Sunset Pavilion. "Are you staying here too?"

"Nope." She grins. "We're just here to borrow the moon."

Before I can respond, she grabs my hand and steps into the moon reflected on the surface of the lily pond. The abyss barely brushes past me when I find myself standing in front of a different hanok.

"How did you do that?" I spin around in a circle. "I don't see any bodies of water here."

Hailey blinks at me in surprise and points to a bowl of water on a small low-legged table in the courtyard. "You don't need a *body* of water. A bowl of it works just fine. Did you not travel this way in the Mortal Realm?"

"I . . ." I don't know how to explain that I hid from my magic— from my identity—for more than a century. I'm not sure how much Jihun knows about me. I don't know how much he shared. "I didn't even know I could moon shift until recently."

"The captain mentioned that you distanced yourself from the Shingae for a long time." Hailey shakes off the forlorn mood. "Well, you're going to have a lot of fun catching up on all the magic you've been missing out on. For the time being, let's get you some practical clothes."

We kick off our shoes and step into a room at the front of the hanok. Hailey throws up a globe of light and walks to an armoire. The room's smaller than mine at the Sunset Pavilion, but it's warm and welcoming.

"I bet black is your color." After rummaging around, she pulls out a pair of black jeans and a black tank top.

"I can work with dark gray if I have to." I grin, taking the clothes from her.

"Those jeans hit a couple of inches above my ankles, so they should fit you okay." She taps her finger on her lips. "And that tank top has built-in support, so you should be fine without a bra."

"Good to know." When Hailey busies herself searching through the dresser, I quickly take my hanbok off and shimmy into the borrowed clothes. The pants bunch a bit at the ankles, but they'll do. "Thanks."

"No worries." She scrunches her mouth to the side. "But I don't think I have any shoes for you."

"That's okay. I have my Converse at the Sunset Pavilion." I hold up my bokjumeoni. "And I need to grab my backpack to put this in."

"All right. Let's get out of here."

We head back out and sit on the stone steps to pull on our shoes. My eyes are drawn to the bowl of water in the courtyard, and I feel a wistful tug in my chest. There's so much I don't know.

When we walk over to the bowl, Hailey takes my hand in hers, then glances at me. "Hey, you want to have a go at this?"

"Moon shift?" I hate how hesitant I sound. I don't have an excuse not to use my magic anymore. "Sure."

I tighten my grip around Hailey's hand and dip my other hand into the water bowl. The abyss sucks me in fast enough to make my head snap back, and I tumble around in countless loops. *Hailey.* As though she heard my panicked thought, she squeezes my hand, letting me know I haven't lost her. Calming my lurching heart, I focus on the Sunset Pavilion, and we stagger onto solid ground by the pond.

"Sorry," I gasp.

"That's okay. It takes a little practice." Hailey shrugs. "At least you got us to the right place."

"Thank gods for that." I jog up the steps to the pavilion. "I'll be right back."

My room is already filled with the warm glow of candlelight—I probably have Miok to thank for that—and I feel a flash of disappointment that I have to leave so soon. Shaking off the indulgent thought, I grab my backpack from inside the armoire, where I'd stashed it earlier.

As I straighten, someone bolts out of the shadows from the other side of the room—so fast that I don't even have time to scream before a blade is buried in my heart, the hilt sticking out of my chest.

A wet gurgle climbs up my throat when I see who is holding the dagger. I open and close my mouth, blood dribbling down my chin. "Y . . . you . . ."

Minju presses her index finger against her lips but rushes to catch me under the arms when my legs buckle beneath me. The historian is surprisingly strong and easily lowers me to the ground, leaning my back against the armoire. She whispers close to my ear, "I'm so sorry, but this is the only way I can know for sure."

I cough and spurt some blood onto her face. She doesn't bother wiping it off as she stares intently into my eyes, holding a small orb of light afloat on her palm. She's muttering under her breath—it sounds like she's counting.

"All right." With a nod, she lifts my right hand, gripping my wrist. She shakes it in front of my face as though to remind me that I possess the appendage. "I'm going to pull the dagger out now. I need you to press your hand on the wound as quickly and firmly as you can. I can't have you losing too much blood."

The room is spinning, and my eyes roll back in my head, but Minju gives my hand another sharp shake. "Sunny, you have to focus. You have to stanch the blood. Do you understand?"

I manage a warbled assent. I don't know what the fuck is going on, but not bleeding out seems like a good idea.

"One, two . . . three." She pulls out the blade in a single, lightning-fast motion and slaps her other hand over my mouth to muffle my scream.

Whimpering against the white-hot pain, I press my palm against my chest. But no matter how much I push down on the wound, warm blood gushes out between my fingers. This might be a fatal wound that even a rare steak can't fix. Minju curses and rests both of her hands over mine. Her eyes closing, she chants an incantation I've never heard before.

As the edges of my vision go dark, warmth spreads across my chest, and a silvery light spills out from under our hands. Sweat beads on her forehead, but the historian doesn't stop the incantation, and soon the pain recedes until only a dull ache remains. She finally stops chanting and drops her hands. I chance a peek at my chest and find the wound healed shut, leaving only a faint scar. That's some impressive magic.

The historian crumples onto her ass across from me, and I drop my head against the armoire with a thud. I don't even feel it. We sit in silence, breathing heavily. But suddenly, Minju jerks upright with a gasp and scrambles to pick up the dagger she stabbed me with. I raise my hands in alarm, too weak to do much else. But she pays me no attention as she studies the blade by the candlelight, as though it holds the secrets to the universe.

"It's gone," she whispers and looks at me with round eyes. "Sunny, it's gone."

"What's gone?" I croak. "And . . . what the fuck, Minju?"

"This blade is a relic of the Endless War." She raises the dagger for me to take a closer look, but I instinctively draw back. Who says she won't stab me again? "It had been contaminated by the Amheuk. I, and every historian who came before me, have been working on purifying the dagger with hopes of understanding how to defeat the ancient darkness. Many of us became obsessed with finding the answer, but none of us have succeeded. Until now."

"You stabbed me with a dagger contaminated by the Amheuk?" I'm too weak to sound outraged, but I really am.

"Yes," Minju says matter-of-factly. "But look, Sunny. The contamination is gone."

"What?" I warily lean closer to the dagger that was sticking out of my chest less than five minutes ago. "What am I looking for? Other than my blood?"

"Nothing." The historian smiles. "It's not there anymore."

"I have no idea what you're talking about, Minju." I speak slowly to make sure she understands that she might be crazy.

"You carry the Yeoiju, the last of the Cheon'gwang, inside you," she says in hushed wonder.

Like lightning striking in my head, I remember the words of the Seonangshin. *He still seeks a power within you—a gift of the Cheon'gwang.* "The . . . the Yeoiju? The gift of the true light is *inside* me?"

"Yes, Sunny." She sighs dreamily as she wipes my blood off the dagger. "Isn't it wonderful?"

"*No.*" I scowl. "Being stabbed in the heart is not a very wonderful feeling."

"I'm so sorry." Minju cringes. "But like I said, there was no other way. Only the true light could've purified that dagger."

My eyes widen in horror as a thought occurs to me. "What if you were wrong and I *didn't* have the Yeoiju?"

"I was fairly confident you had it . . ."

"But what if I didn't?" I whisper shout. "Would I have been contaminated by the Amheuk?"

That would've been a fate worse than death. I'm going to strangle her once I get my strength back. Oddly enough, my limbs don't feel as wobbly anymore.

"No. Why would you be contaminated by it?" The historian sounds perplexed. "The blade only had the barest hint of contamination. My incantation would've stopped any darkness from entwining with your life force even if you didn't have the Yeoiju. But like I said, I was fairly certain you did."

All the fight suddenly drains out of me. I lean my head back and close my eyes. "I don't want the Yeoiju."

"Do you realize how much power you hold inside you?" Minju whispers, her voice brittle around the edges. "How much good you can do?"

"Then you can have it," I say carelessly.

The historian is quiet for so long that I open my eyes. She's staring down at the hands she's fisted on her lap. "Don't ever say that again. If you give up the Yeoiju, you'd be giving up your life. Even though I know that, if you offer again, I might be tempted to take you up on it." Her voice is so soft I can barely hear her. "There is no living being in all the realms who wouldn't want that kind of power."

"I don't—wait." I sit up straight. "I have the Yeoiju?"

"Yes, we just went over that." Minju looks confused again.

"Does that mean I can defeat Daeseong?" Has the answer been inside me all along? I can save Ethan even without the dragon scales? I can go to him now?

"Not yet." She shakes her head slowly. "It's too dangerous to summon the Yeoiju until you learn how to wield its powers. Otherwise, the Cheon'gwang might incinerate you into nothing."

Fear shivers down my spine, but I have no time to be scared. "How can I learn?"

"I don't know the answer to that," she says with soft sympathy. "But I'll work day and night to find out more."

Hope snuffs out inside my chest. The Yeoiju is just another question without answers. I drag a hand down my face as frustration eats through me. I'm running out of time. Ethan needs me.

"Sunny? Are you all right in there?" Hailey asks from the courtyard.

Minju lifts a finger to her lips and gives me a firm shake of her head. She doesn't want her friend to know. Why?

"Yeah, just getting my things together." I peek out through the window. "I'll be right out."

"No worries." Hailey gives me a thumbs-up. "Our thirty minutes isn't up."

"You must tell no one of this." The historian cleans up the blood and mends my tank top with a wave of her hand. Then she gives my shoulder a gentle squeeze. "Not until you can wield the Yeoiju. Otherwise, you'll be signing up for a death sentence—hunted for the rest of your days."

With those ominous words, Minju backs away into the shadows and disappears. I shake my head to clear it. So what if I have the Yeoiju? I don't even know what powers it holds, much less how to wield it. As it stands, it's nothing more than a distraction—a distraction I have to shut out until I have time to figure things out. For now, finding the dragon spirit is our best bet for helping Ethan.

Blowing out a long breath, I tuck the bokjumeoni into my backpack and make sure my hwando is inside. I get to my feet and realize I don't feel any worse for wear. *Wow.* I really need to learn that healing incantation from Minju. Slinging the bag over my shoulder, I rush out to join Hailey in the courtyard.

"Okay." I tug on my sneakers, hopping foot to foot. "I'm ready."

"If we hurry, we might get back before Captain Song." Her expression is full of mischief. "Then we can rub his face in it for being late."

I'm not surprised to find Jihun waiting outside his study when we arrive. Of course he's not late. He's changed into a pair of dark jeans and a gray T-shirt that molds to the contours of his body. My eyes snag on his silky shoulder-length hair fluttering in the breeze. I take in his beauty, a wistful smile tugging at my lips.

My attachment to Jihun has nothing to do with attraction. Sure, he's beautiful. But what seraph isn't? Did I notice? Of course I noticed. I'm not dead. But he and I have a budding friendship, not a romance. I know that now.

Losing Ethan gutted me, and coming to this strange and beautiful realm made coping with it that much harder. So I leaned on the only familiar person by my side—someone as strong and steadfast as the mountains. In some ways, he reminds me of Ben, who was a good friend to me until I got scared and ran. If I give Jihun a chance, will he be a good friend too? And will I be brave enough to keep him?

He catches my smile and gives me the barest tilt of his head. I shake mine but keep smiling. His lips twitch in an answering smile before he turns his gaze toward Hailey.

"Reporting for duty, Captain." Her grin belies the formality of her words.

"Am I last again?" Jaeseok saunters toward us, not sounding the least bit concerned.

"It's the best way to make an entrance," Hailey teases.

He bows his head in acknowledgment. "You know me so well."

Jihun's lips quirk at their antics. This isn't the trio's first mission together. I feel a twinge of envy at their camaraderie. I don't *want* to need anyone, but that doesn't mean I *don't* need anyone. And this group? I could get used to them. Maybe I already have.

Ethan would like these guys. *Are you okay out there?* Of course he is. The alternative is not acceptable. I bite down on my bottom lip to stop it from quivering. I miss him so much that I can't breathe.

"The primary objective of this mission is to obtain the dragon scales." Jihun levels a steely gaze on me. "This is not a rescue mission. We do not confront Daeseong until we forge the sword of light from the sacred ashes and the dragon scales. Is that understood?"

I cross my arms and arch an eyebrow at him, my lips pressed into a mutinous line.

"You will not only be risking your own life," he says softly, vulnerability flashing in his eyes, "but the lives of everyone here."

"Understood." I nod once. He doesn't want to lose his friends any more than I want to lose Ethan. We get the dragon scales, forge the sword, *then* save Ethan from the evil motherfucker. *I will save him. There's still time.* My stomach takes a dip as another thought occurs to me. "Do we have to go through the . . . whatever we went through to get here?"

Jihun hesitates, and I want to throw up. He doesn't hesitate unless it's something really bad. I already know his answer before he says, "It gets easier the more you do it."

"Is she worried about the Gray Void?" Hailey whispers. At Jihun's nod, she waves her hand, and a honeyed cookie appears on her palm. "Here, Sunny. It'll help if you hold this in your mouth as we go through."

"A cookie?" I side-eye her.

"Don't knock the powers of a good cookie." She clicks her tongue and holds it out to me. I have no choice but to accept it.

"Thank you," I say morosely.

"The sweetness will ground you. Remind you that you're still alive," Jaeseok explains. "It took me months to go through the Gray Void without something sweet in my mouth."

"Okay." I offer him a weak smile. Ethan better be alive, because he's the only reason I'm going through that terrifying experience again. Even so, I have to take a bracing breath. "Come on, guys. Let's do this."

CHAPTER
TWENTY-SIX

I come hurtling out of the Gray Void, free-falling toward the mountain peak. How did I forget that the portal is in the middle of the sky? As a scream builds in my throat, Jihun swoops me into his arms, his powerful wings beating behind him. I do okay with heights, but this is a bit much. To my eternal shame, I cling to his shoulders and bury my face in his neck as he flies us down to a clearing on the mountain.

Hailey and Jaeseok land lightly on their feet beside us, despite the fact that they don't have wings. When I stare bug eyed at her, Hailey says with a small shrug, "Flying is part of the high magic we learn as suhoshins."

I nod with a mixture of awe and envy, making my cheek rub against the fabric of Jihun's shirt. I freeze as heat rushes to my face. *Shit.* I'm still in his arms. I relax my death grip on his shoulders and say with as much dignity as I can muster, "You can put me down."

He carefully sets me down on the ground, and I promptly sway on my feet. He steps toward me as though he might scoop me right back up, but Hailey rushes to my side and puts her arm around my shoulders. I let myself lean into her and offer her a grateful smile.

"Chocolate," I wheeze. "Chocolate will work better."

I nearly choked on the damned cookie, but I don't want to say anything. The Gray Void did seem less hopeless and terrifying with something sweet in my mouth. But if I want to be reminded that I'm alive without suffocating on a glob of fried dough, a small piece of chocolate would be perfect. The best solution would be not going through the Gray Void ever again. It's gods awful even with the cookie. Too bad that's not an option.

I glance around the mountain and breathe in a lungful of crisp night air. I missed the Mortal Realm. In this realm—in America—I can carve out a place for myself even if I don't fit in perfectly. But in the Realm of Four Kingdoms, I can't even *exist* without someone vouching for my trustworthiness. I can do without that bullshit.

Unfortunately, I have no choice but to endure all that and more until we forge the sword of light. Or until I miraculously figure out how to use the Yeoiju. I huff a weary sigh. I just have to remember it'll all be worth it to save Ethan.

"Chocolate? That's ingenious," Hailey says, bringing me back to the present. "Why didn't we think of that?"

"Who says I didn't?" Jaeseok wiggles his eyebrows. "I've made bank, peddling chocolate to new recruits for years."

"You did what?" Jihun glowers at him.

"I'm kidding, Captain." Jaeseok turns to Hailey and mouths, *I'm not kidding.*

I take a moment to study my surroundings. A crescent moon casts a silvery glow on the mountain not far from my childhood home—or at least the ruins of it. I can't believe I've only been gone from the Mortal Realm for less than two weeks. Yet my life will never be the same, knowing that the Realm of Four Kingdoms is out there. But I need to hold off on my existential crisis until I have Ethan safely by my side.

"Where are you supposed to meet your informant?" I ask Jaeseok.

"At the base of Mount Baekdu on the North Korean side. Not the Chinese side," he says. "She refuses to step outside Korea."

"We should get going." Jihun nods toward a shallow pond at the edge of the clearing.

I swallow. Moon shifting is worlds better than traveling through the Gray Void, but nausea still clings to me from the trip back to this realm. *Suck it up, Sunny.* I walk gingerly up to the pond and take a wavering breath.

Hailey holds out her hand and raises her eyebrows, but I shake my head. "No, thanks. I need the practice."

I manage not to stumble when I step out on the other side. But my stomach threatens to heave, and I clench my teeth until the urge to hurl passes. I glance around and find a small spring, capturing the water trickling down the mountainside. The moon's reflection shivers beneath the constant drip of water. I'm surprised I was able to shift using it.

Wait. I don't see the suhoshins anywhere. For a moment, I worry that I shifted to the wrong place, but I know I'm at Mount Baekdu. I can feel the powerful rush of its gi flowing around me. Where are the others? I don't let panic get its claws in me. They have to be somewhere close by.

We were supposed to meet the informant at the base of the mountain, but I must be farther up, deeper in the woods. I let my eyelids flutter shut as I open my spirit eyes. My sight is best used for topography, the gi of nature drawing a map in my mind, but I should be able to sense the suhoshins' life force to show me which way to head.

Before I can focus my spirit eyes, I hear the sound of desolate weeping. My physical eyes snap open, and I scan the woods. Did I imagine it? Then I hear it again. I take a step, then another toward the sound.

My heart wrenches as the sobbing continues. There is such sorrow in the sound that I'm reminded all over again of my mother bleeding out in my arms . . . Samshin Halmeom's arm burning to ash as she writhes in pain . . . Ethan disappearing with the assassin before I can stop him . . . The sorrowful crying fills me with helpless rage and grief. I realize it's the sound of han—the twisted gi of a stranded soul.

I catch a flash of white in the corner of my eyes and sprint toward it, shaking away the desolation threatening to drown me. Whatever that thing is, its han is distorting my emotions. I hear quiet sobs to my right and swerve in that direction. Then the sound rings out from my left. The wailing grows louder and louder until . . . a chilling cackle rings out in the night. I skid to a stop, my breath coming in pants, and spin in a circle.

With a strangled cry, I scramble back like I'm trying to climb out of my skin. The woman stands, dripping water from her white hanbok, the long locks of black hair falling over her pale, bluish face. Han rolls off the stranded in sickening waves. She's a water ghost, someone who drowned in her mortal life. I shiver. Gods, she is so creepy.

"What . . . what do you want?" My voice quivers, and I scowl. *Get your shit together.*

"I didn't want to lie to Jaeseok," she says in a thin, reedy voice. "I like him. He actually talks to me like I'm *somebody* instead of running away from me screaming."

"Lie to Jaeseok? You're his informant." My heart sinks like a stone in a bottomless well. "So there's no dragon spirit in Heaven Lake."

"I wouldn't know. I never go in that lake. It gives me the creeps." She paces listlessly back and forth. "But everyone knows about the Cheonji Monster. And human lore is usually at least *partly* true."

"Who told you to lie to Jaeseok?" I slowly withdraw my hwando from my backpack, not wanting to startle the water ghost, and scan the dark shadows of the suddenly sinister woods.

"You mean *what*." She grimaces. "He wasn't human, but he wasn't a stranded either. And that awful yellow unitard. Blech."

"Fuck," I mutter. "Fuck, fuck, fuck."

The ghost crinkles her nose beneath the curtain of her lanky hair. "Language."

"Why?" I pinch the bridge of my nose. "Why did you do it?"

"He said he'll kill the man who raped me." Sobs rack her thin body. "He said he'll kill him in a way that won't let him reach Underworld. I thought . . . I thought that would free me from my han."

"I'm so sorry," I whisper. The poor stranded soul disappears into the night, weeping her endless tears. I hope she finds a way to be free of her han.

This is a trap Daeseong set to lure me back to the Mortal Realm. I feel it in my bones. But why? There's something important I'm missing. It niggles at the back of my mind, just out of reach. I huff a sigh of frustration.

For the time being, I have to get to Heaven Lake. Yes, the water ghost lied. Yes, it's a trap. But there's still a chance that the Cheonji Monster is real and that it's an actual dragon spirit. Because I really need those dragon scales.

I exhale three bursts of short breaths and step into the wavering moonlight reflected in the little spring, focusing unerringly on Heaven Lake. This time I moon shift quicker and land on the other side, like I stretched my leg out to step over a big puddle. No whooshing wind or free-falling through the abyss. And—I glance around to make sure—I reached the right place. Even in the inky darkness, Cheonji glistens like a vast, unending mirror ahead of me as I stand in the midst of a thick grove of trees.

I feel a spike of pride as the torrential gi of Heaven Lake washes over me. I'm getting the hang of this moon shifting business. High magic isn't such a big deal. Maybe I'll figure out how to fly next. My cocky laugh turns into a grunt as someone bulldozes into my side.

I stumble twice before swiftly regaining my footing. And not a moment too soon, because my assailant draws back a fist to plow into my face. I block and sidestep to deliver a jab into their ribs. I think I hurt my hand more than I hurt the bad guy. They don't so much as grunt. They must be wearing some kind of armor, but I can only make out the shadowy outlines of a man.

He's big. Much bigger than me. And stronger too. I block yet another punch, staggering from the impact. I'm not going to best him in a fistfight, but I refuse to draw my sword on an unarmed man—foe or not. The only advantage I have over him is my speed. I need to get close enough to use his weight against him.

I let him land a punch on my torso, shifting my body sideways so I don't feel the full impact of the blow. Even so, all my breath leaves my lungs, and my legs threaten to give out under me. Focusing with every ounce of my will, I clutch a fistful of his shirt and spin around, lifting him over my shoulder. His feet leave the ground, and I use the momentum to flip him.

Before I can gloat, he grabs hold of my arm as he falls, and we both tumble to the ground. We tussle in the dirt, trying to pin the other down and gain the high ground. As we struggle and roll around some more, I hear a sharp gasp from my assailant and rejoice, thinking he got stabbed by a sharp, deadly branch. But he rolls onto his back and holds me against his chest, pinning my arms by my sides. Is he trying to squeeze me to death? I lurch against his hold, but he doesn't budge. I try to knee him in the groin, but he clamps me down with one of his legs. It feels like a hot, muscular log fell onto my legs. I scream in frustration, the sound muffled against his chest.

"Shh," he murmurs in my ears. A shiver runs through me.

What the hell? Scared of my visceral reaction to the bastard, I attack the only way I can with my whole body trapped against his body. I bite his chest.

"Jesus, Sunny," he roars, flipping us over and pinning me to the ground. "You don't play very nice, do you?"

"E . . . Ethan?" My voice breaks on a sob.

I don't give him a chance to answer. He has my wrists in a firm hold on either side of my head as he bears his weight on his forearms. For a fraction of a second, we stare at each other, saying nothing, breathing heavily. The only part of me he isn't holding down is my head, so I lift it up and smash my lips against his. There is no holding back. My relief, joy, and anger combust into all-consuming desire.

Ethan doesn't miss a beat. His tongue flicks out and licks the seam between my lips, coaxing me to part them. I oblige enthusiastically. He deepens the kiss, making a low guttural sound in his chest. I can feel it vibrate against my breasts and their sensitive peaks. I meet every thrust of his tongue and bite of his teeth with my own, reveling in the feel of him—the taste of him.

"Ethan," I breathe.

He raises my arms over my head, holding my wrists down with one big hand, as his other hand travels down the side of my body in a hurried but thorough exploration, as though checking to make sure I'm real. I feel the same need. I can't believe Ethan is here with me. I don't care who he is or why he kept it from me. For now, nothing else matters but this.

I tug on my hands, but he tightens his grip, not hard enough to hurt but hard enough to remind me of his strength. Needing to feel more of him, I arch my back and press myself against him. The dig of his rigid length against my thigh drives me to a frenzy, and I grind my hips against him.

With a growl, he pushes up my tank top, exposing my breasts. He draws in a sharp breath, staring down at them like he's seeing them for the first time, then he dips his head and sucks an aching tip into his mouth. He groans. I whimper and writhe under him as he turns his attention to my other breast.

I blindly reach for his pants and fumble with his belt buckle. Ethan freezes as though someone pressed the pause button on him. He slowly releases my nipple like it's the last thing he wants to do, swirling his tongue around it, then scraping it lightly with his teeth before finally letting go. A shudder runs down my spine and to the tips of my toes. He presses his forehead against mine and brings my hand out from between our bodies.

"Not here," he rasps, his breath coming in rough pants. "Not like this."

He presses a kiss to my knuckles, then lowers my tank top with gentle care. In our tussle, we'd rolled to the very edge of the woods, and the moon casts his face in a silvery light. I should be mortified for losing control like that. But as tenderness replaces the lingering lust in Ethan's eyes, I'm just happy to have him back. Everything else will hit the fan soon enough.

"Are you okay?" I cup the side of his face with my palm.

"I'm fine." He pushes himself off me, and I immediately miss his warmth. I let him help me sit up. I roll my back and shoulders, trying to ease some of the soreness. I didn't even notice how hard and uncomfortable the ground was.

Ethan stares out into the lake, offering me a view of his profile. His teeth are clenched tight, accentuating the sharp lines of his jaw, and his narrowed eyes glint with anger. He looks older, harder. The man who just kissed me as though his life depended on it is nowhere in sight. This is the man who left me in the cave.

"Where were you?" I ask haltingly, remembering how changed Ethan seemed after my house burned down.

"I tried to 'persuade' the yellow assassin to take me to Daeseong. He predictably refused, so I let him escape." His knuckles gleam white on his fists. "I've been following him ever since, hoping he'll lead me back to his master."

"How did you end up here?" I know the answer before the last words leave my mouth. It's a trap for *both* of us.

"I followed . . ." His eyes widen as he realizes the same thing. "Why are you here? Where's Captain Song?"

"We got separated." I can't explain the Realm of Four Kingdoms to him. Not now. "It's a long story."

I scan our surroundings while I desperately think of ways we can come out on top. But I draw a blank. How do we stop a being of the Amheuk who can't be killed? We can't defeat Daeseong—not without the sword of light. I turn my senses inward and try to feel the Yeoiju in me, but I come up empty.

"So here's the deal." I turn to Ethan, who has a dark frown on his face. "We can either moon shift the hell out of here. Right now. And . . . I don't know . . . go back to Vegas and hide out with Ford? Or . . ."

I stop to worry my bottom lip. Why does there have to be an *or*? I have Ethan back. Jihun and the other suhoshins can handle the evil psychopath.

I can even offer them the sacred ashes to do it with. I don't *have* to fight Daeseong. But there is an *or*, because I can't turn my back on them.

"Or?" Ethan says, his eyes straying to my lips like he can't help himself.

"Or . . . we lure the Cheonji Monster—who we think is a dragon spirit—out of Heaven Lake and steal a couple of their scales," I say in a rush before I change my mind.

Ethan steps close and places a palm on my forehead to check for a fever. I exhale with an irritated whoosh and slap his hand away.

"I'm serious." I grit my teeth, wishing this really was a fever dream. "We need the dragon scales along with the sacred ashes to forge a sword of light. That's the only weapon that can stop Daeseong."

"You mean we have to forge a twin to the long-lost Gwangdo?" His eyebrows climb into his forehead. "No one has been able to forge a sword of light since the Endless War."

"Yes, that—" I take an instinctive step back. "How . . . how do you know that?"

"Sunny . . ." Ethan reaches a hand out for me.

"What are you not telling me?" I stumble back another step. *Why did you lie? Why did you leave?* I can't hide from this anymore. "Who are you?"

"I'm *yours*." He closes the space between us and takes my hands in his. "I am yours, Sunny Cho, body and soul. No matter what happens, please remember that."

"Why?" My heart wants to take flight, but I clap an iron vise around it. "What's going to happen?"

"Fuck the prophecy," he growls, his eyes turning dark and wild. "I won't let anything happen to you."

"Ethan Lee." I tug my hands out of his grasp and fist them at my sides. "What in the ever-loving hell are you talking about? Just tell me who you are."

A single tear trails down his cheek. "I'm the one who is destined to kill you."

PROPHECY OF THE END OF DAYS

Darkness takes its final breath,
double dragons reunite.

Fierce shall jade and silver burn
the truth of tears and blood unchained.

Blinding sorrows extinguish dreams,
hope shines forth, the unveiled pearl.

The true heart of the righteous shall
shatter the light that reveals all paths.

CHAPTER
TWENTY-SEVEN

I hear the yellow assassin's approach and welcome the intrusion. Anything to stop Ethan's words from echoing ceaselessly in my mind. *I'm the one who is destined to kill you.*

"Fuck destiny." He grabs my shoulders, fingers tight with desperation, and searches my face. "I will *never* hurt—"

"Yellow's here," I say, cutting him off.

His hands slide down my arms with one last squeeze. His eyes flare with a swirl of silver-and-green fire as he spins around, flexing his hands to summon the axes. I draw my hwando and stand back to back with him.

"Promise me you'll give me a chance to explain everything later," he pleads, his voice husky and broken.

"Later." I can't make him any promises. Not when my head is spiraling with betrayal, hurt, and fear. This isn't a simple misunderstanding after all. No amount of talking will fix this.

Ethan glances over his shoulder but turns back after a split second. He's not an idiot. He can't lower his vigilance. Promises will be meaningless if we're dead.

"What are his other powers?" I ask, tightening my grip on the hilt.

"Teleportation."

The implications of his answer sink in. "You mean the yellow assassin teleported you out of the cave?"

"Yes." He shifts as though he wants to turn around again, but he stops himself. "What did you think happened?"

"I don't know," I mutter a tad defensively. Ethan was summoning axes and shit. Who knew what other powers he had? He can't blame me for assuming he teleported the golem away in some misguided attempt to protect me. Leaving me. Hurting me. But I don't say any of that. "I didn't have much time to mull over the possibilities. I wasn't sitting on my ass, binge-watching Netflix, you know."

"I have . . . powers, but teleportation isn't one of them. Sunny . . . I . . ." He pauses as though struggling to find the words. "I wouldn't have left you. I would never leave you."

"Were you going to come back to me?" I ask, before I can stop myself.

"Once I'd stopped Daeseong," he says. "Once I was sure he couldn't hurt you again. I wanted to come back to you right away, but I knew you wouldn't be safe until Daeseong was dead. I couldn't throw away my chance to have Yellow lead me to him."

My stupid heart does a somersault. He was coming back to me. Then I remember the bomb he dropped on me.

I'm the one who is destined to kill you.

Maybe he was coming back to me to kill me. Maybe I should run far, far away from him. In my mind's eye, I see my childhood home burning. *Run, Daughter. You must run.* My mother wanted me to run. Is this why?

"Sunny, please . . . ," Ethan whispers, as though he read my thoughts.

I can't do this. Not now.

Right on cue, the undead assassin approaches in bursts of yellow smoke, appearing in and out of sight through the dense growth of trees. Fighting in the confines of a cave hadn't done his powers justice. Out in the woods, he moves with terrifying speed and unpredictability.

Yellow's dagger flies at me from overhead, and I block it with my sword a breath away from my throat. The ping of metal against metal rings behind me as Ethan drops a series of daggers with his axes. Then the blades fly at us like bullets from a machine gun, and we have to break apart to deflect them, our weapons blurring with frantic speed.

The assassin can be hurt even when he's not in his corporeal form. In the cave, Jihun slashed the yellow smoke and cut the golem, forcing him to reveal himself. Even as I parry the unending onslaught of daggers, I peer into the darkness for signs of the bastard. Yellow apparates from point to point in plumes of smoke. Then I hear it—a sound like a muted clap of thunder—a split second before the yellow smoke blooms at the point of the sound.

My breath catches in my throat with a sharp gasp as a dagger comes out of nowhere, aiming straight for my heart. I slash my hwando in the air, but I'm not fast enough. Damn it. Not like this. I can't let a walking corpse in a yellow onesie kill me. But instead of embedding itself in my chest, the dagger clatters to the ground a hair's breadth away from me. Knife after knife falls at our feet, and the assassin shrieks with fury.

I gingerly retreat one step, then another until my back meets Ethan's. I open my spirit eyes and see the shimmering outline of a protective dome around us. This is what he did when the North Korean soldiers shot at us. So much magic . . . How is he doing this?

It pisses me off that I don't know—that he didn't tell me any of it. I don't care if he saves our lives. Well . . . I do care. But I can be pissed and grateful at the same time. It must be an untapped talent of mine. Like avoidance. I am a gumiho of many talents. *Fuuuck.* The adrenaline is getting to me again.

"Is there any chance you'll stay in here and let me take care of the golem?" Ethan asks.

When I glance over my shoulder at him, his expression is resigned, with a hint of hope. I give him my answer by stepping outside the protective shield.

He sighs. "I didn't think so."

A muted clap sounds to my left. I leap and bring my sword down with a two-handed grip, then slice sideways without pause. The assassin flickers in and out of view, wisps of black smoke rapidly overtaking the yellow. Good, I cut the bastard. He finally stumbles to the ground and staggers back into a tree.

Ethan's silver axe flies through the air and buries itself in Yellow's shoulder, pinning him to the tree. The golem strains against the axe, his edges blurring, then solidifying.

"Don't waste your energy. You can't teleport with my axe in you," Ethan drawls. I shoot a startled glance at him. How does he *know* that? Again, it pisses me off. But he continues, "Why did you lure us here? Did you want to meet your final death somewhere picturesque?"

"Lure *you*? You were nothing but an insignificant pawn from the start. No, *you* followed *me*. But I'll take credit for luring the beast here." The assassin's mouth stretches into a horrible smile. He gives new meaning to *grinning from ear to ear*. "My master wants her alive, but he didn't say anything about you. Shall we play?"

The golem's face suddenly goes slack. I shake my head in confusion. "Is he dead?"

Ethan takes a step toward him, then halts when a thin yellow snake slithers out of the assassin's mouth. "What the hell?"

It starts out quiet like the wind brushing against the leaves, but soon, the hissing grows deafening, filling my head to the point of pain. The ground undulates like an endless yellow sea—of glistening, writhing snakes. Nausea floods my stomach as the serpents draw near. And a bloodcurdling scream rips through my throat when snakes fall from the sky like unholy yellow hail. Before the reptiles land on my head, Ethan throws another shield around us.

"*Now* will you stay behind the shield?" he asks in a strained voice, a muscle in his jaw twitching. I nod so enthusiastically that my teeth clack. I. Hate. Snakes.

Sweat beads on his forehead, and his arms tremble. Projecting a defensive shield over both of us is taking a toll on him. Worry hits me first, followed swiftly by another emotion. He isn't some omnipotent god or anything. Expending magic too fast drains him. I breathe a sigh of . . . relief? I don't dissect why I'm relieved by that discovery.

"How long until you pass out?" I cast a concerned glance his way.

"Hell if I know," he grits past his teeth. "Hopefully I can last until we figure out how *not* to get killed by a million poisonous snake bites."

"Fair enough," I concede. "Any ideas?"

"I got some . . ." His lips quirk. "But why don't you go first?"

I roll my eyes but can't hold back my answering grin. These glimpses of my Ethan feel like a healing balm. "I don't suppose you can fly."

"I . . ." He clears his throat. "Actually . . . I *can* fly."

I growl, and Ethan has the sense to look nervous. I take a deep breath through my clamped teeth. "Can you fly with me in your arms while holding up the shield?"

"With you in my arms . . ." He trails off with a blush I can see even in the dark. "That might be more distraction than I can handle while wielding powers I don't fully understand."

That makes me smile even as the serpents fall in torrents from the sky. "Well, we're going to have to make a run for it then. If we can get to the lake, we can moon shift out of here."

"But the dragon scales . . ."

"Will be of no use to us if we're dead," I finish for him.

"What's all this talk of death? A bit morbid, don't you think?" Jaeseok says, levitating above our protective dome, bursts of fire streaking from his palms. "I would never let a beautiful female die on my watch."

"I think her point was she doesn't plan on dying." Hailey walks out of the woods, whipping open a folding fan in each hand. The snakes freeze in her wake as she waves her arms in graceful arcs, sending blasts of ice from her fans.

"Save the bickering for *after* we rid ourselves of these slimy reptiles," Jihun orders, his long sword flashing.

Yellow screeches and writhes against the tree as if the sword, fire, and ice are slicing through *his* body. My eyes widen as I step up to the edge of the shield. The slithering minions are extensions of the assassin. That's why he passed out when he summoned the snakes. He's sending his consciousness into them. He feels what they feel.

"Jihun," I shout. "We kill the snakes, we kill him."

"With pleasure." Lips pulling back in disgust, Jihun thrusts his palms out, and gusts of wind slam the scorched and frozen serpents into tree trunks, shattering them into black smoke.

As their captain obliterates the snakes into smoke, Hailey and Jaeseok redouble their fire and ice attacks. The trees sway from the gusts of wind Jihun summons, scattering even the black smoke into nothing. Soon, the rippling yellow mass on the ground disappears without a trace.

With the snakes disposed of, Jihun, Hailey, and Jaeseok run toward us. Ethan drops his arms, withdrawing the shield. I feel him sway, but he catches himself before I reach out. As the suhoshins reach us, he stands tall as if projecting the shield hasn't drained him.

"Are you okay?" Holding me by the shoulders, Ethan scans me from head to toe, fear and fury warring in his eyes. When he tries to turn me around to check for hidden injuries, I shake his hands off.

"I'm fine." I bite my tongue to stop myself from asking if he's okay. But I scan *him* from head to toe from beneath my lashes.

The assassin's bloodcurdling shrieks steal our attention. We turn to him and watch with grim satisfaction as he disintegrates into yellow dust at the base of the tree. Ethan stretches his hand out, and the silver axe rips from the tree trunk and flies into his hand.

With a collective gasp, the suhoshins each drop to one knee and bow their heads to Ethan. "Your Highness."

Ethan's gaze flies to me as I stagger back from the group. Before I can respond to the plea in his eyes, he turns back to the bowed heads of the guardians. He fists his hands at his sides and swallows. "You may rise."

Of course. *Of course.* This is what I've been hiding from. This incontrovertible proof that Ethan and I can never be. The Kingdom of Mountains isn't a fairy tale. It exists in the Realm of Four Kingdoms—as real as the Kingdom of Sky, where I spent nearly half of a moon cycle. The golden axe and the silver axe are real, meaning the crown of gold twines and jade leaves is real too. And Ethan can wield the legendary axes, which means he is destined to wear the crown. He is destined to rule the Kingdom of Mountains.

"Sunny." He looks at me with his familiar brown eyes—the silver-and-green fire extinguished. The undisguised yearning in them threatens to take my breath away. "Please."

"You knew who he was." I address Jihun, not ready to face Ethan. The suhoshin captain never lied to me. He already told me it wasn't his story to tell. But still, I feel betrayed. "You all knew."

"Yes," Jihun says simply. Hailey offers me a wavering smile, and Jaeseok scratches the back of his head.

"You weren't helping *me*." My words catch in my throat. The truth stings like a bitch. "You were helping *him*."

"That's not true. We—" Hailey protests.

"I don't want to hear it." I slice my hand through the air, fighting back my tears. I hardly knew them, but I foolishly let them in because it felt good to have someone on my side for once. I liked *belonging* . . . and look where it got me. Alone *and* betrayed.

Not caring about anyone, forming no emotional attachments, was never just about protecting others, was it? It was about protecting myself too. And for good reason. People let you down. That's what they do. *Unless you get them killed first.* I don't know who I'm angrier with—them, me, or Ethan.

Lost in my thoughts, I don't see Ethan approach until he's standing in front of me. He raises his hand as if to touch me but thinks better of it. Smart move. I pointedly turn my head away.

"When's the last time you've eaten?" he asks softly. "Let's go back to Vegas. I'll take you to Roxy's."

"You want to take me to Roxy's? Right now?" My gaze whips back to him. "You can't be serious."

"We can order steak and eggs." He ducks his head to catch my eyes. My traitor of a heart flutters. And my stomach growls. No, roars. A smile touches his lips. "And a liter of strong coffee."

I . . . bolt for the lake. It's too much. If I listen to him, I might want to forgive him—I already understand why he didn't tell me—and that won't lead to anything good. He's the . . . What is he? The Prince of Mountains? And he's destined to become the King of Mountains. In the Realm of Four Kingdoms. Where my mere *existence* is an insult to the Shinbiin's sensibilities—to *his* people's sensibilities. I can never be enough for him.

"Sunny, wait." Ethan sprints after me.

I step blindly into Heaven Lake, thinking of Roxy's because someone planted the seed in my head. But my foot sinks into the lake up to my ankle. What the hell? Was I not specific enough? I take a step with my other foot—Roxy's Diner in Las Vegas, Nevada. In the United States of America. My foot meets my other foot in the water.

Ethan wraps a hand around my wrist. "Don't go."

"I can't—"

"Please." He spins me around. "Sunny, I . . ."

"No, I mean I *can't* go." A chill runs through me. "I can't moon shift."

"What? I don't understand." Confusion draws his brows together. Snatching my hand before I can react, he takes a step into the lake. His eyes widen when his foot lands in the water across from me. I numbly accept that he knows how to moon shift. And he, of course, tries again with his other foot and ends up with a pair of soggy Converse like me. "I can't moon shift."

"What? You thought I was lying?" I tug my hand free. "Or did you assume the uncouth fox spirit was doing it all wrong?"

His nostrils flare with temper. "That's not fair."

"Fair?" I bark with incredulous laughter, jagged and angry. "I can show you fair, but you wouldn't like it."

"Come now. There's no need to argue." A dark, distorted voice echoes around us, and the surface of the lake shivers. "It would be a shame to ruin this delightful little gathering."

The water turns freezing, the cold piercing my skin like a thousand needles. But the pain is nothing compared to the icy fear that grips my heart. I stand paralyzed until Ethan wraps a protective arm around my shoulders, and I stumble out of the lake with him. The suhoshins rush to our side at the edge of the lake.

"It's him," I whisper, my teeth chattering. "Daeseong is here."

SHATTERED TEARS

Soothed by the sap of the tree, she rests. It guts me to see her hurting. I wish I could hurt for her instead. My eyes wander to the ruins of her childhood home—the fire banked to embers. What the hell happened?

I squeeze the back of my neck and tilt my head this way and that, but the tension knotted in my shoulders refuses to relent. As my hand slides off my neck, I grow still and reach for the base of my throat.

My necklace. My mom's necklace.

I react without thinking. I jump on top of the collapsed house and tear through the still-smoking wood. It doesn't take me long to spot the glow of green within the depth of the embers. I hardly notice the singe of heat against my skin as I dig through the smoldering wreckage.

The leather string has long burned away into nothing, but I gingerly lift the jade disk. Hairline fractures run across the entire surface of the stone. I feel as though those fractures are mirrored in my heart. I close my hand around the necklace, swallowing my sorrow.

I'm sorry, Mom. I'll find a way to fix it.

I don't notice it at first, the disk pulsing against my palm like a heart-beat. Then blinding green-and-silver flames burst through the seams of my fingers, and I'm thrown flat onto my back. The fire surrounds me—then consumes me until it burns inside me. It levitates me off the ground, holding me aloft for a split second before it explodes. I crack like the jade disk. My shout escapes my throat as green-and-silver fire, and my eyes flare with the flames. And I burn.

I *am* the fire.

Then it ends. I know who I am. I know the sacrifices made for me. I know . . . what I must do.

I stand at her side again and watch her sleep. Helpless tears run down my face, and all-consuming rage rips through me. I silence the scream building inside me so she can rest. I fall to my knees beside her and struggle to face the unacceptable truth. I don't want to. I want to run. I want to hide. But there is no running—no hiding—from the blood that stains my hands.

With my first breath, I sentenced my mother to death. And my very existence means the death of my soulmate . . . a love destined by the heavens.

CHAPTER TWENTY-EIGHT

·

Daeseong appears in the middle of the lake and walks toward us—on water. The dark mudang is taking his god complex to a whole new level.

My companions' eyes light up with the gi that sources their magic and their lives. Hailey, the jeoseungsaja, and Jaeseok, the dokkaebi, have eyes that glow red, since they receive their life force from Underworld. Jihun's eyes burn silver, evidencing his origin from Sky. And now I understand the swirl of silver and green in Ethan's eyes . . . He's of both Sky and Mountain.

My eyes, I know, are still brown because I'm paralyzed with terror. I can't breathe. I try taking small sips of air. It doesn't work. I try dragging in big gulps of air. My lungs only burn hotter. I panic and begin to hyperventilate.

My old enemy looks exactly as I remember him. He still appears to be in his forties, with a pleasant face and the distinguished air of a scholar. I figured being resurrected by the Amheuk would've left a mark on him. Maybe a horn or two. Even some long walrus-like incisors would've been less anticlimactic.

But Daeseong is not the source of my terror. *I* am. I'm terrified of the wrath rising in me. It awakens something deep inside me. Something that starts as a pinprick, then grows until it glows white hot in my chest.

My human body won't be able to withstand it much longer, but I still try to douse the magic pushing insistently against my skin.

"The hidden prince is revealed at last." Even from a mile away, we can hear the mudang as though he's standing next to us. "This is an unexpected boon, but it is most welcome. Welcome indeed."

"I hope you're not going to segue into a villainous monologue," I shout, hoping he can't hear the tremor in my voice. "Because we haven't got all night."

"We don't? Is it because you're going to let me take you to Roxy's?" Ethan jokes—because he's got to be joking—with his eyes glued on Daeseong.

"Now? Really?" Hailey bursts out, then bites her lip, lowering her head. "My prince . . . please forgive me. I was out of line."

"No need to apologize . . ." He lets his sentence hang in an unspoken question.

"Hailey," she supplies.

"Like I said, no apologies necessary, Hailey." He shoots her a grim smile. "I agree that my timing is truly horrible, but I'm not sure if there will be a better time."

"Good timing is overrated in my opinion. And if we're doing introductions before our certain demise . . . ," Jaeseok pipes up. "I'm Jaeseok, Your Highness."

"Nice to meet you." Ethan nods. Then he leans close, his breath warm against my ear. "Give me something to fight for, Sunny."

"What? Not dying isn't enough motivation for you?" I snap, even as I shiver at his words. I don't want to have this conversation in front of an audience. Daeseong is spectating our exchange with an indulgent smile on his face. Ugh. What a creep.

"I'll travel to hell and back for even a glimmer of hope of winning you back," Ethan whispers huskily.

Suddenly, I could care less about having an audience. I wrap my hand around the back of his neck and pull him in for a hard kiss. I don't have an answer for him, but I don't want to die without kissing him one last time. Ethan gathers me flush against him and kisses me back, tender and raw.

"Forgive me for interrupting," Jihun says stiffly, "but we have . . . company."

Ethan and I break apart and turn toward the dark mudang, and I immediately wish I hadn't. I can see past glamour, so I've seen all sorts and manners of beings of the Shingae. Some of my kind are definitely not for the faint of heart—even the truly beautiful ones are painfully overwhelming to behold—but these grotesque monsters have my mind grappling for sanity.

Their bodies, if I can call them that, look brutally torn apart, while their limbs . . . four or six of them? . . . hang off at odd, broken angles. They are black in a way that makes the midnight sky seem bright. I'm not actually seeing their forms but the absence of light where they stand. The cloudy white of their pupilless eyes and the red slashes of their screaming mouths are the only colors visible on them. But I don't want to see any part of them.

They fly at us so fast that I'm already bleeding from multiple shallow gashes by the time I draw my sword. There are at least a dozen of them, clawing and snapping their jaws at us. I swing my hwando and chop off what I think is a leg. As I move on to fight the next nightmarish beast, the leg I cut off stitches itself back onto the first one.

The five of us move into a loose circle formation, our backs to each other's. There are gasps and shouts, but I don't take my eyes off the monsters striking out at me. The others are more than capable of taking care of themselves. If anything, I'm the weakest link. I need to focus on not getting too badly hurt so I don't become a burden to them.

As soon as my body heals my cuts, I get shredded with new ones. But I don't slow down. I kick out at the beast closest to me, and my foot sinks into its body. I'm thrown onto my back as I thrash against its hold.

"Sunny," Ethan roars. But he can't break away as three dark shadows close in on him.

I'm . . . I'm *absorbed* into the monster up to my waist. I'm not being eaten. Not exactly. But I feel as though the parts of me that it swallowed don't . . . exist anymore. Fueled by sheer terror, I wrap both hands around the hilt of my sword and bury the blade in the red, gaping mouth of the beast—a scream ripping through my throat. The shadow continues to creep up, past my chest and up to my armpits. Soon, my arms will be swallowed up, and I won't be able to fight anymore.

"Fuck you, nightmare monster," I growl at it, even though it might not have ears. I keep cussing out the beast and sink my hwando into its mouth again and again.

Nothing seems to happen until a cold shiver skitters through my body, down to the tips of my toes. *I can feel my toes!* I thrash around with renewed hope and wrench myself out of the monster. I'm freed so suddenly that I crash to the ground in a graceless heap. I might've cracked a few ribs, but I'm thrilled to feel pain after almost being swallowed out of existence. I manage to raise myself into a crouch as the beast folds in on itself and blinks out in a pinprick of darkness.

"Stab them in the mouth," I yell out. "Hard."

"Which hole is their mouth?" Jaeseok shouts, spinning his spear above his head to keep the monsters at bay.

Hailey launches an arrow from her crossbow into a beast's mouth, stretched wide in a silent shriek. "The big red one."

I shoot to my feet, my ribs screaming in agony, and rush toward the nearest monster. Ethan slams his silver axe into one red slash, then spins to throw the golden axe into another yawning mouth. One by one, the dark beasts blink out into the night.

"Is everyone okay?" Jihun straightens after burying his long sword in the mouth of the last monster.

Everyone is slashed and bloodied except for Ethan. But not for lack of trying. The monsters diligently shredded his clothes, even though they couldn't break his skin. Luckily, the suhoshins' gashes are already closing up, and my ribs are mended enough for me to breathe without wincing.

Ethan's at my side, his hands running over my body. I'm too relieved he's okay to remember that we aren't on touching terms at the moment. Except for the part where I kissed him in front of everyone. But I thought we were going to die, so that doesn't count. I hiss when his palm presses lightly into my side.

"You're hurt." His expression hardens.

"I'll be fine in a minute." I sound breathless. Because of my broken ribs. Not because the warmth of his touch is seeping through my clothes, heating my body. I lift my eyes to meet his, and he holds my gaze as his hands slide down to my hips, his fingers flexing against my skin.

"I wanted to see what you can do, princeling." Daeseong approaches the shore, his steps making gentle ripples on the surface of the lake.

I jump away from Ethan, mortified that I forgot about the dark shaman. I thought we'd won the battle for a second. All I'm gonna say is that Ethan is *very* distracting.

"I must say I'm impressed . . . but your father's worries are exaggerated." The dark mudang waves his hand in a fussy little circle. "I hardly think you and your pretty axes can overthrow the King of Mountains. Not as long as he's aligned with the Amheuk."

Overthrow . . . the King of Mountains? Ethan is meant to overthrow his father to become the new King of Mountains? Is that the *long-awaited* plans that Hailey was talking about? The one Daeseong threw a wrench in? It sounds complicated and heartbreaking to fight his own father. But if the king is really backed by the true darkness . . . it will be suicide to stand against him.

"You're lying," Ethan says evenly, but his body tenses next to mine. I steal a peek at him, but I can't read the hard lines of his face. "The king is too much of a coward to make a deal with the Amheuk."

Yes, the mudang has to be lying. No being of the Shingae would be foolish enough to join hands with the Amheuk. The king is a near-immortal shinbiin, and a *king* to boot. Why would he want to risk everything by siding with an ancient evil? The Amheuk will not stop until every life force is snuffed out in all the realms, including his. Did he play hooky on the day his royal tutor gave the lesson on the Endless War?

"You know your father well then. I was under the impression you two have never met . . ." The mudang tilts his head. "Ah, the Queen of Mountains. Of course. Your mother was a powerful shinbiin. It is rumored that she poured every last drop of her gi into the spell that bound your magic and kept you hidden all this time."

Grief flashes across Ethan's face, and I reach for his hand. He laces his fingers through mine, even as his expression turns insolent and bored. So his magic *was* bound. That means he wasn't knowingly suppressing it. A small knot of hurt loosens in my chest. Maybe I *will* let him explain everything to me. *Later.*

"I see she has also passed her memories on to you." Daeseong looks positively gleeful. "But I wonder how *much* she shared. Maybe just enough to manipulate you into dethroning your own father?"

Does Ethan understand any of this? Why did his mother bind his magic and keep him hidden from the Shingae? How did she pass her memories on to him? How much does Ethan know? Is he . . . is he okay? His grip tightens around my hand, and I feel a shudder go through him. No, he is *not* okay. Far from it.

"How would you know any of this?" I shout, squeezing Ethan's hand in warning. *Don't fall for it.* The dark shaman is baiting him. What game is he playing at? "You've been dead for over a hundred years. And what would a human know about the Kingdom of Mountains?"

"Of course a *human* wouldn't know any of this." He isn't riled by my barb—my reminder that he isn't a being of the Shingae. "But I am a creature of the Amheuk now. I know all about the Realm of Four Kingdoms and its sordid secrets. You can't begin to comprehend the power of the darkness. Even knowledge of the past *and* the future is not beyond my reach."

"No one can see what hasn't been written," I say with more confidence than I feel. What if it is possible? How can we defeat a foe who knows the future?

"I see your mother has lied to you convincingly." Daeseong offers a sympathetic smile. The patronizing fucker. "Perhaps she lied to herself too. Lied so well that she believed the prophecy could be avoided. She might have convinced herself that you could outrun your destiny."

Run, Daughter. You must run. I shake my head to chase away my mother's voice. She didn't lie to me. She wouldn't have lied to me. "The only liar here is you, mudang."

"Even the mighty Queen of Mountains, the most powerful diviner of our time, couldn't foresee the triumph of the Amheuk," he continues, dismissing me and my words. "Maybe it's better she didn't know her sacrifice will come to naught. That her beloved son will never become the King Foretold."

The muscles on Ethan's neck bulge, and I don't know if I can stop him from running headlong toward Daeseong. "Ethan, don't . . ."

"You will not speak ill of the queen or the prince," Jihun says, seething. "You will not speak of them at all."

It wasn't Ethan I needed to worry about. Or he wasn't the only one. I turn around to catch Jihun's eyes, but the wind whips my hair around my face as his wings flare behind me. Before I can stop him, he launches off the ground and raises his sword high above his head. He brings it down on Daeseong with deadly speed.

"Enough." The dark mudang slashes his hand across the air and sends Jihun plummeting toward the lake.

"Captain." Hailey flies out to catch him but staggers under Jihun's weight, and they both sink underwater.

"Jaeseok, be careful," I shout as he sprints toward the lake and dives in after his friends. Ethan and I keep a wary eye on Daeseong, ready to stop him from going after the suhoshins.

"Did you know the deepest depth of this lake is darker than outer space?" the mudang says in a conversational tone. He seems to have forgotten all about the guardians as he draws closer to us.

"Oh, fun." My sarcasm is forced. I don't know how to win this fight. "We're exchanging useless factoids now? I didn't realize this was a cocktail party."

My gaze flits to where the suhoshins disappeared. Not even a lone air bubble rises to disturb the mirrorlike surface of the lake. The rage inside me churns faster, straining against the confines of my control.

"Come with me willingly, Mihwa, and I will make his death swift." Daeseong steps onto the shore.

I was wrong. He doesn't look the same. His eyes are the same black as his monsters—a black hole sucking in all the light, all that is alive and good. Bile rises in my throat.

"She's not going anywhere with you," Ethan growls, raising his axes.

"I assure you, princeling." The dark mudang spreads his hands in a benevolent gesture. Coming from him, even the false benevolence is sacrilegious. "If you stay with her, you'll be laying the path to the destruction of your kingdom—the destruction of the Realm of Four Kingdoms. I'll be granting you a great mercy by killing you tonight."

He'll be laying the path . . . to what? The destruction of the realm? What does staying with me have to do with any of that? Why would I destroy the Realm of Four Kingdoms? The white-hot light pulses in my chest. I shake my head. The Shinbiin might be assholes, but I would never hurt those people. Jihun said I didn't kill the villagers. He said . . . he said . . . Panic threatens to overtake me.

The dark mudang is just trying to distract me and Ethan. He's toying with our heads before he destroys us. I have to focus. I have to find a way to stop Daeseong. Ethan bares his teeth in a snarl and takes a step toward him. But I stand rooted to the ground, desperately study-ing every inch of the dark mudang. We were able to kill his monsters by stabbing them in the mouth. Where is *his* Achilles' heel? Even if I can't kill Daeseong, I might be able to hold him back long enough for Ethan to escape.

"I wonder if you told her. Does she know you are destined to end her, princeling?" The dark mudang laughs with chilling delight.

Maybe I should just stab him in the mouth. It might not be his weak spot, but at least it'll shut him up. While I deliberate, Ethan rushes the mudang and slams his silver axe into his shoulder with enough force to cleave a tree in half. Daeseong staggers as the axe cuts through bones and sinew.

Ethan somehow found the mudang's weak point in a single strike. Or maybe Daeseong isn't so strong without his dark beasts. Either way, hope sparks inside me as Ethan buries his golden axe into the dark mudang's other shoulder.

Daeseong groans and falls to his knees, his hands latching on to the axes in a desperate attempt to pull them out. But his grimace of pain slowly shifts into a demented smile that distorts his face.

"Shall I assist you, Your Highness?" the mudang croons as he pulls the blades deeper into his body.

Oh, gods. Daeseong is like his monsters. He's absorbing the axes.

"No, Ethan." I wrap my arms around his waist from behind and tug him back with all my might. "Let go of your axes."

The dark mudang is a creature of the Amheuk, as his monsters were. Even the legendary axes can't hurt him. No, Daeseong wanted Ethan to strike him with the axes so he could absorb them into his darkness. His death and unholy reincarnation haven't changed his appetite for magic and magical items.

"Let. Go." I grit my teeth as I try to pull Ethan back, but he doesn't budge. "He's going to absorb you if you don't let go."

"He'll die before he lets go of the axes. Isn't that right, princeling?" Daeseong rises to his feet, the axes falling deeper into the depth of his darkness. "Because who will believe him to be the King Foretold without the axes? Without his crown? How else will he claim his birthright?"

"Don't listen to him, Sunny," Ethan rasps. "I can't let these axes fall into his grasp. He will twist their magic and rain down death and destruction on the Realm of Four Kingdoms. The Mortal Realm too. Help me. Help me stop him."

His grip has slipped to the very ends of the axe handles. Soon, his hands will be absorbed. Then his arms. Inch by inch, the darkness will swallow him whole. He won't die and move on to Underworld. He will cease to exist. Ethan will be . . . gone.

Instinct forces my spirit eyes open with a suddenness that makes me gasp. The gi of Mount Baekdu and Heaven Lake blinds me with its power. I raise my hands and cringe back as green fire flares around me. I can't see anything beyond it. My breath comes in harsh pants as panic slashes its claws at me.

Then I feel it. The rhythmic pulse of Mountains in my veins, in my heart. I breathe in time with it and hear my own heartbeat match the gi of Mount Baekdu and Heaven Lake. The wall of green flames banks into a smooth blanket over the landscape. Then I see Ethan. His green-and-silver gi feels like the rush of a waterfall, powerful and pure.

Tears sting my throat. Life is so beautiful. I will *not* let darkness win.

I turn my spirit eyes on Daeseong. Black fire consumes him in a never-ending cycle of destruction. He is born again from the ashes only to be scorched by the flames. His existence is twisted and torturous. His suffering will never stop. That was the price he paid the Amheuk for his resurrection. Foolish, foolish man. Then I see it. A tiny point of stillness in the inferno of pain. I sense a speck of sanity in the depth of his mind.

"Ethan, I have to let you go." I tighten my arms around him for a single breath, then let go. "You need to hang on."

I don't second-guess whether destroying the last of the mudang's sanity is a good idea. I know in my gut that this point is his only weakness. I spin out from behind Ethan, pulling back my hwando in a double-handed grip. Without pause, I rush toward Daeseong and plunge it into his forehead.

A monstrous roar rips out of him. He stumbles and swats Ethan away with a sweep of his hand, sending him flying like a rock catapulting out of a slingshot. Ethan crouches and digs his axes into the ground, skidding to a halt inches before he slams into a tree.

"It worked," I say in a stunned whisper. Ethan and his axes are safe.

Now we need to get far, far away from the dark mudang. I yank my sword out of him, praying that he isn't sucking it into nonexistence. I nearly land on my ass when it pulls free without resistance.

"Shit," I hiss. "Shit, shit, shit."

Daeseong isn't bleeping out like his monsters. A small part of me hoped he'd die even though I didn't stab him with a sword of light. But when am I ever that lucky? Never. The answer is never. Instead, I opened the floodgates to hell. Those horrible nightmare creatures are coming out from the black gash in the mudang's forehead. In *legions*.

Ethan is by my side in an instant, his axes flashing. Back to back, we cut down the monsters as fast as we can swing our weapons. But they keep coming. Ethan crosses his axes across his chest and sends a pulse of energy bursting from his body. A horde of dark creatures drops to the ground and disappears.

"What was that?" I breathe.

"I'm . . . not . . . sure." He collapses to one knee, gritting his teeth. "But I don't think I can . . . manage . . . another one."

My heart sinks when a fresh army of nightmare beasts seeps out of Daeseong's forehead. I swing my sword wildly, piercing through as many red holes as I can. I stumble to my knees with a cry of pain. They cut me faster than I can heal. I would be able to last longer against their assault as my gumiho, but my teeth and tails aren't good for stabbing shadow monsters in their mouths.

Ethan tucks my head under his chin and wraps his arms around me, shielding me with his body. I feel something hot and wet against my palm and draw my hand away from his chest. Blood. I can only lean back an inch—his arms are like iron bands around me—but it's far enough for me to see his wrecked torso. He's bleeding from countless gashes.

"You're bleeding." I don't fight the hot tears that stream down my face.

He grunts as the monsters ribbon his back, but he won't release me. "I'm . . . fine."

"Liar." I arch my back in pain when a beast gets past the shield of his arms.

"I told you I won't kill you," Ethan says faintly. "Consider this my big *fuck you* to destiny."

"Yeah." My vision turns dark around the edges. "You sure showed them."

I shift into my fox form and curl around him. It's my turn to protect him . . . for as long as I can. At long last, I fully appreciate the beauty and power of this body. My gumiho isn't a monster I have to keep leashed. She's a warrior—a guardian. Mihwa was right. We are glorious.

"Sunny, no." Ethan pushes against me, but I don't budge. "They're hurting you."

A low hum vibrates in my chest, liquid and warm. It's not the searing rage that threatened to burn through me earlier. This is calm reassurance—shining certainty that I will protect him with every speck of gi left in me. The hum grows louder, warming me.

I nudge my snout against Ethan's cheek, wiping away his tears, even as my blood soaks through my fur. We're dying. We both know it. If one of us has to die, I want it to be me. But I wish more than anything that both of us can live so I can . . . we can . . . Even my avoidance skills have their limit.

I've fallen in love with him. It's stupid, but it's true. I love him. It's not an infatuation or a fleeting crush. It's not loneliness or horniness. It is passion, friendship, longing, and affection. It's tender and ardent, terrifying and comforting. It is all those things, all at once. It's a confusing mess that makes more sense than anything else in the worlds. It's . . . love, true and everlasting.

I love him. Warmth spreads through my entire body. Gods, I love him so fucking much. And I need to tell him.

"Ethan, I—" My mind goes blank when a blinding blue light streaks past us. "What was that?"

"I hope I'm not interrupting." Jaeseok lands beside us, piercing several monsters with his spear. "But I'm in the mood to dance."

As outrageous as his claim, the dokkaebi indeed dances his way through a throng of beasts, burning them and stabbing them, without missing a step in an oddly familiar choreography. Is that from a BTS music video? But damn, the dude can move.

"Gods, are you showing off again?" Hailey buries an arrow in a gaping, red mouth, then gracefully slides down the dragon's back. "I swear I'll gag you if you tell us about your stint in a Korean boy band one more time."

The dragon's . . . back? My jaw drops open as my mind finally catches up with my eyes.

A dragon just landed next to us.

CHAPTER
TWENTY-NINE

"I apologize for the delay, Your Highness." Jihun grunts as he takes off into the sky from the dragon's back, attacking the nightmare beasts from the air as they emerge from Daeseong's forehead.

"The situation hardly warrants an apology, Captain," Ethan calls out as he struggles to his feet.

I push myself up next to him, and we lean on each other for support, our wounds closing in the reprieve our friends bought us. It dawns on me that we might not die, which frees up some space for things like curiosity.

I try not to stare. I really do . . . but there is a freaking dragon in front of me. Pearlescent scales shimmer on their azure blue body, and the wolflike slopes of their face look masterfully sculpted. The dragon is quite possibly the most beautiful thing I've ever seen.

With the last of their occupants off their back, the dragon unwinds their huge, serpentine body from the ground and streaks to the sky. They move with the fluid grace of a gymnast's ribbon as they breathe blue fire into the mouths of the monsters with brutal efficiency.

"The Cheonji Monster is real," I say in awe.

"Bruh. Did you just call me a monster?" a deep, petulant voice grumbles in my head. Right, telepathy. "Not cool."

"Did you just call me *bruh*?" My gaze snaps to the dragon's face just as their eyes narrow into fiery blue slits. *Shit.* It's probably not a good idea to piss off a dragon, especially when they're keeping a horde of terrifying monsters from shredding you to pieces. "*Bruh* it is. And sorry about the *monster* bit. It's just what the humans call you, and I'm a little shocked that you're real."

"Well, it's my first time seeing a humongous white fox with nine tails, but you don't see me calling anyone a monster."

My gods. Only one form of monster could muster this much angst. "How old are you?"

"How old are you?" they echo right back.

I got my answer. They are definitely a teenager. "I'm one hundred thirty-two."

The dragon doesn't respond right away, busy piercing a beast with their tail. When they're done, they level a sullen gaze on me. "You're really old."

I huff a ponderous sigh as the dragon is distracted by another night-mare beast. I experimentally shift my shoulder blades. I can move my body without the excruciating pain of a thousand bleeding gashes. I love how quickly my gumiho heals. My nine tails swish with pride.

"I really like your fox form," Hailey says, shooting a volley of arrows with her crossbow. "Just so pretty."

"Stunning, really." Jaeseok winks rakishly, then he skewers a beast with his spear and shimmies his shoulders to what appears to be a sexy tune in his head.

"Thanks," I mutter telepathically, touched despite myself that they don't look at me with the same prejudice as the other shinbiins—like I'm an evil trickster or an exotic sex object.

Ethan is back to swinging his axes and plowing down the real mon-sters with steely focus. With a dragon on our side, I splurge a minute to watch and appreciate the spectacle. With his sweat-soaked T-shirt plastered to his torso, I can see every stark line of his muscles as they shift and bunch. The man fights like a *god*. I clamp my jaws together to stop myself from drooling and shift back into my human form.

I jump into the fray with my hwando raised and destroy a pile of monsters. I don't stop until my attacks turn sluggish with fatigue, but the onslaught is definitely slowing. Maybe we have a chance of winning. Hope is a stubborn thing. It keeps popping up. I welcome the burst of happiness it brings, however misplaced.

I chance a glance at Daeseong and suck in a sharp breath. The gash on his forehead is closing, stopping the flow of nightmare beasts. But even before I can register relief, the black of the mudang's eyes spreads across his face, his torso, his limbs. And the darkness keeps spreading until it hides Heaven Lake and the sky above it.

As if by agreement, the five of us gather near the shore, with the dragon hovering in the air behind us. Ethan's hand reaches out to catch mine as we face the towering darkness. The suhoshins shift to stand in front of us, prepared to give their lives for their prince—not that he'd ever accept such a sacrifice. A wasted sacrifice. None of us say it, but we know this isn't a fight we can win. Even my stubborn hope has sputtered out.

The darkness doesn't reach for us. But it doesn't need to move to destroy us from the inside.

Happiness is an emotion foreign to me. Smiles and laughter have never touched my face. I've never known anything but this gnawing grief inside me. I fall to my knees. It hurts so much that I can't catch my breath. There is only pain and darkness. This is all there is. The hot tears sliding down my cheeks provide no relief. My sorrow fills me, a silent scream clawing at my throat. There is no hope. I'm certain of this. There is no end to this pain but death.

A heart-wrenching sob reaches me through the fog of my despair. Ethan's shoulders shake with grief, and he punches the ground again and again. Jaeseok is wailing, tearing at his hair. Hailey drags her fingers down her face, her nails breaking skin. Jihun makes no sound as he cries, staring unblinkingly at where the sky used to be. The dragon is curled tightly in on themselves as they keen—a sound of such suffering and fear.

They're only a kid. Anger sparks in my chest. They're just a kid, trying to do the right thing. I take a full breath as another burst of fury stirs in me. My friends . . . they're hurting so much. They don't deserve this. And Ethan . . . His pain threatens to rip me apart and pull me under the darkness again. Rage ignites inside me, and I transform into my gumiho with a wrathful howl.

Fury urges me to fight, but I sense something behind my anger. Why do I refuse to see a kid suffer? Because there is good in me. Why does seeing the suhoshins suffer make me angry? Because I care about them. They're my friends. Why does Ethan's agony tear me apart? Because I love him. With all my scarred, battered heart.

And what is love? Love is hope. What is hope? Hope is life. What is life? Life is light. My head tilts back as warmth fills my chest and light glows beneath my coat. Liquid heat gathers in my heart, and peace descends on me.

"A beast like you doesn't deserve the Yeoiju. You will never understand its power." Daeseong's voice hisses from the darkness looming over us. "You're a coward. You hid from your powers even as your mother died in your arms. You did nothing to save her. You only used your power to save yourself. You're a murderer. You killed me and my disciples to save yourself. So much blood shed to preserve the life of an abomination."

"Maybe I was all those things in the past," I agree as power hums through me. "But now . . . can't I choose to be better? Can't I choose to be good?"

"You . . . you are evil," the mudang shrieks. "You will kill everyone if you unleash that power."

"No, I won't." My eyes flutter shut. "Because I *choose* to be good."

Even with my eyes closed, the light is blinding. I realize I can't control it. I can't contain it. I'm not wielding the power of the Yeoiju. The Yeoiju is wielding me. It wants to be released, and I have to let it go, even if it tears me apart. I smile. The light will vanquish Daeseong. I will die, but my friends will live. *Ethan* will live. Even the sullen teenage dragon will live. My smile grows.

I give myself up to the light. It seeps out of every pore in my body, pushing against my skin. Then it pulses through me in endless waves until I am nothing . . . but light.

RESTING PLACE

"Am I dead, Mother?" I ask in a little girl's voice.

"No, Daughter." She smiles down at me. "You are just resting."

"But my friends . . ." I want to get up, but I can't feel my body.

"They are all fine." Tears fill her eyes. "You did good. So good."

"Thank you," I say, my words slurring with fatigue. "Am I done now? Do I still have to run?"

She hesitates, then says, "Rest for now."

"Yes, Mother."

Her soft, warm hand smooths my hair, and she hums a pretty tune she used to sing to coax me to sleep. But there are tears in her voice. Why is Mother crying?

As I fall asleep, I realize she didn't answer my question.

CHAPTER THIRTY

"Sunny."

My eyes feel like they're weighed down by bags of sand. My human eyes. I must've shifted back at some point. It's for the best. My gumiho needs her rest.

"Sunny."

Even in my sleep, I hear the urgency in his voice. *Ethan's voice.* I strain to open my eyes and manage to flutter my lashes.

"Thank gods," Ethan cries and crushes me against him. "I'm here, Sunny. Come back to me."

"Is she awake?" Jihun asks, his voice solemn.

"Not yet." Ethan rocks me back and forth in his arms. "But she tried to open her eyes. She just needs time. She's going to be okay."

"Of course she'll be okay." Hailey sounds like she's holding back tears, with mixed results. "Do you think she can handle a journey to the Kingdom of Sky?"

"I have chocolate," Jaeseok volunteers.

"The gi of the realm might help her heal faster," Jihun adds.

"No, she's not strong enough to endure the Gray Void," Ethan says, to my great relief.

I do *not* want a dunk in the gray gunk right this moment. Or any moment for that matter. *Wait.* How does Ethan know about the Gray Void? Has he been to the Realm of Four Kingdoms? Or is it from his mother's memory? Either way, the man has a shit ton of explaining to do. But I'm beginning to understand that he might not know all the answers. *Oh, Ethan.* I try to open my eyes again. I manage a twitch this time.

"Why is her face all twitchy?" *There* they are. Our teen dragon.

"It's a good thing." Ethan brushes his lips against my temple. The corner of my mouth twitches this time. I swear I'm not imagining those lips against mine. "Every movement means she's fighting to come back to us."

"We can't stay here for long," Jihun says even more sternly than usual. What's up with him? "It's not safe."

"Do you think she killed Daeseong?" Hailey sounds nasally. She must've lost her battle against tears.

Good question. I wait for someone to answer. To my great surprise, it's the dragon that speaks.

"Nah. Heaven Lake is legit deep. If you go deep enough, no amount of light will reach it. I bet he dove for the bottom when the really old fox lady—"

"Sunny," Hailey interrupts.

Thank you. And that is why she's my friend. Wait, I have a friend? That's *right*. I have friends now.

"Yeah, okay. Whatever. When *Sunny* unleashed that light thing, that creepy old dude dove to the bottom of the lake." Superpowered teenage sarcasm drips from their words. "So it's an L for you guys."

"And it's a W for you?" Jaeseok laughs. "Like it or not, you're with us, kid. If it's a loss for us, it's a loss for you."

"Bruh." There is so much to unpack in that single word.

"Gods, you're going to be fun to have around, aren't you?" Hailey gripes.

Sounds like the dragon spirit is sticking around. Well, that's good. It's not healthy for a teenage dragon to live all alone in a deep, dark lake. Especially with a demented dark shaman waiting to room with them. And it'll make asking for a couple of their scales less awkward if we're friends. There I go again. How many friends am I going to make?

"I'm just glad I won't be the most annoying one in the group anymore," Jaeseok says with a contented sigh.

"So you *do* know you're annoying," Hailey teases.

"I am nothing if not self-aware . . ." Jaeseok deadpans. "Self-aware and awesome."

Jihun ignores the entertaining discourse and brings them back on topic. "If not the Kingdom of Sky, where should we go?"

"Las Vegas," Ethan answers without hesitation. "Being around familiar surroundings might help her recover faster."

"Las Vegas might not be the most discreet location, Your Highness," Jihun says diplomatically. "The Jaenanpa had to have felt the unprecedented pulse of power when Sunny subdued Daeseong. They might not know about the existence of the Yeoiju, but those magic-crazed psychopaths will soon be after her. They'll torture her—and dissect her if necessary—to find the source of her powers."

"Which makes Vegas the ideal location," Ethan counters. "The crush of people there will help mask our location. That's how we evaded your pursuit, Captain."

"Sweet." Jaeseok coughs to cover his laugh. "Vegas it is. I'm a high roller at the Bellagio, so I'll have them comp us some suites. How does that sound to you, roomie?"

"Dream on, goblin," Hailey says archly.

Ethan stands up, with me cradled against him. "We'll moon shift to Incheon, then lock down our magic. If we take a plane to Las Vegas, we'll be harder to trace."

"Is that what you and Sunny did?" Jihun sounds almost impressed. "She's certainly well versed in staying hidden."

"Did you say we're going to take an airplane?" Hailey squeaks.

"I don't believe this," Jaeseok says slowly. "You can't be afraid of flying. You literally fly all the time."

"With magic," she grits out. "Sitting in a hunk of metal six miles above sea level is a different experience altogether."

"Flying is safer than driving, you know. My dad and I used to take commercial flights all the time," the dragon says. "We were also good at staying hidden. Besides, most of us in the Mortal Realm can't moon shift. The study of high magic was lost long ago."

"And you know all this how?" Hailey asks, her fear of flying forgotten.

"My dad was a very old dragon spirit. He taught me a lot of things the beings of the Mortal Realm have forgotten." The dragon's voice is subdued. Poor kid. I wonder how they lost their dad.

"We can learn more about Draco's life later," Jihun interrupts the interesting discourse. Again. "We need to move."

Wait. Who's Draco?

"I said it once, and I'll say it again," Jaeseok scoffs. "*Draco* can't be their real name."

"I told you," the dragon bellows. "It's my American name. I don't use my Korean name."

"What *is* your Korean name?" Hailey sounds nefarious. "Is it really old fashioned? Like Boknam?"

"Or Cheolsu?" Jaeseok joins in the fun. "You should call yourself John Doe in the spirit of your super-generic Korean name."

"My name is not Cheolsu." The dragon spirit sounds like they're ready to blow.

"*Move.*" Jihun's voice leaves no room for argument. "Second Lieutenant, I'll give you a ten-minute head start to find us a secluded location near Incheon Airport. Then we'll track your magic and meet you there."

"Yes, sir." Jaeseok sounds credibly formal until he adds, "Don't miss me too much, Hailey. You, too, Captain."

Hailey and Jihun don't deign to answer the dokkaebi. Or maybe I've fallen asleep again. Probably the latter, because the next thing I hear is the din of the airport.

"You must be tired, Your Highness. Allow me to carry her," Jihun offers.

"No," Ethan growls. His chests shifts as he takes a deep breath. "No, thank you, Captain. She hardly weighs anything."

"How about if neither of you carry me?" I croak, squinting my eyes against the bright lights.

"Sunny." Ethan nearly drops me before he tightens his grip around me. "How long have you been awake? Are you hurting anywhere? What do you need? Tell me."

Before I can answer any of his questions, he crushes his mouth against mine. I melt against him until I remember with a jolt that he . . . that I . . . We can't be together. For so many reasons.

I turn my head away and push against his chest. "Put me down."

"Are you sure you can—"

"*Now*," I snap. "Put me down or I'll break your jaw."

Despite the threat of violence, Ethan puts me down with utmost care, his hands hovering nearby in case I fall. I lock my knees when they threaten to buckle and clench my teeth to fight against a wave of dizziness. When I'm sure I won't pass out, I push his hands away. Then I stumble over to a row of chairs and sink into one.

I shift uncomfortably in my seat. My clothes are shredded and crusted with dried blood, but someone glamoured me so I don't look like I ran away from a chain saw massacre. I shoot a quick glance at Ethan and Jihun. They're neatly glamoured as well, but my heart shudders as I take in the vicious gashes on their real clothes.

"We got the tick—" Hailey stops midsentence and lunges for me. "You're awake. Oh, Sunny. I was so worried."

I don't have the heart to push her away, even though she kept me in the dark about Ethan's identity, along with Jihun and Jaeseok. We fought together. We almost died together. We *lived* together. No, I can't stay mad at her . . . or at any of the suhoshins. Their loyalty lies with their prince. They did what they had to do.

I return her hug and whisper, "You don't need to worry anymore. I'm fine."

Fine is an overstatement, but I don't feel detached from my body anymore, like my spirit couldn't decide whether to stay or leave. That's something. Ethan hovers nearby while Jaeseok ruffles my hair like an older brother. A gorgeous teenager with hair the same cerulean as the dragon's scales, probably Draco in their human form, gives me a sullen nod. Yup, that's them. Finally, Jihun crouches down in front of me so our eyes are level.

"What you did back there . . . Thank you." His voice is oddly husky as he brushes the hair out of my face. Out of the corner of my eye, I see Ethan step closer. "See, I told you. You aren't a mass murderer."

"Your *thank you* doesn't mean as much when you follow it up with *I told you so* in the same breath." I offer him a wobbly smile. His presence steadies me even as Ethan's unwavering gaze bores into me.

"I honestly wish we could linger for this sweet reunion, but we're late for our flight," Jaeseok gently reminds the group.

"Wow, look at you." Hailey punches his arm. "When did you become so responsible?"

"Well, with the captain preoccupied with simultaneously thanking Sunny and rubbing her face in it, someone had to step up." He grins incorrigibly, all evidence of Mr. Responsibility gone.

"All right. Let's go," Jihun says, getting to his feet.

He offers me his hand at the same time Ethan offers his. I glance up at the two beautiful males holding out their hands, their gazes trained intently on my face—it's like they're having a staring contest without looking at each other. Rolling my eyes, I grip the armrests and push up to my feet without help from either. I'm not getting in the middle of whatever is going on between them. Did they have an argument while I was out?

We make a mad dash—no, we actually make excruciatingly slow progress as I stumble along with Hailey's help—to our gate. We're the last to board the plane, and we prepare for takeoff as soon as we reach our seats.

I stare out the window as Hailey crushes my hand in a death grip, terrified despite Draco's reassurance. I made sure I sat as far away from Ethan as possible, which isn't very far. We're in first class again, and he's sitting in a double suite one row ahead of us. Jihun and Jaeseok flank him in the single suites by the windows. I take evil pleasure in the fact that Ethan is sharing his suite with Draco for the duration of the twelve-hour flight.

But I gasp, making Hailey startle beside me. In a sudden panic, I lift my ass halfway off my seat, ready to jump from the moving plane, when Ethan glances over with a crooked grin. He casually places my backpack on his armrest and pretends to rummage through it, showing me the rainbow bokjumeoni and the "recorder." He must've glamoured it himself.

I give him a subtle nod and settle back in my seat. My heart aches at the disappointment on his face, but I'm not ready to share secret smiles with him over an inside joke.

"Who paid for the tickets?" I ask to distract Hailey as the plane takes off.

"The Bank of the Order of the Suhoshin." She smiles at me, her grip on my hand relaxing a fraction. "All of us who travel to the Mortal Realm are given a black card in case of emergencies."

"Fancy." I grin back. "As far as Suhoshin perks go, it's a toss-up between the black card and the ability to fly."

"Oh, gods. I would give up my black card in an instant if it meant I could just fly myself to Las Vegas."

"You're doing great," I say. "Take a nap, watch a couple of movies, and we'll be there in no time."

I take my own advice on napping. I can't seem to stay awake for longer than a few minutes. And I feel so . . . weak. It's not my favorite. I sleep and sleep, waking up only to eat the fancy first-class food. But it gets harder and harder to wake up each time. When I almost plant my face into the seaweed soup, I give up trying to eat and go back to sleep.

"Sunny," Hailey yells in my ear and gives my shoulders a sharp shake.

"Hey . . . stop." I swat limply at her and close my eyes again.

"Thank gods. You're alive. You need to wake up, Sunny." She shakes me until my head flops around. "We're here. We need to get off this cursed airplane."

"Let her sleep," Ethan says quietly. "I got her."

What does he mean he got me? I actually don't care, since he made Hailey stop shaking me. And I don't protest when he lifts me up in his arms. Instead, I bury my face in his chest and give in to the siren's call of slumber, the steady thump of his heartbeat my lullaby.

Rest . . . for now.

CHAPTER
THIRTY-ONE

My eyes open to tomb-like darkness. Oh, gods. Where am I? I can't hear myself think past the terrified thundering of my heart. I blindly reach out, and my hand connects with a table lamp. I sit up and turn the lamp on with fumbling hands. I sigh with relief when warm light fills the room.

There are no nightmare monsters here. No Daeseong.

I rub my eyes to clear my bleary vision and look at my surroundings, willing my heartbeat to return to normal. *You're safe.* I'm sitting in a king-size bed in the middle of a luxurious bedroom with muted gold wallpaper and plush cream carpet. It's not as nice as my room in the Sunset Pavilion, but it's still a nice room. I guess I have Jacseok, the high-rolling dokkaebi, to thank for the fancy lodgings.

I gingerly lower my feet to the floor and stand, only to have my legs buckle beneath me. It takes a few more tries, but I finally get to my feet and walk to the window. It's covered with blackout curtains. No wonder it's so dark in here.

I pull back the curtains, half expecting it to be bright and sunny outside. But it's dark out. Well, as dark as Vegas gets. An ache spreads across my chest, and tears sting the tip of my nose. *I'm home.*

My room overlooks the Fountains of Bellagio, and the mesmerizing water show distracts me enough to avoid everything I should be thinking about. A smile curves my lips, remembering our dip in the man-made lake. I can't believe I moon shifted us there. It feels like a lifetime ago.

"The view's much better from up here, isn't it?" I spin around at the sound of Ethan's voice. He's standing in the doorway, leaning against the doorframe. "I'm . . . I'm so glad you're awake."

"Why? Did I miss dinner?" I sound snarky, but I don't know how else to act.

"You've been asleep for almost three days," he rasps, looking haunted.

"For three days?" I gape at him. "Why didn't you try to wake me up?"

"I did try." He wipes a weary hand down his face. "I wanted you to eat, but I could barely rouse you enough to take sips of water."

But I don't feel like someone who's starved for three days. I turn my focus on my body. The bone-weary fatigue—the fragile weakness—is gone. And I'm finally wide awake, the relentless tug of drowsiness gone. Thank gods for that. I hated feeling so helpless, even when surrounded by friends. Suddenly, I'm ravenous. My stomach growls on cue, loudly enough to make Ethan's lips quirk into a small smile.

"I'll order room service," he says graciously. "Rare steak with two sunny-side up eggs?"

"Let's . . . let's take a walk." I look down at myself and notice the pink cami set I'm wearing. I blush to the roots of my hair. "Did you . . ."

"No, no, no." Ethan straightens in the doorway and holds his palms out. "Hailey changed you so you'd be more comfortable. Your clothes were ruined in the fight . . . She hung up a change of clothes for you in the closet."

My eyes take in his appearance for the first time. He's not wearing his bloodied clothes from the battle, but his rumpled T-shirt and jeans don't seem like much of an upgrade. His hair is clumped together in places and sticking out in others. He has obviously run his hands through it quite a bit. His eyes are bloodshot, and days' worth of beard darkens his jaws. He's a mess, and knowing why makes my heart hurt.

"I should clean up and change before we venture outside." I wave my hand toward the vicinity of my en suite bathroom.

"Of course. I . . . I should as well." But he doesn't budge from the door, his throat working. "Thank you for coming back to me."

He spins on his heels and walks away from my room before I can burst into tears in front of him. I manage to get my shit together and don't ugly cry until I'm under the spray of hot water. The water runs red, and that makes me cry harder. I don't care if I'm being a baby. It's been a hard few weeks, and it's hard to believe that we're safe . . . even for a little while.

When I'm ready, I go out to the living room, and Ethan shoots to his feet from the couch. His eyes scan me from head to toe as though he needs to reassure himself that I'm okay. He changed into a clean T-shirt and a pair of snug jeans, and I can't help drinking in the sight of him. He's safe. He's healthy. It feels like a miracle.

He takes a step toward me with his hand outstretched. He opens his mouth on a sharp inhale, and I hold my breath. But after a moment, he drops his arm, pressing his lips together. I exhale a little shakily. I stare at the lock of damp hair that fell across his forehead and ache to brush it away. Instead, we nod awkwardly at each other and walk out of our suite without a word.

I feel him stealing glances at me as we stroll down the crowded sidewalk, his hand hovering protectively behind me—not quite touching—whenever anyone gets too close. Our magic is doused. Well, at least mine is. I can't feel the powerful current of Ethan's gi, but it prickles just beneath his skin, ready to burst free. *Of course.* His mother had bound his magic . . . He hasn't had much practice at hiding his magic on his own.

"You need to relax, Ethan," I say softly, reaching for his hand. He shoots me a wide-eyed glance, then rushes to lace his fingers through mine as though I might snatch them away. "Your magic is too close to the surface."

"I . . . Sorry." He exhales a long, slow breath. "I have a lot to learn about my . . . powers. What they are. How to wield them. How to hide them."

I remember snatches of our battle at Heaven Lake—the glow of his silver-and-green eyes, the deadly strikes of his golden axe and silver axe, the burst of unfathomable power that pushed back the nightmare beasts. This male is the Prince of Mountains. He's a stranger to me.

I tug on my hand, but he holds tight. After another half-hearted pull, I leave my hand where it is. The obstinate set of his jaw tells me he won't let go without a fight—and I'm tired of fighting. At least, he's as stubborn as ever. That much is familiar about him.

He holds the door as I walk inside Roxy's Diner, then follows close behind me. When I slide into my booth, he pauses by my side for a moment, and I freeze in my seat. I'm relieved when he settles into the bench across from mine. But when I meet his determined, unwavering gaze, I wonder if it would've been better if he'd sat next to me. I'm thankful for an excuse to look away when Rachel hurries to our table.

"Sunny, I was worried when you didn't come for so long," she says while filling our mugs with coffee.

"Sorry, I had to go out of town unexpectedly." I take a sip of my scalding coffee to hide the sudden rush of tears. Here's another friend I let sneak into my heart. It turns out I'm a lousy loner.

"And look how skinny you've gotten." She tsks when she gets a good look at my face, then narrows her eyes at Ethan. "I hope your young man is treating you right."

"It's not . . . He's not . . ." I turn into a tomato.

"I'll do my best"—he holds my gaze—"if she lets me."

"Well, then." Rachel beams at Ethan, placated by his solemn answer, then at me. "I'll get your steak and eggs started."

"I'll have the same," he says when our happy server looks askance at him.

"And you two are getting an apple pie à la mode on the house." She clucks her tongue. "Really, sweetie. You're all skin and bones."

When Rachel bustles away, I straighten my utensils with great care.

"Sunny," Ethan says, quiet pleading in his voice. "Ask me anything you want. I'll tell you everything."

"So . . . the Prince of Mountains, huh?" I go for flippant but end up with strangled.

"Yes." He swallows but steadily holds my gaze.

"When did you find out?" I manage to whisper.

"The night of the fire." Regret lines his face. "I learned everything that night."

A part of me already knew, but I go limp with relief that he wasn't lying to me from the moment he walked back into my life. I was afraid he was using me somehow, laughing at me the whole time . . . laughing at how easily I fell into his arms. But he didn't know until the house burned down—just hours before he was taken from me. It doesn't change that he kept the truth from me, but I take comfort in the fact that most of our time together was real.

"The jade necklace," he pushes on. "I did lose it when the string snapped in the fire."

"But?" I arch an eyebrow.

"But . . . while you slept, I went back to the house—or what was left of it—to look for the necklace."

I clench my teeth against the sting of his first lie. "Did you find it?"

"Yes, I found it." He blows out a long breath. "But thin, jagged cracks spread along its surface. It felt like my heart was cracking with it. And . . . and I closed my hand around it, desperate to hold it together. It was my last connection to my mom."

I can only nod at him to continue, because my heart's breaking for him.

"I didn't notice it at first, but I felt the disk beating in my hand like . . . like it was alive. Before I could even register the thought, silver-and-green fire burst out of my hand, throwing me onto my back. Then my whole body levitated off the ground."

"Oh, gods." I thought I dreamed about the burst of silver-and-green fire that night. "It must have been terrifying."

But Ethan doesn't seem to hear me. "The fire closed in around me, but it didn't feel like the fire that burnt down the house. It wasn't hot, but it was . . . all-consuming in a way I can't explain. Then the jade exploded into a thousand pieces, and my mind felt like it shattered too."

"You broke the stone," I breathe. "Ben's last words . . ."

"Yes, he wasn't rambling at all. He wanted me to break the stone of tears." Ethan covers his eyes with his hand, his voice catching. After a moment, he takes a deep breath and looks at me again. "The silver-and-green fire . . . the blast . . . it all happened in an instant, but it also felt like a lifetime. Like I've lived another entire life."

I reach for his hand across the table, needing to ease his pain.

"Between one breath and the next, I suddenly knew . . . everything. Everything my mother, the Queen of Mountains, knew before she hid me away. She imbued all her knowledge . . . all her memories . . . into the jade and bound my powers to it. Then with the last of her gi, she enchanted the stone to keep me hidden—to keep me safe—until my time came." His eyes are far away. "I was meant to break the jade disk when I came of age on my twenty-fourth birthday, but Ben died before he could tell me.

"But I . . . I think I've pieced together what happened after I left the Kingdom of Mountains. My mom . . . she was the queen's lady-in-waiting and . . . and my dad . . . they didn't die in a car accident. I think they died saving me. That's why Ben and I had to move to LA so quickly. Even with my mother's magic, the people after me . . . they found us somehow."

"Oh, Ethan." Helpless tears spring to my eyes.

"And I think Ben let himself be killed without a fight because of me." Ethan hunches in on himself. "To keep me hidden until I came into my powers."

"I'm so sorry," I say in a broken whisper.

"Everyone who loved me . . ." He holds his hands out, staring down at them in horror. Like he killed his family with his own hands.

"Everyone I loved . . . died because of me. Then I brought *you* into this nightmare. You almost died because of me too."

"That's not true. It's *not* because of you." I shake my head vehemently. I thought *I* had put him in danger when we were on the run, and the guilt had eaten away at me like acid. I can't let him do that to himself. "*None* of this is your fault. You did none of this. You *chose* none of this."

His gaze focuses on me again, and his bitter smile tells me he doesn't believe me. With a sharp breath, he glances around the diner and changes the subject. "It was my birthday when I found you."

"Oh." Heat rushes to my face. Even considering the circumstances, I'm embarrassed I forgot his birthday. In my defense, I thought he was forever out of my life.

"Don't worry," he says with a ghost of a smile. "You're paying for dinner."

"Fair enough." I smile back at him, then fidget restlessly in my seat. I still don't understand some things. "That night, while I was walking to Roxy's, something set me on edge, and I let my magic surface over a damn alley cat. It was stupid of me, but it was the barest whisper of magic. No one should've been able to trace it."

Yet Ethan found me. The question is how? Yes, he's the Prince of Mountains and is unimaginably powerful. But he found me before he broke the stone. So how did he find me without his magic? I worry my bottom lip, my brows drawing together. I know all of this is hard for him to talk about, but I need to understand.

"The jade disk still bound your magic, but it couldn't contain all of your powers once you came of age—once your magic peaked," I say, puzzling it out. "Maybe that's how you traced my magic back to me. That's how you were able to summon the axes to fight Blue, even though you weren't strong enough to wield them yet."

Ethan nods, his eyes never leaving my face.

"When you broke the stone, you unbound your powers," I continue, even though he already knows all of this. "That's why you were suddenly able to wield the axes so fluidly in the cave. And that's how you knew everything about the Shingae, even about the Realm of Four Kingdoms, when we met again at Heaven Lake."

He nods again.

"Your head must be spinning," I whisper. It's too much. How can he bear it? "Your heart must be breaking."

"Gods, Sunny." He rakes a hand through his hair, his expression haunted. "So much blood was spilled because of me. All to protect me from . . ."

I'm afraid to ask, but he needs to tell someone before he drowns in his torment. "From who?"

I flinch when Ethan meets my gaze. I see the dark fury and jagged violence inside him. In this moment, nothing remains of the kind, loyal man I've come to love. This male, the Prince of Mountains, is hard, ruthless, and implacable. Yet he doesn't frighten me, because my Ethan is still somewhere inside.

"The King of Mountains." The prince's mouth twists into a mimicry of a smile. "My *father*."

"But why?" I choke out.

"Because I am the King Foretold." His bark of laughter is a sound of helpless sorrow, edged with rage. "Because of a *prophecy* that proclaimed I would be the one to unify the Realm of Four Kingdoms."

"I don't understand." How could his own father . . .

"My father feared it would mean the end of his precious reign as the King of Mountains," the prince says with icy calm. "That male killed his wife—and would've killed his own child—to hold on to his power."

Such a bloody legacy . . . I want to hide my Ethan from its toxic grasp.

"Maybe you could . . ." I bite my lip. He could what? Run away with me? If he forsakes his birthright, then the death of everyone he loved would've been for nothing. But the words refuse to die on my tongue. Because if he doesn't go back to the Realm of Four Kingdoms, maybe we could be together. No matter how selfish that makes me, I can't help wanting to hold on to him. "You don't have to—"

"Here we are." Rachel is all smiles as she places our food in front of us. "Now eat up, and I'll bring the pie out when you're done."

"Thank you, Rachel." Ethan pulls himself together quicker than I do. "Everything looks delicious."

She blushes with pleasure, then she hurries over to another table. I watch her go, the thoughts in my head spinning too fast for me to grasp a single one.

"Eat." He pushes my plate closer to me. My Ethan is back. "Rachel will have my ass if I don't fatten you up."

"I'm not a heifer," I force myself to quip, because that's what Ethan and I do. I want to hold on to this brief reprieve . . . this moment of normalcy.

With a soft sigh, I slice dutifully into my steak. I pop the yolks of my sunny-side up eggs and scoop up the rich deliciousness with a slice of rare steak. I close my mouth around the perfect bite and moan, letting the familiarity of the food comfort me. And gods, I'm not gonna lie, it does me a world of good.

We don't talk until the last crumb of the apple pie is gone. I consider licking the melted vanilla ice cream from the plate to stave off the inevitable. Because *this* isn't the norm. Not anymore. The stakes have changed, and so have we.

"I do have to go back, you know." Ethan picks up the thread of our conversation. "The king's hunger for wealth and power knew no end, and it led him to tax his own people to the point of poverty. When my mother became queen, she helped their people as much as she could. They loved her for it, but the king hated her for it."

"But maybe he's changed," I say weakly, not believing for a second it could be true.

"I spoke with Jihun while you were sleeping, and the King of Mountain's reign has grown even more oppressive since my mother died." The prince's face twists into a snarl. "Since he killed her."

I close my eyes against the horror . . . against my own fury. The king hurt Ethan in unspeakable ways. And I want to hurt him right back. I want to make him pay. I want the King of Mountains to burn for what he did.

"Even knowing all this," Ethan rasps, his eyes drinking in my face with heart-wrenching longing. "I would've walked away. I would've turned my back on my people—on my destiny—if you'd asked. But now I can't because I . . . I've bound myself to the crown.

"On that small mountain in South Korea . . . I didn't know who I was praying to, but I prayed to anyone who would listen. I begged them for a way to save you from the blue assassin. I promised to do anything . . . to pay any price. That's when the golden axe and the silver axe appeared to me."

"No . . . ," I say as dark premonition washes over me. *Please, no.*

"When I picked up the axes, I felt the power of the vow lock around me. Even when I knew nothing about the Shingae, I *felt* it." Devastation contorts his face. "So you see, I can't walk away. Not anymore."

"Only a fool would make a vow to the Shingae without knowing the price." My voice is barely above a whisper. *Oh, Ethan. What have you done?*

"Desperation makes fools of us all. And I've always been a fool for you, Sunny. I've loved you since I was sixteen." Ethan's lips quirk at my gasp. "After you left, I convinced myself that I'd outgrown my teenage infatuation. But that lie went out the door the moment you scowled at me from across this very table."

"Don't." I shake my head.

"I'm not asking you to love me back," he rushes to add. "I only wanted to tell you that I love you . . . more than anything, because you deserve to know."

I swallow the sob gathering in my throat and steel myself with a deep breath. "Was it another prophecy that foretold you were destined to kill me?"

"I know what I said before, but that will never happen. I will battle fate itself before I hurt you," he says with quiet conviction. "And my mother believed prophecies were only meant to shine light on one of the many paths to the future. You and I . . . we could travel the path *we* choose."

"So your answer is yes." I swallow past my dry throat. "You were prophesized to kill me."

"The King Foretold is destined to kill the one who possesses the Yeoiju." He drags a weary hand down his face. "I learned of that prophecy when I broke the jade disk, but I only realized who it meant when I found you at Heaven Lake. Seeing you again jarred something in my memory. The lone cypress said you possessed the gift of the Cheon'gwang, and the Yeoiju is that gift, the last of the true light."

I blink at him like an owl. I wish I'd figured out that little tidbit for myself and saved Minju the trouble of stabbing me. I suppress the unhinged laughter bubbling up my throat.

"A part of me still wanted to deny it until you saved us from Daeseong with that gift. I can't deny it any longer, and I don't *want* to deny any part of you." Ethan takes my hand in his warm, calloused one. "I love you, Sunny. All of you. No prophecy can change that. Nothing can ever make me hurt you."

You're hurting me now, I want to say. *Your love is hurting me.*

I close my eyes to hide my pain from him. I understand his vow to the Shingae, even if he doesn't yet. He didn't bind himself to the crown. He bound himself to his *destiny*. No matter how hard I've tried to deny my own destiny, I know I can't hide from it forever. I can't run from it anymore. Ethan accepted his destiny to become the King Foretold. And the King Foretold is destined to kill me because I possess the Yeoiju. The gift of the Cheon'gwang is not something I can choose to give up. It's inside me, tied to my life force. There *is* no other path for us.

I never imagined I could ever love someone and be loved in return. I never knew a love like this even existed. And it guts me that our love cannot be. I can never accept his love or reveal my love to him. Because if I can't outrun destiny, then I intend to fight it.

I refuse to let destiny manipulate Ethan into killing someone he loves. Someone who loves him back. That will destroy him. This has to end now. I'll make him stop loving me, even if it wrecks me. And I will hide my love from him. If Ethan kills me, he'll do it never knowing that I love him. I will spare him that pain, at least.

But I'll love him, even as I die at his hands. I will *always* love him. And hiding that love from him is the best way I can love him. I can't forget that no matter how much it hurts. I pull my hand out of his and will my face into a cold mask.

"Come with me to the Realm of Four Kingdoms," Ethan says in a hoarse whisper.

"I left you and Ben eight years ago for a reason." I arch my brow with disdain, my icy hands trembling under the table. "I don't want any attachments. And I definitely don't want *love*."

"I don't . . . expect anything from you." His crestfallen expression stabs my heart, and stark red blood seeps into my ashen soul. "You're in danger in the Mortal Realm. The Jaenanpa won't stop hunting you until the Yeoiju is in their hands. And . . . and Daeseong will be back." He takes a shuddering breath to stanch the flow of his desperate words. "I just want to keep you safe, Sunny. Let me do that much."

"And how will you do that?" I force a bitter laugh. "The Shinbiin in the Kingdom of Sky don't want my kind anywhere near their precious kingdom. They were disgusted I even set foot in their realm. Do you think your people in the Kingdom of Mountains will be any different? I doubt they would let someone as lowly as me within a mile radius of their prince."

"I will *end* anyone who dares insult you," he snarls, his eyes churning with silver-and-green fire.

"You can't kill everyone in that realm," I scoff. Then I freeze, my stomach turning over. Did Daeseong see something in the future? *If you stay with her, you'll be laying the path to the destruction of your kingdom—the destruction of the Realm of Four Kingdoms.* Could this be what the dark mudang meant? I force myself to continue, "Your people will never accept a creature like me."

"You are *not* a creature." He bows his head, clenching his eyes shut. When he looks back up, his eyes are brown again, but they burn with an intensity that stops my heart. "You are Sunny Cho. My prickly, brave, glorious Sunny. You're my friend. You are my heart. That's who you are."

"Love is fleeting, Ethan," I lie woodenly. "I've lived a hundred thirty-two years. I would know."

"Let me love you for a thousand years and prove you wrong," he says, his voice breaking. "Sunny, please. Don't ask me to leave you here knowing your life is in danger."

"I can take care of myself." My nails dig into my palms as I fight back tears.

"You saved all of us at Heaven Lake, but it almost cost you your life. Don't deny it. You can't face Daeseong and the Jaenanpa alone. Please," he pleads with his heart bared on his face. "Come stay in the Realm of Four Kingdoms. At least until you learn how to wield the powers of the Yeoiju."

"If I do come with you . . . ," I say, wavering. Because despite everything, I want to be close to him. Hiding my feelings from him might ruin me, but being apart from him might kill me. "Will you promise me one thing?"

"Yes." Ethan clutches my hand again. "Anything."

Why is he making this so hard for me? I snatch my hand away. "Promise me you'll stop this nonsense about loving me."

"You might as well tell me to stop breathing." Hurt darkens his eyes, but I recognize the determined set of his jaw. "I promise I won't pressure you in any way, but don't ask me to stop loving you. It's not possible."

Oh, gods. Emotion wraps itself around my throat, and unshed tears burn my eyes. I can't do this. I just want him to hold me and tell me everything will be okay. This is why the last of my mother's gi wanted me to run. She wanted me to run from Ethan. She somehow knew about the prophecy. She wanted to spare me from this heartbreak. Because I can't stop loving him, and it will literally be the death of me.

Maybe it's not too late. Maybe I can run and hide from the Shingae. From Ethan. If he can't find me, he can't kill me. But he *will* find me. He proved that much when he tracked me down at Roxy's Diner through a wisp of magic. My fucked-up destiny is catching up with me. *Mother, I can't outrun it.* And if it means I can stay close to Ethan, I don't know if I *want* to run from it. No one ever tells you that love wipes out your sense of self-preservation.

And Daeseong must be dealt with. He killed my mother. He killed Ben. He will pay for his sins. But it isn't only vengeance I seek. I glimpsed the extent of the dark mudang's power—the extent of his evil. He will unleash the Amheuk from its prison beyond the worlds. It will mean the end of both realms. I know this.

With Draco's scales and my sacred ashes, we can forge a sword of light. I will learn to wield the powers of the Yeoiju. We'll be ready for Daeseong when he returns. And this time, we will stop him for good. I'm still no hero, but I have things to protect now. My home. My friends. My Ethan.

"Fine," I mutter ungraciously, even as my heart beats against my ribs, trying to fly toward him. "I'll come to the Realm of Four Kingdoms with you."

Love makes fools of us all.

AUTHOR'S NOTE

Once upon a time, I was a touch-spoiled, precocious little girl, and the grown-ups showered me with attention. But I knew my mind and didn't bestow my favor on just anyone. My dad was my favorite person in the whole wide world. I was going to marry him.

In Korea, people often sat cross-legged on the floor rather than on a sofa, and my favorite place to sit was on my dad's knee. I must've used him as my personal armchair until I was at least five or six. I wasn't a baby anymore and didn't weigh next to nothing. His legs must've fallen asleep all the time, but he never once told me to move before I chose to get up.

But my dad was an international businessman, and he traveled many months out of the year. So only when he was away would I sit on anyone else's knee. I usually chose my godfather, who doted on me. Other grown-ups would try to coax me and bribe me to sit on their knees, but I rarely agreed. And when my dad came home, I acted as though my godfather didn't even exist.

That was when the grown-ups started calling me a gumiho. They said I was a hundred-year-old fox and my mom was a five-hundred-year-old fox. Gumihos are known for their cunning and beauty, so it was a half compliment and a half insult. I think they just brought my mom into it because she was very beautiful. But the nickname kind of grew on me and stuck until my family immigrated to the United States when I was nine.

I got a new "American" name and a new nickname—"beanstalk," because I shot up in less than a year and was five feet six by the time I was eleven. I was too tall to sit on anyone's lap, and my gumiho was forgotten.

I remember the moment the seed of Sunny's story formed in my mind. It was late fall in 2017. I was a mom by then, and an attorney, because becoming an author seemed like a pipe dream. Because of depression and insomnia, I was up alone in the wee hours of the morning, sitting listlessly on the living room sofa with the lights dimmed. I was reminiscing about my childhood in Korea and wondered, "What if a hundred-year-old fox came to America like I did?"

And that is how *Nine Tailed*, a story about a hundred-year-old gumiho in Las Vegas, was born. I hope you love Sunny as much as I do. Because, even if she doesn't show it, she loves you back.

ACKNOWLEDGMENTS

Let me jump right into thanking everyone who made this book possible.

To my agent, Sarah Younger, I found the courage and motivation to finally write the book of my heart thanks to your gentle nudging. It only took you four years to convince me I could do this! Thank you for always knowing the right things to say to put my anxiety at ease without ever compromising on the truth. Thank you for your enthusiasm for *Nine Tailed* and for giving me the sparks of inspiration to do Sunny's story justice. I wear your support and willingness to go to the mattresses for me like an indestructible armor. I can weather the storm that is traditional publishing because I have you on my side.

To my acquiring editor, Alison Dasho, thank you, *thank you*, THANK YOU for your love and enthusiasm for *Nine Tailed*. I will never forget your tears of happiness and the celebratory jelly beans when I accepted the offer. I knew in my heart then that Sunny and Ethan had found the right home. You are their greatest champion and cheerleader. Thank you. Again. In case I haven't said it enough.

To my *new* acquiring editor, Lauren Plude, I want to give you a flying high five, then tackle hug you. I want us to chest bump and yell "Heck yeah!" in each other's faces. You got me so amped up that I can't manage anything less energetic to welcome you aboard. Go, Team Sunny!!! I couldn't have hoped for a better person to take the baton from Alison to champion *Nine Tailed*. Thank you for loving Sunny and Ethan like I do.

To my developmental editor, Charlotte Herscher, smart, talented, confident, generous, honest, conscientious—you are an absolute dream to work with. Thank you for helping me make *Nine Tailed* the best book it can be. It's so shiny and pretty. Haha. I'm so proud of this book. And thank you so much for responding to my panicky emails so promptly. My family thanks you for neutralizing Mom's freak-outs.

To my amazing critique partners, Gwen Hernandez and Christina Britton, thank you for never leaving my side through the entire harrowing process of writing a book that means so very much to me. I made it across the tightrope with you holding my hands, one on each side. Thank you for letting me pick your brains when I got stuck and for showering me with praise for every little phrase I shared with you. It truly is an honor to have two such talented authors as my dear friends and critique partners.

To my boys, thank you for being proud of me, for believing in me, and for always supporting me. I'm so proud of you guys. I believe you will make this world a better place. And I will always stand by your sides to lend you my strength whenever you need me. I love you guys more than life.

To my husband, I couldn't have done this without your support. Thank you for working so hard for our family. We're so lucky to have you. xoxo . . . xoxoxoxoxo. PS, xoxoxoxoxoxoxoxo.

To my mom and my brother, thank you for never allowing me to forget my heritage and for sharing your knowledge and wisdom about Korean folklore and customs with me. Thank you for cherishing me and loving me unconditionally. I stand straighter and shine brighter because of you.

To my readers . . . WHAT?!?! I still can't believe I have readers—generous, quirky, funny, and kind readers who love my books as much as I love them. *Nine Tailed* is my beating heart, and I trust it to your care. I hope it beats stronger and grows bigger with your love and support.

GLOSSARY

- Amheuk: Ancient force of true darkness
- assi: Noble maiden
- bokjumeoni: Round silk pouch used mainly on New Year's Day for children to put their money in (also known as a "lucky pouch")
- bujeok: Talisman or amulet (often a piece of paper with writings and symbols drawn by a shaman) to bring either good fortune or protection. It can also be used to bring ill fortune to an enemy.
- bulgogi: Thinly sliced, marinated meat that is grilled or pan-fried
- Cheon'gwang: Ancient force of true light
- cheongyang gochu: A spicy Korean chili pepper
- Cheonji: Heaven Lake, a lake that lies on the border between China and North Korea on Mount Baekdu
- dokkaebi: Goblin from Korean folklore
- doksacho: Deadly poisonous herb
- gat: Traditional Korean hat with a wide brim made of black mesh
- gi: Life force, commonly referred to as *chi* (based on the Mandarin pronunciation)
- gimbap: Rolls of rice and seaweed filled with marinated meat and seasoned vegetables
- gochujang: Red chili paste
- gukbap: A Korean dish of soup with rice

- gumiho: A nine-tailed fox spirit
- Gwangdo: Sword of Light
- halmeoni: Grandmother
- han: Grief perverted by resentment and vengeance into something that haunts the soul
- hanbok: Traditional Korean clothing referring to both women's (a cropped top and a floor-length skirt that ties at the chest) and men's (a top and baggy pants)
- hanji: Traditional Korean handmade paper
- hanok: Traditional Korean house
- hwando: Short, single-bladed Korean sword
- Jaenanpa: Faction of dark shamans whose primary purpose is to steal magic from beings of the Shingae
- jeogori: Traditional shirt that goes with the skirt or pants of a hanbok
- jeoseungsaja: Being of Underworld who guides the souls of the dead to the Kingdom of Underworld
- jesa: A traditional Korean memorial ceremony
- Joseon: The last dynastic kingdom in Korea (1392–1897)
- jumak: A tavern serving food and drinks in old Korean society
- jumo: An owner of a jumak, typically female
- makgeolli: A milky fermented rice wine
- miyeok guk: Seaweed soup
- mudang: Korean shaman
- samgaetang: Chicken soup with ginseng
- Samshin Halmeom: A manifestation of the Seonangshin in the form of an elderly woman
- Sanshillyeong: Spirit of Mountains, another manifestation of the Seonangshin in the form of an elderly man
- seonangdang: Tree shrine for the Seonangshin used by humans
- Seonangshin: God of Mountains

- seonnam: Winged angelic being of Sky (male)
- seonnyeo: Winged angelic being of Sky (female)
- seungmacho: Herb used as an antidote
- Shinbiin: Beings of the Shingae in the Realm of Four Kingdoms
- Shingae: World of gods
- ssam: Food wrapped in red lettuce and perilla leaves, topped with ssamjang
- ssamjang: A sauce made of soybean paste, gochujang, and sesame oil
- Suhoshin: Guardians of the Shingae
- Yeoiju: Pearl of Light (the last of the Cheon'gwang)
- Yongwang: Dragon King, the god of Water

ABOUT THE AUTHOR

Photo © 2017 Nichanh Petersen of Nichanh Nicole Photography

Jayci Lee writes poignant, sexy, and laugh-out-loud romance featuring Korean American main characters. Her books have been in *O, The Oprah Magazine, Cosmopolitan, Entertainment Weekly, Hollywood Reporter, E! News,* and *Women's World.* Jayci is retired from her fifteen-year career as a litigator because of all the badass heroines and drool-worthy heroes demanding to have their stories told. Food, wine, and travel are her jam. She makes her home in sunny California with her tall-dark-and-handsome husband, two amazing boys, and a fluffy rescue.